Praise for Rick Boyer
and his Doc Adams mysteries

"There's a lot to like about Doc Adams. . . . [He] is easygoing and unpretentious."
—*The Washington Post Book World*

"Rick Boyer writes with verve. Freshness in both plot and place will keep you hanging on for the violent and ironic conclusion."
—*The San Diego Union*

"The Doc Adams series is one of the most consistently entertaining."
—*Booklist*

By Rick Boyer
Published by Ivy Books:

BILLINGSGATE SHOAL
MOSCOW METAL
THE DAISY DUCKS
THE WHALE'S FOOTPRINTS
THE PENNY FERRY
GONE TO EARTH
YELLOW BIRD
PIRATE TRADE
THE MAN WHO WHISPERED

THE MAN WHO WHISPERED

Rick Boyer

IVY BOOKS • NEW YORK

An Ivy Book
Published by The Ballantine Publishing Group
Copyright © 1998 by Richard L. Boyer

http://www.randomhouse.com

Library of Congress Catalog Card Number: 98-96251

ISBN 0-8041-1044-1

Printed in Canada

First Edition: November 1998

10 9 8 7 6 5 4 3 2

for
TOM AND RAY MAGLIOZZI
the Cheech & Chong of Public Radio . . .
and for
Joanne, Lucille, and Monique
and *all the kids*
and also for the beloved Louis and Elizabeth,
for doing such a great job.
You all are what I miss most about Boston

The author would like to thank Ginny Boyer, John Boyer, and Bill Tapply for their constructive comments on the manuscript. Also, a special thanks is due to the many fishermen and shopkeepers in New Bedford and Fairhaven who were so helpful, especially Mr. Chris Richards of the Fairhaven Office of Tourism, whose knowledge and cooperation were invaluable.

Remembering Bill Rawls

On June 28, 1997, Major William Council Jefferson Rawls II died suddenly in Asheville. A highly decorated veteran of Army Special Forces, Rawls saw service in all corners of the globe, including five consecutive tours in Vietnam. His camaraderie and assistance and expertise in many of the author's books were a big part of what made writing them so enjoyable. He is sadly missed by his fellow members of the Intertribal Veterans Association, members of the Special Forces clubs and associations throughout the country, the Asian-American communities of North Carolina, and by the author and his wife and son.

Oops, Wrong Week!

IN THE PREDAWN DARKNESS OF APRIL 12, 1992, A STATE vehicle belonging to the Commonwealth of Massachusetts Bureau of Prisons was ambushed on Route 2 less than a mile from MCI Concord, a medium-security prison on the west side of town. The vehicle, a van, contained a driver and a guard in front and, behind and separated from them by a thick wire screen, four inmates who were being transferred from the Concord prison to the infamous Deer Island facility.

Most people in Massachusetts will tell you that Cedar Junction, formerly known as Walpole, is the worst prison in the state. This is not true. Deer Island, a two-mile-long blister of granite in Boston Harbor, is not only the worst prison in the state, it is probably the worst prison in America. It is the eastern version of Alcatraz. Here, in the dreary corridors of the old brick complex, the lifers and sickos wring out the rest of their sorry lives in what has to be a living hell. The place is oven hot in the summer months and near freezing in the winter. At least seven inmates are murdered or tortured to death each year despite the strictest security possible. The average tenure of the guards here is only two years because even the most brutal and debased of these cannot stay more than a few years.

A panel truck (rented, as it turned out) swept out onto Route 2 seventy yards in front of the prison van, stopping sideways on the highway and blocking both lanes. Since this is not a new idea in prison breaks, the drivers of state vehicles are taught procedures to follow in such a situation. The guard in the passenger seat pulled his shotgun from its holder and opened his window. The driver put out a Mayday call on the police radio as he drew his sidearm. But before any of these measures could take effect, two men jumped from the back of the panel truck. They each carried 10-gauge shotguns and proceeded to fire four rounds of double-ought buckshot into the front of the van. Both guards were killed instantly. The van slowed to a swervy stop on the grassy median, its blown-out radiator hissing steam. The two men on the road stood guard while two more men jumped from the truck carrying crowbars. They ran around to the rear of the van and attacked the door with savagery and precision; in less than a minute they had the door open and led out the four convicts, who were bound hand and foot with chains, to the center of the median. They studied the four men with puzzled expressions for several seconds before one of them shouted, "Which one of yuz is Ramos?"

None of the men answered. Then one of the felons, a bit older than the other three, said that he thought Christos Ramos was due to be transferred sometime next week, but he definitely wasn't among them. One of the men with the shotguns drew a walkie-talkie from his coat and shouted into it: *"Gawdammit, he ain't heah!"*

After a brief pause, he replaced the walkie-talkie and waved to the rest of the ambush team, who ran across the median, climbed into a dark blue sedan, and disappeared.

Two of the convicts had been hit by buckshot and lay bleeding on the grass when the police arrived. They later recovered. The other two weren't hit and ran across the nearby cornfield and into the woods. They were recaptured the following day.

Christos Ramos, a sixty-year-old convicted drug runner from New Bedford, denied any knowledge of the ill-fated effort to free him. But, needless to say, the deaths of two state prison guards in the attempt did not bode well for him. Two weeks later he was sent to Deer Island—this time in a four-car convoy. He stayed on Deer Island for almost four years, and despite every effort to break him down, he did not reveal anything about the attempted break, claiming always that he was falsely framed for most of the charges (something every lifer claims, of course), and that the effort to free him was more probably an attempt to kidnap him and make him reveal the whereabouts of his treasure.

Treasure?

Of course, this excited immediate interest from everybody, including the press. I recall one *Boston Globe* article that opened with the following headlines:

MODERN DAY CAPT. KIDD MUM ON STASH
Behind Bars on Deer Island, Smuggler Christos Ramos Claims He Has Millions Hidden, but Won't Reveal Details.

After a while the affair died down and most people, including Mary and me, figured it was simply a desperate attempt by the old man to hype his way out of jail.

I got to know Christos in 1991 when I performed surgery on him for an infected mandible, since I do pro bono work at the Concord facility on a regular basis. I came to know and like the old man. I, and a few others who felt the same way, petitioned against his transfer to Deer Island, which we felt was an unjust and harsh punishment for smuggling. The petitions were ignored, or so we thought.

But in late '95, after his second heart attack, the authorities decided to return Ramos to MCI Concord, and even allowed him to spend his remaining sentence on the work farm, which was heaven compared to the hell of Deer Island. Word also got back to Chris about the petitions we'd sent. He sought me out during my subsequent visits to the prison and the farm across the road. He remembered the scrape I had gotten into down around Billingsgate Shoal a long time ago, and we spent more than a few hours talking about the New England seacoast and the always present avocation of smuggling. Naturally, I asked him about his famous stash of treasure.

"Oh, yeah. I got it hid all right. But I can't even talk about it in this place, Doc. You know, they got a mike on everything we say here."

Half a year later, in early April 1997, I was called back to the prison to examine Ramos, who had developed a swelling near the base of his tongue. This one couldn't be done in the prison infirmary; Ramos was once again put inside a heavily guarded vehicle and transferred to Emerson Hospital, where I performed a biopsy that came back with the worst kind of news. Two days later I did what I could for him, and hoped that radiation and chemo would do the rest.

But I doubted it.

Less than a month later Emerson Hospital called my office to say that Christos Ramos was dying. He wanted to see me.

Right away.

1

EMERSON HOSPITAL IS PRACTICALLY ACROSS ROUTE 2 FROM MY office in the Concord Professional Building; I was inside the building in under ten minutes and at the door to his room in less than fifteen. A cop sat in a desk chair at the doorway reading the *Sporting News*.

"You the dawctah?"

I nodded and showed him my ID.

"Bettah hurry—I heah he ain't gawt long . . ."

Inside the room Ramos was propped up in an elevated bed with an oxygen tube under his nose, a food tube up inside his nose, and an IV stuck into the back of each hand. When you see a patient thus rigged, and see him immobile and rigid, with that waxy, sharp look to the face and nose, you generally can guess that the terminal slide is under way. From this point on the medical staff is keeping the patient comfortable. A nurse, a nice young man named Jeremy Thompkins whom I had worked with before, bent down over the old man's head.

"Mr. Ramos," he said in a voice so loud it startled me, "Dr. Adams is here to see you. Mr. Ramos?"

Christos Ramos opened his bleary eyes and motioned me over with his right hand. The IV tube and the rack above it jiggled. Then he looked at Jeremy and said, with half a grin, "Beat it, kid."

Jeremy oozed out of the room, shutting the door behind him. I approached the bed. "Hiya, Christos—how ya doin'?"

"How do you think I'm doin', Doc? Do I look like I'm doin' okay?"

"Could be worse."

"I don't see how." Then he tried to laugh, and the pain just about killed him right then and there.

"Take it easy, guy. Can they give you another shot right about now?" All of a sudden, after his brief bout of bravado and humor, he looked tired and sick as all hell.

"I told them no—not until I talked with you. I know the next dose might finish me. I—*ahhhh!*"

He lapsed into unconsciousness for perhaps half a minute. When he came to, he moved his cloudy eyes around, trying to see me. I took hold of his hand, which was ice cold.

"I'm here, Christos."

"Listen. Listen good. No mikes in here?"

"I don't think so, Christos," I said, scanning the small white cubicle. "Don't think there's much place to hide one."

He drew me close, so my ear was right up to his mouth.

"Saint Bernard's Church—" he said in a whisper so coarse and faint it sounded like somebody using an adz in a nearby warehouse rather than a voice. "—on Morse Avenue—in Fairhaven."

I nodded.

"Repeat it."

I did, and he grabbed me again and pulled me over close.

"There's . . . the keys to the kingdom . . . third row on the left, on the wall side, underneath. You can't see 'em—you gotta dig 'em out."

"Third row on the left, on the wall side . . ."

He grabbed me hard then, arching his back.

"Look out for Claudia, okay? She's all I got . . . Listen, Doc, anything you can find is yours . . . just look out for her . . . and . . . watch out for those fuckin' headhunters—" he arched up in pain once more "—and their goddamn . . . red . . . frogs . . ."

Then he slumped back onto the bed and did not move.

I pronounced him dead seventeen minutes later.

2

MARY AND I WATCHED FROM OUR LIVING ROOM AS JOE'S police cruiser pulled into our driveway in Concord. My wife's brother, Joe Brindelli, is now in his twenty-third year with the state police as a detective lieutenant. I had called him about Ramos's death two days earlier, and he'd said he'd come out when his schedule allowed.

Mary went to let him in while I walked back to the small room next to the kitchen that I use as my study. There, sitting on the leather-topped desk underneath the brass student lamp, was a yellow legal pad with a bunch of scribbling and crossed-out words. When I was growing up, my father kept pads of notepaper with the following saying written across the top:

Confucius say: Poor handwriting better than good memory

How true! Now in my fifties, I was making that painful discovery that most people in advancing years are forced to concede: while memories of early childhood remain as clear as ever (or so we think), memories of recent events, particularly the important details, slip out of our memory banks with alarming frequency. On his deathbed, Christos Ramos, ever worried about hidden microphones, had drawn me close and whispered right into my ear some important directions, which I committed to memory.

I thought.

But when I got home that evening, going straight to my desk to write down the words I was so positive I had remembered verbatim, confusion set in fast.

The first part I was confident about. He'd mentioned Saint Bernard's Church on Morse Avenue in Fairhaven, the town directly across the Acushnet River from New Bedford. That seemed easy enough, and a call confirmed a church of that name on Morse Avenue. So far so good. Then the second part: *The keys to the kingdom. Third row on the left, right near the wall.* That was how I remembered it. But then I thought he'd said "wall side." Did he mean the side of the wall itself, or on the wall side? Then I thought he had said "Underneath—you gotta dig for them." Did he really say "them," or "it"? If it was really keys he was talking about, then it would be "them." And underneath what? Since it was inside the church I assumed that the third row on the left side was a pew. What else could it be? And where else to hide something quickly?

Okay, so we go into the church and find the third pew back on the left side of the aisle. Right near the wall would mean the last seat on the left. Underneath. Well, underneath the seat sounded logical. "You gotta dig" meant exactly what it said. Either I had to scrape around beneath the wooden pew or else maybe even attack the church floor. How to do that without alerting a whole bunch of people?

The only way to find out was to go to the church. And now we had a perfect opportunity: the memorial service for Christos Ramos was to be held the following afternoon at two o'clock at Saint Bernard's Church in Fairhaven.

"So you want me to go to the funeral tomorrow with you? That it?" said Joe, settling down into one of the overstuffed leather chairs in the study with a beer mug full of gin and tonic.

"That's it, Joey," said Mary, who sat facing him with a balloon glass of pinot noir. "We want you to be there to notice anything interesting."

Joe broke into a wide grin. "Tell you what. That guy himself was interesting. Doc, you remember the time you took me over to the prison just to meet him? You were doing something to his mouth."

"Standard third molar extraction. And I knew you'd like him."

"Yeah, I'd heard enough about him down at headquarters. You know, what they say is true: cops have a nose for good and evil. If you have this sense before you become involved in law enforcement, it means you'll be a great cop, a natural. But even if you don't, five years or so on the force and you develop it."

"A nose for good and evil?" Mary asked.

"Sure. At first, the guy in the nice suit who talks correctly and has impeccable manners and lots of charm fools you. You're sure it's the other guy, the guy with raggedy clothes and booze breath and bad teeth who's the villain. But it turns out Mr. Charm is a sociopath, a guy who's perfected his image and his presentation. Underneath he's a monster. With no pity or remorse. A guy who could torture your child to death for kicks and laugh about it later."

Mary made a bitter, puckered face and put down her wine glass.

"What's the matter, Mare? The wine corked?"

"Huh? No; it's what Joey just said—I find it hard to believe there are really people like that out there."

"Well, there are," I said. "Joe and his buddies at the state police have seen them and Laitis Roantis has seen them too."

She shuddered. "Laitis Roantis should know; he *is* one."

"Then how about the other guy?" I asked him. "The guy with the broken teeth and raggedy clothes who don't talk so good? You're saying he's good underneath?"

"Not good especially, but not bad. He's a loser, pure and simple. Poor, uneducated, without skills. Without money or influential friends. Maybe he's an addict or a loner. But anyway, this thing about good and evil relates to old Christos Ramos. A lot of the guys I know who crossed wires with him thought he was a pretty decent sort. Yeah, he was into smuggling drugs when his company went bust. Can't ever forgive him for that. But my friends on the case all had a hunch that if and when things got better, he would have returned to business as usual and left the smuggling alone. Also, a lot of guys thought that it was his partner, Larry Kelly, who was the real kingpin in the drug thing."

"That certainly jibes with what he told me in the joint," I said. "But of course nobody will probably ever know, since Larry Kelly died the year after Ramos went inside."

"You said he gave you a message that you've written down," Joe said, rising and leaning over the desk. "I take it this is it."

He picked up the paper and glanced over it. "There are a lot of cross-outs and inserts, Doc. Can't you make up your mind what he said?"

"No. It sounded so easy when I heard it. But I think what's there is right. Then he added something else. He said look out for Claudia."

"Who's Claudia?"

"Beats me. I know he didn't have any children. Maybe she's a girlfriend who's been waiting for him on the outside all these years."

"I doubt it, Doc. If that were true, he would have mentioned her, don't you think? Also, think about what he said: 'Look out for Claudia.' That could be taken two ways."

Mary lifted her head. "You mean like beware of Claudia?"

"Could be," Joe said.

"I don't think so; right after that he said, 'She's all I got.' "

"Okay, must be a ladyfriend or some relative we haven't heard of. But wait—" He frowned as he stared at the rest of the message.

"What is it?" asked Mary.

Joe looked up from the paper with amazement on his face. "You read the rest of this message? Here it is: 'Listen Doc, whatever you can find is yours. *But watch out for those fuckin' headhunters and their goddamn red frogs.*' "

We sat there for a second, staring at each other.

"I know," I said. "Seemed strange to me too, even at the time."

"Then why didn't you ask him to explain it? Ask him what the hell he really meant?"

"Because he slipped into a coma right then. And then he died."

"Headhunters . . . What do you suppose he means by that?"

"Obviously not the kind that hang out in the Amazon jungles with blowguns and shrunken heads. He means it in the modern business sense."

"To me, headhunters are people who steal executives away from companies and sell them to other companies," said Joe. "Is this what you think he meant? And if so, did Ramos even have a company left, or did the state take it all?"

"Who knows? But there must be a way to find out. There must be some property left, since I would guess he willed it to this Claudia person, whoever she might be. I think he used the term 'headhunters' to refer to vultures who might try to steal this property from Claudia, claiming this, that, or the other under shady business laws."

"Hmmmm . . . could be. It happens a lot. If a guy dies and leaves no heirs, all kinds of creeps come out of the woodwork claiming this and that. But what about those 'goddamn red frogs'? What on earth could he mean by red frogs?"

"It's a figure of speech of some kind," offered Mary. "Everybody knows frogs are green; there are no red frogs, just as there are no blue roses. Therefore, maybe he's referring to people again. Maybe Frenchmen with a socialistic bent . . . I don't know."

Joe scratched his head. "Are there many French down in New Bedford? I know there are Portuguese . . . and some Italians . . . but how about the French?"

I shrugged. "I don't know; it's something to check up on."

Joe got up and paced around the study, then stood looking at us with his hands clasped behind his back. "I'm intrigued by this," he said, "mainly because part of Ramos's last message said that anything you could find, Doc, you could keep."

"You don't really think he had a treasure, do you?"

He shrugged his huge shoulders and took out his pack of Benson & Hedges. "Who knows? But it's worth a shot. At least, it's worth going to his funeral. Count me in."

3

THE NEXT DAY JOE ARRIVED AT OUR HOUSE FROM BOSTON AT eleven-thirty. His wife, Marty, was out of town visiting her brother and his family, so he was glad to have the diversion. As usual, he was hungry and demanded food. Mary told him to wait till we got to New Bedford—we had a small restaurant already picked out. We drove the hour and a half it takes to get to New Bedford from Concord, taking 128 south and then Routes 24 and 25, rolling into town before one. As you come into New Bedford, taking either Route 6 or I-195 eastbound off highway 25, you will top a rise near the airport and see the big red-and-white checkerboard water tank on the hill. Then, a few miles later, below you stretches out the town of New Bedford, almost oozing into the sea toward the south and east, where the hazy horizon sits. Across the harbor lies the town of Fairhaven. With its piers and boat slips, its waterfront factories and warehouses, it is a mirror image of the bigger town across the water.

Among the fishing towns of Massachusetts, New Bedford is similar to its northern cousin up on Cape Ann: Gloucester. Both have a centuries-old tradition of making their living from the sea. But there are differences. Most of the fishermen in Gloucester are Italian; in New Bedford, the Portuguese predominate. Gloucester was never a whaling port; it concentrated on the rich cod, haddock, and halibut fishing grounds of the Grand Banks. And the noble schooners that dominated that trade were built around Gloucester, in the shipyards of Essex and Ipswich. New Bedford was, in the middle of the last century, the premier whaling port in the world, and fell into rapid decline when that industry was cut short by the discovery of petroleum.

Both the climate and the terrain of the two towns differ dramatically, which is interesting since they're only sixty-five air miles apart. Gloucester's harbor is small and granite-rimmed. Looking down at all the vessels crammed inside it always reminds me of the trading floor of the New York Stock Exchange. The shores all around Cape Ann are rugged and high, whereas New Bedford nestles lazy and sprawling in the mouth of the Acushnet River, which meanders through huge estuaries and cranberry bogs. The land is low and flat down here, and the warm currents of Block Island Sound and Buzzards Bay keep the place noticeably warmer than the frigid waters off Gloucester. When it's snowing over most of New England, you can bet that Cape Cod and New Bedford will be getting sleet, cold drizzle, or ice that won't last.

Hurricanes are a big threat down here; the big blow of 1938 almost destroyed the entire town. And to the south, in Narragansett Bay, Rhode Island, it was a disaster of epic proportions.

What happened was this: the huge storm swell of water ran up the bay, and as it headed north to the city at its head, the water shoaled, while the shores of the bay narrowed. These two things meant that the storm surge grew in height and speed as it approached the town at the head of the bay. Narragansett was clobbered by a huge wall of water and was almost totally wiped out. New Bedford was hit almost as hard. Then, in 1954, this section of New England was hit by two hurricanes twice within a week. One was the infamous Carol. I forget the other's name. Anyway, New Bedford and Fairhaven were both years rebuilding. Visitors driving along Rodney French Boulevard at the southern edge of the city are surprised to see sets of gigantic steel gates and rock levees guarding the isthmus that terminates in Fort Rodman. The storm gates and walls are still used regularly to keep the huge Atlantic storm swells out of the harbor.

If you saw the 1950s movie *Moby Dick*, starring Gregory Peck, you might remember the strange church where the sermon is preached just before Ishmael signs aboard the ill-fated *Pequod*. That very church, called the Seamen's Bethel, complete with its unique ship's prow pulpit, still stands on historic Johnny Cake Hill, just as it did in the 1840s during the height of the whaling industry.

Besides the maritime industries, New Bedford has always been known for its metal products, especially copper and brass and all types of wire. Revere Ware, the famous copper-bottomed cookware, originated here. Acushnet golf balls are made here, as are a lot of cutting tools, dies, drill bits, and screws. But, when the 1980s arrived, the town felt the full impact of foreign competition, mostly from Asia with its cheap labor. A lot of these once great companies—Morse Cutting Tools, manufacturers of perhaps the finest drill bits ever made in this country, comes immediately to mind—either collapsed or were forced to cut way, way back. Another casualty was the Atlas tack company. If anybody looks through an old kitchen "junk drawer," chances are they will unearth a red cardboard box the size of a matchbox with a cellophane window on the top and the black letters ATLAS above the window. They made carpet tacks, upholstery tacks, and brads. But they, too, folded in the late sixties.

And this decline in the metals industry obviously contributed to Southeast Massachusetts Towing and Transit's decline as well. And paved the way for Christos Ramos and his partner, Larry Kelly, to look for other ways of keeping their capital equipment running.

We stopped at the small restaurant Mary and I had discovered some years back, a Portuguese joint that served good linguica and Greek salads. We had the hot sausage over rice, big salads, and coffee while we looked at the street map, then got back in the Audi and crossed the harbor on the I-195 bridge into Fairhaven. We found Saint Bernard's Church in a modest but pretty residential neighborhood. It was a white-stuccoed building of moderate size and looked in good shape. We were the only ones there.

"Are you sure it's at two?" said Mary. "There's nobody here."

"Well, he was in the joint for the last six years of his life," said Joe. "That could explain part of it."

We went inside and sat down in the middle, a third of the way back. Our collective gaze was first fixed on the casket, an oblong box made of what looked like brushed pewter that sat right up on the dais so as to be the focal point of the service. But then I found myself eying the third pew from the front, on the far left side. A furtive glance told me that Mary and Joe were doing likewise.

"Looks pretty normal from here, Doc," Joe whispered as he drew out the wooden kneeling bench from underneath the pew ahead of us and knelt down on it. He made the sign of the cross, clasped his hands, and set them on the pew back. His clasped hands were as big as a melon, with hair on the backs of the fingers.

"Of course it does," I whispered back. That's the point. He said 'underneath, you gotta dig for them.' "

We were alone there for almost twenty minutes before two couples came in. One of the men had a cane; they looked about Christos's age. Probably old friends. As they passed by us on the way to the front pew, I heard them speaking softly in Portuguese. Then the organ prelude started and the priest came out. The program said his name was Antero DeSilva. He was a nice-looking man in his late forties or early fifties, dark hair and eyes, and wire-rimmed glasses. I could tell by his slight nod and grin to the four people in front of us that he knew them. When it became obvious that nobody else was going to show, the priest began the service. Of course, as in any Catholic ceremony, there was a lot of bouncing up and down, signing, and bell ringing—stuff that I'm growing to like more and more, incidentally—but from the priest's words about the departed it became clear that Mr. Ramos had helped this church a great deal, including funding and overseeing part of the renovation work that was done just before he ran afoul of the law.

It was during this speech that I heard the faint sound of the front door closing behind us. Then I heard the clack of heels on the stone floor, then silence. I wanted to turn around and look but it would have been bad form. As the service was drawing to a close, Mary leaned over and whispered into my ear.

"How are they going to take the casket out to the hearse, Charlie? There aren't enough people here—"

"I think they'll have arranged something beforehand, don't you?"

Sure enough, after the last hymn had been sung, the Lord's Prayer said, and the postlude began to play, six dark-suited men—no doubt hired from the funeral home—entered from the wings and bore the coffin off down the aisle. We followed.

And it was then, when we turned around to follow Christos out to his grave, that I saw her.

She was standing in the back of the church, right in the middle, wearing a black sheath dress and a dark hat with a short, spider-web veil that almost covered her dark brown eyes. Eyes that were wet and sad. Her hair was long and dark brown with a hint of dark red at the tips. The big deep brown eyes stared straight at us. I think I felt they were staring right into mine. I know I was staring back.

Somebody nudged me in the back. Hard.

"C'mon Charlie, get moving—"

We filed out of the church but hung back to talk to the priest. Joe, as per plan, said he forgot his hat and went back inside.

"Yes, Dr. Adams, nice to finally meet you," said Father De-Silva. "Actually, I'm surprised we haven't met sooner. I went up to Concord and Deer Island quite a few times to see Chris. The whole thing was . . . too bad, really." His face clouded, and I could detect anger underneath.

"Do you think he was unjustly sentenced?" I asked.

"Yes. Yes, I do. He was guilty of smuggling, of course. He admitted as much to me."

"In confession?" asked Mary in a shocked tone. "You're not supposed to—"

"Oh no, not in confession, Mrs. Adams. Of course I wouldn't reveal anything he told me in the booth. But we had long talks before and after he went to prison. He was quite open about it."

"And . . . ?"

"And while he admitted to me that he had done some smuggling, for the life of me I cannot understand the harshness that he was dealt with. Especially when you consider what he did for his church and community. It was a shame. At least they could have let him out when his health failed."

"It seems you were close," I said. "And from the eulogy I gather he was an active parishioner."

"Oh, much, much more than that. He practically rebuilt this church himself. It had fallen into disrepair twelve years ago, and this was never a wealthy parish. A good neighborhood, certainly, full of nice working people, mostly Portuguese, as I am, and as Chris Ramos was. But it was not, and is not, rich. So we languished for years, with Saint Bernard's practically falling apart. Chris and some of his crew put on a new roof, repaired the stained glass, resurfaced the outside, and, two years later, refinished the interior. That was . . . right before he was convicted and sent off."

An old but well-preserved hearse oozed up to the curbside, and the men in suits opened the back door and slid the pewter-colored casket inside.

"Will we see you at the graveside?" asked Father DeSilva. "There won't be many present—surely not as many as poor Chris deserved. We'd love to have you join us."

"Why, certainly we will," Mary said, taking my arm and leading me along the sidewalk toward the car. "We'll follow you."

"What about Joe?"

"He's a big boy; I'm sure he'll be okay until we come back."

"Just let me poke my head inside and tell him where we'll be."

I dashed back up the stairs and into the church. When I went through the big doors into the sanctuary, I saw Joe jump up fast right near the third pew back on the left. His face relaxed when he saw it was me.

"Whew! Scared me, Doc."

"Well?"

He motioned me over with his hand. I came up next to him and knelt down as he instructed.

"I'm afraid it's bad news," he said, motioning me over.

I knelt down on the stone floor and ducked my head way down, then looked up underneath the seat right at the end of the bench—right on the wall side. There, right where the end support met the seat, was a hollow the size of two cigarette packs side by side. The new naked oak was bright where the drill bit and chisel had torn away the old varnished wood.

"Damn!"

"Shhhh! You're in church you know," said Joe.

I rose to my feet. "Look, Mary and I are going to the cemetery for the burial. Why don't you stay here and give the whole place a good going over? Nobody's going to disturb you; we'll all be there."

"Just what I intend to do. And what if somebody shows up? I'm a former priest and a cop. Adios, Doc."

I was halfway down the aisle when he called to me again.

"Keep your eyes open at the grave. See if anybody strange shows up. Know what I mean?"

"Like the headhunters?"

He nodded. "Yeah, with their red frogs!" he laughed. I went back outside and got into the car.

Riverside Cemetery wasn't far away, just about a mile from the church on the water's edge right near the I-195 bridge we'd just crossed. Riverside was the correct term, since the place was on the Acushnet River. But the water was so wide here that it resembled a bay more than a river. We drove through the stone pillar gates and wound downward into the small cemetery that was full of lovely trees and shrubs. It looked like an orchard as much as a graveyard. It was as green and pretty as Concord's famous Sleepy Hollow Cemetery. We parked after two wide turns, then got out and headed toward the olive canvas canopy that had been set up over the grave site.

As we drew up to the service, I noticed two women approaching from the opposite direction. One was the pretty woman with the dark hair. Could this be the Claudia that I was to watch out for? If so, it would be a welcome task. But now she had somebody with her, another woman her age, perhaps slightly older, with medium brown hair in a severe short cut, no makeup, and tiny gold studs in her ears. She gripped the dark-haired woman's arm tightly as they walked, and seemed almost to be leading her. They stopped some distance away from the rest of us and stood beneath a tree.

Mary and I stood beneath the canopy, watching Father De-Silva sprinkle holy water over the casket. I looked up and could see the harbor over the low stone walls that surrounded us. A stern trawler was making her way down the channel, riding high and empty. Her screws were almost out of the water, making a rhythmic splashing of geysers under her truncated stern.

As they worked the mechanism and the casket was lowered into the concrete vault, I couldn't help but wonder what had been hidden beneath that church pew, and who had gotten there before us. Who else had Christos told about his keys to the kingdom? I wondered if his erstwhile partner Larry Kelly had heard about the hidey-hole. But that seemed unlikely. From what Father DeSilva had told us, the renovation to Saint Bernard's had been finished just before the law caught up with Ramos. No doubt when he put the keys—or whatever it was—up under that pew he knew he had only weeks, perhaps days, of freedom left.

And he thought he would be out of jail in time to go back there and get the stash and enjoy himself for the rest of his life.

But he wasn't and so he told me about it. But somebody got there ahead of us. Was this person good or bad? Was he a friend of Ramos or of Kelly? No way to find out now.

"Charlie?" I felt Mary nudging my shoulder. "It's over—time to go get Joey."

I had been staring at the grass at my feet, lost in speculation. I noticed that the two women were leaving the cemetery by another gate.

"Oh, sure." I followed her to the car. "I must have been daydreaming about the keys to the kingdom. I was just wondering who on earth could—"

"Charlie—look!" she said in a hoarse whisper, grabbing the side of my coat. We were almost to the car, and Mary had half turned around and was pointing at an iron fence that bordered part of the cemetery. There, leaning against the outside of the fence, and staring directly at the men in suits as they piled dirt into the new hole in the grass, was a group of eight people. The men were wearing old dress clothes and baggy sweaters against the chill. The women wore brightly colored robes that resembled saris, but were slightly different in a way that I can't explain. All of them were black, but some had a distinctly Asian cast to their features. Three of the men had Rasta hair—huge dreadlocks that jumped from their scalps like angry black snakes waving in the wind. They also had pointed beards. One man and one woman had lighter skin, Mayan features, and absolutely straight hair cut in a bowl fashion. They both wore old trench coats but, to my astonishment, were bare legged and barefoot. Then, as if to top it off, two of the women in the group fell to their knees, wailing and softly hitting their heads against the bars in grief.

We got in the car, and I drove around the curves, heading for the exit.

"Looks like Ramos had more mourners at his funeral than we all thought," Mary said in a low voice. "Hey, why are you going so fast?"

"I want to get a closer look at this curious gathering. Don't you?"

But as we sailed through the main gates again, turning up the street and going way above the posted limit of five MPH, we arrived at the old iron fence to discover that the group had vanished.

"Where could they have gone so fast, Charlie?"

"Dunno," I said, looking up and down the streets as we drove around. "They must have gotten into a car or something."

"It would take a truck to hold all those people. What did they want?"

"I think you guessed: to say good-bye to Christos Ramos."

"Hey, what's that up ahead?" She pointed to a tan squarish car, very large. It looked like an older model Lincoln with a lot of extra chrome on it. What had caught Mary's eye was the fact that it seemed packed with people. We sped up again and drew closer to the old car, which was crossing the bridge back toward New Bedford. We followed discreetly, but close enough to see a brightly colored rectangle that looked like a flag on the rear window. I sped up again, and we caught up to the big car as it slowed down, turning south into the heart of the old whaling city. We followed until we knew we were in the heart of the working-class Portuguese neighborhood of New Bedford: small walk-up bungalows and storefront bars and cafes that are strung out in rows of streets in the lower peninsula of the town just above the ruins of old Fort Rodman. The most striking feature of this neighborhood was that it was all concrete. No trees or lawns, just streets, sidewalks, and the two-story buildings. It could have looked bleak, but it looked clean and orderly instead. The big Lincoln slowed for a turn.

"I'm going to pass it, Mare. Now, get a good look."

We swung out and went past the car just as it was beginning a slow right turn. We both tried to look into the car's side windows, but they were tinted. But the driver had his window open, and as we passed, he shot us a glance.

Picture Bob Marley with another four or five inches in height and another thirty pounds of muscle on him. Bright nut-brown skin. Caucasian facial features with almond-shaped, sleepy Asian eyelids. Dreadlocks you couldn't stuff into a bushel basket. A charm on a shell necklace around his thick, corded throat.

And bright green eyes.

"Wow!" said Mary. "Did you see that?"

"You mean him?"

"Yeah. Wow!"

Fifteen minutes later we were back over in Fairhaven, pulling up to Saint Bernard's. Joe came over to where we had pulled up and got into the backseat. "Well, see anything interesting?" he asked.

"No red frogs, Joe," I said.

"Not surprised," he mumbled.

"But the headhunters?" said Mary. "They're *real*."

4

THE NEXT WEEK HUMMED ALONG WITH ALL THE EXCITEMENT of a preseason minor-league baseball game. Since it was now mid-April, Mary had me till the garden out in back and mix in some builder's sand—an extra coarse variety—to improve drainage in the tomato beds. The roof of the Japanese teahouse needed some new cedar shakes, so I put those on. I also had patients, of course; I'm not totally retired yet. But I only work mornings now, and three days a week: Tuesdays through Thursdays, which gives Mary and me a chance to enjoy a continuous streak of four-day weekends, which we generally spend at the Breakers, our cottage on Cape Cod.

Mary has all but given up her part-time career as a registered nurse, although she still works when the mood strikes or when there is a special need for her services. Our sons Jack and Tony are still living away from home, and neither, to our growing dismay, is showing the slightest interest in settling down to raise a family. Jack is getting his Ph.D. in marine ecology and animal ethology from BUMP, the Boston University Marine Program. Tony is still out west, breaking broncs and spreading his seed God knows where. *Plus ça change, plus c'est la même chose . . .*

But all in all, the Adams family was enjoying itself as never before. Mary and I had put away enough money to do pretty much whatever we felt like. We take at least two serious vacations a year now—one usually to Europe, the other to wherever the mood strikes at the moment. Last year we went to the Maldives. When the weather permits, Mary and I are on our sailboat for hours, sometimes days, at a time. I've always been an avid reader, as is Mary. For her part, she has not only expanded her ceramics hobby but is now also teaching it at Middlesex Community College. She has also taken up watercolors.

No: we have enough to do. We can fill up the time. But it's the other thing. The life of comfort is too easy, and too slow. After a certain age the sand in life's hourglass seems to run faster and faster with each passing week. My life is lacking in adventure. True excitement. The thrill that only comes to some people when they're on the edge—when they're in a situation that demands all their inner strength and resources maybe just to stay alive.

That was sadly missing.

And perhaps—for me, anyway—that was the reason I sometimes find myself these days spending more time doing forensic pathology work for the Commonwealth of Massachusetts. And doing pro bono work in correctional facilities, too. To get a glimpse and a feel of this rough life that I have always been sheltered from, by my parents' design . . . and by my own career choice.

Consequently, we always welcomed the sight of Joe's cruiser pulling into our driveway. For Mary, it was a chance to visit with her kid brother and cook a great dinner with him, all the while reliving their childhood and youth together in Schenectady. And for me it was a chance to hear Joe fill me in on the latest developments in the world of criminals and psychopaths, of brilliant robberies, gruesome murders, slick scams, sordid cults, and gangland massacres.

But when the familiar late-model Ford with too many antennas pulled into the drive the week following Chris Ramos's funeral, the man who exited the vehicle and trudged up the front walk seemed anything but chipper. As we waited for him to approach the door, Mary and I speculated as to why he wasn't his buoyant self.

"I think it's Marty, Charlie. She's been gone almost a week and won't return for another. I know Joey misses her terribly."

"I know that's part of it; when they got married she rebuilt his shattered life in less than three months. But I've got a hunch it's something else."

"Like what?"

"Like something to do with the late Chris Ramos."

She stroked her pretty chin in silence. "You know, I noticed he seemed kinda glum all the way back from New Bedford. I bet he was looking forward to finding that special something that Ramos hid under the pew bench."

"What I've been wondering is, who got it? I had the feeling that Chris was only telling me. I know there weren't any hidden mikes or cameras in that room at Emerson. You and I both work there—we'd sense that in a minute."

"I'm not so sure, Charlie. Remember Emil Haszmanay? We could never imagine in a million years there were so many kinds of sneak microphones in the world until they killed him."

"Well, it's mighty tough to plant a spike mike or bug in any hospital room, since the place is well lighted and buzzing twenty-four hours a day. And besides, he drew me right up to his mouth and whispered very, very softly."

"Then who else could know?"

"I have no idea. Maybe in recent weeks, wracked with pain, facing death, and heavily sedated, he told another person, just as he told me, and later forgot about it. I think if that happened, this Claudia person would be a good bet."

"How would you find her?"

"Not sure. It would seem that Chris's lawyer, if he had one, would know. That's the only thing I can think of."

"I wonder what was in that bench."

"So do I. But since we can't find out, it's best to forget it."

Then Joe walked in, made a perfunctory greeting, doffed his overcoat on the hallway rack, proceeded down the hall, through the dining room into the kitchen, stopped at the oak sideboard in the corner, and poured himself a healthy gin and tonic. This done, he tipped his head back and polished off a third of it.

He turned to face us.

"Well?" asked his sister.

"Well what? Marty's gone and there's nobody at Pinckney Street except those damn cats. I'm working seven homicides and haven't made a dent in them. I was looking forward to this Ramos business—I'll admit it. It would have been a nice change of pace—excitement not involving mutilated teenage hookers."

He sighed, took another swallow, and shrugged. "So we go down there all pumped up only to find somebody beat us to the prize."

"Yeah. It was a bummer." I sighed. "Especially since Ramos was a friend."

"That . . . and—something else . . ." Joe said in a low, dreamy voice. His eyes took on a faraway look as he sat down at the table and looked up at the beams in our kitchen, draped with copper cookware. "There was a feeling about all this—a sort of exotic feeling, that made me eager to get into it, you know?"

"You mean the smuggling, the rumored treasure?"

"Uh-huh. Who couldn't get pumped up about that? But the other stuff, too: the headhunters and the red frogs. Whatever could he have meant?"

"Maybe nothing, according to Charlie. He was half delirious, Joey. And since somebody's already dug out the bottom of the church bench, we know he told somebody other than Charlie. Whoever it was beat us to the punch."

"Why don't you use your sources to try and find this Claudia person?" I asked. "After all, the old partner Larry Kelly's dead, and so's his wife. Ramos's wife's dead also, and he had no children. So this mystery woman is the only one left."

"So . . . you think I hadn't thought of that?" He sniffed, and drew a computer printout from the breast pocket of his suit coat. He put on his cheaters, cleared his throat, and began.

"Claudia Kelly, aged thirty-one. Daughter of the late Lawrence and Ida Kelly of South Boston, Commonwealth of Massachusetts—"

"*What!* Joey! Are you telling us that Chris Ramos felt closest to the daughter of the man who turned state's evidence on him? Who sent him to Deer Island?"

He moved his head slowly up and gazed at his older sister, giving the appearance of a schoolmaster whose patience is being tried by a callow student. "Why, yes, Mary, I admit it does seem strange that he would feel this way toward her. . . ."

He rose from the table and shook out a Benson & Hedges

from the pack in his shirt pocket, slid over to the wall switch that controls the exhaust fan, flipped it, and lit up. Sometimes I get the feeling *chez* Adams is the only place left where Joe can smoke indoors. "But on the other hand, consider this: as much as he grew to hate Larry Kelly, perhaps he always loved his daughter. I mean, they were partners in a successful business for a long time, and Ramos was childless, perhaps not by choice. I bet little Claudia might have called him Uncle Chris when she was growing up."

"You think that woman at the funeral—the one Charlie was drooling over—was Claudia?"

"I was not drooling."

"I'd be surprised if she weren't. In any case, we have her address in Boston. We could look her up. See what she has to say."

"Why did you say I was drooling when I—"

"Quiet, Charlie—we're discussing something important here."

The phone rang. Not wishing to interrupt this tremendously important conversation, I decided to answer it in my study. I walked through the small hallway that leads to Mary's ceramic workshop and on into my small cozy hideaway. I picked up the phone.

"Dr. Charles Adams?" said the voice. But I could hardly call it a voice. It was a hoarse whisper—a voice so low and raspy it did indeed resemble the one Ramos addressed me with on his deathbed. It sounded like the living dead.

"Yes. May I help you?"

"You better. We know Ramos told you where to find it. Now you tell us."

"Who is this?"

"Somebody who's missing his share of the take. Get it?"

I thought for a second. "If what you say is true, why don't we make an appointment to meet someplace?"

"Maybe that's a good idea—" The voice was so low and gravelly it was hard to understand the words. I could detect an accent beneath the horrendous hoarseness, but could not place its origin.

"When we meet, you come alone and tell us where it is. That way, everybody's happy. Nobody gets hurt."

The line went dead.

I stood there for maybe half a minute, holding the dead phone next to my ear. A small voice in the back of my head was saying, *Did that really happen?* I stared at the rows of books on the shelves, the prints of clipper ships on the walls—everything that made me feel so safe and content in my home. But suddenly that feeling of safety was ebbing away. I walked back into the kitchen. Mary was talking as I entered.

"—better if you go, Joey, since you've got at least some legal authority to interview her."

"What if she won't see me? Or doesn't want to talk?"

"Well, that'll end it, I guess. Then we forget the whole thing."

"Maybe not," I said.

"Oh, what's your idea then?"

"Maybe we should meet with the party who just called here."

They both stared at me.

"Well, who is it?" Mary asked.

"I don't know. Didn't leave his name. Just said he knew that I knew where it was, and that I'd better tell him . . . or was it them?"

"No idea who it could be?" asked Joe.

"Nope. It was a guy who whispered. Whispered real low, with an extra gravelly voice, like a guy who's had throat cancer. In fact, it sounded a lot like Ramos himself, come back from the dead."

5

WE STOOD THERE IN FRONT OF THE STOVE, STARING INTO SPACE.

"He said we should meet, and I should tell him where it is," I reported. "That way, he said, everyone will be happy. And nobody would get hurt."

"You didn't recognize the voice?"

"No, Mary. As I said, it was a hoarse whisper, like the caller had cancer of the larynx or something."

"What we'll do," said Joe, "we'll rig up a voice recorder to your phone. It will begin recording whenever the phone rings. That way we'll get his voice on tape next time, and I can take it to the lab for voice analysis."

"Do you think he might be whispering to disguise his voice?" Mary asked.

"There's a chance he's doing just that," said Joe. "When voiceprints first came out, techniques like whispering worked pretty well. But now the electronics are so good we can get a signature on the voice no matter what the caller does to mislead us."

I wandered into my study again and they followed me in silence. I sat behind the leather-topped desk, tapping a pencil on it and chewing on my lip. They sat down; there was maybe half a minute of silence.

"Okay," Joe offered, "in most cases like this, what we have is a partner in crime not known. This person was an associate of Chris's in the illicit side of the business. He was due to get a big chunk of the take when Ramos landed in prison; that could explain the abortive jailbreak five years ago—he wanted Ramos

27

out so he could get his share. But that didn't work, so maybe he was waiting for Chris to get out, but he didn't. Now that he's dead, the partner in crime has nowhere else to turn but you."

"But how does he know Chris told me about the keys to the kingdom?"

"Maybe he doesn't. Maybe he's just bluffing, trying to shake you down. Somehow word got around that you and Ramos were close, and that maybe you were the last man Ramos talked to. And don't forget, Doc, you were seen at the funeral. Whoever this left-out guy might be, he does believe there's a stash somewhere. And he wants his share."

"So what's Charlie supposed to do now?"

"Nothing. Wait until he calls again and we'll get his voice on tape."

"What good will that do?" said Mary. "What if these guys decide to get nasty? Then what?"

Joe stroked his stubbled chin for a second. "Like I said, I think he's bluffing. What Doc should do is say calmly and firmly that he's got no idea what the caller is talking about."

"Okay then," I said. "Get that recorder here ASAP and we'll set it up. Meantime, locating this Claudia might not be a bad start."

Joe headed for the kitchen wall phone. "I'll call in and make the requisition now. That way I can come out early tomorrow and set it up."

While he was talking, I had another idea, and when the phone was free I retreated to my study again and called Emerson Hospital. It took me almost an hour of sifting through the various doctors and nurses who were working the intensive care unit the week that Chris Ramos died, but I finally found the person I was looking for: Jeremy Thompkins. When I returned to the kitchen I smelled that superlative aroma of onions and garlic sautéing in olive oil. It always cheers me up. Joe and Mary were hovering over the giant Swedish enameled stove.

"What's cookin'?"

"We don't know yet; Joey and I are making it up as we go along."

"Well, guess what? I just checked at the hospital; turns out I was not the only visitor to see our friend Ramos before he checked out."

They both turned and looked at me.

"He had two visitors the day before. One was a woman: dark complexion, young, reportedly very pretty."

"Claudia Kelly," said Mary.

"Sounds like it. The other was a man."

They both perked up at this.

"A man? I bet that's the same one who just called you," said Mary.

"Maybe. Maybe not. What they said was, none of the staff would ever forget this person. He was tall, the color of a cigar, with wild dreadlocks down to his shoulders. Asian-shaped eyes . . . but bright green."

"Charlie!"

"Wow!" Joe said, letting out a big breath. "Sounds like a guy like that would stick out anywhere, especially up here in New England."

"Joe, we've seen him. It must be the same guy," said Mary. "Right after the graveside ceremony down in New Bedford, this guy was driving a big old car—his window was open, so we got a look at him."

"Sort of a giant-sized Bob Marley," I added.

"He was neat-looking," Mary said. "Remarkably handsome."

"I agree, but in a sort of predatory way. The way an eagle or a leopard is handsome."

"What's his name?" asked Joe.

"Didn't give it. But apparently Ramos was expecting him."

"Well, did they act like friends?"

"Jeremy Thompkins was the guy I spoke with, Joe. He's a nurse who's a regular at the ICU. All he said was the big scary guy went into the room, stayed for a minute or so, and then left."

"And he didn't hurt Chris, or threaten him?"

"Jeremy was waiting right outside the room, even looked in twice from the doorway. Said they were talking softly, like old friends. After he left, Ramos even seemed chipper."

"Well, this guy is the left-out partner then," said Mary. "This explains what happened: Chris Ramos, about to leave this earth, realizes he's got to tell his close friends where this legendary stash is. So what does he do? On his deathbed, he comes to realize there's just a handful of people he likes or trusts—"

"Yeah, right," said Joe. "He's been betrayed before—he's very suspicious . . . yet anxious to get this information to the right people."

"Uh-huh. And the right people are his beloved 'niece' Claudia, Charlie, and the mystery man."

I went over to where Mary was standing and picked up her balloon glass of red. I took a thoughtful sip, letting the wine roll around in my mouth before swallowing it.

"What is it? Not a cabernet. Not a burgundy. A merlot?"

"Chianti Classico, eighty-nine," said Joe.

I took another slow sip. "What you're both saying sounds logical, and it answers most of our questions. But it leaves one big one unanswered."

Mary took her glass back. "And what's that?"

"If Ramos was so damn fond of all of us, why did he set things up so we're at each other's throats over this thing?"

"Mmmmm. Good point," Joe said.

"Maybe he always had a strange sense of humor," said Mary.

"And another thing. That big guy in the car . . ." mused Joe. "I would think anyone that exotic looking would have some kind of accent or speech pattern that would stick out almost as much as his appearance."

"The caller does have an accent, but it sounded to me like it was from Eastern Europe or somewhere, not the islands or Latin America, which is where our exotic friend probably hails from. I would doubt it's the same guy."

"Same guy or not, let's run down both Claudia Kelly and the Rasta in the big car. You remember the make?"

"Lincoln. Big and boxy. Not new though, maybe six or eight years old. Or older."

"Tag number? Or is that too much to hope for?"

"Tag? Are you kiddin', Joey? With a guy like that staring you in the puss, you think I thought about the tag number?"

"I figured it was a long shot."

"One thing we did see on the back window was something that looked like a flag," I said.

"A flag? Like a country flag?"

"Uh-huh. But I've never seen it before. If it's a country, it's not one we're familiar with."

"Can you give me any more than that?"

"Nope. Brightly colored, with a star—I think a yellow star—in the center. Maybe if I saw it again . . ."

"Okay. When you've got the time, go to the library and look at the flags of the world. What color was the car?"

"Tan."

"More like bronze," added Mary. "It had some metallic sheen to it. And there seemed to be extra chrome on it."

"Any extra antennas?"

"Not that I can remember; maybe there was a cell phone."

"That'll have to do for now. I'll call this in and we'll put it on the wire and alert the New Bedford cops."

"Can you do that, Joe? I mean, to our knowledge, the people in that car have not committed any crime."

"You're right. No, we can't charge them. But I can tell the wire room that this information might be tangential to another case. We'll find out more, anyway."

"All right," I said, suddenly exhausted. "What now?"

"What now? Your sister and I are gonna create a masterpiece banquet for tonight. That's what."

"I think I'll go for a short run and then take a sauna," I said, heading for the bedroom to change clothes.

I did four miles, at a medium slow pace. I just didn't feel like doing more, and was frankly running to shake the combination of anxiety and depression that had crept over me. The whole thing was a letdown. First we follow a hot scent on something exciting and get beat to the punch. Now, Mary and I, who have never wished anybody ill, are being threatened by a mysterious guy who whispers into our phone.

Damn it all.

I was so busy torturing myself with the injustice of it all that I

almost didn't notice the car that swept past me as it turned onto
Old Stone Mill Road. The road our house is on.

Bronze Lincoln. Tinted windows. Couldn't catch the tag
number because by the time I realized what it was, the car was
too far away. I couldn't see the flag clearly, except to see that it
was red and green, with a big yellow star in the middle.

And too far away from New Bedford to be merely coincidence.

"WELL, CHARLIE, HOW DID YOU LIKE THE MEAL?" ASKED MARY,
putting her hand on my knee under the table as we three sat in
the candlelight.

"Great. One of the best."

"Okay, what was it?"

"Huh? I . . . don't remember exactly."

Joe's big face came closer into the candlelight as he leaned
over toward me. The bottom half of the face was purplish black
with his heavy beard.

"What she's driving at, pal, is this: we, uh, sorta can't help
but notice that ever since you came back from that run you took
before dinner, you haven't said much. You seem to be inordi-
nately preoccupied . . . if you get my drift. So what's up, Doc?"

"Okay, I wasn't going to say anything, but since you noticed,
here goes: just as I turned onto our road in the home stretch, a
big old Lincoln swept past me."

Mary froze, openmouthed, her napkin halfway up to her face.
"Not the same one we saw down there after the funeral? No!"

"Yes. Unmistakable. Even to the flag stuck to the back
window."

"Can you describe the flag better this time?" asked Joe.

"Yep: green and red with a yellow star in the center."

"How do you mean green and red? Red, white, and green in vertical panels, like the Italian flag?"

"No—this was different. It seemed to be green on the top and bottom, red in the middle, with the big yellow star in the center of the red. But that's just my hazy memory; it could be different."

"Draw me a picture," Joe said, sliding his open notebook across the table to me. "I'm just wondering how the hell they found out where you live so damn fast."

"I'm getting a sick feeling, Charlie," said Mary, putting her face in her hands and resting her elbows on the table.

"Was the same guy driving?" asked Joe.

"The guy Mary thinks is so handsome?"

"I did think that at first—now I think he's scary."

"I didn't see anything but the car this time—I didn't even realize I'd seen it before until it was far ahead of me."

"Well, I'll say this: things seem to be spinning together pretty fast."

"So, you're the cop; what do we do?"

"Wait until I put the voice-activated recorder on your phone tomorrow afternoon. Then we'll see."

But we didn't have to wait that long; Mr. Whisper caught up with me at work the very next morning.

"Dr. Adams?"

"Speaking."

"I know you remember me, and what I want. I'm calling to arrange that meeting we talked about yesterday."

"First of all, why don't you try clearing your throat? I can barely understand you."

I waited to see if this got a rise out of him. Maybe he'd even drop the fake whisper and I could get a clue to his identity.

"Don't be cute. Half my voice box is gone. You don't help us out, maybe we'll take all of yours away. Would you like that?"

"No. I would not be keen on that at all."

"I didn't think so. Now remember this above all else: this is not a joke. We know Ramos told you about the location of something we want very much. We want this because it's ours."

"What is this thing that's yours? Because I have no idea what Ramos was talking about just before he died; I think he was delirious. He only lived a short time after our conversation; I was the one who pronounced him dead."

"What it is . . . is money. We know the treasure he talked about is real. We want it."

I realized there were voices in the background on his end of the line. Since the call wasn't being recorded, I figured by keeping the conversation going as long as I could, perhaps some other clues or cues would emerge.

"I'll level with you: the only thing he mentioned was 'the keys to the kingdom.' That's all he said in the way of treasure. He said anything I could find of it was mine."

There was a pause here, a long one, and I heard a distant truck horn. A deep hoot like an air horn on a diesel semitrailer tractor.

"Keys to the kingdom? What the hell does that mean?"

"You got me."

"Listen. Take down the number I'm going to give you now. At exactly four-thirty tomorrow afternoon, you call this number. No later, no earlier."

He gave me the number and I jotted it down.

"Now listen: when you call, you'll be told where to go."

"What if I don't call? What then?"

"You don't even want to think about that. Remember: we know where you live and where you work. We want these answers big-time and we're not fuckin' around. Four-thirty tomorrow."

He hung up.

All through the conversation, his voice never changed; not even during quick answers. Which led me to believe that probably his story about losing part of his throat was true.

As I hung up the receiver in my office, I was convinced the man who whispered wasn't faking it. So it seemed that he was being truthful in that, at least. About all the other stuff, who knew? One thing I was positive about: no way was I going to call the number and go where he asked me. I'm not the brightest guy around, but I'm not an idiot. At least not most of the time . . .

I went out past my desk and into the outer office, where my assistant, Susan Petri, was sending out invoices. She looked up at me, licking an envelope. She spread her bright pink tongue all over the paper, then looked up at me.

"Going so soon?" she asked in a husky voice. I looked into those deep brown eyes beneath the mane of chestnut hair . . . the ample bosom, the great smell of whatever she was wearing. Got to be careful with Susan Petri; she's a stick of dynamite with a sputtering fuse.

"I've gotta call Joe, Susan, and I can't do it from our phone here; it might be tapped."

"Ohh . . . Something's up?"

"I don't know, but probably. I'll be back in a few minutes."

She looked at me a little too long, half biting her lower lip. I made a rather awkward exit and went out to the Audi to make the call on the cellular unit so it wouldn't leave a track. The Audi, Mary's old car, is now mine. She went and bought herself a Porsche 911 in Italian Racing Red.

I punched in Joe's number. He wasn't at his office, so I tried his cruiser. This worked. His partner, Kevin O'Hearn, answered.

"Hey ya, Doc; what's happening out in the fields? We're southbound on Furnace Brook Parkway trying to run down a homicide. Hey, you won't believe it—listen: so this guy kills his fiancée. Chops her up and feeds her down the disposer. *No: no shit.* So then—get this—the mother-in-law—the woman's mother, for chrissakes—she can't make the dispose-all work that night, so—"

"Spare me, K. Listen: put Joe on—there's something I got to tell him."

Joe picked it up, then listened. "Christ, they're in your office too?"

"Yeah. And he gave me a number to reach him at exactly four-thirty tomorrow afternoon. He warned me that if I didn't follow through, bad things would happen."

"He gave you a number? That's strange; usually they tell you to be by your phone and they'll call you. I think we're dealing with a real amateur here."

"Amateur or not, he sounded serious. And that voice. I don't think he's whispering; I think something's wrong with his vocal cords. According to him, he's lost half his larynx."

"What else did you two chums talk about? Your families? Your favorite TV shows?"

"He just gave me a warning that I'd better call."

"Give me the number."

I did.

"Hmmm. South Boston prefix. Don't you see why I call him an amateur? Hell, we're gonna trace this number and find the exact—and I mean exact—location of this particular phone. Then, before the scheduled call, we'll have the phone staked out. When he comes to receive your call, we'll nab him. He's walking right into our lap, for chrissakes. This is the first real break we're getting on this puzzle."

"I agree, so why is he doing it this way?"

"Because he doesn't know you have access to the police; he doesn't think you'll locate the phone. But I bet where he tells you to go is just south of Boston—in the Irish stronghold of Southie."

"Uh-huh, where Larry Kelly lived."

"Do tell."

"Why don't you come out for dinner tonight so we can talk about what's going to come down tomorrow?"

"Good idea, but better if you and Mary come into town—there's no telling how late I'll be running. If I'm not home when you arrive, use Mary's key to let yourself in. It's warm and sunny today—nice evening for drinks on the roof."

Mary and I got into town a little after five, parked at the Government Center garage, and had walked to Joe's place on Pinckney Street on Beacon Hill by quarter to six. As he predicted, he wasn't home so we let ourselves in.

Joe's place. What can I say?

I don't know how much it's worth now, but when a young

Joe Brindelli bought this run-down apartment building in 1974, he paid in cash—loaned to him by his father—and got it for a song. Part of the reason was because the odds were 50-50 it was going to be demolished. That's how run-down it was.

Maybe the fact that his father—my late father-in-law—was a supersuccessful builder-contractor cum home building supply retailer trained him to look at real estate as diamonds in the rough. But whatever the reasoning, Joe's purchase was a masterpiece of location and timing. Because from that time on, Boston's downtown was reborn, and Beacon Hill, always classy, (a touch of New Orleans and Charleston up north) was *the* place to be in the Northeast.

Now he rents the floor beneath him—which is divided into two large apartments—for enough money to pay all his living expenses. His top floor is a penthouse with roof gardens on three sides. He has skylights in his huge kitchen and several other rooms. He grows tomatoes and flowers on his deck in the summer, and whenever the weather permits, he dines beneath a grapevine arbor on his Florentine terrace overlooking the Charles River basin. His study holds a great library, flawless Queen Anne furniture, several museum-quality rugs, and $80,000 worth of custom shotguns, mostly of Italian make, all displayed in illuminated, custom-built mahogany cases. Some of them he bought, but a lot of them he won in shooting tournaments.

In his kitchen are several hundred bottles of wine in a rack that takes up an entire wall, an indoor rotisserie, a gas-fired stone oven for making French and Italian bread, and a raised gas-log fireplace.

Not bad for a cop. But this only underscores the double life, the schizophrenic existence he lives. By day he's a hard-boiled homicide detective, tough and savvy as any of America's big-city best. But off-duty, this man retreats to his penthouse suite that drips with art, music, food, and fun. And this is because, basically, Joe Brindelli is a loving, gentle man.

And what's made his life really special in the past few years is marrying Martha Higgins, a woman he was fond of years ago, and found again.

"So what should we do, Charlie, now that we're here?" Mary asked, walking along the carpeted hall toward the living room.

"How about opening a good bottle of red and going out onto the terrace and watching the sun go down?"

"Maybe." She walked back down the hall, opening a door to the master bathroom. She flicked on the track lighting. Joe and Marty had remodeled it since our last visit; it now boasted a sunken marble Jacuzzi bath. The tub was deep and elliptical, with Romanesque trim around the inside lip and a gold lion's head on the tile wall, through whose mouth the water came out into the tub several feet below. It was excessive. It was pompous. It was too much.

I loved it.

Mary turned on the water, then dimmed the lights. "How about opening a good bottle of red and joining me for a while?" she suggested. "Maybe I can teach you the dog paddle."

"Took you guys long enough to get out of that tub," Joe whined as we walked into the living room wearing big fluffy bathrobes and bigger grins. I was remembering Mary's body: warm and smooth and slick with soapsuds. And lithe and dark brown, and packed with hard, smooth muscle at fifty-three.

The Calabrians. Spare me!

Hey, I know they can be mean. They put you in cement and kill your family and stuff like that. But, dammit, the women are knockouts.

Joe rose from the sofa, walked past the Kimball baby grand, and headed for the kitchen. On the way he flipped on his stereo system. Instantly, the apartment was flooded with Vivaldi, playing through Bose speakers.

"Rough life you got here, guy," I mused as I followed my brother-in-law's giant form down the hallway.

"Dammit, I miss Marty. She's not coming back until next week."

"We can stay here till then," offered Mary. "We can get people to take care of the dogs."

"What about my practice?"

"C'mon, Charlie—your practice is shrinking daily. And anyway, you can *commute*. Normal people do it all the time. I officially loan you the Porsche as of now."

I could get used to this, I thought as I entered the kitchen. I saw two packages wrapped in white paper on the counter.

"What's in there, podna?"

"Kobe beef filet mignons and Alaska king crab legs. Thought we might try a little surf and turf tonight."

"Kobe beef? Isn't that the Japanese city where they feed Angus steers beer and massage them three times a day so their meat will be supertender?"

"Yep. Then they kill 'em. Probably cut their heads off in a single swipe with one of those Samurai swords. Probably force kids to watch it. Who knows? Anyway, the meat's eighteen bucks a pound."

"Want them bacon wrapped?" I asked.

"Of course. Then we'll broil this stuff while Mary makes a Caesar salad, and eat it on the patio."

After dinner we went into Joe's study, where he spread a map of Boston out on his desk and drew an X on it.

"We traced the call shortly after you gave it to me over the phone. Here it is: Brian Flynn's pub. I've been in there a couple of times over the years—it's an old standby watering hole that caters to the dockworkers. I remember once I went there looking for a skip and didn't connect."

"A skip?"

"You know, a bail jumper. We needed him badly as a witness. As it was, the guy who looked good for a triple murder walked. I forget the purpose of the other visit. Kevin was with me; maybe he'll remember. Anyway, as far as working bars go, it's about as well known as Anthony's Pier Four is to the higher-class set and, as you can see, not more than a couple blocks from it."

"You predicted the phone would be in, as you call it, the Irish stronghold of Southie."

"Yep. And I found out this too: Flynn's place is not more than two blocks from the Boston headquarters of SEAMATT— Ramos and Kelly's old company."

"What does SEAMATT mean?"

"An acronym from the words Southeastern Massachusetts Towing and Transit."

I leaned back in the leather chair and looked at the ceiling. "I guess what I can't help wondering is . . . How is this phone business connected to that tribe we saw down in New Bedford, and up in Concord in the big Lincoln?"

"Right, Joey. I mean, the guy with the Rasta hair. We don't know where he's from, but no way he's Irish."

"That's obvious," he admitted, "and blacks aren't welcome in Southie, even now. So I think we can rule them out. Hey, I almost forgot—" He got up and started to leave the room.

"Where you goin'?" asked his sister.

"You wanted to know where those tribesmen were from. Wait a sec." He returned shortly carrying his briefcase. He took out a piece of paper and placed it on the desk. It was a color photocopy of a flag that I recognized instantly.

"That's it," I said. "That's the one for sure."

"Positive? Well, guess what it is."

"Haiti," said Mary.

Joe shook his head. "Worse."

"Worse! Bullshit—there's no place on earth worse than Haiti, Joey."

"Oh, yes, there is: Suriname."

"Suriname," I said, letting the word roll around in my mouth. I let it roll around in my brain as well, but it did no good. I'm past fifty now: some days it's all I can do to remember how to go to the bathroom.

"Ah . . . let's see: West African coast."

"No; that's Senegal. Close, but no stogie."

"Isn't it a small country in South America?"

"Right, Mare. Used to be called Dutch Guiana."

"Oh, yeah, those three small countries nestled on the top of the continent right above Brazil. One was French Guiana. I remember that from the movie *Papillon* with Steve McQueen. Remember, honey, Devil's Island was there. What a horrid place!"

"Uh-huh. French Guiana's on the east end. Then there's British Guiana on the west end," Joe added, "which gained its independence from Britain and changed its name to Guyana. That ring a bell, anybody? Remember Jonestown? You recall the wacko Reverend Jim Jones, and the mass suicide of six hundred people?"

"Oh boy—"

"Jeez, Joe. These don't sound like nice places. I mean, Mary and I have taken some exotic vacations lately, but you can probably cross these off the list."

"Ah, but I'm saving the best for last! Suriname is probably the nastiest of the three, located right in between the others. But nobody really knows for sure how nasty it is, since its lower third isn't even explored yet. It's probably inhabited, but not explored. What I heard, the reason is simple: it has high mountains, raging rivers, swamps, and jungles that are beyond belief."

"Headhunters . . ." whispered Mary. "Watch out for those headhunters . . ."

"I think I better freshen up my after-dinner drink," I said, rising from the chair with the big brandy snifter. It seemed that no matter what new development came forth regarding this puzzle, each turn in the road was somehow more sinister.

When I returned to the table with another helping of Talisker and soda, no ice, I heard Joe saying, ". . . but this thing tomorrow, Mary, it'll be easy. Believe me, we've got 'em. Doc can call from the cell phone in the cruiser after Kevin and I settle down for a couple drafts at Brian Flynn's. I mean, we just sit there and wait till whoever it is goes up to answer the phone. Then bingo, we got 'em. I wouldn't worry yourself about this one, Sis. It's in the bag."

7

THERE IS NO OBVIOUS DEMARCATION BETWEEN BOSTON AND South Boston. No signs, no dramatic changes in the streets, architecture, or other landmarks. Also, there is an area called the South End that is part of Boston, and nestles right up against South Boston, or "Southie." The South End is a run-down collection of pawnshops and old warehouses that is being increasingly gentrified. The heart of the South End is South Station, right on Summer Street, where one boards the Amtrak trains for Providence, New York, and points south. But anyway, when you cross Dorchester Avenue heading southeast on Northern, Congress, or Summer Streets, and cross the Fort Point Channel, you're in Southie.

To the north is Boston Harbor and the many piers that line the waterfront. Boston itself used to have a waterfront, way back in the fifties. But now it has marinas, deluxe harbor-view high-rise condos, and the Aquarium, which adjoins Faneuil Hall Marketplace. All this urban redevelopment has made the city of Boston a true gem.

But it's lost a bit of its genuine maritime flavor.

The *real* waterfronts, complete with docks for oceangoing vessels, cranes and derricks for unloading same, warehouses, truck depots, waterfront gin mills, and cheap hotels, are to be found in South and East Boston, Chelsea, and other blue-collar towns.

At quarter to four the next afternoon, Joe and I and Kevin O'Hearn, Joe's longtime partner, were cruising along Summer Street and over the old bridge that spans Fort Point Channel. Nearby were the Children's Museum and the boat replicas for the Boston Tea Party. We hummed along for several more blocks, then angled north, which put us overlooking the dirty, flat gray water of the harbor. The day was cool and cloudy, with an ocean breeze that reeked of brine, old fish, diesel fuel, and exhaust. A typical day in early May on the Beantown waterfront.

It began to rain, slow at first, then hard and loud—so thick we could scarcely see. Joe's cruiser whispered and hissed along the old streets for another four or five blocks. The windshield wipers were going flat out, but still the world ahead of us looked like a Dali painting. Then he swept over to the curb and cut the engine, leaning back in his seat so he could talk to both of us. I was sitting next to him. He pointed up the block.

"That sign up there? Swingin' in the wind? Flynn's place. Way back when, the sign was readable. But now you got to get up real close and stare up at it to read 'Flynn's Across the Water.' Nice name for an Irish bar, eh? I always thought so."

"I'll tell ya now," piped Kevin. "It's still a major place on the waterfront; any cop or politician will tell you that. A lot gets done at Flynn's. Mostly labor stuff, and a bit of the mob. But there's a lotta shit that goes down here for the IRA; you can bet on it."

"So what do we do?" I said. "Like we planned earlier?"

Joe nodded, letting his breath out in a slow sigh. "You wait here," he told me. "Kevin will go in first, since he's right out of County Kerry anyhow. Then I'll join him after maybe fifteen minutes." He looked at his watch. "It's almost four; the traffic to the place will pick up real quick. Kevin and I will arrive separately and fall into the crowd. At exactly four-thirty, Doc, you pick up this cell phone and make the call. We know it's the phone on the wall near the back door; we'll be watching it. Also, I'm wearing a fake hearing aid that's connected to the phone line; I can hear everything you guys say to each other. As soon as we know it's the caller, Kevin and I simply pretend we're going to the john, approaching from two different directions, and escort him out the back door into the alley before he knows what's going on."

"You're not going to show your badge first?"

"We'll show him the badge when we get him outside."

"You sure this will work?"

"Don't sweat it, Doc," said Kevin. "We've done this scene hundreds of times. Don't forget, we got a backup black-and-white cruiser with two bluecoats in it down the block, on the other side. We run into trouble, or don't come out of the place on time, and these uniforms go in there and raise shit."

I looked at Joe. He nodded and raised his right thumb.

"Okay," I said. "Good luck."

Kevin left. Joe and I waited for about twenty minutes, then he left the cruiser. As he walked down the street toward Flynn's bar in the rain, I noticed other dim figures lurching toward the same destination. I studied my watch. At just a hair before four-thirty I switched on the cruiser's ignition and punched the number into the cellular phone. We had already decided that if asked my location, I was to say I was in my car in Concord, waiting to go wherever I was asked.

The phone rang.

No answer.

I tried again, and it was picked up after the second ring.

"Yeah?"

"This is Dr. Charles Adams. I was asked to call this number at this time."

"Just a second."

Then came a horrendous bonking noise in my ear, and I knew the guy who answered had simply dropped the receiver and let it bang and scrape against the wall. Well, what do you expect in a workingman's bar?

"Dr. Adams?" The voice was deep and somewhat raspy, but normal. The man who whispered was not on the line this time. This made me think that perhaps the guy who spoke like Chris Ramos just before he died—with a death rattle of a voice—was a higher-up. He was pulling the strings, but wouldn't be in on the action.

"It's me."

"Where are you?"

"In my car, out in Concord, ready to drive wherever you ask."

"Now listen—HEY!—"

That was the last I heard from him. Then came the bonking sound again, and I knew that Joe had collared him. I shut off the phone and the car, got out and locked it up, and half jogged toward Flynn's. I didn't want to miss any of this.

As I came up to the place, a smallish brick building between two huge ones I assumed were warehouses, I saw the door open and two patrons emerge, each looking with interest over his shoulder, watching something going on inside. I didn't have to guess what it was: Joe and Kevin escorting Tommy Telephone out the back door where they could cuff him. I approached the door, and saw through the two small windows in front laden with neon beer signs that the patrons inside were also looking back over their shoulders. I opened the door. Half the people inside were standing, looking toward the back. Those still seated were also looking in that direction. I worked my way through the crowd as fast as possible, trying to find Joe.

But I couldn't see him anywhere. And believe me, at six-four, two thirty, he sticks out in a crowd. Just as I was turning around, bewildered, looking for the hallway with the john and the back door in it, some guy pointed to one of two darkish doorways and told me, "If you're lookin' fuh ya friends, they went in theyah—"

I went through the doorway and down the dark hall. I heard a scuffle coming from a room at the end of the hallway and I went for it. Just before I opened the door, there came a heavy thump on the door from inside. Not somebody knocking, but the sound of a body being slammed against it. Then I heard a bunch of guys cussing and yelling and a dragging sound.

I opened the door and went in. In the split second before they grabbed me, I saw Joe against the wall being pummeled by a huge man in a knit shirt with the build of a boxer. Kevin was lying on the floor unconscious, blood oozing from his nose and mouth.

A hand shot out and grabbed me by the collar, and I was face-to-face with a man who had a silly-putty nose, a thick neck, and a face like craters of the moon. He hit me on the jaw and I slumped back. He hit me so hard the first time I scarcely felt the second punch to my solar plexus.

The last thing I heard—as if through a mattress—was somebody shouting in the small room: *"Jesus H. Christ! These guys are cowps!"*

8

I WOKE UP WITH THE SIRENS. BEHIND THE SIRENS I HEARD GUNshots in the alley behind the building. Interspersed with the gunshots was a lot of yelling and screaming. The whole world was coming apart. But my first worry was Joe and Kevin.

It was hard to see in the dim room, but I saw Joe sitting on the floor, his back against the wall, his head on his shoulder. His face and the front of his shirt were covered with blood. He was not moving. Kevin began to stir. He put his hands under him and tried to push himself up, but he couldn't. I rolled over and got to my hands and knees and crawled over to Joe. I loosened his necktie and raised his head back. He opened his eyes and drew his huge arm back, getting ready for a haymaker. I caught the arm just in time, but in the condition he was in, I doubted the punch would have had any sting.

"Easy, Joe; it's Doc. Can you see me?"

His eyes rolled around, trying to focus. His arms moved around over his body, as if to tell his brain he was still in one piece. He was in bad, bad shape, especially for a fight that was over so fast. This I knew right away: the guy hitting him was a pro. Had to be. A former prizefighter, bouncer, bodyguard; what the mob calls an "enforcer." Whatever the name, he was a pro at hurting people.

"Kev, can you hear me?" I said over my shoulder.

"Ohhhh . . . that you, Doc?"

"Yeah. Can you get up? We've got to get out of here; they might decide to come back and kill us."

Joe moaned, and I pulled him gently away from the wall and let him down slowly on the floor. "You said there was a black-and-white down the street?" I asked Kevin. "Well, where the fuck are they?"

I got up and went to the door on the far wall. I shoved the brass bar down and pushed. It opened. I saw two uniformed policemen jump out of a squad car and level their shotguns at me. I ducked back inside, fell onto the floor, and rolled away from the door before they could fill me with double-ought buck.

Christ! Getting it from both sides—

A deafening thumping on the door now.

"Brindelli! Brindelli! You in there?"

I yelled back that we were all in here and not to shoot.

"Open the fuckin' door! Now!"

I staggered back to my feet and pushed the bar down, then slid away to the side as the two cops in SWAT vests came storming in. The second cop, obviously high on an adrenaline rush, took in the scene and instantly made the wrong assumption. He saw two badly beat-up comrades and a stranger who seemed fine. Ergo, I was the enemy who had brought this upon his chums. Without a second's thought, he drew a leather sap from his hip pocket and swatted me across the jaw with it.

Lights out for this puppy.

I came to in an ambulance with an EMS lady looking down at me. She patted me on the chest, which hurt like blazes after that punch to my chest by Puttyface.

"Officer Peabody wants you to know that he is very sincerely sorry about the mistake," she said, putting a compress on my jaw.

"Bless his little Nazi heart . . ." was all I could mutter. I hoped it would somehow lighten the scene. Instead, I saw her face cloud over.

"It's just terrible what happened," she murmured. "One officer down . . . one killed. That's why he acted the way he did."

"One cop dead?"

She nodded sadly, and I had the sudden thought it might be Joe.

"How about Brindelli and O'Hearn?"

"Huh? Sorry; I don't know their names."

"Were they in uniform?"

When she nodded, I knew that the men she was referring to were probably the ones Joe had waiting down the street to bail us out. This was awful; Joe would never let it go. Of course, judging from his appearance, maybe his days as a cop were over anyway.

Mr. Scarface didn't have enough time to rough me up very badly; two hours after the fracas I was normal except for a nagging pain in my jaw and a battered rib cage that hurt when I twisted my torso. These would disappear soon. Kevin had a smashed nose and a lot of bruises, but it was nothing that a week at home wouldn't fix.

But Joe was a different story. He wasn't released from Mount Auburn hospital for the better part of a week. Mary called Marty at her brother's place in New Jersey; she started driving back to Boston practically before she hung up the phone and was at Joe's bedside within four hours. The effect on my brother-in-law was, of course, extraordinary; he made great improvement and after four days was released. Back in his luxurious apartment with the woman who had made him reborn, he continued to improve. But it would be a while before Detective Lieutenant Joe Brindelli would cruise the streets again. He had a fractured clavicle, three fractured ribs, a cracked mandible, and a broken kneecap.

And the worst part was this: as bad as the physical injuries were, they were slight compared to his emotional state when he heard that his longtime friend Tommy Mahoney had been hit twice in the chest with a nine-millimeter, killed in the fight at Brian Flynn's.

For two whole days he did not speak—even to Marty. Then he stalked around the apartment, in his circus tent of a robe, putting away an awesome amount of liquor, claiming it was a painkiller. I suppose, in a sense, it was. But Marty was beside herself, seeing her husband, who had been dealt way more than his share of bad cards in his life, going straight down the chute.

But the worst blow didn't come until the following week, when the Internal Affairs Division of the state Bureau of Public Safety approached Kevin with what they claimed was "sworn testimony" by some of the bar patrons that the "two arresting officers"—Brindelli and O'Hearn—failed to follow standard procedure by not showing the man at the wall phone their badges before attempting to escort him from the premises. This was a serious mistake because it gave the man the impression he was simply being bullied by a couple of drunks, not being detained by law enforcement officials for questioning.

O'Hearn blew it, too. He at first vehemently denied the charge, then later admitted the mistake. IAD then officially notified both of them that there would be a full investigation.

This hit Joe like a twelve-pound sledge. He instantly felt the full guilt not only for the bungled arrest, but for his friend Tommy Mahoney's death.

Great.

And not only that, but if the cops ever did catch up with the thugs who beat us up in the back room at Flynn's, it was extremely doubtful they could make anything stick due to this breach in procedure.

Which certainly tells us all something about the state of our criminal justice system.

Anyway, just as things looked their bleakest, two things managed to float into my aging brain.

One: No matter if the mark at the phone could have mistaken Joe and Kevin for thugs, there was no way in hell the triggermen in the alley behind Flynn's could have mistaken the uniformed cops who jumped out of the first black-and-white. The punk who shot Tommy Mahoney *knew* he was shooting a cop. Pure and simple.

Two: If IAD persisted in persecuting Joe and Kevin, I would—with the aid of a sharp lawyer like Brady Coyne—approach Captain Mahaffey at the Bureau of Public Safety and tell him I was prepared to make a sworn deposition—probably in the presence of one of the *Globe*'s leading city reporters—

that I was brutally assaulted by Officer Leonard Peabody with a blackjack—which is illegal for Boston police to carry in the first place—without so much as a word from him before he struck me.

I didn't mention any of this to Joe. Instead I called on Kevin O'Hearn at his walk-up duplex in Medford the next day to see what he thought. In short, he thought it was bully, and was almost beside himself with joy and relief when I left.

On the way home, I phoned Brady's law office from my car phone to see if he could meet me for a drink at the Library Bar in the Copley Plaza around four.

"Absolutely! I'll tell you about my trip to the Rogue River next month. There's still time for you to make a reservation, Doc."

"I'll consider it. But we're in a bit of a pickle right now, and I need your help."

"Unnnnnh," Brady sighed into his glass of Tennessee whiskey on the rocks. He took a slow sip and let it slide down his throat. He was already tan from fly fishing the rivers of Massachusetts: the Deerfield, the Westfield, the Swift, and so on. He lives for this sport, loving nothing better than dressing himself up in waders, felt-bottomed boots, a vest (or maybe a float tube), an entire array of surgeon's hemostats and other tools (which I provide him with), portable fly-tying kit (to "match the hatch"), nets, magnifying glasses, spare leaders, tippets, spools, books on stream entomology, and the rest. Until he can barely move. Then he wades into these icy currents and flips his thousand-dollar rod around until he catches a fish.

Which, of course, he immediately *releases* back into the river. Then does the whole silly thing all over again, returning home with nothing to eat—just a sore arm and ice-cold lower body.

Is this stupid, or what?

Once he took me fly fishing and I wanted to keep the fourteen-inch trout I caught. He would have none of it. I asked him if this river was catch-and-release. He replied in the negative. I then informed him I intended to keep the fish and eat it.

He stopped in midcast, turned around, and looked at me in horror.

Then I realized that if I did keep the fish, he might cry himself to sleep for a whole week. So I put it back.

"But, hell, Brady, can't I at least *maim* it a little? You know, cut off a fin or something?"

A joke, of course. But he scarcely talked to me the whole drive back to Concord. He says that there is still hope that I will grow up someday, and stop acting like a thirteen-year-old. Come to think of it, Mary and my friend Moe Abramson keep saying the same thing about me. I just don't get it.

But anyway, Brady's words pissed me off so much I almost sneaked out and let the air out of his tires. But I didn't because I'm a true friend and a nice guy. Lucky for him.

"Tell you what," he said after listening to my tale. "I'll call one of my sources. You know the name Dianne Liebermann?"

"Sure. She writes for the *Globe*. I've seen her picture, too. Nice. You banging her or what?"

A slow grin spread over his face. "Please, Doc. I'm a professional; don't insult my sense of propriety."

All I needed to hear. Definitely banging her.

"I would never even consider such a . . ." He droned on and on about his moral precepts, etc.

Banging her and her *daughter* . . .

". . . anyway, she has a law degree from Georgetown and is a hell of a good reporter, too. Specializes in city scandals. Public outrages. She's a first-rate investigative reporter. She'll scare the shit out of the whole state police. What I'll do is, I'll call her and get her to approach Mahaffey with a statement you have written and signed. When you get the draft done, fax it to my office and I'll dolly it up so it looks all legal and threatening, then fax it back to you. With this document, she'll storm into this Mahaffey's office and that'll be the last you or Joe will ever hear of this threat of investigation."

"Great, Brady. I knew I could count on you."

"It'll cost you about seven hundred," he added as an afterthought.

I stared at him. "I thought we were friends, Brady."

"We are. But Dianne doesn't come cheap. Good people always cost, Doc. You ought to know; you live in a big country house in Concord."

"And you're not getting any of this fee?"

"I didn't say that. I may take a small percentage," he said, finishing his drink. "After all, fishing the Rogue isn't cheap, you know."

I trudged up to the bar for our second drinks thinking about lawyers.

Banging her, her daughter, and her daughter's *dog* . . .

9

TWO WEEKS LATER JOE WAS SUBSTANTIALLY HEALED, AND MORE importantly, the threat of the Internal Affairs investigation had vanished in a twinkling after Dianne Liebermann paid a brief visit to the police brass.

A welcome upshot of the whole thing was that the state bureau granted both Kevin and Joe three weeks' paid time off. It was not a punishment or suspension of any sort; it was simply a well-deserved break after what they'd been through.

But the police on all levels—local, state, and federal—were humming. A cop had been shot to death, and all of his brothers—and sisters—in the profession were out to get the killers. One guy, the huge enforcer, had been positively identified by the three of us. His name was Gary Walsh, a thirty-seven-year-old native of Charlestown. As I suspected after watching Joe cave in under his punches, he had been in the ring as a heavyweight for almost a decade before age and injuries forced him to retire. A compulsive gambler, his debts soon overwhelmed him and he went into dealing drugs until he was caught at it and did a stretch in the federal pen at Atlanta. When he got out, he found a new avocation as a collection agent for the mob, getting loan shark victims to come up with their "vig" every week. Now he was still on the loose, but photos of him hung in every police department in the Northeast.

We all knew it was only a matter of time before he was caught. As for the others, a composite sketch of two of the men had been worked up with help from the three of us and some of the patrons of Flynn's. While no mug shots of these desperadoes turned up, the law was confident they would be found shortly as well.

But the man who had called me on the phone, the man who whispered, was still a mystery. Was he the guy Joe and Kevin collared before the ruckus started, or only an underling? Was the guy with the shattered voice box even near Flynn's tavern at the time? Joe said he doubted it.

After going through all this, I decided that we all needed a break. So Joe and Marty joined Mary and me at our cottage, the Breakers, in North Eastham on the Cape. It was now the last week in May. The days were long and sunny. The ocean was cold, but on the Bay side, where we lived, the water was shallow and sometimes warm enough for a brief dip. None of the usual summer crowd had arrived yet. This was the best time to be on the Cape except for fall. The no-see-ums were bad now and then when the breeze didn't keep them away, but then we could retreat to the screened porch that overlooked the water.

"Hey, Doc," murmured Joe as he reclined on the wooden lounger in the afternoon sun, a pair of Armani sunglasses wrapped around his head. Looked just like an Italian film director. "I just want to thank you again for saving our ass. It was nice of you. Also, if I do say so, it was brilliant, and the three weeks off feel good already."

"Shut up. You're just kissing my ass so I'll buy the food tonight."

"Nah. Wrong." He wagged his finger at me. "Marty and I already bought it this morning in Wellfleet."

"Well? What?"

"We're not telling. But while there I made a call to your old chum who runs the Olde Curiosity Shoppe downtown, right near the old customshouse."

"Bill Givens?"

"The very same. I remembered how he helped you with his explanations of the ivory trade two years ago. I had a wild hunch that a guy who'd traveled as much as he has might have some inside info on a godforsaken place like Suriname. And, of course, I was right."

"He's been to Suriname?"

"Twice. His cousin died there."

"Died there?" This did not sound promising. "Of what . . . or don't I want to know?"

"You don't want to know." He gave a slow yawn and shifted his position in the sun. "But he may tell you anyway, over dinner."

"He's coming here?"

"Uh-huh. We didn't think you and Mary would mind."

"Of course not; he's always welcome."

"He said he'd bring one of those mini-kegs of Grolsch."

"In that case, he's extremely welcome."

At a little after five a white Rover sedan pulled up behind our cottage and a powerfully built man in his seventies emerged from it, waving merrily at us. William Givens was deeply tanned, and his broad, leonine head was ringed with silky white hair. He was, of course, a member of the infamous Boston group of intellectuals known as the Bald-Headed League, or the Society of Bald-Headed Men, or simply "The Baldies." This dubious group first formed as an offshoot of the local MENSA Society, and included many luminaries. Perhaps the most famous and beloved of these was the late Isaac Asimov, who was also renowned for forming his own New York–based mystery reader's society called the Trapdoor Spiders.

Joe helped him lug the two-gallon can of Grolsch beer from the trunk of the car (which Givens insisted on calling "the boot") and up the steps to the cottage deck. As soon as we were settled, Givens drew out a leather case from his coat and took out three cigars that carried distinctive black bands with white dots. He handed one to Joe and one to me and I caressed the semi-oily wrapper and sniffed at it. Smelled terrific.

"What is this?"

"*Cohiba*. Cuban. Castro's personal favorite."

"How'd you get it?"

"Never mind," he said in his clipped British accent, brandishing a Davidoff cutter and snipping the ends off both of them, then lighting them with a long cedarwood match.

"Know why I'm here?" he asked through a cloud of pungent smoke.

"Yes. Because we enjoy your company," I answered.

"You're too kind, Doc. And too good a cook. I'm here because Joe mentioned that you all are rubbing elbows with Suriname."

"Yes, in a way."

"Well, don't do it. I've been all over the world—a single visit to my shop will prove that. I've been to places I've loved and places I've hated. I choose to live in New England, at least for the present. Perhaps, as my bones get stiffer and my disposition lapses, I may have to make a choice between Tuscany, Andorra, or Provence. But I would certainly avoid the tropics as well as the very cold climes. At all costs, I would avoid the northeast coast of South America, Doc. There are good places on that continent. Parts of Peru and Ecuador. Sections of Brazil and Argentina . . . Uruguay is a delightful place if you don't mind an aristocracy composed mostly of German fascists. But I would avoid those three little countries perched atop Brazil."

"Too hot?"

"In every sense. The capital city is Paramaribo, on the coast. I was there in the late fifties lending my cousin money so he could start a trading station there. He'd done the same type of venture successfully on the island of Timor, and thought he'd try it in the West. Well, the nation was still under the Dutch at the time, so it had some hope. But even then, it was difficult. The insects alone would drive most people crackers."

He paused to fill his big mug with Holland beer and sat back, puffing and sipping. "From the low coastal plain, which is really swampland and loaded with malaria and yellow jack, the ground rises as one heads inland. Now, as I recall, there is a narrow strip of land between the lowlands and the high mountains of the south that seemed quite pleasant at the time. Perhaps an enterprising soul could undertake some kind of ranching there if he could find a strain of disease- and heat-resistant cattle. But then, since independence in 1975, the reports I've heard about the political and economic situation are not encouraging."

"What are the mountains like?" asked Mary. "I bet the air would be better up there. Charlie and I went to Caracas on one of those cruises a few years ago and it was delightful."

"You're absolutely right, Mary. I'm sure the mountains in southern Suriname are delightful. If one could only get to them. But where are the roads? There are no landing strips there yet, and may never be. As for the rivers, they are all raging torrents surrounded by impenetrable jungle and forest growth."

"Well, actually, Bill, we're not planning on visiting there," she said. "It's just that we've sort of brushed up against some people who might be from there. That's all."

"That's all?" He gaped at her, his eyes wide. "That's *all*?"

She nodded and leaned back, watching the ocean.

"Believe me, madam, that's quite enough, I assure you. Because in a moment, I'll show you what probably happened to my poor cousin, Robert Oldham."

"Why not show us now?" Joe asked.

"Perhaps we better have a little more beer first."

"Then can you tell us, rather than show us?" pursued Mary.

"He went into the interior a number of times to see if there was any way to open up some kind of trade route to the mountains. But each time he was met with disappointment. He told me of his attempts; that's why I'm so familiar—albeit in a second-hand way—with the terrain of the place. One thing that kept recurring in his travels was the mention of precious stones in the hills: diamonds, emeralds, rubies, and sapphires. South America is one of the few places on earth where all four types of first-water gems are found. Colombia has long been famous for its diamond mines. Brazil, for diamonds and especially emeralds. But according to what Robert heard repeatedly, the mountains and foothills of Suriname were rich beyond belief. Naturally, he was eager to get his hands on the raw stones and then set up a cutting and finishing business."

"And nobody had a similar idea?" asked Joe.

"Certainly they did—the people of the Netherlands in particular did. As you know, DeBeers is by far the world's largest diamond company. In addition to their vast holdings in Africa, they are always seeking new fields to exploit. I think that's a major reason they acquired Suriname, and only let the country gain its independence when they saw the futility of getting at the stones that apparently lurk in the mountains."

"How was it so futile?" I asked. "If the rewards were even half as great as rumored, why didn't they build a narrow-gauge railroad or something?"

"They tried it; all the crews either died or simply disappeared."

"Died of what?" asked Mary.

"Malaria in the old days. In more recent times, cholera, parasites, jungle fever, snakebite. It's not a user-friendly place."

"I have read this," I said. "Most of the books on jungles and the tropics say the fiercest places of all are in the Amazon Basin of South America."

"And right they are. How do you like your Cohiba, Doc?"

"A lot," I said, leaving the deck to take a leak. I don't see how some people sip at beer. It's not meant to be sipped like wine, but drunk. On my way back from the bathroom my eyes fell upon a large cigar box sitting on the table in the darkened hall. It was half covered by Bill Givens's light jacket. It looked like an ordinary cigar box of the highest quality, made of cedarwood. Yet it had no brand markings on it, and it was quite large: as large as a cake box. I slid it over to the edge of the counter. Thinking that perhaps it held more of the contraband Cohibas, I opened it.

And wished I hadn't.

I went back out on the deck and put my hands on the rail, leaning over, trying to steady myself.

"Hey, Doc, you okay?" asked Joe.

"Yeah—fine."

"Well, c'mon and help me get the steamer kettle ready. It'll be a while before it's hot enough to put the lobsters and clams in."

I helped Joe get the clambake kettle set up, but I was not my chipper self.

The dinner was great. So great that halfway through I actually got my appetite back. Steamed lobsters with clams and hot French bread, washed down with tumblers of Grolsch, did the trick. Afterward, as we sat inside with a big fire going in the rock fireplace, Givens said it was time to show us what had probably befallen his ill-fated cousin, Robert.

"I'm not sure that's a good idea, Bill," I warned. "I already had a peek."

He looked up at me, a maniacal grin on his round, tanned face. "Ah, me lad! And what did you think?"

"It's, uh . . . different. Not what I thought it would be."

"Quite so. I admit it's one of the more curious of my curiosities, don't you think?"

I nodded, and settled back in my chair while Bill Givens opened the box and drew out the smallish, brown object. In life it was considerably larger, of course. The eyes were sewn shut, as was the mouth. Tendrils of delicate straw twine cascaded down from them. Crude sutures, perhaps, but effective. The hair was still in place, luxurious glossy black, and so straight it could have been ironed.

"Good God!" Mary gasped. "It's not real, is it?"

"Afraid so. I bought it from a chap in Paramaribo just before I left. He claimed to have got it in the interior. Most people know there are headhunter tribes in the Amazon Basin. The most notorious are the Jivaro from Ecuador. But as you can see, they are also alive and well in the uplands of Suriname."

"And your cousin . . . ?" said Joe, his eyes transfixed by the shrunken head.

"Can't really say," shrugged Givens. "Since no trace was ever found of him or the six natives who went with him. And I *do* apologize if this display shocks you. But . . . I suppose that was half my purpose in bringing my little friend with me. Because, believe me when I say Suriname is not for the faint of heart."

"Headhunters!" whispered Joe.

"Headhunters!" said Mary.

They both looked at me.

"Okay, Charlie—tell Bill what Chris Ramos said just before he died."

"He said to me: 'Watch out for those fucking headhunters, and their goddamn red frogs.' "

We all sat in silence while Bill Givens placed the head back inside its cedarwood home. Even from where I sat, I could again smell the smoky, spicy sandalwood odor that I had first noticed when I opened the box.

"Well, he was correct, of course. However, the reference to the red frogs is a mystery. I don't know of any red frogs anywhere on this planet . . . and I consider myself well traveled. But as to the headhunters—yes, he was right on the money."

More silence. Then Mary spoke.

"Bill, what do the people from Suriname look like?"

He placed both palms on his knees and sat back, staring at the ceiling. "Let's say for starters, Mary: *exotic*. You see, the original natives, the Indians of the river valleys, are still there. The headhunters I and Chris Ramos mentioned are among these. Then the next group would be the black Africans originally imported as slaves from the sixteen hundreds on. You may not know this, but of all the slaves imported to the New World from the west coast of Africa, only sixteen percent went to North America. The other five-sixths went to plantations in the Caribbean or South America."

"Really? Only one-sixth of them landed here?"

"Absolutely. So the black Africans are a very large group. The third group are the Malays who came from Indonesia when the Dutch ran both countries. They provide the Asiatic influence on the genes. Finally, of course, there are some remnants of the Dutch European occupation. Though by far the smallest group, it remains, as any student of history might expect, by far the wealthiest and most influential. So we have the native Indians, the blacks, the Malays, and the Dutch. Truly a worldwide representation of humanity. But the lines blur over the ages, and I would say a hefty percentage of people from Suriname would reflect this fourfold input."

"Well," Joe said quietly, his hands interlocked across his

ample stomach, "that would describe our friend in the Lincoln to a T."

"I would be extremely careful if whatever endeavor you're undertaking deals with people from this place who could in any way oppose you," intoned Givens solemnly as he drew on his jacket, tucked his little friend in the cedar box under his arm, and headed for the door. "Remember again: Suriname is exotic, and promising—has been this way for centuries. But as I said before, it is not for the faint of heart. Good evening, all, and thank you for another glorious evening."

After he left we cleaned up the dishes, then gathered around the fire once more with mugs of coffee. I lit a pipe, and let the fragrant blue clouds wash around my head.

"I think we should rethink this whole thing," Joe finally said.

"What do you mean, rethink it?" asked Mary.

"I mean we should forget it."

"All of it," I asked, "or just parts of it?"

"Hell, Doc, you can't forget parts of it. Don't you see by now? All the parts are intertwined. We've got a nasty gang in Southie who's committed to finding out where Ramos hid whatever he managed to squirrel away. We've got this weird group down in New Bedford cruising around in the Lincoln who are probably from Suriname . . . and, dammit, who probably *are* headhunters. We don't know exactly what they're after yet, but we can sure as hell guess."

"Joey? Do you think there is some kind of treasure Ramos left behind?"

"Yes, I do. I'm positive of it. Why? Because other people, bad people in the know, are after it. And they're willing to murder cops to get to it. Now, thinking of this, doesn't the attempted 'jailbreak' of Chris Ramos back in ninety-two make all kinds of sense now? I mean, all kinds of sense?"

Mary and I admitted that indeed it did: it wasn't to get Ramos free; it was to kidnap him and make him lead the breakout artists to the stash.

"That's right. And after he led them to it, do you think they would have said, 'Thanks, Chris, you can go home now'? No, they woulda killed him and dumped his body into Fort Point

Channel. That's what. Look at me: now I've got a beat-up partner and a dead colleague. And my name is shit at work because
of it, never mind that I feel that way already because of what
happened in that alley behind Flynn's. And I could be next.
Doc, Mare—you could both be in a lot of danger already. I say
we let it go."

"Okay," I said. "If you think it's best. We'll all just bow out."

"Good, Charlie. That's the first sensible thing we've done."

But our resolution didn't do any good. Because as soon as I
showed up at the office, another element to the puzzle surfaced.

I had no idea how she found me.

10

"SOMEBODY HERE TO SEE YOU, DR. ADAMS."

I could tell immediately by the tone of Susan Petri's voice
that she wasn't overjoyed at the patient who'd just arrived in the
outer office.

"Who could it be? I don't have an appointment until two. Is it
a salesman?"

"I don't think so; she doesn't look like one."

"She?"

"Right. She, uh, says it's very important."

"Well who is she? A referral? Is she from Concord? Lexington?"

There was a pause as Susan covered the mouthpiece. Then
she came back on the line.

"Claudia Kelly. From Boston."

The name sent an electric charge through me.

"I'll come out."

There she was, sitting with her ankles crossed on the sofa

reading *Car and Driver*. She looked up at me as I drew near. Same brown-black eyes. I got a closer look at her this time. It was worth it. I took Claudia to be in her late twenties, or maybe early thirties. As typical with people with darkish skin, she appeared youthful—it would be hard to fix her age—but then I remembered Joe had said thirty-one. She was wearing a beige knit dress that clung to her nicely. Around her neck was a silver chain from which hung a Castilian cross. The dark brown hair still cascaded down to her shoulders. Also, even from several feet, she smelled great.

"Hi, Claudia. This is a pleasant surprise." I was not lying.

She stood up, came over to me, and offered her hand. It was cool and dry, and firm. I looked at her face again up close. Something was familiar about it. I thought I had seen this face before—not just at the funeral in Fairhaven, but somewhere . . . and close up. Where was it . . . and when?

"Yes?" she said, almost in a whisper.

"What?"

"Ah, nothing," she laughed. "I just thought you were really studying me there for a second."

"I suppose I was. Probably my habit as a person who works with faces and jaws."

"I guess I should tell you why I'm here, Dr. Adams. There's a lot I have to tell you, and frankly, I think you'll be interested to hear it. I was hoping we could go somewhere, maybe for lunch, if that's not too inconvenient."

"Well, I . . ." I stammered, looking at my watch. It said ten-thirty.

"Okay then, maybe just coffee? I feel I should treat you to something, after showing up here unannounced. It was sort of a last-minute decision on my part."

"We'll go to a little restaurant at the old train station. They've great coffee and pastries. Susan, will you get by till we get back?"

"Sure." The tone was flat; she was looking down at some papers on her desk. Not exactly thrilled at this interruption out of the blue.

We walked out of the office and into the parking lot, where Claudia showed me to a new model Cadillac coupe, dark blue with tan leather interior. This made me wonder about her financial status. Everything I'd heard about SEAMATT was that it went bust—then the partners, first one then the other, tried to put it all back together again by going outside the law. When they got busted, the law apparently took everything they left. That is, except the fabled stash belonging to Chris Ramos. Either Claudia Kelly had a very nice job, or a rich boyfriend, or something else going for her. She oozed money. She also oozed a lot of other things, all of them greatly appreciated by a fifty-plus-year-old man.

Ten minutes later we were seated at the Cafe au Beauchamp, having hot blueberry muffins and Sumatran coffee.

"Okay," she said, "here it is. First: I recognized you and Mary right away at the funeral; I've heard so much about you over the past six or seven years it's not even funny, Doc. Can I call you Doc?"

"By all means."

"So, I knew I had to see you sometime. However, I didn't think the funeral was the proper place to force the introduction."

"Wait a sec. Who told you about me? Your father's been dead for years; I never met him or your mother. The only person I knew was Chris—I never even met his wife, either."

She put down her coffee cup, reached over and placed her hand on mine, and squeezed it. Then she brought her head closer to me. I saw then that her eyes were wet, just the way they were at the funeral service. She looked a lot like Sophia Loren just then. Sign me up.

"Doc—" She stopped, looked down to wipe away a tear, then looked at me again. She reached her other hand over and grabbed my other hand. Then—and as I look back I still can't believe she did this—she drew herself up to me and kissed me, then brought her left hand around to the back of my head and held me there, in a very sincere kiss. So there we were, kissing over a coffee table at a prominent restaurant in my town. Great.

"Claudia . . . what the hell's going on?"

"Can't you figure it out? Daddy spoke of you so often. Oh, he loved you, Doc!"

"Why? I never even met Larry Kelly—"

"Not him—!" she spat. "My other father. My *real* father. Doc, look at my face again. Who do you see?"

Right then I realized why I had stared at her so hard before. I did know that face. From across the table, Christos Ramos jumped right out at me, come back from the dead in the person of a very luscious young woman.

"So that's it! Chris Ramos was your father, not Larry Kelly. Then his suspicions about Chris and your mother were true."

"Hell yes, they were true! And that's why he had Chris framed, Doc. Larry Kelly was a drunken brute by the time I had my earliest memories of him. My mother, Ida Kelly, kept telling me he was a very nice man when she married him. Maybe that was the case once upon a time. But from the time I could remember, he was a bully. And since I was the product, the evidence of what he saw as a traitorous infidelity, he couldn't stand me either. Thank God the booze finished him when I was twenty-five, and set Mom free. I was hoping, since Chris's wife was no longer alive, that he would marry Mom and make it official. But he didn't. As much as he loved me, Doc—and nobody loved his daughter more than Chris loved me—I think he regretted the infidelity. He was a very devout Catholic. So much so I think it hurt him sometimes."

"I have something to tell you that you'll find interesting, Claudia. Just before he died—in fact, as he was dying—your father told me three things. One was to look out for you. He said he left you everything he had—"

"That's true; I'm very comfortable because of him."

"Then he told me to beware of some headhunters. Headhunters and their damn red frogs. Do you make any sense out of that?"

She looked at me over the lip of her coffee cup. She put it down slowly. I thought I heard her clear her throat very softly, as if buying time to think.

"He told you that?"

"Yep. Sounded like nonsense at the time—not the part about you—the part about the headhunters and the frogs. You ever hear of red frogs?"

She shook her head. "No, but his business took him to some

exotic places. Either that or he could have been pulling your leg."

"On his deathbed?"

She shrugged. "You said three things. What about the third thing? Or don't you want to tell me?"

"The third thing was a set of directions to find something he had hidden in your church in Fairhaven."

"Saint Bernard's? He loved that church. And Father DeSilva too."

"I gathered that from talking with the padre when we were down there."

Now I had to ask her. Because Joe had come up empty looking under that third pew—finding nothing under the bench but a bunch of chisel marks where someone else had dug out the treasure. So I took a breath and asked, "Did he ever mention anything to you about hiding something under the third pew back on the left side?"

"No." She took a bite of her croissant. There seemed to be no artifice in her voice, no shifting of the eyes or body that might indicate she was lying. On the other hand, if she were a good liar—and there are a lot of these about, as we all know—then she wouldn't betray her lie. "Why, did you check it out?"

I stared at her for three or four seconds before answering. Each second seemed like a minute.

"Yes," I finally said. "We checked it out. Somebody got there before us."

"I'm sorry."

"Sorry? Hey, don't you resent the fact that I was searching for something your father had hidden?" I had to ask; she seemed so neutral, but I was certain that underneath she should be resentful.

She smiled at me, then leaned way over the table and kissed me on the cheek.

"Hey, stop doing that. This is where I live, you know. Somebody will see us and word will get back to my home."

"Sorry. But you're rather kissable. I was showing you exactly how resentful I am, Doc. For you getting him out of that filthy hellhole and letting him come back to Concord, where he could at least be outside part of the time and breathe fresh air. If I'm sorry about anything, I'm sorry I didn't get in touch with you before to thank you."

"Well, at least I'm thankful he took good care of you."

"Yes, he did. But most of what I have from him he gave me before he went . . . inside. That's what they call prison you know: inside."

I nodded.

"I have his house, a two-bedroom bungalow in the Harbor-view section of Fairhaven. It's not far from Saint Bernard's and it overlooks Buzzards Bay. Also, there's his warehouse—an old, two-story stone building that's right on the wharf in Fair-haven. It's deserted now, but who knows? In a few years, I hear they'll start gentrifying New Bedford's waterfront. You know, transform the warehouses into condos. Put in a big marina. Just like they did to Boston in the seventies. The climate's nice there; it's practically an extension of the Cape."

"That's true. Of all the smaller cities in Massachusetts, New Bedford's become my favorite."

"Then there are the boats and barges . . ." she said almost absently. My interest was ignited though; I've always been in love with boats—any kind of boat.

"I have three big barges and two smaller ones. They're for sale. Have been for months. Guess there's not much of a market for barges nowadays in the Northeast."

"What about the boats?"

"Want one? There's a small tender vessel of forty-six feet. Used to refuel vessels when they're at sea, or anchored off-shore. A good part of Daddy's business in the last few years was the refueling of fishing vessels at sea."

"Why at sea? Why not just refuel after the haul?"

"Because if you're on to a school, or dragging scallops in a hot place, you want to stay there, let the fueling vessel come to you."

"I see. So you'll keep that boat?"

"I think so. I have a guy running it for me. I give him a modest salary and he keeps a cut of all sales. Sort of like a commission. It's working."

"Good."

"Then, there are two other vessels . . ."

"I can tell you've been around pros, Claudia. Only professional fishermen or navy people use the term 'vessel.' "

"Right," she laughed. "Got that from Daddy. Anyway, there's an oceangoing tugboat. Seventy-two feet. Hull still sound. Needs new engines. I'm trying to unload that for a hundred fifty thousand. So far, no takers. But it's a steal."

"Why hasn't it moved?"

"Same thing as the barges, Doc. The hauling business is dead in the Northeast. What plagued the business in the late seventies and forced Daddy into smuggling is still with us. There's just no market now for hauling scrap iron or other heavy stuff. Fuel costs are too high—the market's gone away, too. Face it: industry is leaving this country. At least this part of it. The politicians will tell you it ain't so. But it is."

I nodded in sad agreement and buttered half a croissant.

"The other boat's a big one," she added nonchalantly. "A freighter."

I looked up from my plate. "A freighter? An oceangoing freighter?"

"Yep. One hundred fifty-seven feet. The *Santiago*. I've got pictures of it at home I could show you. Pretty vessel. Not big, but just right for hauling fruit from the West Indies, or rosewood from Brazil . . ."

Suddenly, her words made a vision swim into my head. There I was, standing on the bridge of the *Santiago*. Panama hat on my head, Brazilian cheroot clenched in my teeth:

I look over the rail at the stevedores far below on the ancient stone quay. The skinny brown natives sing a plaintive song as they load copra and hides into the hull. Everywhere in this river port the water is hot and brown, and stinks. Birds and monkeys scream in the forest. Wizened Indians paddle alongside the hull in log canoes with wild pigs and 'gators tied in the bows. White monkey bones are stuck through their noses; glorious plumes erupt from their matted hair. I hear a samba from a waterfront cafe. The hot, deep basso beat humps the moist air. A barefoot woman saunters from the cafe, leans seductively against the Spanish stone pillar, her black eyes gazing up at me. Funny . . . she looks just like Claudia. . . . It is hot in Belém . . . but soon we'll be under way, headed for Rio. The sun is sinking in the west; the sky is red-gold and the ocean a rich purple. . . . Frigate birds soar above me on slender bent wings. The woman opens her gorgeous lips, mouthing words I cannot hear but understand. She cannot wait until tonight. Ah, duty calls. I shrug and flip the cheroot overboard. It hisses out in the brown water, startling a giant loggerhead turtle that makes its way toward the bollards with slow strokes of his flippers. I descend the gangplank . . . walking toward her with the smell of musk and gardenias in the sultry air. The samba beat grows more intense—

"Doc? Doc, you okay?"

"Huh? Oh—yeah. Fine."

"You seemed . . . gone for a second."

"I always wanted to be a skipper of a tramp steamer. What a way to see the world, eh?"

"Could be . . . with the right person." She was smiling.

"And is there a right person in your life?"

"There . . . could be. I'm not sure. I just met a person two months ago who I'm still seeing. And who is very nice—almost perfect. But there's something . . . I don't know what it is, that makes me hesitate to make any real commitment."

"Hey, you're sounding like a guy, Claudia."

"I know. Hey, you know what? I think women are beginning to think more like men, don't you?"

"I do. I think as they assume more business roles, and are drawn away from the traditional female roles, the thinking seems to go in some of the same channels, anyway."

"I think the thing is that perhaps this person's too interested in money to suit me."

"Your money, perhaps?" I knew I was being nosy now, but I couldn't help it.

"Well, money in general. But, yes, my money too."

"Well, you're certainly better off than a lot of people. Are you planning on selling the *Santiago*? That could bring a substantial hunk of change, I would think."

"I'd sell the dear old tub in a heartbeat if I could. Gee, I hope Daddy isn't up there hearing this. He just loved her."

"Well, why can't you sell it? It's yours."

"Can't find it; that's the problem."

"Can't find it? As in, can't find your glasses or your car keys? C'mon, Claudia, it's pretty damn hard to misplace a hundred-fifty-foot freighter."

"The last we saw of her was just before Daddy was sent to Concord for the first time. She was leaving New Bedford with only a fractional cargo, headed for the Bahamas."

"What's a fractional cargo?"

"What it sounds like. You can either be full, which is best of course, or half full when you leave port. If you're less than full, or three-quarters, you'd better expect a prompt and lucrative load awaiting you at your destination. Otherwise, you'll lose money. And time is money in the shipping business. If you have to wait somewhere like Manaus for a week because the cargo isn't on the dock waiting for you, then you lose money. A fractional cargo is a euphemism for a vessel that's just about empty."

"Why was the boat leaving almost empty?"

"Because, Doc, there was nothing to haul from New England. That's what I've been saying all along. It's dead up here: New England's gone high-tech; there's no room for heavy maritime hauling. Daddy would let *Santiago* go down to the Bahamas, even as far south as Trinidad, going very light if he could get a good cargo coming back."

"Like what?"

"Fruit and wood, or coffee."

"And later on, drugs?"

She stopped chewing.

"Yes. Drugs. For a very, very short time, until his conscience got the best of him and he quit the drug trade."

"But your dad—your mother's husband, kept it up?"

"Oh yeah, Larry kept it up till the end. He talked Daddy into it for a while, but my father never did it again."

"How long did he smuggle drugs? Eight years or so?"

"No. He did it for about four years. Mostly ganja from Jamaica and the Bahamas, not hard drugs. He knew what hard drugs did to people. He wasn't so down on hemp, though. When he was skipping the *Santiago*, he spent a lot of time in South America and the islands—sometimes weeks at a time waiting for cargo. Marijuana is just part of the culture down there, like alcohol is here. But Daddy saw that the rum in those ports caused a lot more damage and misery than the ganja. So he wasn't particularly guilt-ridden about that. He was a good Catholic; he never wanted to hurt anyone. In fact, he wanted to help."

"That was in the eighties?"

"Uhhhh . . . before that. In the late seventies."

"But I thought he was into smuggling for longer than that. Unless the others lied about him. The story was that he was an active smuggler for over a dozen years."

"First of all, the other side did lie. I think Larry got Daddy into smuggling drugs for two reasons. One was, obviously, to improve SEAMATT's bottom line; the company was almost bankrupt. But the other reason, just as strong if not more so, was to get the goods on Chris Ramos for smuggling. This way, if Larry was caught, he could turn state's evidence and get a lighter sentence, at the same time putting Chris behind bars, which was perfect revenge—in Larry's twisted, alcoholic mind anyway—for Daddy's escapade with my mom. In short: perfect revenge for *me*."

She had a hateful look in her pretty eyes. She also looked about to cry. I reached over the table and squeezed her hand.

"Ohhhh, I wish to God that bastard had never been born!"

There was a minute of silence while she dabbed her eyes. I looked around the room and was distressed to see Tom Costello, my stockbroker, wink in my direction from a far corner. Great. How long before gossip about this tête-a-tête would reach a certain pair of ears on Old Stone Mill Road? I looked at my watch. No wonder the place was filling up: it was lunchtime.

"But . . ." Claudia continued. "You're right, Doc. Chris didn't stop smuggling. He just stopped smuggling drugs. It was dirty money and he knew it. So he concentrated on something else."

"What?"

"People."

"People? Illegal aliens?"

She looked up at me softly, her big brown eyes still damp. Her face flushed over her deep tan. She looked hurt now, and aching with old memories. "Please, Doc—don't make them sound like freaks from outer space."

"Sorry. Didn't mean to."

She bent over the table, playing with the wadded-up napkin in her hands. She spoke to me looking down at her hands.

"There's a lot you may not know about my father, Doc. I'll tell you something of his early life—then what I'll say later will make more sense."

"That would be nice; I'd like to hear it."

11

"HE WAS BORN IN PORTUGAL," CLAUDIA CONTINUED. "SINCE he lost his accent here in the States, most people never knew this. He was born and grew up in the town of Peniche. It's on the coast, about thirty miles north of Lisbon, where his family were fishermen. At seventeen he married and was ready to start a family. But when she was four months pregnant, his young wife died. It practically killed him. He decided to emigrate to America, and it was a decision he never regretted. You knew what a hard worker he was, Doc, and how much he loved people. Anyway, he always thought America did so much for him. Naturally, he gravitated to New Bedford, where so many of his countrymen had settled. He tried fishing at first, but soon realized he hated it. He always told me the fish were too fickle, unpredictable. So he got into hauling scrap steel from the wire factories in New Bedford to points south, like Camden and Philadelphia. It was a single barge operation then, using a small tug to push it. Later on, when he had more scrap, he would go as far south as Baltimore and Newport News."

"And that was the beginning of Southeastern Massachusetts Towing and Transit."

"Uh-huh. Small at first, but it grew and grew. Pretty soon he owned two small tugs and several barges. He did a lot of business with shipyards then. Anyway, Baltimore, Philly, and especially Newport News were all shipbuilding towns, and the scrap metal business was important to them."

"I can bet."

"But the most important shipyard of all was up north, on the Maine coast."

"You must be talking about Bath Iron Works."

"How'd you know?"

"Hell, Claudia, anybody who drives up the coast of Maine can't miss the place. They've got the biggest crane in the world, for one thing."

"Yeah . . . Well, right away Daddy realized that he could make a lot of money hauling from Maine to Newport News via the Cape Cod Canal. But he needed a partner north of New Bedford."

"So that's when Larry Kelly joined the company."

"Yep. Since Larry already had an oceangoing tug—it was an old steam tug from the First World War—it complemented the business perfectly. The two made a really good living from then on. Things got slow in the mid-sixties, but then Vietnam came along and business boomed again. But after seventy-two there was a big drop-off. And a gradual decline since then. Daddy said foreign yards in places like Singapore and Malaysia, and yards on America's Gulf Coast, were doing so much of the shipbuilding now that it was almost dead in the Northeast."

"And heavy manufacturing declined as well. I've lived here long enough to see that. So, tell me about the people smuggling."

She clasped her fingers together on the tablecloth, and stared down at them as she talked.

"It started slowly, by accident. Daddy was skipping the *Santiago* and was laid over in Trinidad. This was in eighty-two or eighty-three. He was barely making a living. Though it wasn't official, SEAMATT was really split then, with each partner taking his own profits from his own boats. Daddy knew Larry was making tons of money in the drug trade, but as I said, he didn't want any part of it."

She paused to take a sip of coffee.

"Halfway through his layover in Port of Spain, three men approached his crew in a tavern one night and made it known they would pay almost anything for passage into the United States. Word got back to Daddy, who decided, more out of curiosity than anything else, to go to this tavern and meet them."

"Aren't some of those waterfront dives tough places?"

"They're all tough places, Doc. Every one of them. But Daddy was stout and tough. He was also friendly. And don't forget he spoke fluent Portuguese, which meant that with a little practice, he was also fluent in Spanish. Besides, you know how dark he was. After a few weeks in the tropic sun, he was almost black; he fit right in among the people down there. So, in this bar he asks the men what they could pay for this passage, which everyone knew was going to break the law. One of the men, who was apparently their leader, took a small leather bag out of his pocket and slid it across the bar."

She stopped her narrative, as if waiting for me to say something.

"Well?" was all I could think of.

"Well. Would you like to see the bag?"

"Why, of course."

Claudia pulled her purse off the floor and onto her lap. She rummaged in it for a second or two, then lifted out a tiny leather bag with a drawstring closure. She tossed it lightly over to my side of the table. It made a faint beady rattle as it landed. I picked it up, drew apart the top, and spilled a cluster of stones onto the white tablecloth. Some were dark, others light. Some had a greenish hue, some were bluish. Some were almost clear.

None was smaller than a pea, and some were almost as big as marbles.

"Are these what I think they are?"

She nodded. "These aren't the best ones. But they're representative of what those desperate natives gave Daddy to take them to America."

"The greenish ones are emeralds?"

"Right. And the blue ones are sapphires. No rubies. But the pale ones are diamonds."

I stared at them, poked at them with my finger. "So, how much are these worth?"

"In the uncut state, not tremendously much. Of the twenty-three stones you see, some may not be of very high quality. Only a master gemologist or an expert cutter can tell. But in the real world, the only way to tell is to cut the stones. It's only in the cutting and finishing stages that the experts can get a real handle on the price."

"Why is that?"

"Because it's only then that the light can pass through them in certain patterns. Still, by weighing the rough stones, and examining them carefully through a loupe, the skilled dealer can place a rough value on them. These stones, for example, would fetch at least ten thousand from a field dealer."

I gave a low whistle. "That's a lot."

She shook her head slowly, a soft grin on her pretty face. "Not really, Doc, when you consider that one or two of these stones may end up in a New York jeweler's showcase with a fifty-thousand-dollar price tag."

I snapped my head up, staring at her. "Seriously? Why the huge markup?"

"One, it's the nature of the business. The first thing you learn about precious stones is that in the retail jewelry business, the markup from wholesale to retail is a hundred percent. So right away, we know that the stone with the fifty grand label on it in the showcase cost the retailer around twenty to twenty-five thou."

"I knew it was high, just not how much."

"The other factor is the cutting. It costs a lot to cut stones. It costs even more to cut them expertly. There are three centers for the global market in diamonds. One is New York, where Jewish gem dealers, who have run the business in the States for generations, routinely walk around Manhattan's trading district with thousands, sometimes millions of dollars' worth of stones in their pockets, buying, selling, and trading handfuls of ice every working day, right on the street. Hand to hand, with no written contracts. Deals are consummated with a handshake, nothing more."

"And the deals are worth millions?"

She nodded. "Yes, and the dealers' words of faith are what make the wheels go around. Needless to say, outsiders aren't welcome in this trade. It's strictly a closed circle, almost an extended-family business."

"And the other centers. Would it be Holland?"

"Holland and Belgium. Amsterdam and Antwerp are the other world capitals of the diamond trade. You've heard of DeBeers—they practically have a stranglehold on the big diamond fields, most of which are in Africa. Amsterdam is also the home of the world's most skilled diamond and gem cutters."

"So I've heard; a friend came down to our cottage on the Cape last week and told us about the Dutch and their diamonds. That was supposedly a major reason for their colonization of Suriname."

There was a silence. I looked up; she was staring at me with a frozen look on her face.

"Claudia? Something the matter?"

"What . . . Why did you mention Suriname?"

"I don't know . . . Just popped into my head, I guess."

She continued eying me, and the warmth of her earlier smile was replaced by a colder look. A look of scrutiny and . . . One could almost say fear.

"Now, Doc, I've been forthright with you. I would appreciate the same in return. Of all the countries in the world, why did you mention Suriname?"

I sensed I had touched a nerve. As much as I found Claudia

attractive, and as much as I wanted to cooperate with her, I decided then and there to string her along for a few more seconds to see why she was so anxious about this tiny South American country that, according to Bill Givens, was hell on earth.

"Well, it was one of the countries Bill mentioned that the Dutch explored for diamonds, since rumor had it that they abounded there. But apparently, the place was—just too much for them. I gather it is not exactly hospitable."

She lowered her eyes, and her voice. "No. It is definitely not a kind place. Not in climate, nor in terrain, nor in . . . anything."

"Did Chris have any dealings in Suriname, Claudia?"

"Yes," she said without hesitation. "He did. And with a lot of other countries between the Bahamas and Brazil. The Dutch left Suriname because they couldn't operate on a massive scale there. Big companies have economies of scale—if a place is too . . . treacherous, or politically unstable . . . if there is too much disease or danger, why, they abandon it. But the natives who live there, in the wilderness and the mountains, along the hot rivers where Europeans won't go—they pick up stones as they go about their daily lives, understand?"

I nodded.

"And before you know it, each desperate fugitive in those nasty countries has a handful of precious stones, which he'll trade away for a ticket out."

"Was there a—special connection with Suriname?"

"I don't think I should tell you that. Not yet, Doc. When I tell you—you'll understand."

"Fair enough." This seemed an honest answer. Honest enough so I ventured to tell her more. "Your father told me just before he died to look out for you. You may take offense at this—but ever since then, I've been wondering just how he meant that phrase. Am I to look out for your interests and your safety as a friend of his? He obviously loved you very much. Or . . . am I to beware of you?"

She laughed softly, and brightened up again. "You don't need to do either."

"And why not? He specifically told me—"

"Forget it. First of all, you needn't beware of me. I'm not a mean person. Secondly, he left me comfortably well off. I have a nice condo in the Back Bay that's all paid off, and the other property I mentioned earlier."

"The tugboats and the warehouse buildings."

"The boats, and the warehouses that I'll turn into condos for rentals—yes."

"And that's a lot, I guess."

"It is. So you don't have to watch over me. And then, of course, there's something else."

She opened her purse again and drew out a fabric-covered jewelry box that opened clamshell fashion. The kind necklaces come in. She slid this across the table to me.

"Don't tell me you have more goodies?"

"Open it."

I flipped open the box. It was lined in light blue plush fabric. Nestled snugly inside were eight huge diamonds. Not lumpy and pale like the rough ones, but all cut and sparkly and brilliant. The kind women kill for—and men die for. *Ice.* I gave a low whistle. Couldn't help it. "These were also payment from the people he smuggled into America?"

"Yes, but not in this cut state," she said, flipping the box shut and sliding it aside. "Daddy became an expert at judging diamonds in the rough. They're called field-grade stones. Anyway, by the end of his career, he was as keen as any expert when it came to looking at rough stones—be they diamonds, emeralds, or sapphires—like I showed you earlier. He'd take the rough stones and fly to Amsterdam to have them cut."

"Why not New York? It's closer."

"Uh-huh. And riskier, too. People talk. The IRS and the FBI pay attention when these people talk. Follow?"

I nodded.

"Nothing is easier to smuggle than gems. Their size and composition make them impossible to detect electronically, and you can fit them anywhere on your person or in your luggage."

"So he'd fly the rough stones into Amsterdam, wait a week or so, then fly back with the finished pieces?"

She shook her head. "He wouldn't wait. He'd trade the rough

stones for finished ones. Toward the end, some of the finest cutters in the world were waiting on pins and needles for Chris Ramos to fly in each month with another load."

"So," I couldn't help asking, "how much do you think he accumulated in all?"

She shrugged. "Doc Adams . . . I have no idea whatsoever." She paused a bit, then leaned close to me over the table. So close I could smell whatever perfume she had on. So close I could see the gloss on her full lips, look into those deep brown eyes. Smell that great dark brown hair that cascaded down to her shoulders. I felt an attack of the fantods coming on . . .

"But whatever the amount . . . you can bet your ass it was *awesome*!"

I guess I gulped.

"Now do you see why you also don't have to beware of me? I've got more than I could ever want."

"Well, I guess that's a relief. But let me say this: since you've got all this, has it ever occurred to you that there may be people out there who would like to take it away from you? And who might . . . hurt you in the process?"

"Yes. Daddy warned me that any business as lucrative as his was risky. He had many associates, you know. In the shipping business, you deal with a lot of people. When he was into moving . . . people . . . there were others in the chain."

"Chain? What do you mean?"

"It was sort of like the underground railroad in slavery times. There were contacts along the route. At every port, every stopping place or embarkation point, there were people who were involved."

"Ah, I see. And, perhaps, these people have heard of the rumor of your father's wealth, of the treasure people talk about. And maybe they want their cut?"

"Exactly. Of course, he paid these contacts well; he never held back from them. He was an honest man."

"I agree. But there are those who would say that any man engaged in an illegal activity is not honest."

Her nostrils flared a bit. "So, the people who helped run the underground railroad were dishonest because they were breaking the law?"

"A good point. But the question is, did they make large amounts of money off it?"

"Well," she said after a pause, "let's just say he was as honest as a fellow in his position could have been."

"I don't doubt it."

"So, part of the reason I called on you this morning was to give you something for helping Daddy."

"No need for that."

"Yes, there is." She slid the jewelry case in front of me and lifted the lid. "Here. Pick any three stones."

"Naw," I waved her off. "That's not necessary, Claudia."

"Oh, but it is, Doc. I insist. Just take three."

"Why three?"

"One for your wife. You might want to have a ring made. And you have two boys, right?"

"Who told you that?"

"Guess. Their names are Jack and Tony. And, as far as Daddy could recollect before he died, neither one of them is married. Yet. But when the time comes, won't they want engagement rings?"

"Gee, I don't know about this, Claudia . . ."

"C'mon, pick three, Doc. It's the least I can do for what you did for Daddy."

I went to pick one off the fabric.

"Not that one. Try another."

She kept giving me not-so-subtle hints until I had selected three jumbo-sized diamonds. She wrapped them in a paper napkin and handed them to me. "Don't forget and throw this away, Doc. You'll regret it."

I paid the bill and we walked into the parking lot. I felt tired from the interview.

We got into her Caddy and drove to my office building. She leaned over and kissed me good-bye before I got out.

"You've got to stop that, Claudia," I said sternly, but without a lot of feeling. "It could get habit-forming."

"Suits me," she said with a wink and a smile. "Listen, my

name's still Kelly, but by the end of the month I'll be Claudia Ramos. Then I might even put my name in the book."

"That's good. Chris would be proud," I said, getting out. But I stopped at her window and leaned over. "Listen, Claudia, do you have any idea who could have beat me to the stash that was supposedly hidden underneath that church seat?"

"A lot of possibilities, Doc. But no firm answers. Did he indicate to you that it was the treasure, or a key to it?"

"He didn't say at all what it was. Just the location. He said anything I could find was mine. I'm not saying that to lay claim to it—I'm just telling you what he told me."

"I know. I know you're telling the truth. The only other man I think he would tell would be Father DeSilva. He adored him."

"Hey, right. I should have thought of that. If he got the stash, then all is as it should be."

"But what if he didn't? What if some other person got it?"

I shrugged and began to walk away.

"Doc."

I returned to the window.

"Tell me more about Suriname. How did you come up with it?"

I told her about the strange group of mourners looking through the fence into the cemetery after the funeral, and the big Lincoln Town Car with the flag on the back window.

"And the driver of this car, Doc. What did he look like?"

"Like a guy you'd never forget. Handsome, in a way. Exotic. Thin, with Rasta hair and Asian eyes—but green."

"Oh, shit," she said. "It's Smitty."

"Hmmm? Who's Smitty? If Smitty is a nickname for Smith, he sure didn't look like a Smith to me."

"His name is Smits, not Smith. Smits is a Dutch name. He's from Suriname, and a mixture of all those people who inhabit that godforsaken place."

"Smits?"

"Missaels Haagmann Smits. His father was a Dutch mining engineer who was hanged for murder. His mother was half African and half Indonesian Malay."

"How do you know about him?"

"I've met him. Remember what I said about the chain, Doc? Well, Smitty was a major part of the chain. The southern leg of the chain, from Suriname and Trinidad up to Haiti and the Bahamas."

"So he was a friend of Chris's?"

"More than that: a partner."

"Have you spoken to him lately? What is he doing in New England? What's he after?"

"C'mon, Doc, the answer's obvious: he wants Christos Ramos's treasure. He knew that Daddy socked away a huge fortune somewhere. Now that the original owner's dead, Smitty wants it."

I leaned closer to the window.

"Know what? The orderly at the hospital said that Smitty visited your dad just before his death. Right before I did. What do you think about that?"

"I don't know what to think. Maybe they parted friends. Maybe Daddy revealed the church hiding place to both Smitty and to you. I'm sure he didn't want to reveal it to me."

"Why's that? He loved you the most."

"Yeah. But he left me sitting pretty. And because he loved me, he wanted to leave me safe as well. Get it? He wanted to leave me entirely out of the hidden treasure stuff. He knew it would be hell to pay when he was gone. A lot of people were involved. All of them feel they are entitled to a piece of the action now. I hate to say this, Doc, but maybe Daddy didn't do you much of a favor by telling you about this."

"I'm sure he didn't think anyone else would know."

"Well, somebody does. The treasure was gone, wasn't it?"

I nodded.

"Look, I read about the incident in Southie two weeks ago with you and your brother-in-law. I'm sorry. But I can tell you now, for sure: that bunch of thugs were associated with the late Larry Kelly. Bet you anything."

"I think you're right."

"And believe me, they're rough. I don't know which is worse, them or Smitty."

"So Smitty's mean?"

"He's killed people. Daddy told me as much. So watch out, Doc, for God's sake. You're a good man. I'm sure your family is great. It's too bad you're stuck in the middle of this whole thing."

She mouthed a kiss at me and drove off.

Feeling the napkin-wrapped diamonds in my shirt pocket, I started to go inside to the office. But then I changed my mind and walked over to the Audi, climbed in, and drove to downtown Concord. Those stones had me thinking.

12

"WOW!" EXCLAIMED TOBY GUSTAFSON AS HE LOOKED THROUGH the jeweler's loupe. He shifted the stone and brought it into the beam of the high-intensity lamp again. "Double wow!"

"See anything good?" I asked, trying to be nonchalant.

I was standing at the counter in Toby Gustafson's shop. Concord Jewelers was a small but very high-end little shop right on Main Street.

He frowned at me, put the stone down on the foam pad at his worktable—it looked and felt just like a "mouse pad" for computers—and picked up the second one. He put it under the light, turning it slowly this way and that as he peered through the heavy lens.

"Holy . . . I don't believe what I'm seeing here, Doc! You say a young woman gave them to you? Gee, whatever charm you have, make sure you keep it. Or maybe you can sell it . . ."

I nodded. "Well?" I asked, legs crossed at the ankles, leaning casually against the counter, blowing on my nails. "How about it?"

Perhaps I would buy a Porsche to match Mary's, only in Stallion Black.

"Fakes," he said flatly. "Great looking at first, but fakes. Cleverest I've seen; must be worth several hundred dollars."

"Shit," I said, gazing vacantly out the window onto Concord's Main Street, watching townspeople and tourists walk up and down it, looking into the little trendy shops. Two heavyset middle-aged men stopped and peered into the shop window. They looked up at us, then moved on.

"Whatsamatter, Doc? Disappointed that they're not worth a couple hundred grand?"

"No—that's not it. It means Claudia lied to me. And I thought she was a neat person, not the type to lie. And she had a lot to say about a problem we're having now—"

"—you and Claudia? Uh-oh, better not let you-know-who find out."

"No. Not Claudia and me. Although it does concern her too. These stones were supposedly part of a vast collection that her late father amassed over the years."

"Hmmmm. A vast collection, you say? This Claudia sounds more and more interesting."

"But since they're fakes, that means she's lying to me. Or, perhaps more disturbing, that her father lied to her. Or, it could even mean that certain people in Amsterdam lied to him . . ."

Toby picked up the last stone and held it under the light. "I just don't believe this," he said softly.

"Frankly, neither do I. I was so convinced she was telling me the straight scoop."

"Relax, Doc. They're not fakes. I was just teasing you."

"They're not? You were?"

He nodded; the loupe stuck in his eye socket jiggled up and down with his head. "I've never seen stones of this size and quality. You mentioned Amsterdam. That's right on the money—pardon the pun—if she mentioned that city. I think that's the only place on earth where three stones of this magnitude could have originated."

"Do tell," I said. I was about to add that there was more where those came from, but caution stopped me. Like Chris, I wanted Claudia to be safe. If word got out that she had maybe a couple dozen more of these crème de la crème diamonds, her life might not be worth a Confederate nickel. This was especially true since it seemed that everything I said, or even thought, lately, was being picked up on by thugs of one description or another.

I slapped my hands on the counter. "Okay, Toby, ol' buddy. How much?"

"How much what?"

"Will you give me for the diamonds? How much for all three?"

"I couldn't buy them. I have nowhere near that much cash on hand."

I looked around the small but elegant confines of Concord Jewelers. Silk wallpaper with red mahogany trim. Classic Oriental rugs on the floor. Leather chairs for clients to wait in. Also, he carried good lines. I don't know the jewelry biz, but I do know some good brands. Rolex, Beaume & Mercier, Ebel, Tudor, and Omega were pretty good names for watches. I guess he did not carry Cartier or Patek Phillipe, but I could overlook that. He had a large stock of Mikimoto pearls, and a whole lot of gold pieces as well. Not gold plate, but solid, 18-karat stuff.

"No kidding? Uh, how much cash would that be?"

"Who knows? Diamonds this special, the usual laws of carat, cut, clarity, color, and brilliance all go down the tubes. Doc, these three stones weigh—" He plopped them one by one on a small electronic scale that had a digital readout. "—almost twelve carats total. But it's not their size that's so amazing. They're flawless stones. Brilliant and colorless. They're pure, pure, brilliant white. What we in the trade refer to as 'diamonds of the first water.' "

"Is that good?"

"Is Stradivarius good? Is Rembrandt good?"

"So how much for a dealer to buy them?"

"At least a hundred thousand for the three—assuming he would sell them for upwards of two hundred. And if he were clever and kept them as a set, there's no telling how much they could fetch at the right store."

"This isn't the right store?"

He shook his head without hesitation. "Naw. This is a good store, of course. We feature quality brands and merchandise in good taste for the affluent of this small village. But, by nature, New Englanders aren't flashy. You know this. A major New York house, or perhaps one of the biggest in Boston, might take them on. Boy oh boy, are they something."

"I think I'll put two of them in my safe deposit box for now and leave one here for you to make into a ring for Mary."

He brightened at this, saying it was a good idea and a sound investment. "But not to get personal, Doc—I hope you have some kind of safe at home to keep it in when it's not on her finger."

"Nope. I have a gun safe in the basement. Will that do?"

He made a face as if sniffing dog doo and replied flatly that it would not. Then he rose from his work chair and disappeared into the back of the shop, reappearing with a catalogue of jewelry safes.

"There are some nice smaller models in here that aren't expensive and more than pay for themselves in peace of mind," he said softly, turning the pages. "I would recommend a small one that can be installed in the wall or floor of your bedroom, and cemented in place."

I left thirty minutes later, having given Toby enough business to make him a happy man. It was worth it; Toby Gustafson had an absolutely impeccable reputation; I didn't mind paying for his services.

And Mary would love the ring.

I got back in the Audi and headed back to the office. Gee, it was now past two. Susan Petri would wonder where I had been. And maybe a few other Concordians might wonder why I was talking so sub rosa with this attractive woman over coffee. Of course, all they had to do would be to talk with Tom Costello, who would fill them in. I was happy about the diamond gifts from the lovely Claudia, but I sensed trouble coming my way.

In the parking lot of the Concord Professional Building a guy was trying to change a tire on a late model station wagon right near the side door I use. I heard him mumble something about not knowing where to put the jack.

"I think it goes on the side of the body, not in back," I said. "There should be a special indentation on the frame where the tongue fits—" I squatted down on my hams to look under the car. No good; I wasn't low enough.

"Here, I'll look. Thanks for your trouble," he said, getting down on his belly and feeling around underneath the rocker panel. He was well dressed, and I pitied him somewhat; he would trash his slacks.

"Hey, pal, can you bring that jack up close to the frame? I think I found it—" He was lying on his back now, his feet stuck out toward me.

I got the jack, which was one of these screw-lever types rather than the old ratchet kind, and moved it close to where he was lying on his back.

"Great! Hey, pal, thanks. That looks just about right."

There was a slight pause. Then he added, "In fact, it's perfect—ain't it, Al?"

The first thing I thought was that my name wasn't Al. Then I saw the shadow on the pavement come over mine as I squatted on the asphalt. As fast as I could think I pulled the lever from the jack and was rising up, ready to spin and swing at Mr. Shadow behind me, but it was too late.

I felt a noisy blow on the back of my head, and that instantaneous taste of copper on my palate—two inches behind my nose, exactly where I taste a fine cigar—that always comes with a knock on the head that's way too severe. Then I knew that, just like the book title, I was going to "lie down in darkness."

I awoke to the sound of Susan Petri's voice, which was full of alarm, yet soothing. She knelt down beside me and cooed at me, rubbing the back of my neck with her cool hand.

"What happened?" she asked.

"I got mugged, right outside my office."

"Gee, that seems strange. Why would anybody want to mug you?"

"I haven't the slightest—*oh my God!*"

I sat up to check my breast pocket where the folded-up napkin was supposed to be. Gone. The two remaining diamonds of the first water were taken. A quick check revealed my wallet was still in place.

"Shit," I mumbled, and tried to rise again, but she held me down.

"Don't you move, Dr. Adams; I've called help."

"Where's Moe?"

"Don't you remember? He went to New Jersey to visit his mother."

"Why the hell does he always take off when I need him?"

Then a hurry-up wagon from the hospital arrived, swooshing into the lot with lights a-blazing. They arrived fairly quickly. Big deal; they'd come all the way from across Route 2. I stood up, wobbly and woozy, waving them off. But it didn't work; they forced me inside and on my back, making me ride back across the street to the emergency ward, where they checked me for concussion. This involved a lengthy wait, lying motionless while they watched my pupils dilate and took my pulse every few minutes. Then they X-rayed my noggin and CAT scanned it. By about four in the afternoon they pronounced me fit enough to go home—under Mary's supervision, of course.

By dinnertime I was sitting in the living room with a big earthen mug of Hacker-Pschorr lager. I had a crowd around me: Mary, Joe, Marty, Tom Costello—whose presence was disconcerting, to say the least—and Brian Hannon, Concord's chief of police.

"You're not supposed to be drinking that beer, Charlie. The doctor said water only—and bed rest."

"Doctors are full of shit," I replied, taking a long, refreshing pull at the beer. If there's a better German lager made, I haven't tasted it.

"You're a doctor."

"I rest my case."

Brian Hannon was staring at me from the big red armchair across the room. With his doughy Irish face, thinning hair, and beat-up nose, he looked remarkably like Ed Asner, and sounded even gruffer as he drummed his pudgy fingers on the arm of his chair in annoyance.

"Well ... you've gone and done it again, hotshot," he growled. "You go to school for this, or what?"

"Don't be cute, Brian. It's not funny. I was toting two hot stones in my breast pocket that were given to me earlier—"

"Ah, I bet I know by *who*!" said Costello, almost shouting. He had a sly grin on his face. I put a finger to my lips, as if feigning a headache.

"Please don't shout, Tom. Please don't say anything—"

"Ohh—sorry—I, uh, understand . . ."

I was safe for a second. Costello would say no more and the lunch with Claudia would go undiscovered by Mary. It's not that I wouldn't tell her eventually, of course. Just not right now; there were too many things going on.

But then Mary turned her head like a battleship gun turret in the direction of Tom Costello. Uh-oh.

"And who might that be, Tom? Who would casually give Charlie two hot stones? Hmmm? And was this person by any chance female?"

"I, uh, can't remember." Good old Tom. But it was too late and we both knew it; Mary crossed her arms over her very ample bosom and looked at us. One, then the other, back and forth. Her black eyes boring into each of us.

"You're a stockbroker and you can't remember? Aw gee, Tom. Try harder."

He looked at me desperately; I had to rescue him.

"What happened was this, Mare. Claudia Kelly showed up at my office—totally unannounced—early this morning, saying she had to talk with me."

"Claudia Kelly came to your office?" said Joe. He had amazement in his voice. "Hell, we been looking for her for the past couple weeks. How'd she find you?"

"They just seem to, Joey—especially the pretty ones."

"Right. Anyway, she had some unfinished business to discuss."

"Oh, I bet," said Mary though clenched teeth.

"Really. Truly. She told me all about Ramos. His life history, and the history of SEAMATT. She admitted he did smuggle drugs, but not for long. She revealed what he really smuggled—"

"Diamonds!" cooed Marty. "So there really is a treasure!"

"Wait a sec, Doc," said Joe. "How come she knows so much about Chris Ramos if he and her father were on the outs?"

"Because—you ready for this?—she's Chris Ramos's daughter. That's why she looks so much like her late father."

There was a chorus of "ohhhhhhs . . ." as it sank in. Then everyone agreed that it made perfect sense, and explained why she was at the funeral.

"And she gave you these two diamonds," pursued Mary. "Why, pray tell, did she do that?"

"As a token of appreciation. From Chris."

"Hmmmph!" was all Mary said. I noticed Marty sidle up to her, offering support. Now, listen: I've watched enough wildlife films on the Discovery Channel to know exactly what was going on. This was a female thing: the two alpha cows in the elephant herd were going to drive the old bull out. Let him wander alone in the bush until the poachers got him. Serve him right.

"It just seems odd, Doc," said Joe's wife, "that gorgeous women keep bumping into you."

"Must be karma."

"You're gonna get it, Charlie. As soon as these people leave, you're gonna get it. They'll hear your screams all the way to Ayer—" Mary said.

"She didn't give me two stones, my dear. She gave me three. Guess where the third one is?"

"Where? Up your ass?" she said this in a hiss, like an irritated black mamba. Then I told her. Her eyes softened, with a hurt, wet look. She came over to me and planted one on my cheek. "Ohh, Charlie. I'm so sorry—"

"The ring ought to be ready in a couple of weeks. That is, unless the two thugs go into Concord Jewelers and knock Toby on the head and steal it. Hey, what are you two talking about over there?"

The two cops, Joe and Brian, were huddled near the armchair, whispering and nodding to each other. They turned to face the group. Joe spoke first: "Doc, doesn't it strike you as odd that the two thugs managed to catch up with you almost immediately after she gave you the diamonds?"

I rubbed my chin, trying to think about this.

"And also, when you look back over the events of this morning," continued Brian, "doesn't it seem funny that this woman, who Joe has been searching for without success, turns up unexpectedly at your office, without even calling beforehand, and makes this sudden effort to befriend you?"

I continued to urge the old gray matter forward, trying to see the point they were making. But it wasn't working; my head hurt too much.

"What exactly are you driving at?" said Mary.

"Well, this woman shows up to repay Doc for all the good things he did for Chris Ramos. That's fine, except she shows up suddenly at Doc's office. Funny she'd know exactly where he works. But that's okay; maybe her dad told her. Anyway, she gives him these diamonds, which maybe are real, maybe they're fakes—"

"They're not fakes; Toby himself looked them over. Said they were diamonds of the first water. He said the three of them were worth at least a hundred grand, maybe much more."

"Well, anyway," pursued Brian, "she makes this generous gift to you when she first meets you. That in itself is a little fishy, you ask me."

I shrugged. "I dunno, Brian. Way she talked, I think she has more where that came from."

"But to continue," said Joe, "right after she gives you these flawless stones, they get taken away from you. As if—as if the whole thing were planned beforehand."

"Ahhhh!" I said, the light finally dawning. "You guys are convinced that Claudia is in league with the guys in the parking lot. She gives me a great gift knowing she'll get it back shortly. It was only my detour to the jewelry store that saved the one diamond."

"Exactly."

I leaned back in my chair and closed my weary eyes. I did not want to believe this. I did not want to believe that Claudia

Kelly—excuse me, Claudia Ramos, lovely daughter of Chris—would go out of her way to dupe me like that.

"Why? Why would she do this?"

"We're not sure," said Joe, "but Brian and I, being in law enforcement, think in somewhat the same patterns. This just sounds too much like the old con games, the Murphy jobs that we've dealt with all our careers. It doesn't ring true. Maybe you better warn your jewelry store friend that these two thugs are on the loose."

"Come to think of it, I did notice two rather heavyset guys looking in the store window when I was in there. So you think she set me up?"

"There's a good chance. A very good chance."

"Well, let me ask you this: how does this explain the man who whispered on the phone? The guys who ambushed us in Flynn's? They made it look like we were setting the trap—when really they were setting it for us. Huh?"

Joe thought a minute before replying.

"If they were remnants of Kelly's gang, she could have informed them about how to set the trap."

"Claudia told me she read about it and she does think they're remnants of Kelly's gang. But she hated Kelly after the way he treated her mom. She was on Chris's side. If I'm sure about anything, I'm sure about this."

"What about the guy with the Rasta hair?" asked Mary.

"His name is Missaels Smits, otherwise known as Smitty, a former partner of Ramos's. He's sniffing around because he wants his cut of the fabled treasure."

"How do you know all this?" Joe asked.

"Claudia told me. And he's from Suriname, too."

I filled everybody in on what she had told me over lunch. They sat like sparrows on a wire, staring at me, gobbling up all the details.

"A human chain of escape?" asked Marty. "Like the underground railroad?"

"People picking up these gems in the heart of the rain forest," said Tom, "and trading them by the fistfuls to get to America?"

"She has an oceangoing freighter that she's *misplaced*?" said Brian Hannon in awe.

"Yes," I said, reclining gently back with a nonchalant look, "all this and more. Much more. But time grows short . . ."

"What do you mean, time grows short?" snorted Mary.

"We need to eat," I said, glancing at my watch.

"Hey, everybody, he does have a point," said Joe.

Good old Joe. He walked his lazy, shifting elephant walk toward the kitchen. I finished the Hacker-Pschorr and got up and followed him, still not believing that Claudia Ramos could have tricked me.

Although Mary and I had four unexpected guests for dinner, it was no problem. She took out a huge frozen lasagna and put it in the oven. I went to the market for French bread and salad greens while Joe made anchovy toast and minestrone. We opened big jugs of dry red that had an earthy straw and wheat aroma and tasted like an Italian farm in Tuscany.

It was a splendid meal, with the talk mostly about diamonds, Claudia's role in this whole thing, and what to do next.

This last question was answered in part by the ringing of the phone. Mary went to answer it.

"I hope it's not the guy with the missing vocal cords again," I said, diving into my salad of romaine, black olives, feta and Parmesan cheese, and a balsamic vinegar and oil dressing. "Last time we were eating here together, that's what happened."

"Oh hi!" I heard her say in a pleasant voice. "You what? Oh, really? No kidding, Father . . . Well, that's, uh, interesting. I'm sure Charlie will want to know—"

"Sounds like she's talking to her dad," mused Tom, taking another giant-sized mouthful of lasagna. "My God, this is splendid. Absolutely blue chip!"

"She's probably not talking to her dad," said Joe. "Our dad died almost fifteen years ago."

"But she said 'father'—" said Brian.

"That must be Father O'Flaherty," I said.

Mary came back in and sat down.

"What did he want?" I asked her.

"He wants for you to call him back in the morning. I said you were too busy and exhausted tonight. He was sorry to hear that you'd been hit on the head."

"God bless him."

"Do you think you'll be well enough to go down there tomorrow? I'll drive if you want."

"Naw," I shrugged. "I'm feeling much better already. I'm sure after a good night's sleep I'll be fine. I'll cancel the office, but I'm sure I can handle Concord center, don't you?"

"Concord center? Why are you going there? Oh, I bet you're going to warn Toby Gustafson about those—"

"Wait a second, Mary. Wasn't that Father O'Flaherty?"

"No, it was not. It was Father DeSilva. Remember him? From Saint Bernard's Church in Fairhaven?"

A hush fell about the table.

"Yeah? So?"

"He just got a call from Claudia."

"And?"

"Well, he said that he knew about the place underneath the third pew from the front."

"He did?" I said, dropping my fork into the salad.

"Yes, he did. Seems Chris was a bit drugged up toward the end, poor man. God knows I see enough of that in the final stages of cancer. Apparently he told Father DeSilva the same thing he told you."

"And . . ."

The silence was deafening.

"Well, after he got back to the church, the first thing he did was check the spot."

"*And . . .*" said Joe.

"And what he found was, nothing. Just the same as us."

"You mean he dug into the bench with a chisel and found nothing?" I pursued. Good God, sometimes it's very hard getting the straight dope from a woman.

"No, silly. He found what we found: the chiseled hole."

"Aha!" said Joe.

"Aha *what*?" I asked him.

"I don't know," he admitted.

"You mind telling me what the hell you're all talking about?" snarled Hannon. I think he was in a bad mood because we were drinking wine and he couldn't. But then again, his personality isn't exactly cuddly anyway. "What the hell is this thing about the pew?"

We told him and Tom the background. A great cacophony of voices followed, like that produced by a nesting colony of jackdaws. It was full of sound and fury, nothing else.

"Just a minute—" came a soft contralto voice. We all looked to Marty, always the eye in the middle of a storm. She cleared her throat softly and said, "If he told Mary that he had dug out the hole himself, and found nothing, that would be an answer of sorts. It would tell us that there was indeed no treasure, or key to the treasure. It would mean that either Ramos was lying or, more likely—as Mary indicated—that in his condition he was somehow giving wrong directions . . ."

"Yes, yes," said Joe. "Go on, honey—"

"But, what he saw was a torn-apart structure underneath the pew, just like Joe saw . . . and showed you," she said, nodding at Mary and me.

"So what now?" Mary asked.

"Well, it means somebody got to the treasure before us. From what Claudia told Doc, I think that person is this Smits fellow, who sounds dangerous."

"And is," I said.

"According to Claudia, who is probably lying," said Joe.

"She is not lying; I just know it," I said.

"So all is well," continued Marty. "Since this Smits has the treasure, he is presumably happy, and the matter will therefore drop."

There was a moment of peaceful silence.

But not for long.

"Well, I'm not happy, honey; I want the treasure. Or at least the excitement of seeking it," said her husband.

"I think you and Doc have had all the excitement you can stand for a while," she said. "You're both lucky to be alive."

"And that reminds me," added Joe. "The Kelly gang doesn't know Smitty's got the golden egg—they still think we have it. Else why would they be calling us and beating the shit out of us?"

"Good question, Joey," said Mary.

"Here's another good question," I said. "If Smitty's got the treasure, or the key to it, or the whatever, then he should be happy as a pig in poop. Right?"

Everybody nodded.

"Well, then, why is he riding around in his big old Lincoln up here in Concord, cruising along our very own road? Eh?"

Another silence. This one no fun at all.

"Because," I said, answering my own question, "I think Smitty was the first one Ramos told, and the first to go to the church. He was the one who dug the hole in the wood. He found nothing. What then? Well, he naturally supposed that he was looking in the wrong place, and that maybe I had already looked in the right place, and have the loot. See?"

"And so . . . he'll keep after us until we tell him where the stash is hidden," said Mary, looking down at her plate. Somehow, her appetite had suddenly dwindled. Same with mine.

And everybody else's, too.

13

NEXT MORNING JOE AND I HEADED DOWN TO FAIRHAVEN TO see Father DeSilva. Joe had time on his hands, and I knew the whole business of Chris Ramos and his hot stones intrigued him—a welcome break from the constant bloodbath stuff he worked on around Boston. We told the wives we were spending the night at the Breakers; it would be a nice break for both of us.

Now all the blooms were out in New Bedford and Fairhaven. The place, like the Cape, was just far enough south and stuck out into the water to be ahead of Concord by about a week and a half. Joe parked his car in front of the church, and we went two doors down to the modest parish house, where we found Father DeSilva doing the dishes from a big noon meal with several teenagers. The kids looked rough, but not mean. I supposed they were victims of families shattered by alcoholism, drugs, divorce, neglect—or all of the above. Seems like about half the kids are part of this sad saga nowadays.

Listen: except for advances in medicine, you can have the twentieth century.

Joe and the padre sat down over coffee at the kitchen table, and Joe talked about his several years as a priest. Father DeSilva was entranced. He also couldn't believe Joe had quit the cloth for the badge.

"Ah, now, Father, we must remember we're both in the same business, just other sides of the doorway on it," said Joe, following the priest out the front door and onto the porch, which overlooked rows of neat houses with nice lawns and clipped shrubbery. It really was a lovely little town. They sat down and Joe lit a Benson & Hedges.

"Now, who was the guy again? The entrepreneur who gave so much money to this little town?"

"Henry Huddleston Rogers. John D. Rockefeller's right-hand man. Controlled six of the thirteen spinoffs of the original Standard Oil. Have you seen the library? Right out of Renaissance Florence. He gave us that. And most of the parks and schools. Yes, I like it here. I am fortunate to have this community as my parish. I only wish Chris were here now to enjoy it with us. You ever meet him?"

"No; I missed out, unfortunately. But everyone I know who met him loved him, including Bozo here."

He nodded his head in my direction.

"But you can call me Doc."

"Good, and my friends call me Tony. I'm sorry I couldn't be of more help to you with regard to the hidden treasure in the church. It seems someone got there before us."

"Ah, yes. And who do you think that was?"

"I have no idea. I was under the impression that I was the only one Chris told."

"Well," said Joe, half suppressing a chuckle, "maybe his sense of humor lives after him. You see, Doc thought the same thing. Maybe he did this to set all of you after each other."

"Could be. But I must say, gentlemen, I do believe that no matter how many people he told, he ultimately wished his stash—whatever it might be—to go to our church. I say this not only because he hid it in the church, but because he cared very deeply for this parish and all its members."

"Excuse me, Tony," I said. "I get the same feeling. But if that's so, then why so few people at the service?"

The priest leaned back in his chair and clasped his interlocked hands behind his head. He seemed to be looking heavenward, wearing just his black garments and the white collar. The sea breeze blew wisps of his thinning black hair around.

"Several reasons. The main one, I'm sure, is that a lot of Chris's best friends are now gone; it's an old parish, age-wise. The few people you saw were in their eighties. Secondly, Chris had been gone quite a while, and he left under—difficult circumstances. Our parishioners are like most people, Dr. Adams: they are quick to condemn and slow to forgive. In short, they aren't perfect Christians."

"If they were, you'd be out of a job," Joe said.

"Ah, true! Still, you would think more of them would remember the work he did for the church, especially the renovation."

"Other than the two of us, who do you think he told?" I asked.

"Probably Claudia Kelly."

"Really? Why?"

"Because they were extremely close."

I thought a bit before saying anything.

"Exactly how close?" Joe asked.

"You might say like father and daughter," answered the priest with a wry grin. We grinned back. Then we all laughed.

"I, uh, take it that you may know about their special relationship?" he asked me.

"Yes. Claudia and I had coffee together yesterday."

"So then you know why she was so special to Chris. I think she would be the obvious one he would have told."

I decided to lay the cards on the table. I looked at Joe and he nodded.

"Father—I mean Tony, Claudia told me he did not tell her. She suggested that perhaps it was Smitty."

The priest's eyebrows lifted. "Smitty? I'm surprised she even mentioned him."

"So you know about him."

"Oh yes, met him several times. A Catholic. But I wasn't aware that he and Chris had any doings recently."

"A nurse who was on duty at the hospital said that Smitty came to see him before he died."

"Well, well. So did I, of course."

"Right. So if he told both of us, why not Smitty as well?"

"Hmmmm. I still think Claudia might be a better bet. There was nobody on earth he loved more than that girl."

"I gather. But you know, he left her sitting pretty. She owns what's left of the shipping business, Chris's house here, and a condo in Boston. Also, she said she even owned a freighter, if she could find it."

"Then why wouldn't he tell her about the hiding place in the church?"

"Because he felt it might be dangerous."

"Why?"

"Because people kill for diamonds."

"Diamonds? You're certain it's diamonds?"

"All but certain; that's what he left her. That's what she gave me."

"She gave you diamonds? My, my, she must like you."

"She said it was from Chris."

"That's what she told me when she gave me mine," DeSilva said, smiling.

"Well, the girl does get around, doesn't she?" said Joe.

"Joe thinks Claudia might not be on the up and up," I said to DeSilva.

"She is, uh, mysterious. But in case you're wondering where

my diamonds went, those kids in there are the answer. An architect here in town is already drawing the plans for the addition to this parish house for runaway kids."

"Gee, you should meet Moe Abramson; you'd get along famously."

"Dr. Morris Abramson, the psychiatrist?"

"You know him?"

"Of course. Anybody in the charity field knows him well. The most Christian man I ever met."

"Well, if you don't know already, I got news for you, padre," said Joe. "He's Jewish."

The priest thought for a second before replying. "That's funny. So was Jesus."

Minutes later the three of us were in Joe's car, riding down to the Fairhaven waterfront. We were going to have a look at Chris Ramos's warehouse and then his seaside cottage.

The headquarters of SEAMATT were located on an old stone pier just north of the Union Wharf area, right behind the little island called Crow Island, which isn't even on most maps. The quay had a high cyclone fence around it topped with barbed wire. There was an abandoned section of railroad track leading into it—the railroad spur that any company dealing in scrap metals would need. But I could tell by the rusted steel of the rails they hadn't seen any traffic in a long time, and the big swing gates, also of cyclone fencing, were closed and locked with rusty chain and padlocks. The building that housed the company offices was also stone. It was a two-story structure, but the windows were closed and shuttered with plywood. The base of the building extended all the way down into the harbor water, and I knew it must have been built a long, long time ago. The faded letters SEAMATT could still be seen on the roof, now a faded, pale green.

"Let's get out of the car and walk around," said Father De-Silva. And so we did. The odors of marine paint, gasoline, diesel fuel, and old fish were everywhere. I heard the sputter and crackle of welding rods—almost everywhere you looked along these docks, the bluish white brilliance of the welding flashes bounced off the buildings or flashed right in your eyes.

"Most of the seafood industry, which is mostly scallops right now, is located over in New Bedford," said DeSilva, pointing to the pastel-colored steel freezer warehouses across the bay. They had names painted on them: Frionor, Bay State Seafood, Sea-Rich, Fairway Fish Company, and so on. "But over here, as you can see, we specialize mostly in boatyard work. Repairing hulls, rigging, mending nets and trawls, salvage work, and so on. Also, we've had a lot of growth in recreational marinas. See all those sailboats?"

The place bristled with boats of all descriptions. Not having spent much time in this town, I found it hard to believe how huge the harbor of these twin cities was, and how busy. So it came as no surprise when he told me it was the busiest fishing port in the East.

Joe walked over to the big steel fence surrounding SEA-MATT's wharf and peered through it. "When's the last time you were in here, Tony?"

"Years and years ago. Just before Chris went away. I don't think anybody's been in there since. As you can see, all kinds of vessels are tied up to the wharf, so they're using the outside of it, anyway."

"Doc, you say Claudia owns this now?"

"According to her, and some barges, a tug, and the freighter."

"Well, she might get a pretty price for this property alone. I—"

He stopped, staring at the fence on the other side. He motioned us to follow him, and soon we were all staring at a section of the fence that had been cut out, and then wired back into place.

"The casual observer wouldn't notice it," said Joe, examining the bright metal where it had been sheared by cable cutters, "but somebody's cut their way through here, and within a week, it looks like."

"Maybe we should call the police."

"Tony, I *am* the police."

Joe used his cell phone to put in a call reporting the breach in the fence. DeSilva and I walked along the wharves, watching men rig the great stern trawls that sat suspended in giant spools over the sterns and sloping transoms of the new-generation draggers. One fishing boat, a steel-hulled giant named *Friend-ship*, was hauled up in dry dock for refitting and a paint job. We walked beneath her; her bows rose up three stories in the sky above us. She was around ninety feet in length, deep hulled and massive.

"Well, it looks like American fishermen are finally narrow-ing the gap with the rest of the world," I said. "When I first came down to the Cape in the late sixties, all we had were those forty-foot wooden side trawlers, most of them old and beat-up. Back then the East Germans, Russians, and Japanese were beat-ing the hell out of us. Thank God we're catching up."

He nodded, then stared a while without saying anything. Fi-nally he spoke. "But you know, Doc, it's the big syndicates who put these vessels together. They cost millions and millions. That means the little guy doesn't have a chance anymore. We may have caught up, but the family business of fishing is almost dead."

"I realize that. And you know what? The family business in almost every field is vanishing. Family farms, family retail stores, family restaurants. Everything."

"You're right. And this town's been hit especially hard because the Portuguese community was built on family businesses."

We heard a honk behind us and went to the car. Joe continued driving slowly along Middle Street, which fronted the water. When it ended, he swung left on South Street and then right on the next one, which was Fort Street. Instantly, there was an in-credible change in the neighborhood. In place of the modest two-story walk-up bungalows, package stores, and taverns of the working waterfront, there were now spacious homes—mansions would be a better word—set on deep wide lawns with walls around them, and their own private docks and tiny beaches.

"Hey, what the hell happened?" said Joe, wide-eyed.

"This is Fort Street, one of the oldest in town. This is where many of the early whalers and industrialists built their homes."

"They sure are pretty. Which one is Chris's?" I asked.

"We're not there yet. His place is much smaller, around the point ahead."

We went by old Fort Phoenix, a Revolutionary War fort that had been restored, and then looked back at the massive break-water that bridged the bay, stretching from the old fort all the way across to New Bedford. Right in the middle of the massive stone structure was the sea gate. It was a little over a hundred feet wide. Tony explained to us that two giant, curved walls of steel were housed in the buildings on each side of the gate, and could be closed by hydraulic mechanism in the event of a storm.

"It closes up as tight as a Diebold bank vault," he said. "The whole thing took almost ten years to build."

"I can't help wondering," Joe said, "how Ramos could have smuggled anything into this place with a breakwater like this guarding it. I mean, every boat that comes or goes must pass through this narrow lock. Right?"

DeSilva nodded.

"Well, they're right under the noses of the authorities. They could tell any boat to stop, and then search it."

"No. The Coast Guard would have that authority, but they don't operate the gate," said DeSilva. "They're the Army Corps of Engineers. They have no law-enforcement function."

"Ahhh—I see. So a gutsy skipper could sneak things into this harbor."

"Definitely. They do it all the time."

"What, mostly?"

"Drugs. Marijuana and cocaine. Some heroin. I see the effects of it every day. Joe, keep bearing to the left—follow the point around; the Harborview section is right on the other side."

Harborview lies at the bottom of the peninsula on the Fairhaven side of the bay, and a little to the east. From some places here, you can just barely see Butler Flats Lighthouse, which sits out in front of the huge breakwater guarding New Bedford Harbor. It's a caisson design light, built in 1898, stuck right out in the middle of the sea. It was this light that guided Mary and me on many sailing expeditions to New Bedford. Father De-Silva guided us down through the small streets until we emerged on a road that swept by the ocean, with small shingle-sided

Cape-style cottages that looked recently built. We parked the car and walked along the shore, enjoying the cool sea breeze that seemed a constant here.

"Up there, fourth one on the right," he said.

We walked along the sandy front lawns and noticed the fine view these new tenants must enjoy. I asked Tony why Chris Ramos chose such a modest house, since, during most of his career at least, he seemed to have plenty of money.

"He was always a modest man. Also, when he went into illegal activities to support the company, he figured a lavish house would alert the authorities."

"Hah!" Joe laughed. "That's the one thing that most drug dealers and wiseguys still can't get into their heads: a big house with three flashy cars out front invites suspicion. I'm getting the feeling more and more that Ramos was really buttoned up; he knew how to hide his assets."

"Speaking of assets," I said. "Did Claudia ever mention the small freighter that belonged to SEAMATT? It was called the *Santiago*. She says it disappeared."

He turned to face me, the wind whipping at his clothes and hair. A ship hooted in the distance. "I'm all but positive I've seen her twice in the past month, Doc. New paint, new name, but the same shape underneath."

"You've seen her here?"

He nodded. "Both times over near the state pier on the New Bedford side."

"What's her name?"

"Esmeralda."

We were now standing in Ramos's front yard. The place appeared to be well maintained, and Father DeSilva said that Claudia made sure the grass was cut and the place looked after when she wasn't in residence. We walked up to the front porch and sat on the pine-backed rockers, looking out over Buzzards Bay.

"You wouldn't have a key, would you?" asked Joe, leaning over and placing his hands around his face and against the windowpane, trying to peer inside.

"Sorry. I gave the only one I had to Claudia a long time ago."

"Nice place inside?"

"Great. Nice and cozy. Chris used to invite me to dinner a lot. We'd sit out here and drink some wine, watching the sun go down, then go inside for a great meal."

"You miss him, don't you?" I said.

"Oh, very, very much. For one thing, he was a local success. And Portuguese too. And he was always caring, always very generous. A great man."

"Did you ever suspect," said Joe, leaning forward now in one of the rockers, "that he was set up to serve a prison term that was overly harsh?"

"I don't suspect it, Joe; I know it. Maybe it was Larry Kelly and his gang who did it. But somebody did. And I hope that somebody pays the price. Excuse me. As a priest I should not say that. Sometimes my feelings get in the way."

"But now that Larry Kelly's dead," Joe pursued, "is there any-body out there you could name who's still after Ramos's cache?"

"Especially somebody who's got a strange voice," I said. "A man with almost no vocal cords left. A man who whispers?"

The priest shook his head.

The wind shifted then, bringing with it the odor of something dead, so we left the porch and walked across the road down to the beach. A big trawler was returning with the usual cloud of screaming gulls whirling around it. It was a lovely day, the air cool and crisp, the clouds giant puffballs that sailed fast overhead.

"Ummmmm," mumbled Joe. "Smells better here. Don't you think it smells better here?"

We both nodded. "Must be the breeze," said Tony.

"Hey, Doc, maybe we should invite Tony to join us at the cottage. Whuddayah think?"

"Great idea. Can you take a night off?"

"Not tonight. But maybe tomorrow. Sounds like fun."

We got back in the car and Joe started it. Then he rolled his window down, looked at the house again. Rolled the window back up, shut off the car.

"I'll be right back," he said, walking toward the house.

Tony and I talked while Joe went around the house, then came back. He reached for the radio mike under the dash.

"This is Detective Lieutenant Brindelli. Yes, request immediate assistance at Thirty-two Farmfield Street in Fairhaven. Suspected homicide. Over."

DeSilva and I stared at each other. Then we all got out and sat on the rocks bordering the beach while Joe lit a cigarette.

"The smell," he said. "I thought it must be something dead here on the beach. But I couldn't see anything dead, and the smell got stronger near the house. Quite strong toward the rear of the house."

"And you think . . . ?" whispered DeSilva.

"I don't think, Tony. I know. I been doing this too long not to know." He spat into the sand at his feet, flipping the cigarette away. "Shit. And I thought this was going to be a nice break."

"But it's not your beat," I said. "Be thankful of that."

"Right. I called it in, but I don't hafta handle it."

The first vehicle to arrive was a local Fairhaven police car, marked, with lights on top. But they weren't on. The car slid noiselessly up the street and parked behind Joe's. A handsome young man with a dark complexion got out, instinctively feeling for the tiny radio on his belt. He introduced himself as Officer Partmos. He and Joe walked toward the house slowly, talking so low we couldn't hear. I saw Partmos remove the little radio from his belt and begin speaking into it as they disappeared around the building.

"Can we go see what they're doing?" Tony asked me. "I mean, are we allowed to?"

"Sure, as long as you don't touch anything. But, personally, I would rather stay here and watch the ocean, Tony. I've been on enough of these discoveries to know they're no fun. And what you'll see and smell might make you sick."

When the two returned, another cop car had arrived, and a big black truck with no markings. Three men got out wearing what looked like green jumpsuits. That would be the lab team. As they opened the back double doors for some equipment, I noticed there was a litter in there. For a minute or so we all stood in an almost silent circle at the foot of Chris's driveway. I thought we were pretty discreet. But already I could see window shades going up (or down), and several women standing on porches or stoops looking at us.

"I can pick the lock in front without touching the knob," said Joe. "I think that'll be the best way to get in."

Tony and I walked over to the seawall and sat listening to the gulls and the faint whine and growl of far-off diesels as they pushed the distant draggers across the horizon.

"Any idea who might be in there?" I asked Tony.

"None. I hope it's not Claudia. She comes down here often to get away."

"I doubt it; she was alive and well day before yesterday. Whoever or whatever's in there must be several days old at least."

But all the same, I realized that a cold chill was sweeping through me. I couldn't recall anyone I'd met who had so impressed me, or attracted me. She'd had a tough time too. I realized my mouth was dry now and my lower legs were trembling slightly.

"Say a prayer, Tony," I added. "Pray it's not her."

He bowed his head, and I put mine down in my hands, shutting out all the light. I heard footsteps approaching and was afraid to look up. Joe was looking down at me.

"Tell me it's not her, Joe."

He shook his head, grim-faced.

"It's not her. White male, maybe mid-forties. He looks strangely familiar to me. I think maybe you might recognize him."

"Me?"

"We'll wait until the place airs out a bit, then you can come back inside."

"Should I come too?" Tony asked.

"I don't recommend it, Tony. But we'd like you to see his face when we bring him out of there. Then you can administer the last rites."

He began to walk back, then turned, a sour look on his face.

"Of course, the first thing we'll have to do after they take the pictures is cut him down. Then after that we have to . . . put him together again. It'll take a while."

"Cut him down? Put him together?"

"Come see for yourself, Doc. Tony, we'll call you soon, okay?"

Joe and I walked slowly around the side of the cottage. He explained it to me, trying to keep his voice steady.

"First, remember the rules: don't touch anything. Go only where they tell you. Stand where they tell you, nowhere else."

"Right."

"He's in the back room with all the windows shut and the curtains drawn. Thank God it's been cool here or the smell would be much worse."

"How . . . far gone is he?"

"Not too far. No gross bloating or discoloration and no insect infestation—thank God! Mel Ables, the head of the New Bedford lab, places death at between forty-eight and sixty hours ago."

"I take it he was murdered. How?"

"You'll see. Get ready, though. It ain't a Monet painting . . ."

We entered by the back door, a white-framed door on the top of a little wooden deck stoop with white railings. The odor got more intense right away, but wasn't overpowering. I heard an exhaust fan whining in the kitchen, which was the first room we entered after going through the little screened porch in back.

Off the kitchen was a narrow hallway.

"First door on your left, Doc. The rear bedroom. Get ready—"

I steeled myself. Even before I got to the doorway, I saw the constant flashes of strobe lights from the cameras bouncing off the walls, and heard the low intense murmuring that is always present when a lab team is at work.

I turned the corner and could not believe what I saw.

A man was hanging, naked, suspended from the ceiling by a wire line. The giant fishhook at its end was thrust through the man's upper torso from the back, its bloody, barbed point exiting the chest just beneath the collarbone. His head lolled to one side, eyes open and blank. Below him, all over the carpet, were his entrails; his belly had been ripped from sternum to crotch, and he was all spilled out.

The men turned to see me standing there, grabbing on to the doorjamb to keep from falling. A hand lifted my arm away, and the man helped me over to a wooden stool.

"Here, sit here," he said softly. "Do you think you need to go into the bathroom?"

He was asking me if I was going to vomit. "No. I—don't think so."

So I sat there for several minutes while the crew dusted and vacuumed. I thought I heard a low scratching sound coming from down the hall.

"Look at the face, Doc," said Joe. "Tell me what you think."

It didn't take long to place that face. As I looked at it, I found myself once again in that back room at Flynn's waterfront tavern down in Southie, getting the shit beat out of me. The same silly-putty nose, the huge neck and battered ears that marked the professional boxer. Finally, the horrendous acne scars all over the pale face that looked like a street in battle-blown Bosnia.

"It's him. The guy who whacked me at Flynn's."

I looked up close into the face. The eyes, pale gray-blue, were empty of all emotion. Irish eyes that weren't smiling.

"Hey, what's that?" One of the lab men bent his head over and stuck it out into the hall. "Somebody leave a dog or cat in here, or what?"

Joe's big paw caught me on the upper arm and led me out of the room. "We'll go see," he said.

Halfway down the hall we came to a small door that appeared to be a closet. Joe knocked on it. I heard an eerie whine on the other side.

"A cat," I said. "There's a cat in there, for God knows how long."

Joe leaned over, listening close.

"Not a cat—I heard a chattering. Almost like a child . . ."

We looked at each other. I wished I were home, sweeping the basement. Joe listened again, then straightened up. "I don't like this, Doc."

He called for the team. Then there were five of us standing in front of the door. Joe knocked again. An intense scratching on the other side. A frantic pawing of feet ... or perhaps small hands.

"Hey, boy! Hey!" called Joe.

Then came a scream, frantic with rage, hurt, and fear.

"Holy shit, they've locked a kid in there!" Joe said, turning the knob and swinging open the door.

None of us were ready for what happened next.

A reddish brown blur shot out of the closet, screaming. The monkey, eyes wide with fear and rage, sprang upon one of the lab men, clutching its wiry arms around his neck, and bit him on the face. The man screamed and fell backward. Then the animal jumped down, shot down the hallway, found an open window in the porch, and flew through it. Gone.

14

I CAUTIOUSLY OPENED THE DOOR TO THE GUEST ROOM AT THE Breakers and peeked in. Joe was still asleep. Or, rather, passed out. Place smelled like a distillery. I wondered when he'd surface.

I was worried about my brother-in-law. The night before, when we got to the cottage, he started putting the booze away big-time. It wasn't that long ago that he went on a binge because of Tommy Maloney's death, which he felt was his fault. Now, this lab guy from the New Bedford department, Devlin Conroy, gets bitten on the face by a rabid monkey. We weren't certain it was rabid, but it was doing a hell of a good imitation. There was mucus and foam all over Conroy's wound: two big fang marks on his right cheek. Monkeys have awesome fangs. Next time you're at the zoo, take a look at the big male baboons when they yawn. Yikes.

So what it meant was, if they couldn't find the monkey, dead or alive, and find out if it was infected, poor Conroy was going to have to undergo the series of inoculations for rabies and pronto, too. And sometimes they leave the patient partially paralyzed. When Joe was told this, he lost it. When we got to the cottage, he made three of his monster G&Ts in a row, sitting out on the deck watching the horizon of Cape Cod Bay, muttering.

"Why the *fuck* did I have to yank open that door, Doc? Huh?"

"Because you thought there was child in there, nearly suffocated, that's why. You're a great cop; you care for people. It was an accident. If anyone's to blame, it was the jokers who put the animal in there in the first place."

"Yeah? Well, this little puzzle of yours is jinxing me, that's what. First Maloney and now this Conroy. And he's not even a cop! No lab guy figures he's taking a big risk dusting for prints."

He paused for a big swallow and to light a cigarette. Two years ago he quit, and recently started up again. It broke Marty's heart. But she knew when she married him that cops are nervous wrecks inside. They're not afraid; they're brave—it's just that their job is so high-stress it eventually eats them up inside. Read any Joseph Wambaugh book and you realize this. And Wambaugh knows; he's been there. He was with the LAPD for sixteen years.

"What do you want for dinner, then?"

"Nothing. I'm not hungry."

Then I knew we were in trouble. When Joe Brindelli goes off his feed, he's had it. Look out. I went out to a clam shack and got a clam roll and fries. When I came back, he was in bed, passed out.

Now here it was nine-thirty, and he was still comatose. I crept in and opened the windows another notch. When I turned around, he was looking at me with those melancholy Marcello Mastroianni eyes.

"What time is it?"

"Nine-thirty. You okay?"

"Do I look okay?"

"No."

"Well, I feel like shit. Do I look like shit?"

"Close. Look, Joe, you can't go around blaming yourself for all these misfortunes. Now I think the best thing for you—for *us*—to do at this point is just to back off. Just forget all about Chris Ramos, Claudia, Smitty, the guy with no voice box, Father DeSilva, the whole shmear. Okay?"

He shook his big dark head. The whites of his eyes looked like stoplights.

"And close your eyes; you'll bleed to death."

"I am going to mix a bloody and take a mouthful of Tums. Then I'm going to walk and walk and walk on the beach until I feel a little bit human . . ."

"And?"

"And then I'll eat a little lunch. Then take about three sauna baths . . . then we'll talk about dinner."

"That's my boy."

He did as he promised. While he walked, I jogged. It was during the sauna baths, when we were both in there wrapped in towels, that the kitchen phone began to ring. We tried to ignore it, but it wouldn't shut up. I went out to answer it, half afraid even to touch it after recent events. But I returned to the sauna with a light heart, and when I told Joe the news he jumped off the bench and hugged me.

"Well, well, well," said Joe, easing himself away from the groaning board after putting away a pound of scrod, four russet potatoes, a heaping double handful of green beans (with sour cream, Parmesan cheese, and lemon on them), and half a loaf of French bread. He had skipped his ration of grog, and instead had only two glasses of chardonnay with the meal.

"Feeling better?"

"Much. So tell me again, how did they catch the monkey?"

"It went down to the beach and tried to drink seawater. I suppose it was almost dead from thirst; that's why it was making such a ruckus in the closet."

"Wow! It must have been *really* thirsty after that."

"Yeah. They say it's a howler monkey. Red-handed howler monkey; they're famous for their screams."

"I can see why. God, what an awful noise!"

"Uh-huh. So, after it drank a few mouthfuls of seawater, you can imagine the thirst it had. So much that it sneaked into a house and drank from the toilet bowl."

"Must've got that trick from your Labs, Doc."

"Anyway, the housewife heard the noise and opened the bathroom door. When she walked in, the monkey climbed up the curtain and perched on the curtain rod, screaming bloody murder at her. She simply closed the window and walked out, shutting the door behind her, and called the police."

"And the monkey isn't rabid."

"They don't know for sure. But a vet they called in said he'd be extremely surprised if it were. It actually was really tame and friendly after they fed and watered it."

"So it's a pet. An escaped pet—"

"Pretty rare for a pet. Howler monkeys are only found in zoos. Other than their natural habitat."

"Which is? Don't tell me . . ."

"You got it: Central and South America."

His face froze. "Uh-oh . . . I'm getting that feeling again."

"So am I."

"The South American connection. No red frogs so far, but monkeys. You suppose he was a pet of one of the murderers and got stuck in that closet by mistake just before they split?"

"Could be. Or else they put it in there deliberately, maybe as a sign or warning."

"Well, listen, Doc: I'm not letting go of this thing now. It's gotten way, way under my skin. I'm a little more than pissed off about it if you'd care to know."

"I, uh, couldn't help getting that impression."

"Uh-huh. I'm gonna stick with this problem like—like— what would Hannon say?"

"Like white on rice."

"Yeah. That's it."

"Like stink on shit."

"Exactly."

"Like bubble gum on your shoe."

"Couldn't put it better. And I've got a couple weeks or more to devote to it. So starting tomorrow, bright and early, we're going to find your pal Claudia Kelly."

"Claudia Ramos. And she's not my pal."

"Hell she isn't; she gave you those hot rocks."

"And, according to you and Brian, stole them right back."

"We'll see who's right, hotshot."

Then the phone rang again. Joy of joys. We debated answering it, but finally Joe staggered to his size thirteen-and-a-half feet and went over to get it. It was the Bobbsey Twins, Mary and Marty. Just checking up on us. Joe told them about the murder victim in Chris's house, and the monkey. While he was thus engaged, I went into the living room and got on the other extension.

"There was a piece in the *Globe*, but an even juicier one in the *Express*," Marty was saying.

"About what?" I asked.

"About your friend Claudia Kelly," said Mary. Her voice had the tone of one of the head honchos at the Spanish Inquisition.

"She's not my friend. Why does everybody keep saying we're buddies?"

"Only because you drooled over her from the start, Charlie. And because she took you out to lunch and gave you three huge diamonds. That's all."

"Get back to the subject," demanded Joe. "And quit picking on Doc."

Good old Joe. Always standing by me.

"It's hard enough being a nitwit," he added. "He doesn't need any more aggravation."

"Anyway, the Boston cops and the FBI detained Claudia for questioning about the murder."

"Really? How did they finally find her?"

"That's the big news: she's been staying at the apartment of her special friend," said Mary.

"That explains why we couldn't find her," said Joe.

"What's his name?" I asked. "He's probably the one she referred to over lunch."

"That's just it, Charlie; it's not a he, it's a *she*."

". . . oh?"

"Go into Wellfleet and buy the papers. You'll see," added Marty.

"Anyway, Charlie, I guess I feel a little safer now about Claudia Kelly, or Ramos, or whatever her name is. You guys try to stay out of trouble for the next twenty-four hours, okay?"

Joe and I cleaned up the dishes in silence. We went for an after-dinner stroll on the beach. The tide was coming in softly, making little slurping noises as it crept up the flat sand. The sunset was killer: a bloodred sun that looked double-sized was going down in banks of purplish cumulus clouds. One big advantage of living on the bay side of the Cape is the great sunsets. Several mewing gulls were silhouetted against the red and gold sky. There was nobody else on the beach.

I tried to talk about the sunset and the ocean, the groaner buoy at the foot of Billingsgate Shoal, the old wrecked Liberty Ship on the horizon—or what was left of it—and Joe tried to answer. But we each knew what the other was thinking. Finally Joe said, "I need cigarettes; let's go into Wellfleet."

So we did. And while he bought smokes, I examined the racks and bought the *Globe* and a copy of the *New England Messenger-Express*. This was a fairly new paper, about six years old, and designed to be the regional gossip rag. As might be expected, it was in tabloid format, heavily pictorial, and full of trash about local icons. The obvious targets were, of course, the Kennedys, the Boston Brahmins—what was left of them—and the sports heroes of the Sox, Celtics, and Bruins. It was, in short, the *National Enquirer* for Eastern Mass. Underneath the masthead was a logo picturing a man in colonial costume riding a swift horse. Apparently it represented Paul Revere. Under the logo was the credo: *Bringing the Truth to Our Citizens.*

Joe took the *Globe* and read aloud. "Ms. Kelly, who is legally changing her name to Ramos, was found at the residence of Ms. Katherine Winger on Memorial Drive in Cambridge. Ms. Winger accompanied Ms. Kelly/Ramos to the John F. Kennedy Federal Building. Ms. Winger told reporters afterward that it was impossible that her friend could have been involved with the murder, since the two had spent the past several days together in the city, scarcely leaving each other's sight."

The *Messenger-Express* was more blunt, and full of innuendo. First, there were several photos of the women walking closely together, embracing after the police interview, and speaking together afterward, both wearing sunglasses. I thought Claudia looked a dead ringer for Sophia Loren, especially with the shades on. Then there was a photo of the elegant apartment on Memorial Drive, a stone building behind those gorgeous sycamores, and a white circle around a set of front windows. The caption read:

Love nest where the two women spent the last week together. "We've been inseparable for the last month," says Kathy Winger.

And so on.

On the way back to the cottage Joe asked me, through a cloud of smoke, if I was disappointed.

"How?"

"You know, that Claudia's a lesbian.

"We don't know that for sure."

"Not for sure, but things certainly point in that direction, I'd say."

"Yeah, I guess I am a little bit. She sure is gorgeous, the type of woman any man would have fantasies about."

"Especially you, Doc."

"Lay off, Joe. Let's concentrate instead on finding more pieces to this puzzle."

"Uh-huh. Like where Smitty lives. I bet it's in New Bedford."

"Me too. And, fortunately, we're not that far away."

"We'll start by tracking down the Lincoln. My people at Ashburton Place were working on it; let's hope they have an answer."

15

"WELL?"

Joe and I sat staring at the picture on the screen.

"No. Don't think so," I said.

The slide projector shuffled and clicked like the step of a soft-shoe dancer, and brought up another picture.

"Hmmmmm . . ." said Joe.

"Any good?

"Nope."

Shuffle-click.

"That's more like it. What year is that?"

"That's an eighty-one."

"Do you have any rear views? Doc saw it mostly from the back each time."

"Sorry. Most are three-quarter shots from the front. What about this?"

Shuffle-click.

"Hey! That could be it."

"Eighty-three Town Car," said Officer Wardwell. "Joe, have you seen this vehicle?"

"No. And it's too bad Doc didn't have time to notice the tag number, or even the first three digits. He and my sister were too taken with the Surinamese flag on the back window."

"If you can sketch the flag, we can get a copy to all the departments and have them alert their men."

"We did that last week with no results," Joe said. "I think they got wise and took the flag off. What's the difference between the Continental and the Town Car?"

"Not that much. Town Car usually has four doors. The Continental is usually two doors and has the European-style tire well flare on the trunk."

"Doc, you remember the tire well or not?"

I shook my head.

"Problem is, there's almost eighteen thousand Lincolns registered in this state. We've got one break; we list the color on the registrations. So we've got body color to rely on besides model and year."

"Let's go through a few more slides," said Joe. "If nothing pops up, I say we take a flyer and get a printout of all Lincolns over ten years old registered in New Bedford, Fairhaven, Dartmouth. Can you do that?"

Wardwell nodded, and Joe and I left the viewing room at One Ashburton Place and went over to a local sub shop for lunch. Joe ordered two small subs: an eggplant Parmesan and an Italian sausage with green peppers. I ordered a small steak and cheese with tomato and lettuce, hot peppers, oil, vinegar, and spices. And Tums for dessert.

"They finally ID'd the gutless wonder at Chris's cottage," he said, picking up the first sub, taking a huge bite, and chewing in ecstasy. Apparently the thought of the ripped corpse didn't deter his appetite. "Name's Jacob Breitz. Like our other dear friend from Flynn's, he was a former boxer turned informer and enforcer. Drug addict most of his life. His arms showed marks and collapsed veins."

"They sure do select the quality types, don't they?"

"Yep. Wish they'd nail the other guy, this Gary Walsh character. Then we could pump him for the info we so badly need."

While we were having our second cup of coffee, Joe suddenly said, "Speaking of info . . ." and went over to the pay phone and called Tony DeSilva. He returned with a map of the area and spread it out on the table between us.

"Tony says there are two black neighborhoods in New Bedford. One is on the west side where Route 6 comes through town. This is predominantly African American. These blacks are mostly descendants of those who came up right after the Civil War."

"Really? No kidding. Then it's an established community."

"Oh yes. Now the other one is the one I think we should pay special attention to. It's down here, roughly halfway between the state pier and Fort Rodman—especially around the area of Purchase and County Streets—where they intersect."

Joe drew a circle on the map halfway down the narrow peninsula that extends down from the center of town into Buzzards Bay. "If any of these old Lincolns show a registration address in this area, I say we go check out that address. Maybe stake it out."

"Why this neighborhood and not the other one on the west side?"

"Because the African Americans probably aren't involved with our friend Smitty and the rest from south of the border. The blacks who live in the south end are mostly descended from natives of the Cape Verde Islands and other former colonies of Portugal, like Brazil."

"How long have they been living here?"

"A hundred fifty years at least. Since the whaling days, Tony says. They've been a part of the whaling and maritime industries all along."

"Gee, I didn't know all this exotic stuff was so close to home."

"Speaking of home, let's take the ladies out tonight. Give them a break."

We had just finished stuffing ourselves with pot-stickers, black mushroom soup, baby spareribs, Hunan pork, Peking duck, and shrimp toast at the Yangtze River in Lexington when Joe waved a cautionary finger at us.

"Here's the way I see it. This thing is beginning to have all the hallmarks of a classic gang war between remnants of the old Kelly gang and the organization Smitty runs. We don't know at this point how they're still connected. My guess is that it's the rumor of Ramos's vast treasure. Up until now I assumed it was mostly bullshit. But now I'm not so sure. It seems that people— rough people who are in a place to know—are slugging it out to get it. So far they're mostly focusing on each other. But if they get nowhere, sooner or later one or both gangs are gonna come down on top of us."

"I thought this outing was to cheer us up, Joey."

"It is. But all I'm saying is keep your eyes peeled. And if I call you and tell you to get out fast, leave Concord and come into Boston; you can stay with us for as long as needed."

As we left to get in the car, Mary remarked that my earlier hypothesis regarding the so-called keys to the kingdom was probably true.

"Because, face it," she said, "if Smitty was the first to look under the pew, which I believe, and he found the treasure or the means to it, he would have left the scene by now. Gone back to Suriname or Jamaica or wherever his permanent hangout is."

"Gotcha," said Joe, stifling a burp.

"But he's still around. I mean, who else would kill the guy in the cottage but Smitty or his gang? Who else would leave a monkey behind?"

"Right," said Marty. "And the Kelly gang now probably thinks that Smitty, not Doc, has the answer."

"So we're in the clear," said Mary.

"Never assume that," warned her brother. "Not when people are disemboweling each other and hanging each other up by fishhooks. Never assume you're safe."

"I don't think anybody knows where this treasure is," I said. "I think Ramos was sufficiently out of his mind that he gave the wrong directions. Either the keys to the treasure are somewhere else than the pew, or there is no treasure at all."

"There's a treasure, Charlie. I know it. I feel it. Why else are these bad guys so worked up?"

I was reading street names from the map as Joe drove south along Kennedy Highway from the state pier in downtown New Bedford toward the address he'd been given earlier by Officer Wardwell: number 319 on a street called Rivet. Out of sheer frustration, the guys at headquarters had followed Joe's suggestion and simply done a search of owner names of older Lincolns in the New Bedford area. Of the four that sounded most promising, this was our second try.

The neighborhood was interesting and unique. There was not a lawn or tree to be found in this cement, concrete, and asphalt layout of streets and blocks. Wide sidewalks bordered the streets, and houses and stoops sprang up from these sidewalks. A few shrubs and flowerpots were the only green living things visible. However, the area was not run-down, and had a safe, "close neighbor" feel to it. It was a little like Boston's Italian North End except the buildings were not as high, and the place had a more spacious appearance. On every block were signs in Portuguese for restaurants, butcher shops, grocery stores, taverns, hardware and clothing stores, all catering to the daily needs of this small and tight community.

"You're going to turn right on Potomska Street," I said, squinting at the small print, "and then south again on Purchase."

He did, and the streets got narrower. We decided to park wherever we could as we approached Rivet Street, which was just a little over a block south. After turning right on Rivet, we got to the intersection of Rivet and County Streets, which seemed to be almost the heart of the neighborhood. Joe managed to wedge the cruiser in between a van and a motorcycle, and we got out. Joe stretched languidly and walked back in the direction we'd come. I asked him why.

"Because it never makes good sense to go marching into a neighborhood too fast. For one thing, it screams 'cop.' Even though we've got regular clothes on and an unmarked car, chances are these street people have already got us pegged. What Kevin and I do, we walk around a little, maybe go into a little shop and get coffee—sort of get the mood of the place first. Then, we do business."

So I played shadow. We walked back to Purchase and Rivet, then down a street and back over, then snaked our way back by the opposite direction. The neighborhood was as it appeared: safe and close. There were a lot of bars, but they were working-men's pubs, not rough hangouts. There were plenty of churches and, at half past three, kids walking home from school together chatting and singing.

"I like this place," he said. I agreed.

We did a quick walk-by of 319 Rivet Street. A two-story

walk-up with a stoop on the lower level and a narrow railed balcony on the upper. Light blue composition-shingle siding with faded white trim. The place wasn't fancy, but it was clean and neat. We went on by, and later Joe looked in the book.

"Owner of the eighty-four Lincoln is Mrs. Maria Ibenez. Age forty-six. Doesn't say whether she's married or not, or whether she's got any kids. So far, looks on the up and up, wouldn't you say?"

"Uh-huh. But I don't see that big bronze Lincoln anywhere. Do you?"

"Negative."

We circled around the block then, trying to see if there was an alleyway where the car could be parked. And, of course, there was the possibility she was using it in her job, whatever that was. As we walked we saw kids playing hopscotch, kick the can, "double Dutch" jump rope, and stickball. All of those inner-city pavement games that have been lionized in recent years. I guess so. Better than watching Mutant Killer Space Rangers on the tube, or shucking dollars' worth of quarters into video games that depict violent dismemberment and death.

We checked out the rear of the buildings on Rivet Street. There was a narrow, car-clogged alley there, but no Lincoln. It was on our way back around the front that we heard the child crying.

She was sitting on the bottom step of the stoop that led up to number 319. She looked to be no more than six years old, dressed in a light-colored frock, with lots of curls around her pretty dark face. A man in jeans and a T-shirt was standing over her, his booted foot stuck up on the lowermost stair where the child sat. At first, I felt an instant dislike toward the man, thinking he had punished her or was scolding her. Joe stopped beside them, waiting silently. Then I realized the girl was not speaking English. It was obviously Portuguese—sounding a bit like both Spanish and Italian but neither. Finally the man, whose face showed growing concern, looked up at Joe. Joe leaned over close to the pair and spoke softly. I heard enough to know he was speaking in Italian-Spanish. He learned Italian as a kid, forgot most of it by the time he was a teenager, then relearned most of it when he became a priest and finally a cop. If you speak Italian, it's only a hop and a skip to Spanish. I knew the man and the girl understood him. The man nodded. Joe took out his badge and spoke to the man after stepping between him and the child. He put his hand on the man's shoulder.

Then I realized once again why Joe Brindelli is the best cop in Boston. Despite what the television shows may portray, being a cop is not a gun or a car job. It's not being cagey or tough. It's being a people person. And he's the ultimate people person. It was obvious that he had, in a few seconds, gained the utter faith and trust of the man in the T-shirt.

I felt like a fifth wheel standing there; I gave Joe the high sign and went across the street and into a small bar with a Portuguese sign outside. Joe would know where to find me. I slid onto a stool and kept watching the three of them talking and gesturing across the street. The kid behind the bar came up.

"Hey. You wanna beer or somethin'?"

He looked Portuguese, but was obviously of the new generation.

"I'd like a coffee, please."

"Sure. You want regulah, latte, or mocha?"

Wow. I wasn't expecting this. Even the working-class joints were now getting into the upscale coffee thing. I asked for a latte, and when it came asked the kid if he'd been working there long.

"Nah. I just help out my old man in the summah when I'm off college."

"Where do you go to school?"

"U. of Rhode Island, Kingston."

"Good for you. Your major?"

"Physics."

I nodded, impressed.

"So what brings you here?" he asked. "You a salesman or what?"

It was a friendly question, but I could sense the kid wanted an answer. He wanted to know why these two strangers were in his neighborhood. "I'm with him," I said, jerking my head sideways in Joe's direction.

"Is he a cop?"

"How'd you guess?"

The kid shrugged. "I dunno. Hahd to say—I think he's just got the look."

"Listen, you ever see anything . . . interesting over there in that blue and gray house across the street?"

He stood there, looking at me. "Are you a cop too?"

"No. A friend of his. Have you heard about a murder over in Fairhaven day before yesterday?"

He nodded.

"Well, we're following up on some leads."

He leaned over and put his elbows on the bar, his arms crossed in front of him, hands on biceps. "A couple live there, upstairs. The husband's sick, in bed a lot. So they don't get out much. They rent out the downstairs to Mrs. Ibenez. She's a nice lady; her daughter works in the Hi-Tech plant up in Acushnet. They make coils."

"Coils? Coils of what?"

"Capacitors. Like for your car's spark plugs?"

"Does she drive an older Lincoln, kind of bronze colored?"

He nodded. "Well, she used to, but now her daughter drives it."

"And who does the daughter hang around with?"

"She's about twenty-something—that's her little girl over there with your friend. Anyway, it's a group of younger people. But lately there's been a new batch of dudes hanging around. They seem nice enough, but weird looking, man."

"Black, white, mixed?"

"Kinda mixed, yeah, like most of us."

"Do they party, or what?"

"Not sure, 'cause I haven't been back that long," he said, scratching his curly head. "I think they just kinda come and go. Hey, your friend's waving at ya . . ."

I looked out the window and saw Joe motioning me over with his arm. When I saw him reach around under his suit coat and pull his police radiophone off his belt, I knew we had something.

"Well, take care," I said, sliding off the stool. "I hope everything is okay."

As I crossed the street, I realized it had warmed up a bit. Joe was talking on the phone. I caught the last of the conversation.

". . . Well, we intend to look inside if we can. From what the granddaughter tells me, and the neighbor, I think we have just cause. Uh-huh . . . yeah . . . We just don't want to go in alone without the locals. Okay. We'll wait."

He slid the antenna home and replaced the phone, then introduced me to Raymond Salazar, the neighbor in the T-shirt, who sat down on the stoop and held the girl on his lap, softly singing to her while Joe and I walked ten yards or so up the street.

"I don't think this looks good," he said under his breath. "Every day the grandmother is home waiting for little Anna. But today nobody seems home, and the mother isn't back from work yet. I kept asking her where her grandmother could be. She said she's always home except today. I think we better get a look inside."

"The guy tending bar told me that her daughter drives the Lincoln to her job, which is why we didn't see it."

Soon a couple of black-and-whites whispered up to the curb and the locals got out. Joe introduced me as "a forensic dental expert for the commonwealth." I suppose that was officially true, even though it occupies about five percent of my time. He did it to get me an entree. One set of cops spoke Portuguese, and they sat down with Salazar and the girl and spoke to them softly. Little Anna handed one of them the key she carried with her. The men made sure that the girl stayed with Salazar. She did, and an officer accompanied them as they went two doors down to sit on another stoop and wait.

We got inside with the key. In the small hallway there was a stairway leading upstairs and a door straight ahead of us. We unlocked that door with the same key and went on inside. The place was modest and neat, with white doilies over the arms of the living-room chairs and the kitchen smelling like Pine-Sol. A crucifix hung in the dining room over the small Formica table. Off the dining room was a small bedroom with a small bed. Stuffed animals and dolls were on the bed, which I assumed to be little Anna's. The bathroom was next, and then another bedroom with an unmade bed, a dresser with makeup and a mirror on it, and some photos in frames. As soon as I got a look at them, I grabbed Joe's arm.

"On the far left, Joe. That's him."

"Who? Smitty?"

"Yep, without all the hair and beard. But it's him."

Joe and the other officers thought they could use the photo as a basis for a mockup bulletin if needed. Also in the room was a stereo system and lots and lots of tapes. The music was mostly Senegalese—a band named Yousin D'or. There was a lot of reggae as well, and some American pop stuff. I felt a tap on my arm and followed Joe's pointing finger to a long Plexiglas cylinder lying on a high shelf. He went over and sniffed at it.

"Bong," he said. "So the daughter, Celia, is a doper."

"So? Half the kids under thirty are."

"I know. But I bet I know where she gets her pot."

We stood around in there for a few more seconds, then went to the last door at the end of the hall. This was the bedroom Anna tried to open to find her granny, but couldn't. We walked down there and Joe placed a clean handkerchief over the knob and, holding it by his cupped fingertips at the edge of the knob, turned it and pushed. No go. He dropped to one knee and peered through the keyhole. He rose and pushed the door again, from all different directions and up and down along its knob side.

"Locked from the inside, but not at the location of the door lock. Probably a bolt lock that's been fastened at about eye level. I can tell by the way the door feels when I push on it."

"You going to force it?"

"Not unless we have to. I wish we knew where the daughter works."

"At Hi-Tech, up in Acushnet. The kid in the bar told me."

"Splendid, Doc! Let's get a phone book and call the plant. Maybe we can talk to her."

So we did. But when we finally got to her supervisor, we were told that Celia Ibenez had left work early, unexpectedly. Joe asked if she had seemed upset when she left. The supervisor answered yes, very upset. Something about a family emergency. When had she left? Around ten-thirty. Joe thanked her and re-placed the cell phone in his coat pocket.

"Ten-thirty this morning." He sighed. "That's over five hours ago."

"No good, is it? I wonder where she could be?"

"No place good, Doc. No place good. Well, let's have a look around in back before we force the door."

We walked around the block again, back to the alleyway, leaving one officer inside, the other two with us. The fourth was still with the little girl and her neighbor friend. A worn picket fence ran across the property line in back. The backyard was mostly sandy dirt with a little grass on it. There was a crude swing that hung from a four-by-four frame. Joe skipped all these and went straight to a closed window about eight feet up. He studied it.

"This is the old lady's bedroom," he said. "If it's unlocked, I want to push it up with a stick and take a look inside."

One of the uniformed officers offered Joe his nightstick, but it was too wide. Finally Joe remembered he had seen a stout yardstick in a garbage can in the alley. We got that and Joe held it under the innermost sash and pushed. The window slid up a few inches.

"What I was afraid of," he said wearily.

"How come?" I asked.

"Well, Mrs. Ibenez could have locked herself in her own bedroom. But it wasn't her habit. Now that the window is unlocked in the back, I'm thinking someone was in there with her and they locked the door and left via this window. Doc, you and the guys see if you can't scare up a heavy trash can with a good lid in the alley. Something I can stand on."

We came back with one and Joe stood on it. It didn't take him long to ease himself back onto the ground. He looked at me with a baleful eye. "Here we go again, sport."

So the grim scene was repeated: the lab truck came around back, and the first thing Joe had them do was check the window, the sill, the whole back of the building for evidence.

"And then, I guess the only thing to do is force the door," he said. He sounded as if he hadn't slept in months. "How's Mr. Conroy doing?"

"Fine. There won't even be any scars, Joe."

"Well, good for that. Tell him again how sorry I am about it."

"Holy Jesus!" whispered the lab guy as he looked into the apartment. "You see what's in here?"

"Yeah," Joe said, looking at the ground and holding the bridge of his nose with his fingers. "I saw her."

Part of the lab team dusted the windowsill while the other half went inside. Joe and another cop butted the door open with their shoulders. As Joe suspected, the only thing holding it was a small barrel bolt lock—the kind you screw onto the surface of the door. The door swung back and they went in. I heard nothing for a few seconds, except whispered oaths. Then Joe's voice: "Doc, it's worse than I thought; you may not want to come in here."

I almost accepted his offer to decline, but then noticed all the other men looking at me like I was a spare piece of furniture. I had been introduced as a forensic expert for the state. So I went in.

Maria Ibenez had been a pretty woman. Like most dark-complected people, her skin, even at fifty, was still wrinkle-free and glowing. Her hair was dark brown and curly, and cascaded down the side of her face as she sat in the chair, her head nestled down on her left shoulder. Her eyes must have been pretty too, but I could only see one. The other had been removed. In addition to the gouged-out eye, her arms, strapped to the chair, were covered with burns, and her fingernails had been pulled out. Beneath her body, still held tightly to the chair with thin cords around her legs, waist, and chest, was a puddle of blood and urine. The gag was still in her mouth.

We all stood there, stunned, for the better part of a minute before Joe spoke.

"We've got to make sure little Anna doesn't see this," he said. "I'll go next door and stay with them a few minutes while you take pictures."

"What about upstairs?" asked one of the cops. "Ain't anybody living up there?"

"I don't know," said Joe.

"I do, and they are," I said. "An invalid couple who own this place."

"Well then, we better have a look," he said. I followed him up the stairs. The door at the top of the landing was open. Joe started inside. I asked him if he shouldn't knock first. He shook his head.

"No need, Doc. I got a pretty good hunch they can't hear us."

We found them both in the bathtub. Their throats had been cut; the small tile room was awash in crimson.

16

IT WASN'T LONG BEFORE THE SCENE ON RIVET STREET, DOWN-town New Bedford, echoed that of across the bay in Fairhaven two days previous: the yellow vinyl police ribbon around the premises, the silent parade of body bags on litters carried out of the small two-story house, the collection of police cars and vans, some with lights winking.

Joe saw to it that Raymond Salazar, the neighbor, kept Anna away from the scene until other close relatives could be located. Of course, the closest relative—her mother, Celia—was no-where to be found. This especially had Joe down.

"It doesn't look good, Doc, her and the Lincoln missing after all these hours."

"What do you think happened and why?" I said. We were sit-ting across the street in the same little bar I had found earlier. It was filled up now with the regulars and, not surprisingly, the cu-rious. Joe had talked to as many locals as possible, writing down names, descriptions, and events as fast as he could in his little pocket notebook.

"It's a revenge killing, of course, for the murder of Jake Breitz. But it was more than that: it was death by torture. Maria Ibenez was worked over by a sicko who really knows his stuff.

He knows just where to pick and pry to induce the utmost in horror and pain to his victims. If nothing else, I want that sick bastard on a slab before this thing winds down."

"They tortured her to find out where Ramos hid his stash?"

"I doubt it. They wanted her to tell them where Celia was. So they sneaked in there early this morning, hoping to get the daughter, but she'd already left for the plant. They had to kill the couple upstairs first so they wouldn't hear anything. Even if they didn't say as much, Mrs. Ibenez knew they were after her daughter—so it's no wonder she held out. You saw what they had to do to her to get her to talk—"

I sighed. "Let's hope she died of coronary arrest before they finished."

"I dunno, Doc, she looked pretty healthy to me. Then, after they found where Celia worked, they called the plant and told her of some emergency. Probably something about the daughter, so Celia would leave work immediately. That's when they nabbed her."

"And they'll kill her too, once they have what they want?"

"Damn right they will. In fact, the chances that she's alive right now are just about nil. Christ! That poor little kid . . ."

"Maybe we better call Mary and Marty and tell—"

"Hey! What the hell do you think I did an hour ago, as soon as I had a free five minutes?"

"You called them?"

"Hell yes, I called them. Told them to get to 'the place we talked about' ASAP. I didn't mention place names—there's no telling how sophisticated this gang is at bugging phone or radio messages. I told them to drop everything and get out of your house inside ten minutes. No packing, no deciding what to wear, no female last-minute delays. Get out!"

"Good for you."

"Then I called Brian Hannon and requested a cruiser to watch over your place night and day for the next several days or until I called him back. The men are to detain anyone hanging around your digs."

"Wow!"

"Whadduyuh mean, wow? You and I have seen what these

people do to each other. If we're lucky and wait long enough, maybe they'll kill each other off. But I don't know. Pretty soon now they're gonna figure that maybe it's Dr. Adams, close friend of the deceased, who has the answer. Now let's get out of here and go up to Boston. We'll camp there for the next week or so until this latest dust storm settles."

We didn't get to Joe and Marty's apartment until after eight. This wasn't surprising considering we didn't leave New Bedford until five-thirty, then had to stop at headquarters to check in. Joe wanted to find that Lincoln, and Celia Ibenez, too, if she was still alive. There was an all-points bulletin out for the car, including tag number this time. When we got to Beacon Hill, Mary and Marty were waiting for us. Over a drink we told them what we'd found. This was probably a mistake; it sure didn't set a festive tone for the remainder of the evening. The women hadn't cooked because they had no idea when we'd return. Now we were all too tired and depressed to cook, so we went out to Locke-Ober's.

We walked down there from Beacon Hill. It isn't far; nothing in downtown Boston is. Boston is the perfect walking town. We ambled down along Charles Street to Boylston, then up Tremont, then took a right at the tiny street called Winter, and there it was. Locke-Ober's remains the quintessential snooty Boston restaurant. Until the early seventies, women were not allowed in the main dining room; they had to retreat upstairs. Now that was all changed, and we sat right in front of the big bar with the huge silver coffee urns, and all those waiters in tuxes bringing you that fresh French bread and the best butter in the world. I had braised duck with cherry-brandy sauce and wild rice.

We walked back slowly; I had my arm around Mary, and we stopped at every shop window on Charles, looking at the antique furniture and lamps. I'm always struck by how similar it is to Royal Street in the French Quarter. By the time we returned to the penthouse apartment and sat out on the roof under the moonlight, looking at the silvery glow of the Charles River basin and all the lights below, we felt a lot more chipper. A slow, rather sad piece was playing over Joe's Bose all-weather speakers. Mary asked what it was, and he told us it was Mozart's *Stabat Mater*.

"What's that?" I asked. I had heard of the *Stabat Mater*, and was vaguely aware that it was some sort of musical set piece. "Mater" was Latin for mother, of course. But other than that, I couldn't decipher it.

"It's Latin for 'standing mother,' " Joe said. "It is Mary, standing before the cross, looking at her dead son."

Mary put her hand to her head. "Well, maybe we could switch to something else then."

"Does anybody want to play cards?" asked Marty. No takers. I retired into Joe's study to listen to music and read Stephen Ambrose's book on Meriwether Lewis. When I got sleepy—finally—I reminded myself to call Brady first thing tomorrow. And of course I also had to call Susan Petri bright and early and tell her I wouldn't be in until ten. When I left the study, I found the apartment semidark and silent. I crept into the guest room bed to find Mary asleep.

"I'm going to church," Mary announced over the coffee and English muffins next morning.

"Why now?" I asked.

"I just want to go for a little while; get my head straight after all this mess. When are you leaving for the office?"

"In a half hour," I said.

"Oh no you're not," announced Joe. He was using his most authoritative policeman's voice when he said it. "You're not going anywhere near your office until we get to the end of this thing, or at least a lot further through it. Are you forgetting your recent bop on the noggin in the parking lot? Clearly both sides of this gang war know where your house and office are. Let's not tempt them into torturing you like they did poor Mrs. Ibenez."

"He's right, Doc," said Marty, placing my poached eggs in front of me. "We didn't bring you and Mary all the way into town just to have you go back out there."

"Maybe it's not safe even to have Susan there," said Mary. I thought about this and agreed. Consequently, I called her at home and told her not to come in. There is a special punch-in phone code that changes the message on the office's answering machine, telling callers that due to unforeseen circumstances, the office will not be open. That was that. Now, what to do all day?

"Charlie, why don't you and Joe just wait here till I return from church, okay?"

"You gonna say a novena for us?" he asked her.

"Maybe I will," she said. "We all need it." Then she left.

She returned in forty-five minutes, her face flushed. "C'mon guys, we're going to New Bedford!"

"What?" said Joe, looking up from his *Sporting Clays* magazine. "Listen, Mare, in case you don't remember so good, Doc and I just got back from there yesterday. Seems every time we pop down for a visit, mutilated bodies start turning up. I, for one, am getting rather sick of the place."

"Me too," I said.

"C'mon, let's get a move on. We can call Father DeSilva on the way."

"Mary? Can you tell us why we need to go?" asked Marty.

"Okay. I think I know where the keys to the kingdom are. Remember Charlie said we probably looked in the wrong place? Well, that got me thinking—and I'd like to go back to Saint Bernard's. Now. If you guys don't want to go, I'll go alone."

"You believe this woman, Doc?" said Joe. "Thinks she can order all of us around. Ha!"

"Ha!" I agreed.

"Ha!" said Marty.

"Tony? Is this Tony DeSilva?" Joe asked over the car phone.

"Oh, really? Well, do you know when he'll be back?"

We were humming down Route 24 toward New Bedford after exiting the Southeast Expressway. I sat next to him, amazed at the continually increasing variety of electronic communications gear he had up front in his cruiser. The latest, besides all the different phones and walkie-talkies, was an eight-inch CRT monitor that could be fed data from the computers out in

Framingham, or even the FBI and the crime wire services. Amazing.

"In about a half hour. Good. Perfect. Please tell him to wait in the parish house for Detective Brindelli and Doc Adams. "Uh-huh . . . That's right, dear. He'll know who it is. Thanks."

Joe replaced the phone, then talked over his shoulder.

"This better be good, Mary. I'm beginning to feel like a mailman on a route."

"Just be patient."

"Can't you tell us?" pleaded Marty.

"No. I want to wait till we get there."

We pulled up in front of the parish house and went inside. More street kids cooking meals, doing housework, pretending to do their homework. Just like home. We had to wait almost half an hour for Father to show up, but when Mary explained why we were there, he quickly led us over to the church.

"It was the *Stabat Mater* that gave me the idea," said Mary, walking up the center aisle. "You said it was Mary, looking up at her dead son on the cross. Well, that reminded me of something we overlooked." She swept her hand around the walls of the church.

"The stations," whispered Joe. "The Stations of the Cross. Hey, it's worth a shot. What do you think, Doc?"

For a minute I couldn't say anything. I just kept staring at those fourteen plaques up on the walls. Most churches don't have these depictions. As far as I know, only the Catholic and Episcopal churches do. They are panels depicting the various events in the final hours of Christ's life: the stripping off of his garments and his scourging, then the journey up to Golgotha, the place of execution where he was to die. To die horribly, in the worst of all tortures then known to mankind.

The panels are generally bas-reliefs, done in wood or plaster, and numbered in Roman numerals from I to XIV. They generally start on the "Joseph" side of the church, which is to the right if you are facing forward from the pews, and end on the "Mary" side, which is to the left. They can either be placed seven on each side or, in some cases with more modern buildings, extend all across the rear wall of the church as well as the sides.

"Thing is, which do we check first?" I said.

"C'mon, you guys, we know that already. The third back on the left, just as Chris said. Now go on up and look at Station XII. See what it shows."

So we did. We walked around to the left side, the side with the statue of the Virgin right up in front. The Joseph side usually has a statue of Joseph, who is easily recognizable because he is holding a carpenter's square. We stared up at the scene shown in Station XII. It was titled "Jesus on the Cross." There, at the foot of the cross, were Mary and two attendants.

"Well, there it is," I admitted. "Third back on the left, right near the wall. Why didn't we look there earlier?"

"Too high up," said Joe. "And besides, I thought he said third *row* back."

I shrugged. "Maybe he did. But what made us stop looking— which was our mistake—was seeing that somebody had dug out the wood under the pew bench before us. So we assumed that that was the hiding place, and we simply got there too late."

"You can see how I got the idea," explained Mary. "I kept imagining how the *Stabat Mater* would look: the scene of Mary looking at her son on the cross. When I visualized it in my mind, I realized that I had seen this very event before. Many times before. But where? I couldn't recall until just before I fell asleep last night. I remembered it vividly as a girl back in Schenectady at Our Lady of Angels: looking up at that Station of the Cross."

Father DeSilva gently cleared his throat behind us and began to speak.

"You know, it's interesting, but during the renovation of this building, Chris took a keen interest in every phase of it. He should have; his donations paid for most of it. But these stations—we first saw them advertised in a national newsletter. They are made of solid birch, and carved by a shop up in Minneapolis. They were quite expensive, but the old plaster ones we had were falling apart, and Chris thought these would add the extra touch to the new church. He ordered them himself, paid for them, and even installed them."

"He installed them himself?" said Joe. "Then I do think

Mary's on to something. How are they fastened up there, and how heavy are they?"

"I can't answer either question," said Tony. "I suppose we'll just have to get up there and see. I do know they're each two feet by three wide, and a couple inches thick."

"Wow, that's about forty pounds at least," I guessed.

"Maybe not," said Joe. "Don't forget a lot of wood has been carved away on the front face. But one thing we should think about: considering the circumstances that have surrounded this, I think we should wait until after hours when the door is locked to undertake this."

A moan came from the women, who didn't want to wait. But Tony agreed. He said that the church was locked at ten, and re-opened at quarter to six before the first mass every day.

"We used to let the door remain open day and night, but like most churches nowadays, we can't risk the danger of theft and vandalism. It's just a sad fact of life."

"Okay, we rendezvous back here around ten," said Joe. "Tony, can you get some of your kids to help you get two stepladders brought into this building before then?"

"Sure. But we have a custodian too."

"Use your own judgment, but I like the kids better; the janitor could get suspicious if he's left out. If you can get two ladders, so Doc and I can each get on a side, that would be perfect. Just say it's for some minor repair."

"That'll be no problem."

"Fine, now can you come with us to our cottage until then?"

"I'm afraid not; I'm booked up until dinnertime."

"Well, then, come for dinner."

Tony shook his head, smiling. "Sorry, but I have dinner with the kids over in the parish house."

We went out to the street and said good-bye to Tony.

"You know," he said wistfully, "if indeed anything is behind that station, I keep wondering why he chose that one, since he could have picked any of the others. I can't help but think that maybe he felt a little like Jesus then. This was just before he was to begin his sentence. I'm convinced now about one fact. I know somebody—perhaps someone high up in government or law enforcement—betrayed him and gave him that harsh sentence."

"It's something to think about," admitted Joe. "A lot of us have thought so all along. Take care, Tony; we'll see you later tonight."

"And, Father," whispered Mary as she got into the cruiser, "shhhhhhh! Mum's the word!"

We drove over the Bourne Bridge and along Route 6 all the way to North Eastham, where the Breakers sits on the edge of Sunken Meadow Beach. It was a little over an hour's drive and helped kill some time. But we had a lot of time to kill; it was scarcely after noon. We tried to chill out, but we had a whole eight or nine hours until after dinner when we would wend our way back to Fairhaven and try to rob the church. We couldn't wait.

But we were skittish as a flock of doves on opening day. Joe and I tried beach walking for a couple of hours, and that helped a little. Mary and Marty busied themselves in the kitchen making the famous Adams clam chowder—with three sticks of butter in the kettle, half a package of bacon, six Idaho potatoes, four onions, a gallon of milk, nutmeg, three dozen surf clams and their liquor, cracked pepper, a half bottle of dry white, and a cup of brandy. It's the best chowder ever, and will kill you, of course.

But that's life.

Finally, around four-thirty, when the tide came booming in, Joe and I waded out into the cold waves with twelve-foot surf rods and cast those nickel-plated spoons way out there, and waited for strikes. The spoons had strips of mullet on the treble hooks for added attraction. And wouldn't you know it: just before dinnertime, when we *had* to go in and eat due to the pressing schedule, we each got strikes. Joe managed to haul in a good-sized striper, and I had a blue of about four pounds. Then we had to quit. We scarcely had time to dress and fillet the fish and put them in freezer wrap before diving into the chowder and fresh-baked bread.

Then we got back into the cruiser and headed to New Bedford, stopping at a discount store on the way to buy two inexpensive wood chisels and a mallet.

"The fact that we've bought this stuff probably means we'll strike out," observed Mary. "But we'll soon see."

We met Father DeSilva at the parish house at ten. It was a few minutes before he could get away, so we waited in the church, watching Station of the Cross number XII. When he arrived, we locked the door and turned off the main lights, leaving only the small spots that illuminated the gorgeous stained glass windows from inside.

Then Tony led us through the door to the back of the vestry where two aluminum ladders were laying on the floor. We carried them into the sanctuary and set them up on either side of the two-by-three-foot bas-relief that was seven and a half feet above the floor. Joe and I climbed up and tried to wiggle it. No wiggle, but some play. Joe shined his flashlight behind it.

"I see two big bolts, or rods, extending from the wall, Doc. Maybe if we lift up . . ."

We did, and after raising the wood two inches, it came free. The bolts were lag bolts with hex heads, which fitted into metal-lined recesses in the wood.

"He hung those himself," said DeSilva. "I think he knew what he was doing."

Joe and I each half turned on the ladder rungs and held the plaque, which weighed maybe thirty pounds, out a foot.

Then we looked behind it.

There it was. A white patch in the wood the dimensions of a pack of cigarettes, right on the bottom edge, in the center.

"What do you see?" Mary asked.

"We see," I said, "that you're obviously a genius. There it is, underneath, just like Ramos said."

"Yep," said Joe, unable to hide the rising excitement in his voice, "and now we got to dig 'em out just like Chris told us."

We climbed down, holding the plaque between us, then rested it on the floor with the face leaning against the wall. *Oooohs* and *ahhhhs* all around. Joe and I each took a chisel and began what we assumed would be a major, and delicate, job. It was neither; the white stuff in the mortised hole was silicone caulking. The stuff peeled out of there almost as easily as Silly Putty. After an inch and a half of scooping, we saw a plastic container. I pulled it out. A soap dish. A common, five-and-dime plastic soap dish with a cover. The kind you carry in your luggage for wet soap.

"All this for a bar of Ivory?"

"Shut up, Charlie! Open it!"

"No, you open it, Mary; you're the one who broke the code."

She took the box in her trembling hands and removed the lid. Inside was a wadded-up plastic bag.

"I . . . see . . . *sparkles*!" she shrieked.

"Shhhhhhh!" said Tony, with a huge, shit-eating grin on his priestly face. "You'll alert the neighbors!"

"Diamonds, diamonds! I just know they're diamonds!" giggled Marty.

Mary fiddled with the bag. We all heard clinking.

"Metal," said Joe. "Maybe it's gold."

"Gold? We don't want gold; there's not enough of it. We want diamonds!" said Mary.

Finally she opened the bag and looked inside. Her face fell.

"Oh, no!"

"What?"

"Keys. Three—no, four *keys*!"

"That's it?" asked Tony.

"That's it—" She tipped up the bag and let the contents fall into her outstretched palm. Four keys landed there. One huge brass key that looked like an antique, a common house-lock type key, and then two almost identical keys that were simply flat metal with slots cut in them. Cheap keys—the kind used to lock gym lockers or cabinets.

" 'The Keys to the Kingdom' . . ." I said in a half whisper, "just like Ramos told me . . ."

We all stood there for a second or two not saying anything.

"Jeez, what a letdown," murmured Joe. "Four lousy keys."

"But Joe, they must be important," said Tony. "Or else why would he take such pains to hide them?"

"Like Charlie says, they're the keys to the kingdom; somehow, they'll unlock the treasure."

"Yeah, but what do they go to? Where do we find the locks they're made for?"

"Well, he didn't tell me that part," I said.

"He sure didn't, Doc. So . . . I guess we've got a lot of looking and thinking to do."

"Right," said Tony in a soft voice. Obviously, he was let down too. No doubt he was thinking about all the lodging and attention he could get for the cast-off kids with the treasure—had we found it.

"Wait a minute," said Mary. "There is a treasure hidden somewhere. These keys prove it. So let's clean up this mess, replace the plaque, and go home to figure this out."

"Just one question," said Joe. "Who gets to keep the keys?"

"There's an obvious answer," said Tony. "Doc and Mary keep them. After all, Mary figured it all out."

Mary handed me the four keys.

"But remember," said Tony, "I'm still convinced that, should any treasure come of this, Chris would want a substantial portion of it to go to this parish."

We all nodded at him.

"After all, he hid the keys here, didn't he?"

17

JOE AND I WERE DRIVING IN CONGESTED TRAFFIC IN THE TOWN of Chelsea, which is just northeast of Boston. Demographers who have studied this town estimate that as much as one-quarter of all its residents will never in their lifetimes make the trip across the Mystic River Bridge into Boston. They will be born, live, and die in this little working-class enclave of two-story walk-ups, neighborhood bars, and mom and pop grocery stores stuck between Everett and East Boston.

The residents look out for each other, though; this is not a frontier-town type of place with rival gangs guarding each street corner. In many ways I suppose it resembles the neighborhood in New Bedford where the Ibenez family lived, but much less dynamic.

"What's this guy's name again?" I asked. I was used to the cruiser now. I knew every doodad and switch that flooded the panels in the front seat. I was getting tired of it. I felt as if I, like the people in Chelsea, was doomed to spend the rest of my life in one place: Joe's cruiser.

"Name's Nick Bronzini. Known as Nick the Pick."

"What a charming name."

"He's a charmer all right. Charm his way right into your house and walk off with half your worldly possessions. That's why he's spent half his adult life in the slam."

"How'd you get him to meet with us?"

"He's been in trouble with his parole officer—I said I'd put in a good word if he helped us out."

"He's the best lock man in the area?"

"Probably the best on the East Coast. I've arranged for Jimmy Hoolihan to come meet us at this little pub Nick likes on Marginal Street right next to the Andre McArdle Bridge. You ever meet Jimmy Hoolihan?"

"Nope. But you've mentioned him a lot. I guess he was your mentor in lock picking."

"Sort of. But I was his mentor, too."

"Where's Hoolihan live?"

"Charlestown. His family's lived there for generations. So he said he'll pop over the Mystic bridge and meet us at Shirley's at two." He looked at his watch. "Hey, it's quarter till. The timing's perfect."

"Nick the Pick is still on parole?"

"Hell yes. I doubt he'll ever get off parole. In his prime, I doubt there was any lock or security system he couldn't bypass.

Excepting, of course, the big bank vaults. His specialty was transfer stations."

"Transfer stations?"

"Uh-huh. Companies like Brinks, Wells Fargo all have stations where cash is stored en route to other places. They're heavily guarded, but not like banks. Nick and his associates would knock off these little transfer stations all up and down the seaboard from here to Miami. They'd net between a hundred and two hundred grand a haul."

"I take it he's retired."

"Who knows? Who's to say he doesn't sneak out some nights and pull a couple lucrative B&Es just to keep his wire hand in shape?"

"Wire hand?"

"Sure. Remember I told you the basic principle of lock picking is to put lateral pressure on the pin cylinder with the tension bar while raking the pins upward with the pick. Remember?"

"Sort of . . ."

"Well, anyway—ahh, here we are, just up ahead. See the sign?"

A suspended neon sign announced the establishment named Shirley's on the next corner. The view they had was of the Chelsea River, and East Boston on the other side. Frankly, it wasn't much. I thought the street's name, Marginal, was pretty appropriate. We pulled up and parked and got out.

"Hey, this reminds me a little of Flynn's," I said.

"Hold your tongue!"

Shirley's was a shot and beer joint with the bar all along the far wall and a TV on each end, up above the bottles and racks of snacks. The Red Sox were playing on one set and a "daytime drama" on the other. There were about twelve people in there, mostly men. The place smelled of booze and cigarette smoke. They had menus up on the wall, but it didn't seem like the patrons were there to eat.

"There he is, in the second booth."

I followed Joe down the aisle between the bar stools on one side and the booths on the other to the second one from the rear, where a short, dapper man with slicked-back brown hair was sitting in front of a cup of black coffee. He wore a checked sportcoat over a silk Hawaiian shirt with black and pink and yellow flowers on it. He was smoking a cigarillo with a white plastic tip. It was sitting in an ashtray to the man's left. It smelled like doo-doo.

Joe introduced us. Nick nodded in my direction and mumbled, "Hey, yuz—" but didn't get up. We slid in opposite him. Close up, his face was smooth and tan. He was thin, almost skinny. The kind of build you often see on people who smoke and drink coffee, as opposed to the people who swill beer and eat bag after bag of chips. His deep brown eyes darted back and forth between us fast, never still. He made constant grunting and hacking noises in his throat, and continually wiped the front of his mouth with his right hand while holding the burning cigarillo with his left.

He looked like a bookie. Like a street guy right out of Damon Runyon.

"Well, how's it goin', Nick?"

The man glanced at Joe, then kept shifting his eyes. "Can't complain. Come see, come sah. Mostly sah."

"You staying out of trouble?"

The little man glared at Joe. "Do I look like I'm in trouble, Joe? Do you see me in trouble?"

"No. Actually, you're looking good. And prosperous."

"Whatzat supposa mean?" he growled, the cigarillo bouncing up and down in his mouth as he spoke. "You tryna say I'm woikin' again?"

"No. I'd never accuse you of that, Nick."

"Good, 'cause I ain't. I been playing the ponies wit some success, I'll hafta admit. You evah go to Suffolk Downs? I don't evah see you theah."

Joe shook his head. "No, but I bet you see my partner there: Kevin O'Hearn."

"Oh yeah. A regulah. So what's up?"

"Jimmy Hoolihan and I want to ask you about something."

"I ain't done it. Whatevah it is, I ain't done it."

"No, Nick, we're not talking about a job here. My brother-in-law, Doc Adams here, has come into possession of four keys. Three are simple. The fourth is a mystery. Even Hoolihan is stumped."

"Maybe he ain't as smaht as he tinks," mumbled Bronzoni as he fought his way out of the booth's confines and went up to the bar. Joe looked out the window and announced that Detective Hoolihan, of the theft division of the state police, had arrived and was walking across the parking lot to Shirley's. He came in and joined us just as Nick the Pick returned from the bar with a fresh cup of coffee, which he complemented by lighting up a fresh cigarillo.

Hoolihan was tall, thin, and blond, with a healthy complexion and trim body. Like another cop in his office, Bernie Manning, he obviously worked out with weights and ran to keep fit. He was wearing a handsome tweed suit and Scots brogues. Did not look like a cop. Lawyer maybe. But not a cop.

"Hiya, Nick. How's tricks?"

"She's fine. So let's get on wid it."

"Doc?"

I took the ring of four keys from my pocket and placed them on the Formica table of the booth. Nick the Pick looked at them for a second or two, then up at Joe and Hoolihan, who had eased himself in beside Nick, much to the latter's consternation.

"You guys gotta be kiddin'," he said.

"Why's that?"

"Why? 'Cause they're all a cinch." He picked up the ring and grabbed the house key. "Schlage pin tumbler door lawk. Ten pins inna cylinder. Piece of cake."

Hoolihan and Joe nodded at him. "We know," said Hoolihan. "What about the flat keys?"

Nick grabbed them, studied them for a few seconds. "I don't fuckin' believe this shit—" he mumbled. "What is dis, a friggin' joke? Dese heah are for levah lawks. Cheap-ass levah lawks for *gym lawkahs*. You know, put yuz clothes inna lawkah when yah woik out. So?"

"Why two of them?" asked Joe.

Nick glared at him and shrugged. "I'm sposa know dis? The numbahs on 'em say one-oh-six and one-oh-seven. Next to each othah. I dunno, you bozos deal wid it."

"I take it you, uh, don't think somebody would hide a large sum of money, or a . . . treasure . . . in a gym locker, do you?"

Nick looked insulted. "Whadduyuz? Crazy?"

"Okay, Nick," said Joe, "how about the big brass puppy? What about it?"

"Yuz don't know?"

"Frankly," said Hoolihan, "we're stumped."

Nick held the big brass key for some time before speaking.

"I would hafta say . . ." he mumbled, turning the big key over and over in his quick hands, "that this is probably an *admiralty* key."

"Admiralty key?" said Hoolihan. "What the hell is that?"

"Well—harrumph!—" he said, clearing his throat. "I spent mosta my life around the watahfront. Heah in Chelsea, sometimes ovah in Eastie—you know. I nevah did much woik around da dawks . . . but I seen dis kinda key."

"What's it to?" asked Joe, leaning over close.

"I'd hafta say . . . some kinda boat. Not a dinky boat. But a big boat."

"A ship?" I asked.

"Yeah, a ship. And prawb'ly a ship not made in dis country."

"A foreign vessel?"

"Yeah, dat's what I jus' said, Hoolihan. Not made heah."

"We don't make ships that use this kind of key?"

"Not dat I know of. I'd say England—maybe Holland."

"That's it?" said Joe.

"Yep."

"Well, thanks, Nick. We'll be in touch."

"Yuz gonna fix it so I don't hafta report no moah?"

"We'll see what we can do."

"Hey, don't break yah necks ovah it."

"Nice to meet you, Nick," I said, sticking out my hand.

He took it and shook it weakly. "Yeah, me too. Must be my lucky day."

"Only one way to find that out," said Jimmy Hoolihan.

"How's dat?"

"Go out to Suffolk Downs."

We left Shirley's and headed home.

None too soon, you ask me.

18

JOE AND I HEADED BACK TO MY NEW HOME AWAY FROM HOME, his apartment. It wasn't far, just across the Mystic River Bridge on I-95, through Charlestown, then pick up I-93 southbound over the Charles River basin and into Boston. Get off at the Charles Street exit and there you are. Problem was, it was between three and four o'clock. So it took us more than a while. But on the way back I was again struck by all the rivers that empty into Boston Harbor: the Charles, the Mystic, the Chelsea, the Island End River, Fort Point Channel, and the peninsula that comprises the city of Boston sticking out into the harbor. All these factors make Boston truly a watery place, where you are never more than a mile or so from bridges, shipyards, docks, and ships and boats of all descriptions. Just as we were exiting the Southeast Expressway onto Charles Street, Joe got a call from Ashburton Place.

"He *what*?" Joe said into the mike. "How many hours before?"

Silence. Then, "So the ME says TOD is four to six hours prior to the incision, but still has not determined cause of death?"

More silence.

"So, why can't he figure it?"

We pulled onto the parking ramp near Pinckney Street.

"Thinks it's neurological but isn't certain? Well, call me back when you have more."

He said nothing more until we were all seated, the Gang of Four, on the rooftop terrace overlooking the Charles River.

"Apparently the medical examiner has come up against a problem with regard to your dear departed friend, Jacob Breitz, Doc."

"Who's he?" asked Marty.

"The guy with the putty nose who worked Doc over, while Gary Walsh was working me over. He was the guy we found spread all over the back room in Chris's cottage in Fairhaven."

"Ummmnm," I said. "Should have had a sign on him saying 'some assembly required.' "

"What the guys in the lab say is that he died at least several hours before he was cut open. They say in all likelihood he died elsewhere, was taken to the house, strung up and gutted as a message, or warning."

"What did they do, shoot him first?" asked Mary.

"That's what's so strange. They can't find a specific cause of death. The blood work, all the other factors indicate he suffocated. He simply stopped breathing. This almost always indicates a collapse of the nervous system. But so far, they can't identify the neurotoxin. Nor can they discover how it got into the bloodstream."

"Well, does it make a difference? Seems to me dead is dead."

"Yeah. But this is still an interesting development."

"Have they looked for traces of curare?" I asked.

"Yes, they did. One of the first things they looked for, in fact. Especially considering the howler monkey, since curare is derived from plants in the Amazon. But they found none."

"I wonder if those guys are staking out our house in Concord," said Mary. "And if they are, we better warn the boys not to come home."

"Good idea," I said, and went to the phone in the kitchen to call them. When I returned, Joe was holding the ring of keys.

"So you think the big brass key goes to the freighter that Claudia can't find?" asked Mary.

"It's a good guess. Trouble is, we can't find out without the ship."

"Tony swears he's seen her in New Bedford recently," I said, "under a different name. Maybe she'll come in again, and we can board her."

"That's tricky, Doc. Then you're treading on other people's turf. That stuff's strictly Coast Guard, Treasury Department, DEA. We could make a case, but it would have to be pretty watertight, not just based on hearsay."

"What about this key, Joey?"

"That's your standard house key. We know it's not for the cottage in Fairhaven; Claudia produced that key when she was questioned and they're not the same. I'm betting it's to the warehouse; that's why I've already requested a search warrant for the place."

"Then how about these little ones?" asked Marty, taking the ring from Joe and looking at them closely. "They sure don't look important."

"Probably not. Nick said they're locker keys. I think he's right. My guess is Ramos just had them on the same ring as the others when he hid them all. If there are lockers in the warehouse we'll try them. Otherwise, we'll ignore them, concentrate on finding that ship, and then approach the Coast Guard."

"When do we expect clearance on the warrant?" I asked.

"Tomorrow morning. Then it's off to New Bedford again."

But Joe was wrong; next morning, when he drove into headquarters to get the writ, the brass at Ashburton Place maintained that since the warehouse had an owner, that owner must be notified that the search was about to take place, and even "be present at the scene" during the search. The reason was this: it was determined that Joe had insufficient evidence to authorize a search of these premises, and therefore "insufficient probable cause" for the search, and that it violated the owner's due process. So he came back to Pinckney Street empty-handed and grumpy.

"Well, we've got two options here," I said. "One, we can simply go down there, walk through the snipped wire fence, and go inside with the key, if indeed the Schlage key on the ring is the proper one. If anybody questions us, we flash the badge."

"Sounds good to me," said Joe. "I mean, what can they do, fire me?"

"Ohhhh, Joe, honey," cooed Marty, "you know nothing on this earth would make me happier than that. I'm so sick of you being in danger all the time. And your vocabulary! My God, what an improvement in your speech if they canned you!"

Joe turned to face Mary and me. "I can see she's delighted with my career choice."

"I hate your career choice, honey."

"But are you forgetting something? I wouldn't have met you if I weren't a cop."

"That's true. But now that we've met and married, get out of it. You've got enough money for a sumptuous retirement. We could start really living."

"Not to change the subject," I said, "but option two is to contact the owner and get her permission."

Nobody said a word for a few seconds.

"Well?" I asked.

"Listen, Doc, Claudia Kelly-Ramos is dubious at best right now. I just don't see where that would get us."

"It would get you inside the building, Joey. Now what's the problem?"

"The problem is, I don't know whose side she's on."

"Why do you keep saying that? Chris Ramos befriended me before he died. He also grew close to Tony DeSilva and Saint Bernard's Church, right?"

Joe nodded.

"Well, Claudia visited me and paid her respects, explained Chris's early life and recent history, then gave me a hundred grand worth of stones."

"Which she promptly had stolen back."

"You're not sure of that; you're just speculating. And Tony DeSilva got diamonds, too, for those poor street kids without homes. On top of it all, she's changing her name to Ramos. Now what more do you want?"

A pause here.

"Maybe he wants her to be hetero," guessed Marty.

"I know Charlie does," whispered Mary.

"Oh, for chrissakes," I said. "I think I'll pop up to Copley Square and see Brady Coyne; maybe it's not too late to go on that fishing trip."

I got off the Green Line at Copley Square and walked the short distance to Brady's office. When his secretary, Julie, let me in, I entered the plush, carpeted office to see Brady, lighted Winston dangling from his mouth, with a giant fly rod in each hand, whipping them up and down gently, testing the action.

"I was told you were working."

"I am working. Working on my saltwater rods. Here." He placed them in my hands. They were very long and heavy, with exquisite cork handles and varnished mahogany reel seats below the grips. Probably two thou apiece.

"Which do you prefer, the Loomis or the Sage?"

"How about a J.C. Higgins?" I said, twitching the rods, which made little whippy jet noises as they cut through the air. "By the way, when do we leave for the Great Trout River in the Sky?"

"You're too late, Doc; we've already got the lodge filled."

"Awww. Breaks my heart," I said, putting the toys aside and sitting down across the desk from him. "I have a problem."

He snuffed out the Winston—smelled terrific when he did it—and looked sympathetically in my direction.

"You don't *have* a problem, Doc." He leaned back in his swivel chair and clasped his hands behind his head. "You *are* a problem."

Being the mature and good-natured soul that I am, I ignored this jibe. "Yeah yeah yeah yeah. Listen to what I have to say. Then help me."

I explained Joe's getting shot down on the search warrant in New Bedford. I told him I thought this development was curious considering Joe's reputation, and the rash of violent deaths associated with the Ramos affair.

"But remember, Doc, Joe's been in hot water recently with the department. Also, the powers that be are correct as I see it. The warehouse has been deserted for years. Ramos was in prison for a long time, and now he's dead. Joe lacks enough direct evidence—the probable cause—to enter that building without Claudia's consent. Not getting said consent constitutes a violation of due process. Listen: the cops have to be very careful nowadays. Look at the Rodney King disaster—and the shit Joe stepped into at Flynn's bar. Cops just can't barge into any old place they feel like anymore. That's just the way it is. Hey, speaking of Claudia, what about that article in the *Express*, eh?"

"So you think she's a lesbian too."

"Hell yes, I do . . . until some other evidence comes my way."

"Look, Brady—if we can't find Claudia, how do we get inside that warehouse?"

"Well, Joe can't do it. He's already in Dutch with the brass and he's been ordered not to without Claudia. So he's out."

He paused to extract another coffin nail from the pack and light it. "So that leaves you, sport."

"Me?"

"Who else? Your fairy godmother?"

"What happens if I get caught?"

"You're in deep shit. You need me to explain this?"

"Would the fact that the warehouse has been deserted help me?"

"Maybe a little. But a B&E is still a B&E. A felony."

I thought about all this for a while, then decided to risk it.

"If I told you a secret, would you keep it?"

"Depends on the secret. If it involved criminal activity, or future illegal activity, or malice aforethought, then it would be my duty as amicus curiae to report it."

"Amicus curiae? What's that?"

"It's Latin for 'friend of the court.' We lawyers are bound not to participate in illegal things. You can see why that's part of our oath."

"Okay, here it is: on his deathbed, Chris Ramos gave me some keys. I think they fit the warehouse and things inside it."

Brady froze, then leaned forward over the desk. In my face.

"Gave you keys on his deathbed? How did he do that? Have them ready underneath his pillow?"

I explained the clues, and the discovery of the keys. His eyes lit up, then continued to glow.

"Wow, Doc. No wonder you're so anxious to get inside that building . . . Just imagine what could be in there . . ."

"Maybe nothing."

"Yes, but . . . Listen, maybe we can find room for you on this fishing trip after all. Now if you need a partner . . ."

"Forget it. Now: is the gift of the keys sufficient, or at least helpful, in justifying my trying them on the building?"

"I would say . . . yes. Here's why: deathbed acts and confessions are given special weight. Secondly, the giving to you of the keys constitutes a de facto consent."

"What the hell does—"

"Okay, a de jure consent would be a written statement authorizing you to enter the premises. But obviously Ramos had neither the time nor means to draw up a statement. So he told you where to find the keys. That's an act that takes the place of the written instrument."

"So I can go ahead."

"I . . . didn't say that."

"Yes, you did."

"No. I said that it could eventually be construed as justification. I am not advising you to do this. I am merely assisting you in suggesting possible legal interpretations."

"So you're not willing to stick your neck out and say it's okay?"

"Absolutely not. We lawyers never stick our necks out."

"Of course not. Just your palms."

I rose from the chair. Brady was looking at me sideways, biting his nail. I grabbed one of the fly rods again. Twitched it around. "How much does this cost?"

"About seven hundred."

I shook my head. "I got a suggestion for you, Brady."

"Can't wait to hear it. Some impossible sex act I should perpetrate on myself?"

"No. Take up bowling."

He made a face so unpleasant I was sure he was about to

throw up. I grabbed his brass and teak wastebasket and slid it underneath him.

"Here, sport. Puke in there."

19

I COULDN'T REVEAL MY PLANS TO JOE; IT WOULD PUT HIM IN an awkward position. Although it wasn't too long ago that he had actually coached Laitis Roantis and me on how to bypass the security systems of a suspicious fish warehouse up in Gloucester, I knew in light of recent events it was pushing the envelope to include him in this scheme. Consequently, I couldn't tell Mary or Marty or anyone else in the family either.

But I wasn't that worried about it. Brady's words of assurance buoyed me up, and I knew that if the key fit, getting in there would not be tough. And the key was my badge of authority.

I also realized that the more I sneaked around, the more suspicious I would appear. If I went at night, everyone would want to know why. Also, if I dressed up in one of Roantis's ninja suits, I was sure to stick out. So I decided to wear a suit and tie, with my physician's ID in my wallet, and walk in during the bright of day. Walk in as if I owned the place.

Mary and I each had our cars in Boston garages. I thought about borrowing her Porsche, but knew it would be conspicuous. So I took the old Audi and headed south. Mary had asked me why I was wearing the suit to go to the cottage. I informed her I was going to call on the offices of the *New England Journal of Medicine* on my way down, inquiring about an article I had submitted.

"I think a personal visit will give them the motivation they need," I had explained.

"Isn't Joe going with you to the Breakers?" she had asked.

"Maybe tomorrow afternoon—I thought I'd use some of this idle time to do some more writing."

She had said she was proud of me, and I had scooted.

I parked my car just off Main Street in Fairhaven and began a leisurely stroll down to the docks and shipyards a block and a half away. It was late afternoon, almost early suppertime, and sunny and cool. Boston had been quite hot, but here the cold waters of Buzzards Bay and a refreshing ocean breeze made walking delightful. Soon I was at the premises. It was easy to spot because of the big letters SEAMATT in faded green paint on the roof of the old stone building.

First I tried the Schlage key in the padlock that secured the big swing gates in the cyclone fence. No go. But I did not expect it to work. I went around to the other side of the property to the spot where Joe had noticed the breach in the fence. Slipping a pair of wire cutters from my coat pocket, I snipped the wires holding the fence together. Uh-oh, *breaking*. And soon to come, the *entering*. I put it out of my mind. A few vigorous shoves and kicks and the fence gave way.

I walked through the three-by-five-foot gap and onto the raggedy asphalt. I was in a parking lot/working yard that was beat up and full of potholes. Old junk was lying around in the corners. Rusty chains. Discarded block-and-tackle rigs. Two massive diesel engine blocks flecked with rust. Discarded wheel rims and auto parts that people had thrown over the fence because they wouldn't fit in the trash bins. The building looked pretty much intact except for the broken and boarded-up windows.

I made myself walk around the building and look it over, in plain view of everyone. Actually, there weren't any spectators that I could see; most of the workmen were behind other buildings or on board the big draggers, bent low over their work, or stuffed under the damaged hulls of hauled-out vessels. They couldn't care less about some real estate appraiser (which is what I was trying to resemble) looking over an abandoned building. The front door to the offices of SEAMATT was on the bay side. It was under a small projecting porch roof that had once been painted white. Windows were on either side of it. Both were covered with plywood. Turning around, I saw the nice view that Chris and his employees had had of the harbor. There was Crow Island straight off across the water about eighty yards away, complete with the abandoned radio station on its tiny summit. SEAMATT's stone quay extended out forty yards, but was now entirely taken up by other vessels. I guess "maritime squatters" was the term I was searching for.

Then, as calmly as I could, I pulled out the Schlage key and tried to insert it into the lock cylinder. It wouldn't go in. Wrong key. Tough luck. I felt my body slump all over. Then I noticed that the window on the left side of the door had its plywood partially shoved in. Under closer examination it was clear that it had been forced in under great pressure, and the resulting gap was big enough to let a man inside. That was true breaking and entering. I then returned to the lock cylinder and leaned over, looking into the key slot. It had been stuffed with wood. Probably toothpicks jammed in there and broken off. The thieves saying to me, or anyone else with the correct key, *If we can't use it then you can't. Nyahhhhh!*

I wanted to climb right through that gap in the plywood. But, somehow, this act would not seem very legit if anyone saw me, suit or no suit. Keys or no keys, a guy shimmying through a partially blocked-up window in the light of day would result in the cops being called *toute suite*. Nope—better try the back.

I walked around to the back, or street side, which was where I had come in. The rear of the building had a door as well, but it didn't seem to be the main one. Just a back door, I supposed. It was solid, thick wood. No windows. It had a lock cylinder on it too. I bent over and looked. This one appeared to be clear. It couldn't be . . . But it was worth a try.

I looked around me casually, took out the ring of keys, and selected the Schlage. I inserted it into the lock on the back door. It seemed to fit; it went in without any fuss. I turned it and heard a muted clack; the door unlocked. I felt my pulse rev up. I opened the door slowly. It was dark inside that stone building. I felt for a light switch on the wall and found it. It was dead, which was no surprise; I was certain the power had been off for years. I took the small halogen-bulb flashlight from my other pocket and went inside, closing the door behind me.

I was standing in a short hallway. There was another solid door directly in front of me, three feet away. To my right was a stairway leading up to the second floor. The door had a knob, but no lock underneath it. So I tried the knob and shoved. No budge—not even a millimeter. So there was definitely a lock on the other side. No way I could get in there without a sledgehammer.

The stairs were the only option; there was nowhere else to go. Maybe this upstairs was a private office, or perhaps even a small furnished apartment for Chris. I decided to check the upstairs first, then try the front door again when I came back.

If I came back.

I realized after the first two steps that I wished I had brought my Beretta along. It was eerie indeed going up those dark steps— all I could see in my head were the two blood-soaked bodies of the couple in the upstairs bathtub in the house on Rivet Street.

Well, I made myself climb those dirty stairs, which went up to the right for half a flight, then turned left at a small landing and continued up to the top. There was light up there, which made me feel better. I crept up and up. The farther up I went, the more anxious I felt. Finally, I was standing on the floor of the second story, looking around at the big room there. It was full of cots. They were mostly bunk beds, but some single cots, simple iron frames with built-in spring metal supports, covered with thin mattresses in blue and white ticking. The place was a shambles; somebody had tossed it, and done a thorough job.

What light there was came in through the few unboarded windows. I walked deeper into the big room. I was looking for gym lockers, but I saw none. There was a row of sinks along the right wall, and next to them commode and shower stalls. Underneath the row of sinks lay a section of stout rope about twenty feet long, doubled in half. It was almost two inches thick—as thick as a towing hawser. One end had an eye-splice in it. The rope was the only object I could find; everything else was simply bunks and mattresses.

Then the answer came to me: this dormitory was not for Chris's employees, but for his *cargoes*. This was the place where the smuggled Haitians, Guatemalans, Brazilians, and Surinamese stayed for the interim period between disembarking the *Santiago* and sneaking ashore with their fake IDs to start life anew in America. It could only be that; the fact that there was no place to store personal belongings said as much. These desperate immigrants had nothing but the ragged clothes on their backs. Those, and a pocketful of uncut diamonds and emeralds that they handed over to Captain Ramos for passage . . .

I sat down on one of the bunks and thought about this. I knew I had to get in touch with Claudia again and discuss all of it. I then counted the bunks. Twenty-two. I thought it was doubtful that all of them had been full at one time, but I wasn't sure. I looked more closely at the mattresses. Each and every one, whether left on the floor or replaced on a bunk frame, had been ripped open with a knife and searched. Looking into the commode stalls, I noticed that all the toilet tank lids had been removed so the insides of the tanks could be inspected. The pillows were also torn open. Whoever went over this place left nothing untouched.

And then I noticed the most curious thing in the rear corner of the room: a trapdoor in the floor. It was cut into the old plank floor with such care that upon casual inspection it might not even be noticed. I tried to lift it up, but there was no ring or finger hole to grip. I then dismissed it, thinking it had been nailed shut and forgotten long ago. But before I left the upstairs, I examined it again more closely. There were no signs whatsoever of pry marks around its perimeter. I again examined the torn-up mattresses. The stuffing seemed bright and fresh, as if they had been ripped apart recently. On my first tour of the room, I had noticed footprints on the floor, made in the dust. They, too, seemed recent. As recent as the snips made on the metal fence.

But the trapdoor that excited my curiosity was untouched. Why? The only answer I could think of was that the intruders had entered the building at night. They had only flashlights to guide them, and these they had to use with caution, since the flashes could be seen through the few remaining windows from the outside. They had tossed the place in semidarkness. They had simply missed the trapdoor; they failed to see it.

I tried it again with no luck. I rapped on it, then the floor next to it. The trap had a lighter sound to it—as if there were no sub-flooring underneath. I was excited again. Now for the down-stairs. But just before I went back down the stairs I chanced to look up at the ceiling. Above the trapdoor was a large hook set in the rafters. I went back and got the big rope. Moving the nearest bunk frame over, I stood on it and slipped the eye-splice over the hook. The remainder of the rope sat in a large coil upon the trapdoor.

Interesting.

But not as interesting as the question that now entered my mind: if there were no signs of forced entry on the door, and if I had the only key to the lock, how then did the midnight raiders get inside the dormitory in the first place?

Interesting.

Interesting and unsettling.

I went back outside, locking the door behind me. Soon I was around the front side of the building once again, standing in front of the jammed-up door. Soon I realized the longer I stalled, the more conspicuous I was. To hell with it. Suit or no suit, I reached up and grabbed the plywood, then pulled myself up so that I was standing on the windowsill. I leaned in, and felt the ply-wood give. Trouble was, it was still fastened at the bottom; I couldn't get my foot through. I leaned in again, only harder. There was a creak and a groan and some popping, and the board gave way more. I did it again. Soon I was performing a swaying kind of dance against the wood.

Then there was a horrendous cracking as the plywood gave way, and I fell into the building.

I lay there for a few seconds, listening. With the big board gone, there was enough light in the place to look around. I found myself in a room half as big as the one above, and darker because all the windows on the lower floor, except the one I had punched out, had been boarded up. I got to my feet, sneaked over to my newly opened window, and peered out. Nobody was screaming "police" or milling around the place. I heard hammers booming on metal hulls. Boats hooting in the bay. Seagulls mewing overhead. The crackling and sizzling of welding electrodes. No—there had been plenty of covering noise. I was okay.

I walked around in there. The desks and chairs, still in their places against the wall, determined that this was the office. However, like the room above, the place had been turned inside out: drawers were removed from the desks and dumped on the floor. The couch on one wall was sliced open and disemboweled. Papers were everywhere under my feet, but I had not the light nor the time to examine them. I assumed they were nothing of major importance. There were three doors on the far wall; the one in the center had a frosted pane in its upper half, while the others were solid wood. The one on the left turned out to be a bathroom. On the right was a closet. I feared the one in the center would be locked, but it wasn't. I opened the door and went inside. Shining the light along the walls, I saw a countertop with a coffee machine on it and cupboards above. Not surprisingly, all the cabinets and drawers were open, the contents scattered over the countertops and the floor. These included canned goods, coffee filters, cleaners and brushes, and so on. This room was obviously a sort of kitchen and lounge. Then I shined the light on the far wall.

My heart skipped two beats.

There, lined up like sentinels at attention, was a row of big lockers.

They were dark gray, all twelve of them, with brass plates affixed to their centers with numbers 101 through 112. I walked up to them slowly. Most of them were either all or partially open. Despite the dust and grime on them, they were in excellent condition. They were also substantially larger than standard gym lockers; the tops were taller than I was, and they were each about a foot and a half wide. With a vague trembling in all my limbs, I advanced to lockers 106 and 107. Number 106 was open partway. I carefully swung back the door. It was empty. Nothing at all inside. Number 107, however, was closed. I inserted the key from the ring in the slot that was centered in a round cylinder with a tiny metal lip around its circumference.

Joe had told me from the appearance of the keys that these were lever locks—the same kind found on safe deposit boxes. Almost impossible to pick, yet from the keys, which were merely flat, stamped metal, they appeared to be very simply made. I turned the key, lifted the locker handle up, and pulled. It didn't budge. Turning the key again, the handle came up and the door swung open. It had been closed but unlocked. Like number 106, this locker was also empty. I shined the light all around the interiors of both of them to make sure. But there was nothing in either one.

So that was that. Unless the big brass key that Nick the Pick had identified as a ship's key panned out, there was nothing at all to the "keys to the kingdom" that Christos Ramos had enticed all of us with. Or, if there had been something here, the burglars had taken it already.

But somehow I doubted this. I doubted it because when Joe saw the cut fence on our first visit here with Tony, he guessed the breach had occurred at least several days previous. And it was on that day that we discovered the mutilated corpse of Jacob Breitz—dead only a couple days or so at the most. Therefore the burglary took place before all these recent killings. So it was the same old story: the rival gangs—however many there were or would eventually be—still hadn't connected and were getting more and more pissed off with each passing day.

I walked around the premises once again. I discovered a door in back with two big slide-bolt locks on it. I had a hunch what this was: the door I had seen when I first came through the back way. I threw the bolts and opened it, and was correct. There were the back stairs. So that explained how the burglars made their way upstairs, then returned here, locking the door after them. Other than that, I drew a blank. I was disappointed, of course, but inwardly relieved as well. We could now drop the whole thing and, with luck, return to a normal life again in a few weeks.

I decided to examine all the lockers before I left, just in case I had overlooked anything, no matter how small. After all, Ramos was a clever man. He was adamant about the keys, and they were carefully hidden. So I went down the row, from 101 to 112, checking them out. Some had old bell-bottomed blue jeans and striped jerseys in them. I supposed these were navy surplus clothes Ramos bought on the cheap to dress his fugitives in, giving them the appearance of crewmen. In locker 104 I found a curious piece of wood. Under normal circumstances, I would not have paid it any mind. It was a one-by-two about eight inches in length. It had been altered only in this fashion: one end of the stick had a semicircular hollow dug or drilled out of it about a half inch in diameter. I stood for a while in the near darkness, looking at the scrap of lumber, then at the lockers. The only connection I could make was that the horizontal metal bars in the lockers—used for coat hangers—that ran horizontally across each one about four inches below the top shelf, were the same diameter as the groove in the wood.

After five minutes of puzzling, I left the stick in locker 104 and went over to the corner of the room and shined the light upward. There was no sign whatsoever of the trapdoor above.

Aha! But I knew there was one. So Ramos was clever at hiding things.

I pulled a small table over to the corner, then went looking for a long board or pole. I found a push broom in an alcove near the lockers, leaning right next to a handsome brass fire extinguisher fastened to the wall. It was the old-fashioned, soda-acid type. I tried to jiggle it to see if any solution remained inside, but it was absolutely immobile, which made it useless anyway. I took the broom, returned to the far back corner, stood on the table, and placed the handle end of the broom about where I figured the lip of the trapdoor would be. I pushed, and the door opened with no effort. I pushed farther, and the light's beam revealed the rope dangling above the door, just where I'd left it.

What it all meant I wasn't sure. The only thing I found out for certain was that three of the four keys on my ring were worth about as much as a Confederate nickel.

Back in the front room I looked around once more, then put my foot up on the windowsill and stood up. It looked bright and cheery outside as I jumped down onto the asphalt.

When I stood up, I saw a flicker of movement out of the corner of my eye. I turned to see a uniformed patrolman. Looking to the other side, I saw his partner.

"Please turn around and face the building," he said. "Lean forward and place your hands on the wall."

20

"DR. CHARLES ADAMS," INTONED THE EXPEDITING SERGEANT as he read me the canned speech, "you are hereby charged with breaking and entering, a crime deemed a felony in the Commonwealth of Massachusetts. You have the right to remain silent..."

And so on. Right out of two dozen or so TV crime dramas. I looked down at my hands. Surgeon's hands that had taken decades of training and practice to reach their potential. They were locked in manacles. I was led down a corridor of the Fairhaven police station and placed in a holding cell. Damn thing was smaller than a closet, and I could feel the claustrophobia begin to build inside me. Suddenly the town of Fairhaven wasn't so pretty. Then I thought of Steve McQueen in the movie *Papillon*, locked up in those dark silent punishment cells on Devil's Island. Devil's Island . . . in French Guiana . . . right next to . . . *Suriname!* There it was again. No question about it—this whole thing was jinxed.

The jailer peered at me through the bars.

"What wuz you doin' in that building, dawktah?"

"Trying to get a lead on these recent murders," I lied.

"But you're nawt a cowp."

"Believe me, I'm making that painful realization. Listen, those keys you took from me. They were given to me by the owner of that building on his deathbed. I was the attending physician, and a personal friend of Chris Ramos."

"Who?"

"Listen, I know Tony DeSilva, the priest at Saint Bernard's."

"Yeah. I know him too. Nice guy. So?"

"Can't I call him? Aren't I allowed one phone call?"

He said he guessed so. So I was "escorted" back down the corridor to an ancient dial phone stuck on the wall that had a hundred thousand numbers and gross words scrawled on it. I looked up the parish house in the extremely well thumbed directory, dropped the quarter, and waited. One of the street kids answered and informed me that Father DeSilva wasn't in.

"Do you think Father will call you before tomorrow?" I asked, crossing my fingers.

"Oh yeah, he calls in alla time."

It was not the kind of message I wished to leave, especially with a man of the cloth, but I did anyway. I was desperate. I told the kid to write down that Doc Adams was being held in the Fairhaven jail, and needed help and money.

Not expecting much to come from that quarter, I next tried to reach the mastermind of this foolish expedition: Brady Coyne. My former friend. His secretary, Julie, answered.

"Julie, this is Doc Adams. I need to speak to Brady right away."

"I'm sorry, Dr. Adams, he's away from the office now."

"Well, page him then; this is an emergency."

"I'm sorry; I can't do that. You see, he left for Oregon this morning. He'll be back week after next. Shall I have him call you when he returns?"

I told her not to bother; by then I would be in the Big House.

On my way back to the holding cell, I vowed I would take Brady—the guy who told me I had a de facto right to enter Chris's warehouse but wouldn't actually stand behind me—on a fishing trip. He would be the guest of honor. But what he wouldn't know was this: I was going to bludgeon him and cut him up into tiny pieces and use him for bait. That's what. After all, wasn't he an old *chum*?

I needed time to think. Well, for the first time in a while I had plenty of it. They came by my little cage and told me I would have a bail hearing with the magistrate, who would determine the amount of the bail, and so on. But she would not be in until tomorrow. So I had to spend the night behind bars no matter what. Or I could call someone able to pay the court a nominal fee of two thousand dollars, and get out tonight. Who could I call? Joe was the logical one, and could probably get me sprung. But it wasn't fair to him. He was in enough trouble already at headquarters. Mary was out of the question; she would blow her stack.

I considered my elder son, Jack. He was close by, responsible, mature, and not given to outbursts, idle gossip, or foolish adventures—in short, everything his father was not. He was ideal. And, therefore, I ruled him out. No way did I ever want Jack to find out his daddy had gone to the slam for a B&E. Second son Tony was more like me; Mary and I still worry about him daily. He would certainly understand my plight. Trouble was, he was in Montana working on a horse ranch and shacked up with a luscious young thing named Jenny Littlefeather. No help there.

So I sat there, trying to get comfortable on the miserable cot, thinking about who I could possibly call. I tried pacing the cell but gave it up for two reasons. One: It was one pace wide and two deep. Not a lot of room to fling the old legs around. Two: I had to hold up my pants while I walked, and be careful my shoes didn't fall off. They had taken not only my wallet and personal effects, but my belt and shoelaces as well. Afraid I might hang myself.

Suddenly, it didn't seem that remote a possibility. I tell you, after living most of my life as a surgeon, a revered calling that pays well, and enjoying the fruits of that occupation, being married to a goddess, having wonderful children and everything in the way of material success I could ever wish for, finding myself suddenly locked up in a steel cage in the bowels of a stone building and having my liberty and dignity taken away. Well . . . it was quite a shock indeed.

They came by again and it was oxymoron time: they said

they were taking me to a "more comfortable cell." This one was only slightly bigger, but had a sink and toilet. And no privacy.

So I sat on the edge of the bunk with my head in my hands, feeling mightily sorry for myself, and realizing that what I needed was not a friend, or the money, but a *miracle*.

I fell asleep praying.

"Dr. Adams, wake up."

I opened my eyes, then realized that it was not a bad dream. It was the real thing. I tried to curl into a fetal position and go back to sleep. Even a bad dream was preferable to this.

"Dr. Adams."

There was no darkness in the jail; the light shone twenty-four hours a day. There was no music, no beauty. Nothing green or natural. No window to the outside world. No songs of birds, or even the distant honking of car horns. I opened my eyes again to see what was going on. Were they bringing me breakfast? Were they going to fit me for a uniform with stripes? What? I saw another jailer standing outside my cell inserting a key into the lock. Must be the night-shift guy. What a job.

"What's going on?" I asked. I thought maybe I had a phone call. But that was probably too much to hope for.

"You're free to go, Dr. Adams. Somebody's paid your bail. All's you hafta do is sign some papers, get your stuff, and you're outta heah."

I sat up on the bunk rubbing my eyes.

"Somebody's paid the bail money?" I couldn't believe my ears. "Are you sure?"

"You wanna ahgue about it?" the guard said, swinging open the bars. Hell no, I didn't. I scooted out of there fast, holding up my suit pants as I hobbled along in my untied brogues. What a stupid mess, I thought. Maybe the damn clothes caused it. One of Henry Thoreau's lesser-known but perhaps wisest sayings goes like this: *"Beware of enterprises requiring new clothes."*

Aha! How true! I got my shoelaces and belt back, then my wallet, handkerchief, and the infamous ring of keys. Felt like throwing them out the window.

"This way, sir," said the night clerk, holding open the thick steel door with the wire-mesh window in it. Who the hell could it be? I thought, walking up the stairs. The only person I could think of was Father Tony DeSilva. But how did he get two grand just like that?

Then I walked into the lobby, still in a daze, and a lovely, throaty voice behind me said:

"Hey, hotshot, you glad to see me?"

I turned around and was again looking into those deep brown eyes. Saw that gorgeous reddish brown hair all around her Latin face.

Claudia Ramos was up next to me before I could say anything. She put her arms around me and kissed me on the lips. Hard, and a bit too long. I hated every millisecond. Then she put her arm around me and delivered me from that hellhole.

We were walking in the dark underneath the sighing trees. We passed a park on our left. Again I smelled the ocean, heard the night swallows going *breeent! breeent!* above us. The air was dark blue, and Claudia let her head rest on my shoulder as we walked along the cool sidewalk. Fairhaven was beautiful again. Claudia smelled great. I put my arm around her, too, and we were walking slowly, like lovers.

"You're an angel," I said. "Really and truly you are. How did you—"

"We'll talk later, Doc. Here's my car. You must be beat."

The next thing I knew, I was seated on that soft leather, looking at the glowing dashboard of the new Cadillac. I couldn't believe this was happening.

"So what happened was," she casually explained as she wheeled the big boat through thinning traffic, "I called Tony's office like I do every other week or so, just to touch base. And what do I find out? Doc Adams has been jailed for a B&E! He needs two thou to bail him out. So here I am—to the rescue."

"God bless you, Claudia. You delivered me. And now my family won't have to find out either."

"What's so bad about them finding out? Won't they understand?"

"Well, maybe not. See, you don't know me very well yet, but

I have a history of ending up in the soup like this on a regular basis. In short, I'm sort of a jerk a lot of the time."

"You are not; you're a wonderful, generous man, Doc."

I felt myself crashing; I was coming to realize that the warehouse entry and the ordeal in jail were merely the culmination of a series of fiascos, blunders, and grisly crime scenes going on for a month now. It had finally gotten to me. I had had it. I was exhausted to the bone. In my deepening stupor, I managed to ask her where we were headed.

"I was about to ask you that, Doc. You know, I thought of taking you to Daddy's house down here. But after what's happened, I sure don't want to; I don't think we could get in even if we tried."

There was a slight pause as we whispered along the road toward I-495. I saw the signs to Boston and the Cape. Then she asked the question. "Didn't I hear you had a cottage down on the Cape? I think that would be the perfect place to go since you're so tired. What do you think?"

What did I think? I gazed over at her. She was wearing a sleeveless cotton blouse, well-fitting tennis shorts and cork-soled white leather sandals. She was brown as a nut and curvaceous in the extreme. What did I think?

"I think that's not a good idea, angel. I don't want to get into any more hot water. And you're simply too gorgeous."

She looked over in my direction in the dim light of the car. I could see her eyes soften. Her lips slowly opened halfway. An oncoming car's headlights lit up her face for an instant. Be still, my heart—

No! came a shrill voice in my head.

Dammit, Doc, it's time to grow up, for chrissakes! For once I was going to listen to that little whiny voice in my head that always warned me when these situations arose. I suppose it's my conscience. Anyway, it was always there when I least wanted it. Sort of like a funeral march. But this time, by God, I was going to tread the straight and narrow; I wasn't even going to get into a tempting situation. And I really meant it this time, so help me. I would do whatever the little whiny voice said.

"It's really sweet of you to say that, Doc. I've thought the same about you ever since we met."

Uh-oh . . .

"I knew I liked you even before I met you from the things Daddy told me. But now I can know firsthand what he meant. And I find you very attractive."

"Well, thanks, but, uh, see . . . It's just not a good—"

"I don't see why you're so afraid of anything happening, Doc. If you read the papers, you know I'm gay."

It took a second or two for it to sink in. Yes, that's right, I said to myself. I said it to the little whiny voice as well. That's right; she's a lesbian. What possible interest could she have in me? Then I remembered Mary's very own words: *"Anyway, Charlie, I guess I feel a little safer now about Claudia Kelly, or Ramos, or whatever her name is."* I said it again to myself in my head. Then over and over again.

And guess what?

That little whiny voice vanished.

Just like that.

"Well, Doc?"

"Okay, angel. Head for Eastham. If I'm asleep, wake me; I'll guide you there."

"Good boy," she said, placing her warm hand on my leg just above the knee. I let it stay there.

21

I GUESS I DOZED A BIT IN THE CAR. IT WAS OFF AND ON. I REmember the Bourne Bridge all lit up, the sign for Marstons Mills. Then the signs for Brewster and Dennis. So we were headed in the right direction, anyway. I felt Claudia nudge me when we came into Eastham. I directed her to the Breakers, and we walked up to the cottage. I unlocked the front door and we went in. Claudia was strangely silent. I knew what I wanted: a big drink and then to go to bed and fall dead asleep to the sound of the ocean.

"Do you want a drink, or some coffee?"

"I'll have whatever you're having," she said in a low voice. I knew then she was as tired as I was. I asked her if a scotch and soda was okay. She nodded. I made the drinks, and we went out onto the deck and sat in the chairs in the dark, listening to the small waves working up the sand.

"It looks like I owe you two grand," I said.

"Forget it."

"I guess you're curious to know why I got arrested today."

"The guys at the desk said breaking and entering. Naughty, naughty, Doc."

"Ummmm. The place was your dad's warehouse. Actually *your* warehouse. Now maybe you're not so happy you bailed me out."

"Well, did you steal anything?"

"Nope. But almost. I saw a curiously shaped piece of wood in one of the clothes lockers in the back room of the first floor. I thought it might prove—interesting. But I didn't take it; I returned it to the lockers."

"In what way interesting?"

"It appeared to have been made especially for the lockers—a sort of brace or lever—here, I forgot to show you these . . ."

I fished the notorious key ring out from my pants and handed it to her. It wasn't two seconds before she jumped up and headed for the back door.

"Claudia?" I got up and followed her as she made her way into the kitchen, holding the keys under the stove light.

"Where did you get this, Doc?" I saw she was holding the big brass key, turning it over and over, with the light from the appliance bulb winking off it.

I told her of Mary's brilliant deductions and the finding of the keys to the kingdom under the twelfth Station of the Cross.

"Wow! Doc, this is *it*!"

"The big brass key? You know what it goes to?"

"Hell yes, I do. This is the ship's master key to the *Santiago*."

"Ahhh so! So Nick the Pick was correct."

"Nick the Pick? Who's he?"

I explained, then held the other three keys for her to examine. "You ever see these before?"

"Maybe." She shrugged. "I don't know. They don't look that remarkable to me."

"They're not. One's the key to the warehouse door, the other two—the little cheap-looking flat keys—fit two of the twelve lockers in the warehouse."

She looked up at me expectantly. When I said nothing, she said, "Well? So did you find anything?"

"No. Absolutely nothing. Just some old sailor clothing."

"The clothes were for the fugitives. To make them look like crewmen so in case the ship was boarded, they'd have half a chance at deceiving the Coast Guard."

"I guessed as much. But did you ever see the dormitory on the upper floor?"

"Once or twice, when it was empty. But that was just a place where they could spend a few nights until the time was ripe for them to scoot out of there and mingle with the population of south New Bedford."

"But how did they do it? How did they just walk out of that warehouse and mingle? Didn't they need fake IDs?"

"Oh, yeah, and Daddy helped provide them with them; that was part of the deal: transport to America and a forged green card when you got there."

"How did he get the forged green card?"

"In Panama. Where you can get just about anything on earth if you have the ready cash."

"No kidding?"

"No kidding."

"Gee, the world sure is a different place than the one I read about growing up."

"Yep. And getting worse. You ready to turn in? I'm more tired than I thought."

Trying not to appear nervous, I led her back inside the cottage and showed her the guest room upstairs, the first right at the head of the stairs. Jack's room. She walked in there, looked around, sat on the bed, and in two shakes had pulled her top off. She folded it up neatly and laid it on the bed beside her, never once glancing in my direction. But you can bet I was glancing at her. She knew it too. Listen: Women are the most dangerous things on the planet. Trust me on this.

"Is there a toothbrush I could borrow?" she asked demurely, sitting there with a very full bra and all that dark olive skin.

Watch out, Doc. WATCH OUT! the voice said. I tried to listen to it. I was trying with all my might to listen to it.

"Uh, sure. Right in the john there, in the cabinet. Look, Claudia, I've got to go downstairs. I just have to. Okay?"

"Sure," she murmured, lowering her eyes as she fiddled with her shorts. I was out of there fast, almost falling down the stairs. I reached the living room and took three big breaths. Didn't do a damn thing. This was truly exquisite torture.

Here's what I've managed to figure out since that night: never, ever, *ever* let a desirable woman who is off-limits into your house after three in the afternoon. If you do, and she finds you desirable and starts going into those female routines, you have had it. Because one of two things is going to happen:

1. You'll end up in the sack together, going at it like you're seventeen again. This feels great at the time, of course, but if you care anything for your wife and family—and I care a helluva lot for mine—then you'll regret it soon, and forever. And you can never really repair that rent in the fabric, even though you'd like to think so.

2. You listen to your conscience and are a good boy, shunning her hints and advances—which makes you feel like a total jerk and does the same for her—and then go off to your bed alone, thinking about that luscious morsel just doors away who is probably still there waiting for you, willing to give you another chance to do what you really want to do because *that's the way you're made*.

But you don't; instead, you injure her self-esteem and spend the most miserable night imaginable (more miserable than sleeping outside nude in a horde of mosquitoes and black flies), only to awaken with the horrendous regret of a chance lost and life not being lived to the fullest.

So the bottom line is, in these situations: either way, you lose. And you lose *big*.

So I did the second option, hating myself and feeling like a chickenshit every second that ticked by. I could not get my mind off her, wanting like crazy to see her with her bra and her shorts off, to put my arms around her and smell her and . . .

My only consolation was the knowledge that if I did this, I would probably feel even more miserable.

I went into the master bedroom on the first floor, brushed my teeth, then slid into the covers naked with the windows open, feeling the cool sea breeze and hearing the building surf of an incoming tide. I was asleep in no time.

Sometime in the deep of the night I had a dream that I was bodysurfing, riding the waves as they buoyed me up and down with a gentle rhythmic motion. Then I began to awaken, certain that it was the sound of the breakers coming up the beach causing this dream.

But I was mistaken. It was the bed that was moving, even though I was not. I heard the hiss of sheets being pulled down and up behind me, and turned to see a dark mass of hair on the next pillow. Out of long habit I reached my hand over and found the bare buttocks next to me, and commenced stroking them. Mary responded even more than usual, snuggling up close to me and encircling my chest with her arms. I kissed her . . .

She smelled different.

She felt different.

She kissed different.

And then I knew.

Now the little whiny voice in my head was going ballistic.

I rose up and turned on the light. There was Claudia, on her back, smiling up at me. She stretched her arms above her head languidly, displaying a chest I have never seen the equal of.

"Ohhh noooo," I said in a whisper.

She pouted slightly. "What do you mean, 'oh no'? You seemed to like it."

"Claudia, this can't happen. I have way, way too much at stake."

"She won't have to know, Doc. I promise. Nobody has to know."

I got up out of bed and slid into my underpants. She gave me a low wolf whistle. I turned to look at her, now sitting up in bed. Boy, did I regret this. Claudia Ramos was certainly world class.

"You're hurting my feelings, Doc."

"And you are hurting my marriage, and all that I hold dear. Do I wish I weren't married right now? You bet. But that's not the case."

I went over and sat down on the foot of the bed. "See, the thing is, I've just had too many close brushes like this. And every time, without fail, Mary has shown up. And if she doesn't show up, she finds out. Every time."

Claudia laughed, and her breasts, which she made no attempt to cover, jiggled and swayed enticingly.

"In fact, I'm shocked that I don't hear her coming in the front door right now, even as we speak."

She tossed her head back. "Well, Doc, seems to me you're not very experienced at this. Maybe you need some practice."

"Uh-uh. Now c'mon, Claudia, scoot back to your room. Gorgeous as you are, if I give in, I'll regret it forever."

She got slowly out of bed and walked toward the door. But as she passed, me, she made a quick grab, kissed me hard on the mouth, and went out. I heard her voice from the hallway.

"Better luck next time, hmmmn?"

I was awake before dawn, jumping out of the sack and hustling over to the window, scanning the road to our cottage. I knew that any minute now, Joe's cruiser or Mary's Porsche would swerve up the drive. They would enter the premises, find

Ms. P.O.A. (Piece of Ass) on said premises, and that would be that for Charles Adams, MD.

So I dressed as quickly as possible and hurried upstairs to wake Claudia and get her the hell out of the house. But when I looked into the guest bedroom, I found it empty—and the bed perfectly made. I went downstairs and into the kitchen. Also empty. No Claudia. Just some coffee waiting for me in the carafe. Then I saw the note:

I meant no harm. What I said was true. Stay in touch.

And then a phone number. Considering Joe's problems in finding her earlier, I assumed this number was important, so I copied it in my address book under T (for Trouble), then tore the note into little bitty fragments and put them in the wastebasket.

Then I spent the next half hour going over the place for any sign, no matter how minute, of her presence. I did the place the way I have seen the state police lab teams work. I left no drawer unopened, no closet unchecked. The bathroom she used got an especially thorough going-over. The wastebaskets, the shower stall, the outside approaches to the house. Everything was perfect. Claudia had obviously listened to me, and was extremely prudent.

It also made me sad. I think she truly did want sex not for the thrill—although God knows it was there—but because she wanted to know me better. And now that she was gone, so quickly and efficiently, it hurt a little. She took my message a bit too much to heart.

"Well, you jerk, you did the best you could," I mumbled to myself, sipping coffee and putting on my running shoes. "It's just a no-win situation."

So I flipped on the sauna and went for an hour's run along the hard-packed sand at the water's edge. It feels good at first, but it's murder on your feet because the sand has no spring, it only gives and leaves you sore and tired. I couldn't believe my good fortune: I had been rescued from jail by a beautiful woman who was obviously fond of me. We had a near encounter that I dodged due to my excellent conscience (I must remember to give myself a Gold Star for Good Behavior), and, best of all, *Mary had not found out*.

It wasn't until I was in the sauna sitting in my own sweat that I realized all was not well. I knew it: if things seem too good to be true, they aren't.

I was still in a helluva pickle, due to the following three items:

1. My car was in New Bedford, parked right behind Chris's warehouse. How was I to get there to retrieve it? And if Mary and Co. showed up, they would sure want to know how I got home. Uh-oh . . .

2. Despite the fact that my bail was paid, I was still charged. I had to get a lawyer, go to court, etc. No fun. Worst of all, with all this legal and criminal accusation against me, how could Joe Brindelli, of the state police, not get wind of it from his cronies?

3. Search as I might, I could not find the cursed ring of keys. I wondered who on earth could have absconded with them.

Three guesses . . .

So there I was, up to my ass in alligators again.

As I sat there on the deck, watching for the cab that was coming to fetch me from New Bedford, I pondered yet another riddle: If Claudia Ramos was a lesbian, she obviously wasn't a very dedicated one.

What did all this mean? What sort of person was Claudia underneath? Was she my friend, my delivering angel? Or was she a schemer who had taken this opportunity to befriend me and take the keys her father had hidden in the church? In short, was Joe correct about her? Was she working for one of the gangs? Or for herself? Could I trust her? She was a lot like her dad: colorful, yet enigmatic.

I shifted on the deck uncomfortably, watching for the cab and hoping it would arrive before the Boston contingent.

My butt hurt. At first I thought it was the running. But then I realized it was those alligators—biting me on the ass.

22

JOE CAME DOWN THAT AFTERNOON AS WE HAD PLANNED. HE told me the women were going to depart in time to be at the Breakers for dinner. We were out walking along the beach in swim trunks and T-shirts, soaking up the sun.

"Well, how did the writing go?"

"Ummm . . . Okay," I said, offhandedly, rocking my spread palm back and forth.

"Get a lot done?"

"Not too much, actually. Only a couple pages."

We stepped over a big tile culvert pipe and continued south. The concrete hull of the old World War II Liberty Ship *James Longstreet*, aground and full of bomb crater holes, lay directly off our starboard beam. It was formerly a target for the air force, but I think they abandoned it when it got so full of holes it was hard to see.

"Mind if I read over those pages?" he asked.

I slowed my walk, trying to pretend I was looking at the horizon. "Read the pages? C'mon, Joe—don't tell me you actually want to *read* that stuff."

He stopped, then turned to face me. "Yes, I do, and I'd like to explain why."

Instantly, I felt uncomfortable. I didn't like the tone in his voice. It was not the voice of my brother-in-law. Of Joe the Nice Guy, who always poured oil upon turbulent waters. No: this was the voice of Joe the Interrogator. Joe the Cop.

"I'd be curious to know," he said in a low voice, "how much writing you got done in jail last night."

Suddenly my knees felt rubbery. I went over to the remains

of an old wooden pier and sat down on an ancient bollard, beckoning him to join me.

"How did you find out? I figured you might."

"How the hell do you think I found out? Crystal ball? Look, bonehead, every cop in southeast Massachusetts knows your mug by now. We've only been on the scenes of the two most grisly and bizarre murders in the last twenty years, for chrissakes. Last night Marty answers the phone and tells me I've got a call. I thought it was routine until I was told by Lennie Ungar, who works the New Bedford area for the state, that my companion, a certain Dr. Charles Adams, had been arrested for a B&E in Fairhaven."

I got that sinking feeling again. That feeling that, once again, no matter how innocent the circumstances, Mary would discover everything and my goose would be cooked. And I was trying so hard to be *good* . . .

I just sat there on the piling with my head in my hands.

"Well," he continued, "I thought I would just let it go. Let you stew in your own juice overnight and come get you in the morning."

"That would have been the best thing, Joe. I know you've saved my ass before and I—"

"*Quiet.* Don't say anything." He paused to light a cigarette. I noticed that his hands trembled slightly. Joe was steamed. And he was big and strong enough to pull my head off and stick it on again backwards.

"So, anyway, like I said, I was going to let it go. That is, until he told me who paid your bail. No, he didn't get her name, Doc. But he didn't have to. The description was enough."

"It's true Claudia came and paid my bail. But I didn't call her. I called two people to help me out: Brady Coyne and Tony DeSilva. Neither one was in. But a kid at the halfway house wrote down my message. It so happened that Claudia called him, as she does on a regular basis, got the message, and came and got me."

"She found out from Tony DeSilva?"

"Yep; when he returned from his church convention—he obviously called her."

"She's been calling Tony regularly, just to stay in touch?"

"What she tells me."

"Yeah? Then why hasn't Tony told us about this cozy relationship? It's been my impression that he's not that close to Claudia—that maybe he feels as I do: that she's a little slimy around the edges."

I shrugged. "I don't know how else she found out. I didn't call you because I didn't want you involved."

"How kind. But now—as even you can plainly see—I am involved."

"Well, sorry about that. But I did get a good look inside the warehouse."

"Great. What did you find?"

"Nothing. Nada. Rien. Zip."

He stroked his stubbled chin. The raspy sound of his purplish black whiskers could be heard over the waves. "When's your trial, or don't you know yet?"

"I guess I'll find out soon, but since Claudia paid my bail, and she owns the property, I doubt there'll be one."

"Yeah . . . Maybe you're right. So tell me, just for the record, of course, what did you and Claudia do after she sprung you?"

Here was the tricky part; I had maybe two seconds to decide how much of the previous night's misadventure to reveal to Joe. If I tried to cover it all up and he found out, there would be storm clouds over the family for months, maybe years. So I told him everything, from start to finish, exactly as it happened.

I did, however, omit the part about her sneaking into my bed naked in the middle of the night. Since this was only a minor detail, I felt it would be—less awkward—to leave it out and thus avoid any misconstruing of motives and character, etc., etc.

"And that's it? She just up and left early this morning?"

"Yep. And took the ring of keys with her."

"Took them?"

"Apparently; I can't find them anywhere. She identified the big brass key as the master key to her missing freighter, the *Santiago*."

"Really? Didn't Tony say he'd seen that ship around here?"

"Yes, under the new name *Esmeralda*."

"Doesn't the fact that she absconded with the keys make you just a bit suspicious?"

"I'd rather she hadn't taken them, Joe. But remember: the ship is hers. The warehouse I broke into is hers. Seems to me she's got a right to them."

"Tell me exactly what you found in the warehouse. Take your time; try to remember everything."

So I did. He then asked me a whole bunch of questions, including many about the row of lockers. "Think about this especially: did the lockers look like they'd been there from the start, or added recently?"

"They were certainly added after the building was built. My guess is, from the stone construction, it dates from the whaling days."

"Did they appear more recent than the other fixtures in the building?"

"Definitely."

"And they were all open, and you found absolutely nothing inside any of them?"

"Nothing but old sailor clothes Ramos dressed his cargo in. And also a funny-shaped stick with a notch in it."

"Yeah? Tell me more."

So I did, and his interest never lagged. "Did you try to manipulate the lockers in any way, other than opening and closing their doors?"

"I tried pushing and pulling and looking for hidden levers or catches but came up empty. But we have to remember that the light was bad and my time was limited."

"I hope Claudia doesn't lose those keys."

"As far as the warehouse goes, it wouldn't matter; the lockers are unlocked and the window is now open."

We walked on again in silence. Finally Joe said, "So Claudia didn't try to come on to you?"

"Are you kidding?" I said, avoiding a direct answer to the question. I hoped he couldn't see my ears turn red or my nose grow. "Are you forgetting her—uh, sexual orientation?"

"Oh that's right! Of course she wouldn't. Did she act kind of, you know, mannish?"

"Hey, between you and me: a bull dyke if I've ever seen one."

"No shit?"

"No shit."

Since I had never knowingly seen a bull dyke, and wasn't even sure what it meant, I had again avoided a direct lie.

But I wasn't kidding myself: I was on thin ice. Very thin.

We walked on again. Finally Joe asked, "How much of this do you think we should tell the wives?"

"As little as possible. And if there are no charges pressed, and no further mess, anything you could do to keep it under wraps would be appreciated."

"Figured you'd say that. And that's what I intend to do."

"Thanks, Joe."

"But something's still bothering me. It's this sudden closeness—or alleged closeness—between Claudia and Tony."

"Well, remember that she gave him some diamonds a while back. It's how he's building the halfway house."

"Ummm. Forgot about that. Okay, suppose they are close. That still doesn't make Claudia clean in my book. Maybe these two, while pretending to be mildly interested in Ramos's hoard of gems, are secretly as eager as everybody else. Remember that after we found the keys Tony reminded us that Saint Bernard's should get a major share because Chris had hidden the keys there."

"He's got a good point."

"Right. Now, if this is so, then Tony wants the keys as badly as we do. But he couldn't come out and ask for them. He could merely hint. Also, he says that he went to look underneath the pew as we did. And, like us, found it already dug out. We are then to assume that Smitty, the green-eyed monster that doth apparently feed off other people, was the person who first carved out the seat bottom in vain. Follow?"

"Yes."

"Ah, but from everything that's happened so far—from the very beginning of this case until now—I deduce that Smitty still thinks somebody else found the keys."

"Which is true."

"Yes, but I mean before we actually found them. In short, I doubt that Smitty was the first person to look underneath the third pew on the left. He was not the one who dug out that wood. I'm remembering now that it was done carefully. With a sharp chisel and mallet. I've been thinking that whoever made that hollow in the oak—the hardest native wood—that person might even have removed the entire bottom section of the pew and turned it upside down on a pair of sawhorses to do such a good, neat job. A person with all the time in the world. A person who could work on it any time he wanted."

"Tony DeSilva. You're saying that he's a thief and a liar."

"Not a thief, just a liar."

"But he's a priest, Joe."

"So? I've known lots of priests who lie."

"Really?"

"Sure. In America, they lie mostly about their sexual preference. I'd say twenty, maybe thirty percent of Catholic clergy are gay. In some places it's much higher. In this country they can't be honest about it; if they were openly gay, I think it might destroy the church in America. Now in Italy, if a young man realizes he has attractions toward the same sex, he goes into a monastic order. Simple."

"So Tony is . . ."

"Nah, I seriously doubt it. That's not the point I'm making. The point is, if he's been less than honest about his desire for a share of Chris's treasure, it would not surprise me. And I'm sure it would go for a good cause. The point I'm making is this: if Claudia and Tony DeSilva have some undercover cabal going, then we should work around it. Let me ask you this: when you broke into the building, were you aware of anyone seeing you?"

"I waited until I thought nobody could see me. But I made some noise going in—and I left that plywood ajar."

"Right. But I still think it's odd the way you were tagged going into a building that's been deserted for a dozen years or more. I think somebody made a phone call. I say you're being watched, Doc. Just the way you were mugged carrying those

giant diamonds Claudia gave you. The timing's just too good in
both these cases. So then she shows up after you've been behind bars for a few hours. Here comes friendly Claudia to the
rescue."

"And takes off with the keys next morning before I'm awake."

"Yep. It's all just a little too convenient. But listen: we'll tell
Mary and Marty that the keys fell out of your pocket as you left
the warehouse. How's that?"

"It's terrific, is what it is." Good old Joe.

"Fine. Now let's go back and take a sauna, shower, go buy
some killer seafood and deluxe white, and start making dinner.
We'll have it mostly under way by the time the better-halves get
here."

"Sounds good to me. Let's turn around and start back right
now."

So we did.

23

SOMETIMES IT SEEMS THAT NO MATTER HOW HARD YOU TRY TO
stay out of trouble, it just keeps following you around like a bad
smell. This business about Ramos and his treasure hoard was
certainly one of those instances.

It was a roaring pain in the ass, is what it was. It was enough
to make me wish I'd never met Christos Ramos, despite the af-
fection I felt for him.

Likewise for Claudia. Sure, she was pretty. In fact, she was a
killer knockout: the kind of woman who, when you first see her
on the street, you look back twice to make sure it wasn't a mi-
rage. Your knees are wobbly afterward; you realize you're breaking into a cold sweat. And you keep thinking about her vision

for a long, long time. That's a killer knockout. Mary is one. She'll be a knockout till the day she dies. I admit I'm a sucker for them. Even though women are the most attractive yet dangerous things on this planet. By far. And Claudia, attractive as she was, only brought trouble.

Now, as Joe and I walked along the sand in late afternoon, we finally spied the gray-shingled dot ahead that was the cottage. I'm sure then that he felt as I did: that soon we'd be back safe in its confines, having a drink, making dinner, and gazing out at the sunset, which would commence in about two hours and promised to be gorgeous. But no sooner were we in hailing distance when we spotted a car that looked all too familiar. It looked like Joe's. Different color but same make, and parked next to his wheels.

"Oh, shit," he mumbled. "I've got a feeling either I'm about to be fired or my brief vacation from the state bureau is about to come to an end."

"It's an unmarked cruiser, isn't it."

"You bet. I say it's Keegan, sent out here to find me."

Detective Lieutenant Paul Keegan was Joe's counterpart for Barnstable County, which is Cape Cod. I had been associated with him on two previous occasions: one dealing with a drug-running ring from Jamaica, and the other an extremely painful episode in our lives when son Jack was a suspect in a murder case. Both ended well, and Paul was a nice guy and a true professional. But I must confess that his cruiser sitting there on our turf set me on edge. I knew something was up. When I saw him come down from the rear deck and walk toward us in his suit, waving at us to hurry up, I knew something big was up. We sped up, and he cupped his hands and called to us.

"Joe, you're back on duty. They found the Ibenez woman's car down by Fort Rodman."

We hustled up to him, and the three of us went back up the deck stairs.

"Have they found her?" Joe asked.

Keegan shook his head. "No, and that's the interesting part." He then turned to me. "Doc, a man named Missaels Smits was picked up outside your house in Concord early this morning."

Joe looked at me. "Now aren't you glad I made you and Mary scoot into Boston? So where's this Smits now? Does Brian Hannon have him in custody?"

"Yep. Hannon's the one who called it in. He says Smits wants our help in getting the woman back. I guess they're engaged."

Joe's face assumed a sour look. "Get the woman back, eh? He really thinks he's going to get his woman back? You heard about the scene at the Rivet Street residence in New Bedford, didn't you?"

Keegan nodded, tight-lipped.

"Well, I think poor Celia is probably mutilated beyond all recognition now."

"We think not," said Keegan. "This Smits claims to have heard her voice over the phone yesterday afternoon. She told him she's being held hostage and they'll kill her if he doesn't meet with them."

"*Meet with them?*" exclaimed Joe. "C'mon, Paul, nobody in his right mind would meet with the Kelly gang after what happened at Rivet Street. And none of them would dare meet with Smitty's contingent after they hung up that well-ventilated corpse in the Ramos cottage. Who's jerking who around here?"

"I'm just telling you what happened, Joe. He obviously thinks that you, Doc, can help him. He was picked up ringing the front doorbell to your house in Concord this morning. Hannon tells us he's been watching the place on instructions from Joe."

"So Smitty came looking for me, eh? Then I think maybe he's been talking to Claudia."

"Not her again," snorted Joe. "What a busy little bee she is. How come she's all over the place and I can't ever find her?"

"Smits is being brought down to New Bedford for questioning regarding the recent killings," said Keegan. "He claims to have been at sea for the past three weeks and so had nothing to do with them. But we'll check on this."

I said nothing at this piece of news. But inwardly I was excited. If he was the one who'd absconded with Claudia's coastal freighter, then maybe the ship was nearby.

"You say they found the Lincoln at Fort Rodman," said Joe. "Seems Doc and I drove past there several times and couldn't find it. Is the fort still there?"

"Hardly. It's a ruined wall behind a few wire fences. If you'd like to go now, I can take you."

Joe sighed and went into the living room, where he sank into my favorite reading chair in the "study corner."

"Actually, Paul, I'd rather not go there right now, and I'm sure Doc feels the same way. We've kind of been through a lot. Can't it wait until tomorrow?"

"Maybe. But Smits is probably in New Bedford right this minute, waiting to talk to Doc."

"If he thinks I can help him, he's crazy."

"Look, can we all start for New Bedford early tomorrow, Paul? I mean, I thought I was officially still on vacation, and Doc here's had a—difficult past few days."

"So I heard. Breaking into that warehouse in Fairhaven."

"And another thing," Joe added. "If you'll promise not to mention Doc's recent incarceration in the Fairhaven slam to our wives, who are due here shortly, we'll treat you to an excellent dinner here. What say?"

We convinced him. Inside of twenty minutes the three of us were bound for Wellfleet, to the fish market and the wine store. We even convinced Paul it would be better to meet Smitty the next day—it would give us all time to think about what to ask him, and maybe think of some plans in advance for rescuing Celia, whom we all hoped to dear God was all right.

Mary and Marty arrived on schedule, and we had as good a time as possible considering recent developments. All during the meal I was in mortal fear of Paul spilling the beans about my jail time. But he didn't.

Later on that night, after Mary and I made love, she said, "Gee, Charlie, you were really eager tonight. Is it the fish diet or what?"

No, I told her, I was just glad to see her, and the cottage and the sound of the ocean always made me horny.

"I can't wait to see Smitty up close," she said.

"Before you become smitten with Smitty, remember he's dangerous. Claudia told me so."

"Claudia tells you everything, doesn't she?"

"Nope. But she told me that. When she gave me the stones."

"Joe thinks she's no good."

"No, Mary, he does not. He thinks she's not totally on the up and up, but he does not think she's no good. And Father Antero DeSilva thinks she's special."

"She gave him diamonds too. You told me. No wonder he thinks she's special."

"I think," I said slow and deliberately, "that Claudia Ramos is fulfilling certain family obligations by giving those stones away. Just as she was by telling me all about her father's early life. I personally think she's on the square. I will continue to believe that until new evidence says she isn't."

"Do you think she's a lesbian?"

"Oh, definitely."

24

ALL OF US WENT INTO NEW BEDFORD THE NEXT MORNING. From Paul Keegan's evening visit to the cottage and the news about Smits, we all knew there was going to be change in the operation. But it was nothing like the change that actually occurred.

Meeting us at the state office in New Bedford was none other than Captain Mahaffey himself, who had driven down from Boston just for the meeting. He stood there at the head of the briefing room, his thin body leaning back against the desk, his keen aqua eyes sweeping over all of us, Mary and Marty included.

"Since the developments of yesterday, I have given this situation top priority in the entire state," he said. "With the death of one of our uniformed officers and the vicious assault on Detective Brindelli last month, and the brutal murders that have ensued as a direct result of this case—not to mention the unsavory publicity it's meant for us and the state we represent—I have given the detectives in this jurisdiction carte blanche to pursue any and all avenues they may encounter. Detective Brindelli, I regret this means putting you back on active duty so soon—but from what I hear, you and Dr. Adams have been busy anyway."

There was a slight guffaw around the room. It was corny, but showed that the spirits of the men were high. Everybody involved wanted to put a cap on this thing and do it quickly.

"As most of you know, Doc Adams has been associated with our department as medical examiner of Barnstable County, a position he relinquished a few years ago . . ." Here Mahaffey paused and reached down into his pants pocket. "Well, I want everybody here to know that, at least unofficially, he's back with us."

He stepped forward and handed me the flat leather folder that I had turned in before. I opened it. As expected, I saw the badge of the Massachusetts Bureau of Public Safety. It was gold with the blue seal of the commonwealth in the middle. It was exactly like Joe's except that it said "Special Investigator" on it instead of "Detective Lieutenant."

He finished the speech with more fanfare, urging us to be diligent but cautious at the same time, and bring the business to an end without endangering the public.

Then he left.

Well, it was a railroad if I've ever seen one. There I was, getting slapped on the back by all these cops, most of whom I'd never met before, and holding this badge in my hand that felt more and more like a red-hot rivet every second I held it. Still standing there speechless—and not a little annoyed—I felt Joe's breath in my ear. He spoke low, so nobody would hear.

"I'll explain it all later," he said. "Basically, it's to keep you out of trouble. Gives you some authority."

"Keep me out of trouble? How will it do that?"

"Let's put it this way: If you had had that badge with you when the cops nailed you at the warehouse, you wouldn't even have been charged. They would have called our office instead. Sure, there'd have been some ugly red tape, but basically, as a state investigator, you would not have been locked up."

"Gee, I thought Mahaffey would be pissed off at me."

"He *is* pissed off at you, dummy. And me, too. But he's smart enough to realize two things. One: We've got to make some headway on this case, and fast. Public outrage and the low morale of the state bureau demand it. Two: Even though you're a constant screw-up, you are, somehow, one of the central actors in this thing."

"Yeah? Who are the others, then?"

"You can name them as well as I: Claudia. Smitty. The bad boys from Southie. Maybe even Tony DeSilva."

"And . . . ?"

"And the biggest one of all: the man who whispers."

I just stood there like a dumb cluck, turning the heavy metal badge over and over in my fingers.

"But, Joe, I turned this in two years ago. How come it keeps coming back at me like a goddamn boomerang?"

"Ever hear the expression 'you can't fight city hall'? Well, now you know."

"So I'm stuck with it?"

"You're stuck with it. Even worse, we're stuck with you. Now let's go down the hall and meet the notorious Mr. Smits."

Joe and I went alone, much to the chagrin of the women, who had been talking of little else besides Smitty.

Joe searched for the correct door and, having found it, opened it to discover it empty and smelling like old cigarettes. Gee, I'm surprised he didn't get homesick: it smelled remarkably like his old office at Ten Ten.

"Well, where the hell are they?" he said under his breath.

"They're having coffee down the hall," said a female officer who was walking by. We followed her into a lounge area. I saw three men in there who wore plain clothes but were definitely cops. It's just a look they have, and if you hang around enough cops, you get to know that look. It's a cynical, world-weary look with a glint of sadism and humor thrown in. The fourth man in the room was slumping in a chair with his long thin legs stuck way out. He was wearing black high-top Converse gym shoes without socks, loose cotton pants in dull gray, and a silk flowered shirt with colors so bright it could give you a retinal hernia if you stared at it too long. I knew it was Smitty; his Rasta dreadlocks took up the whole back of the chair. When he saw me, he jumped up, came over, and shook my hand firmly and with warmth.

"Dr. Adams, how nice of you to come. I have been waiting to meet you for some time. Captain Chris told me much about you."

As we shook hands, I felt how huge his paws were, wrapping around my big hands with ease. I was looking up at him; he was at least six-four, possibly six-six, but thin—not over 190 pounds. His voice had that singsong musical cadence that most speech from the islands has. He had a strong British accent and a deep basso voice that resonated like a prize bass fiddle. His teeth were white and even, his skin the color of natural cigar leaf. The eyes were bright bottle green with a sleepy-lidded look and an Asian cast to them. And the dreadlocks . . . Well, they waved and danced like a nest of water moccasins on his head. Now and then he shook them out of his eyes with a flip of his head, or sent his thin hand sweeping back over them, as if putting them back in their nest.

I would say he was both handsome and scary. Since he seemed well disposed toward me—and had in fact sought me out in Concord—I thought he was handsome.

"Smitty, we are all very sorry about Celia's abduction. This is my brother-in-law, Joe Brindelli. He's a detective on the case, and will be doing everything in his power to get Celia back safely."

His lively eyes fell at the mention of his fiancée. But he quickly recovered and shook Joe's hand, looking him dead level in the eye and full of charm and grace. Then I was struck with his personality. He was obviously a leader. Articulate, quick, and possessed of great self-control, this was a man whom most people would naturally gravitate to, and fall in behind. I sensed also that quality that Laitis Roantis has in abundance: the ability to stay cool, even dead calm, in a crisis. I imagined Missaels Smits would make a first-rate ally in a fray—or a fearsome foe.

"Coffee? Hah hah hah"—he had a jiggly, guttural laugh that interspersed his speech, like a deep waterfall—"the coffee is good here, for a police station—hah hah hah . . ."

"Joe," said one of the seated detectives, "Mr. Smits has established a firm alibi for the past twenty-two days. He was at sea on a trading voyage to Jamaica. We've checked the story with the maritime officials. It's solid."

Joe drew up a folding chair with one hand, holding his Styrofoam cup in the other, and sat down in the circle. I did likewise.

"Mr. Smits, as these men may have told you, Doc and I discovered the body of a Mr. Jacob Breitz in Chris Ramos's cottage over in Fairhaven. Did they describe the scene to you?"

"Oh, yes, indeed, sah. Hah hah. It was not pretty."

"Well, do you have any ideas as to who killed him?"

"Not presently, but I'll ask around. You see, there are many possibilities. Mr. Breitz was not unknown to me. Celia told me that he was the head of much crime in the area of south New Bedford. Mr. Breitz was selling drugs to the kids, you see, and running a prostitution ring. More than once he attempted— quite unsuccessfully, I am proud to say—to recruit Cape Verdean girls for the trade."

"We never heard that," said one of the detectives.

"Your misfortune. And the misfortune of the Cape Verdean community here as well. You see, gentlemen, there are thousands of people in this city from the Cape Verde Islands and Senegal—seafaring folk who drifted about and washed up here. They are very good people. Hardworking and proud. And if pushed too hard, they can be terrible avengers. This man Breitz went way over the line. He had it coming to him. Hah hah hah."

"Who did Breitz work for?" asked Joe.

Smits shrugged.

"Could it have been remnants of Larry Kelly's organization?"

Smits closed his eyes and leaned back dreamily in the chair, as if waiting to hear from a muse. "I don't think so. The word on the waterfront is a man named Iktass—Akassis—something like that."

The detectives all looked at each other, then shook their heads.

"We haven't heard of him," continued Joe. "He from around here?"

"He used to be, a long time ago. But then I heard—and it is pure conjecture—that he moved to Florida."

"Can you give us a description?"

Smitty shook his head. The snakes went wild. "No. I don't think anybody knows his appearance."

"Have you any idea who kidnapped Celia?"

At once Smits's face grew stern. His wide jaw worked back and forth under the nut-brown skin.

"Yes. I am positive it is the people who you call the remnants of the Kelly gang."

"You knew Larry Kelly?" asked Joe.

"No. He was before my time. I'm only forty-two, although I look younger—hah hah hah—but yes, those are the people who took Celia. They say they will call me back, and these gentlemen here say that when they do, we will have a way to determine where the call is being made."

"How do they know where to reach you, since you just got off the ship?" I asked.

"Everybody knows that I can be reached at the Seamen's Bethel when I'm here. The fact that they left a message there so soon after I arrived means they are watching everything around these parts very closely."

Joe nodded. "At least we're hopeful that we can trace the call when it comes in. Since you seem sure about their identity, Mr. Smits, can you guess their whereabouts?"

He took a long time answering the question, and finally said that he was convinced it was somewhere nearby. "I think this because these terrorists seem to know—the coming and goings of many of my friends. To trick my beloved Celia into leaving her job, they must have been keeping a close eye on her. And to enter the house of her mother and do those terrible things—they must be very well versed in these parts—you see?"

The questioning went on for another hour. Through it all Missaels Haagmann Smits was a picture of composure and honesty. Only toward the end of the interview, when we discussed various options on how to get Celia back, did his emotions show. I'm not claiming to be an expert, but as a physician I am well trained in the basic job any doctor has: to observe. To observe and then deduce. I deduced that what Smits told us in that room was at least ninety percent truth.

But, of course, he could be a first-rate liar. There are lots of con men around, and Smits was a known pirate, just as Ramos was. So he was a good candidate. After the interview, we introduced our exotic new friend to Mary and Marty. They couldn't take their eyes off him. Smits was conscious of this attraction, and poured on the charm and smiles. He had a great smile. I knew the women would have something to talk about for the next week. We talked for almost an hour. Then the detectives called him back.

We left the New Bedford office and drove down to the ruins of Fort Rodman. We cruised along Rodney French Boulevard and swerved off near a small park, then kept bearing right through a gap in a high cyclone fence. Another fifty yards or so and we saw the ruins of a high stone wall with ancient gun embrasures covered in vines and brush. This vague honeycomb pattern of stone was the only indication that a fort had once been there. But I saw all this later; when we arrived, I was transfixed by the old bronze-colored Lincoln that sat at the edge of the brush beneath the stone walls. When we walked up to it, I was positive it was the same one we'd seen earlier and that I had seen while running in Concord. A close examination revealed a clear patch on the back window where the Surinamese flag had been stuck. The attending officer told us that no blood, torn clothing, or other evidence of violence had been found in or near the car. That was good news, I suppose, but given the recent events relating to the two rival gangs, I was not at all optimistic about the return of Ms. Ibenez in one piece. Neither was

Joe, who left us to huddle with his fellow detectives and scribble detailed notes about how to proceed the next day. Then we drove back to the cottage, a glum and silent foursome.

That night we had a farewell dinner of sorts at the Breakers. Joe and I would be going our separate ways for a while. He was being assigned full bore to the kidnapping of Celia Ibenez. He was already working with Paul Keegan and two other detectives on it, plus a whole passel of other people—state, local, and, of course, federal. The FBI had come in immediately when they heard of the kidnapping. J. Edgar Hoover made kidnapping one of the very first federal crimes when he created the Bureau. So Joe was tied up. I was free as a bird, and with a badge to boot.

I was not particularly thrilled by it. And neither was Mary, to put it mildly.

"Now you're going to go and get yourself killed, aren't you?" she said, sniffling and blowing her nose over her plate of cala-mari. "You couldn't just retire like a normal doctor. Worry about your golf handicap and the crabgrass in the lawn. The state of our portfolios. Or even our two boys. Noooooooo. You've got to go running around getting knocked on the head—finding slit-open corpses—howler monkeys that bite people on the face—Rastafarians who kill people . . . Good God, Charlie, you've found everything but the red frogs Chris was talking about."

I sat beside her, putting my hand on her knee. "Don't forget, Mare, that it was your brilliant discovery of the keys that plunged me into this."

"Speaking of the keys, who's got them, you or Joe? I want to see them again."

There was an awkward silence until Joe broke it by saying that I had dropped them inside the warehouse just before I left it.

"Warehouse? You were inside a warehouse? What warehouse, Charlie? I thought you told us you were coming down here to revise a paper for the College of Oral Surgery—"

"I was. I mean I did. But then I got bored and tried to explore the SEAMATT warehouse in Fairhaven to give those keys a try."

Mary's eyebrows went up. "Really? What happened?"

"They fit the lockers in there all right, but there was nothing inside the lockers, or the warehouse."

"So you mean the keys aren't worth anything at all, even after Mary's brilliant discovery?" asked Marty. She sounded as disappointed as Mary.

"It seems that's the case," I said. "I was hesitant to mention this episode to you because I knew you'd both be disappointed."

"Well, we are. And I bet you are too. Right, guys?"

We both nodded.

"How about the big brass key? The one that Nick the Pick said went to a ship? I bet that's the one that counts."

"Well, unfortunately, we don't have it anymore. I suspect that sooner or later Claudia, who owns the building, will go exploring there and discover the lost keys herself."

Mary stood up fast. "Wait a second! What's going on here? I find the keys and hand them over to you. The next thing I know, you're sneaking into Claudia's warehouse—which even I know is illegal—without telling us. Then you claim to lose the keys on the way out. Is that correct?"

"Yes," I said, without a whole lot of feeling. I had the growing suspicion that Mary was in the process of unearthing the truth, and it made me extremely uncomfortable.

"Well, then, why don't you just hustle back to the warehouse and look around for the keys, then? If you got in so easily the first time, why can't you do it again?"

Joe bent his big head low over the table in a gesture of mock horror. He covered his ears, resembling one of the three Chinese monkeys. "I'm not hearing this," he said. "I shall not be a party to an illegal entry."

"What's so illegal?" chimed in Marty. "I thought you just told Doc he could go almost anywhere he pleased now that he's got his state badge back. Well?"

"No. He cannot make an illegal entry onto private premises without a search warrant."

"Well, let's get one then," said Mary.

"We need probable cause," answered her brother. "And we

don't have it. What we do have is a more pressing issue—namely, the return of Celia Ibenez."

"Well, I sure don't like the idea of Claudia having the keys that I found," said Mary.

"I don't like the idea of Claudia in general," said Marty.

"Hear, hear," answered Mary.

"In fact, Doc," said Marty, "I think this whole business about how you lost the keys sounds a bit fishy."

"I was just thinking the same thing," said my wife, staring at me like a white-tipped shark. "I don't think you guys are leveling with us."

"Maybe we'd better get in touch with Claudia ourselves and find out what's really going on here," suggested Marty.

Mary answered that it sounded like a great idea.

"Hey, you guys are getting upset over nothing," said Joe. "Why don't Doc and I clean up while you go for a walk on the beach? Then, when you get back, we'll have dessert."

"Why are you trying to get rid of us all of a sudden?" asked Marty.

And so on. It was the oldest conflict in history reemerging: the war of the sexes. They did take off, though, leaving Joe and me to clean up.

"Jesus, Doc—what if they do get in touch with Claudia?"

"Don't even talk about it," I answered, trying to keep my hands from shaking as I carried a load of dishes over to the sink.

"Boy! That would just about finish you—if Mare finds out about Claudia paying your bail and—"

"*Shush!* I just wish some outside event would come along right now and shift the attention away from those keys."

The phone rang. I went to get it.

"Is Dr. Adams in?" said a vaguely familiar voice.

I hesitated for an instant. The way things were running, I was sure it was bad news.

"Uh—who is this, please?"

"Father DeSilva—Saint Bernard's Church—"

"Oh. Hiya, Tony. What's up?" I was glad indeed I had answered the phone. If Mary had picked it up, there was a chance Tony would have mentioned the jail episode.

"What's up is this: the *Esmeralda* is in New Bedford. Moored right up next to the state pier. Thought you might like to come over and have a look at her."

"No kidding? When?"

"Whenever you like. Come by the church and pick me up."

"I'll be there tomorrow morning at nine."

"Perfect. See you then."

I hung up the phone. Of course, what I was dying to ask him was if he'd seen Claudia recently. But I thought I better save that question until I saw him in person.

25

NEXT DAY I PICKED TONY UP AT THE CHURCH, AND WE DROVE across the bridge to New Bedford, parking near Johnny Cake Hill and hoofing it past several warehouses until we approached the wharf just beyond the state pier. There she was: the biggest ship I had ever seen in New Bedford.

"I don't know who's aboard," said Tony as we walked past it, "so just keep walking and talking, and don't stare."

"You know that Smitty's in town."

"Really? Well, then, that proves it; Smitty did commandeer Claudia's boat. I bet his men are aboard right now. Maybe even Smitty's aboard."

"Well, we met yesterday and he could recognize me," I said as I deliberately faced away from the vessel as we walked past.

"Notice especially the stern of this boat, Doc. She's high and rounded for such a small ship. Chris told me she was built in England to be a North Sea coaster. A coaster is a small ship that doesn't make long trips across open water. But he said the high stern was for the rough seas around England."

We walked on past, went on the far side of a small building, then stood at the edge of it looking back at the *Esmeralda*. Her hailing port was Port of Spain, Trinidad. I suspected she was of Panamanian registry.

"You're convinced it's the *Santiago*?"

"Absolutely. The stern is distinctive. See how high it is for such a small vessel? And then the size. There aren't that many freighters—even short-haul vessels—on this side of the Atlantic under two hundred feet."

As we watched, two black men in sailor uniforms came to the port quarter rail and leaned over it, smoking cigarettes and laughing. I stared hard at the ship, trying to fix it my mind. I knew Claudia had pictures of it; I could compare the two images.

"What will you do now, Doc?"

I turned to look at the padre, his thinning dark hair being whipped about by the ocean breeze. "I was about to ask you the same thing. We can't just board her. If I could get the keys back, we could maybe get aboard her and try it. If it fits, then that would seem to be proof positive that the vessel belongs to Claudia."

"Well, where are the keys? When you left me last, Mary was carrying them."

"I lost them in the warehouse."

"What warehouse? You were in a warehouse?"

"Hell yes, I was—the same night I got put in jail for it. That's why I called you in the first place—"

"You called me?"

There was a blank space of about three seconds when nothing was working in my head. Mary claims this is my natural state. Anyway, when his words sunk in, I faced him, up close and personal.

"Tony, you mean to tell me you don't remember my calling you Friday night from jail?"

"You couldn't have called me then; I was at an archdiocese council in Brockton."

Another pause. Our faces were inches apart. We were staring at each other like two gunfighters in a Randolph Scott western.

"I know. But . . . You did get the message from the kid I left it with, right?"

Nothing from him. Just a bewildered stare.

"And you did tell Claudia Ramos . . . Right? And that's why she came and paid my bail. Don't tell me you can't recall this. Because if not, then one of us is nuts."

"This is the first I've heard about the whole thing."

"Jesus Christ!" I gasped, hitting my palm with my fist.

"Doc! Watch what you say!"

"Oh. . . . I'm very sorry, Father. I forgot."

"You say Claudia paid your bail?"

I told him everything then, and he didn't show much reaction, which rather surprised me. All he said was, "Well, I guess they're her keys, Doc. And her warehouse. And even her boat."

He sighed then, and we began a slow walk back to the car.

"I guess what I would do in your position," he said, getting out at the church, "is to call Claudia and tell her the *Esmeralda*'s here. Also mention Smitty. Then try to arrange to go aboard the boat with her. That sounds like the most logical move. Here— I'll write down her number for you."

As I drove back over the bridge into Fairhaven, my thoughts were a jumble. So Claudia had not talked to Tony. What did it mean? Whose side was she on? Or was she just out for herself? Maybe even Joe's theory was correct: she was following me, or having me followed. Followed by God knows what sort of thugs.

I went over and over the situations when Claudia and I had crossed paths. All I could come up with was this: either Claudia Ramos was the best ally I had in this thing, or she was one sneaky, deceptive bitch.

Out of my pants pocket, I fished the scrap of paper that Tony had given me when I dropped him off. Claudia's number in Cambridge. After thinking it over for ten minutes, I finally grabbed the cellular phone off the dash and punched in the number. There was nobody there, so I got a canned message from the answering machine. It was a female voice, but brassy and authoritative, not cozy. It said I had reached the residence of Kate Winger and Claudia Ramos. Please leave a message, etc.

So they *were* living together. Maybe Claudia was a lesbian after all and merely acting the other night.

Once again, as I do almost every other week, I wished for my ideal invention: a machine that could tell me, at any given time, what a woman was thinking. If such a device existed, it would be worth a hundred thousand billion dollars.

Then I thought of a plan that might be helpful. It would be a distasteful invasion of privacy—something that under normal circumstances I would never even consider. But it was a possibility, and in this situation—considering a hostage's life was hanging in the balance—perhaps necessary. What I could do was this: approach Joe and, first of all, tell him Claudia hadn't talked to Tony DeSilva. This I knew would get him stoked up; he already eyed her as a "possible" anyway. Then I would ask him to see if his people at headquarters could do some research on Ms. Katherine Winger. See what they could find. If she were a known homosexual, or even bisexual, then the odds would be probable that Claudia was too. This in itself, of course, would be unimportant except to a blackmailer.

But it would be meaningful to me in this sense: it would reveal if Claudia had been sincere in her advances to me, or merely acting. And if I knew this, then at least I would have a good idea of which camp to relegate her to.

I did leave a message, though. It was brief, and merely stated that Mr. Smits was in town, and so was the *Esmeralda*—and for her to call Tony or me ASAP.

Then I went back to the Breakers to await developments.

They weren't long in coming.

The first development was from Joe. Katherine Winger had been dismissed from her position as associate professor at Wellesley College for "inappropriate advances toward a student." The student was a female. Also, Ms. Winger was active in the Boston Area Gay/Lesbian Alliance. The people who found this information told Joe off the record that they believed that it was Winger's background that provided the basis for the insinuation in the *Messenger-Express* that she and Claudia Ramos were having a tryst. So: Claudia probably was lesbian, and therefore her behavior that night at the Breakers, while convincing and enticing, was put on. This, coupled with her saying she'd contacted Tony DeSilva when she hadn't, meant that she was not on the up-and-up. Where she stood in this jumble of enemies and furtive plans was unknown. But she had to be watched, and watched carefully.

The second development was a call from Claudia to me at the cottage, saying that she very much wanted to sneak aboard the *Esmeralda* in the dead of night and try the key while searching for things in the ship that looked familiar, all to prove that the ship was indeed the *Santiago*, and therefore hers.

Oh, and the keys? A mere mistake, she claimed. She'd absentmindedly put them in her purse when she left early in the morning, without realizing what she'd done.

I believed her, of course. Just as I believe that Elvis is alive and living in Muscatine, Iowa.

But here was the complication: while I was lucky that she called me when Mary and Marty were out on the beach sunning themselves, and I extracted from her the solemn promise (which, considering her behavior so far, probably wasn't worth a damn) that she would say nothing about the jail, the bail, or the sleep-over at the cottage, I realized that I absolutely had to include Mary in on this caper.

The reason was simple: I was planning to take our catboat, the *Ella Hatton*, from Wellfleet down to the Cape Cod Canal and into Buzzards Bay, then sail into New Bedford Harbor with the aim of approaching the moored freighter from the water in the dead of night. I could not do this without Claudia. Now, if Mary discovered this plan, and knew Claudia was aboard with me in the little craft for at least one night together, then, lesbian or no lesbian, she would go ballistic. Therefore, she would have to come along.

So now I had the prospect of sailing with these two luscious females for a couple of days. Ordinarily such a prospect would have cheered me up. But now I had second thoughts.

I remembered the poor tiger at Brookfield Zoo.

When I was a kid, still living in the Chicago area, a male tiger died at the zoo. Actually, he was murdered. Murdered by the

two female tigers with whom he shared a barless rock enclosure
with a dry moat around its outer edge. The keepers came in one
morning to find the five-hundred-pound beast dead in the
bottom of the moat. Then they discovered the wounds all over
his body. Knowing that neither female would be a match for the
big, healthy male, they came to the grisly conclusion that the
two females had momentarily set aside their rivalry and dis-
patched him. Why, they never figured out. But there had to be a
reason. Perhaps he was abusive. Maybe each "wife" got sick
and tired of his constantly frolicking with the other woman.
Whatever the case, they ganged up on him and did him in.

I still remember the picture, a photo in the *Tribune* that showed
the once mighty beast all limp and crooked, shrunken and dis-
torted from his fall, smashed up there on the concrete of the dry
moat at Brookfield Zoo.

Was there a possible parallel here? I sure hoped not. But the
upcoming voyage with these two Latin beauties had me more
than a little concerned.

26

"WELL, WHERE THE HELL IS SHE? I THOUGHT SHE WAS SO DAMN
eager to go."

Mary was nervous and it showed. Whether she was unnerved
by the prospect of sharing a twenty-two-foot boat with another
woman who was young, unattached, and almost as pretty—
something she sure was not accustomed to—or the fact that the
lovely lady might make an advance toward her, I couldn't tell.
But Mary was used to being confident and in control; she knew
from childhood that most men did whatever she wanted. The
fact that I didn't might be what attracted her to me—but in any

event, I now saw Mary pacing the small dimensions of the *Ella Hatton* nervously, sorting through the cardboard boxes of clothes and provisions, diving down the main hatch, sorting things here and there. Beside herself.

"You don't have to go, you know."

Her face appeared immediately in the hatchway.

"Oh no you don't, Charlie! I'm here for the duration of the voyage."

"Well, the voyage will be briefer than originally planned—that's why we trailered the boat to here in Sandwich. That saves us four hours at least."

"If I'd known that, I would have asked Marty to come along. Maybe then she wouldn't have gone back to Boston."

"The truth is, Mare, that neither Joe nor Marty is that big on sailing."

"I know, but I still feel a bit like I'm ditching her. Anyway, why the rush? The sail across the bay is always so pretty."

"We don't know how long the ship will stay in New Bedford. Therefore, time is short." I looked at my watch. We'd told Claudia to meet us at the Sandwich marina at eleven. It was now almost a quarter after. "We'll be on the Buzzards Bay side of the canal after lunch, which will leave us plenty of time to get to New Bedford by dusk."

"Look, there's a car swinging into the park."

"That looks like her," I said, watching a new midnight-blue Cadillac swerve into a parking place in the marina lot.

Claudia hopped out of the car dressed in white cotton shorts and a striped jersey. She opened the back door and grabbed a big duffle-type white satchel, which she slung over her shoulder, then started a girlish, bouncing run across the harbor lot toward the pier gangway.

"Awwwww . . . how cute," said Mary between clenched teeth. "What a lovely nautical outfit. Bet she ran to Jordan's to get it as soon as you proposed this trip."

"Now, Mary, sarcasm ill becomes you. We need her; she has the keys and owns the boat."

"What if you get killed on that boat, Charlie? What if they

cut you open or take your eye out, like they did to those other victims?"

I flashed her my badge. "Are you forgetting this?"

"Ha! You think these people give a flying fuck about a state badge? After what they've done to each other? They'll put to sea and dump you and that badge overboard, weighted down with enough chain to take you straight to Davy Jones—forever."

"Nah. Never happen." I was trying to retain my confident air, but her words were unsettling, to say the least.

Now Claudia was on the pier, walking briskly toward the *Ella Hatton* moored at the far end.

"Where's she gonna sleep? I mean, after the caper. Assuming you're still among the living—"

"There are the two bow bunks, and somebody can sleep on the settee cushions. Personally, I like to sleep in the cockpit."

"Well, I don't like it. And the fact that she's . . . gay . . . makes me nervous."

"Shhh! Here she comes. Now act nice. She's a good person."

We stowed Claudia's stuff, cast off, and within a half hour had entered the northern terminus of the Cape Cod Canal, at seventeen miles the longest sea-level canal in the world. Sixty feet behind our stern rode the tiny dinghy, a fiberglass boat barely eight feet long, fastened to our catboat by a towline. This would be the sneak-boat I would use to creep up on the *Esmeralda*.

The voyage promised to be pleasant. After an initial icy silence, the two women got along surprisingly well. Of course, I know just enough about women to know that underneath they could still hate each other. But Claudia especially made a real effort to be friendly and helpful, and gave Mary every indication that she had no amorous intentions toward either of us, and that she respected Mary's age and wisdom. We made cold ham sandwiches on French bread and washed them down with chilled Heinekens. I smoked a Royal Jamaica petit corona. We soaked up the sun. Mary was now very dark and Claudia showed a reddish brown blush on her face and arms. Once inside the canal I lowered the sails and started the Westerbeke diesel.

Cranked up, it would push the *Hatton*'s pumpkin-seed-shaped hull over the water at over five knots.

We motored along to the hum of the engine underneath our feet, watching the rich green bluffs on either side of the canal slide by. We hailed passing boats, and they hailed and hooted at us. The pace was slow, the ride absolutely smooth. Canal travel is the nuts; it's a shame it went out of business. I've heard portions of the Erie Canal are still navigable. I would love to take a trip along that historic waterway, especially in an old horse-drawn barge. We watched the gulls and terns through the binoculars, and looked up the birds we didn't know in Peterson's *Field Guide to the Birds*.

"Hey, you guys," said Mary, scanning the hilly bank through the glasses, "did you know I can see houses in there through the trees? I never knew people lived along the canal. Here, take a look."

I saw trailers and small cabins interspersed among the pine trees and scrub oak. Up ahead loomed the huge Bourne Bridge. It looked impressive enough when you crossed it—passing underneath it in a small sailboat was absolutely intimidating.

"My dad had a crony who lived along here somewhere," said Claudia, taking the glasses from me. "Name was Ivan. I think he worked for SEAMATT. Dad liked it that he could watch the SEAMATT boats and barges pass through here for him, you know? He could call Ivan and ask him if the barges were running on schedule. The skippers would say one thing, but Ivan could look out his window and see them slide by."

"How come I don't see more big ships in the canal?" Mary asked.

"I think it's because you can't leave a wake here," answered Claudia. "The ships now are huge and fast; they can make it around the Cape in less time than going through here. It's just another reason SEAMATT, and lot of other small carriers, went under."

"Charlie? Isn't there a danger of flooding here? I mean, if the ocean rose real fast?"

"No more than we have on the beach. Hey, Claudia, is your dad's friend still there?"

She shrugged. "I haven't even heard about him in years. I think he's dead. He had TB really bad, and it surprised me. I thought nobody got TB anymore. Hey, is that a kingfisher?"

We passed below the Sagamore Bridge and soon exited the canal. Once outside the canal's southern end, we were in Buzzards Bay. Hoisted sails again and hauled southwest for New Bedford. By shortly after six we were standing off the harbor, headed for those clamshell gates in the giant breakwater that guarded the teeny opening in the wall of rock. We passed through the storm gate and had arrived.

But no *Esmeralda*. I scanned the docks of the New Bedford side of the harbor again and again with the marine binoculars. But no freighter. She had gone, perhaps out to sea again for another two or three weeks. Perhaps for good. I sat at the helm, stumped and feeling like a fool.

"I can't imagine why it would leave so fast," I said. "Maybe when Tony and I were watching it yesterday, somebody spotted us and got wise. I don't know . . ."

"No! Look everybody; there she is!" said Claudia, pointing to the other side of the harbor. Sure enough, there was the freighter, sitting very high up and at an odd angle. "See? She's being hauled out for repairs." Claudia came off the foredeck and headed aft to where we sat in the cockpit. She took the glasses from me and studied the scene.

"That's not far from Daddy's wharf. I know the place; it's the nearest thing to a drydock we have here. It's a huge, sloping ramp. They use big cradles on rails to haul the vessels up with a stout cable and a huge winch."

"You're convinced it's her?"

"Oh yeah. Hundred percent. See, she's moving. Ever so slowly, almost like the minute hand of a clock . . ."

Claudia was right. As we sailed straight for her and the big yard, we could see her inch up the ramp. We motored on and moored in a marina just a hop and a skip away where we could watch her closely through the glasses, and settled down to wait.

By eight o'clock two things were clear. One: *Esmeralda* was hauled up as high as she would go considering her size. She sat there, nose in the air, stern down toward the harbor water, ready for whatever repairs she needed to her hull. Two: There was nobody aboard her. At least, it sure didn't seem like it. We saw no one on her decks, superstructure, or nosing around her hull. If anybody were still aboard, he or she would be stuck in an uncomfortable, stuffy dark shell of metal. They had power lines aboard to keep some light on her, probably to discourage vandals. The fence around the yard looked easy to breach. But most of the power I assumed to be for the welding equipment, which would probably sputter and flash into action next morning when the workmen showed up.

Studying the big hull through the glasses, I decided my best route would be to take the dinghy and row over to the ramp around one in the morning. Then I would scale one of several ladders that already were rigged to the ramp, and hop aboard. Testing the big admiralty key and snooping quickly around wouldn't take more than ten minutes; the boat was too small for an extended visit.

This was made clear simply by looking at her: she was deep enough in the hull to be an oceangoing vessel; that was obvious. But she appeared cut in half, short and stubby. She had only one set of derricks, while most freighters have at least two or three. Furthermore, as Claudia explained to us, all the personnel, officers and crew alike, were housed in the aft area structure that supported the bridge and funnel.

"The crew was between nine and twelve," Claudia said, "depending on the cargo and the length of the voyage. Daddy was captain. He had two mates and a bosun, and a crew of four to eight. At sea, three of the crew were cooks and stewards. Three men ran the engine room and the electrical system. The remainder kept the ship up."

"So when she's hauled out, how many on board?"

"I don't think anybody, Doc. I mean, she's all canted up; nobody could sleep in her like that. There's nothing in the holds—they made sure she was light before they hauled her."

"So if I climb aboard in the wee hours, nobody's going to know or care?"

"I don't see why. There's not enough to justify a watchman. All the cabins and corridors will be locked. The bridge, radio shack, the hatches down to the engine room—all those will be locked."

"Ah, but I can open them," I said, holding the big brass key.

She shook her head.

"That key was only for the officers' quarters and bridge. I bet they've put new locks on."

"Then why are we bothering with all this?"

"Listen: all you have to do is get aboard and get a look at the doorways leading to the officers' quarters." She pointed up at the higher of the two decks on the aft superstructure. "That deck right there. The forward cabin is the captain's—it spans the entire beam of the ship, and he has the forward upper deck there for himself. It's so he can look at the ship whenever he wants. Aft of the master cabin are two smaller ones, one starboard, the other port. They're for the mates. The bosun and the crew all bunk on the next deck down. There's nothing forward but holds and the 'tween decks, all for cargo. The only other bunks on the ship are found in the engine room—the duty watch sleeps down there, so if the engines act up, they'll know right away."

"So I get aboard, make my way to the upper deck, and see if there's a lock on any of the doors that fits this key."

"Right. They'll have new locks installed, but the old ones were installed when she was built. They'll still be there. If you try the key and you hear the lock mechanism working, that's all we need."

"What will we do then?" asked Mary. "Go to the police?"

"Go to the Coast Guard," Claudia said.

"No," I said. "Better to go to Joe and have him contact the maritime authorities. A cop will carry more weight."

"What if somebody's aboard, Charlie? You could get killed."

"No way." Then a long silence. So I added: "But if I'm not back in, say, an hour, you two—call the cops."

"Are you taking the Beretta?" Mary asked.

"It's at home. Don't worry; I won't need it."

We locked up the boat and walked into Fairhaven, getting a nice seafood dinner at a local workingman's diner close to the water. Then we walked around the parks. As we approached a group of buildings ahead, I got a sudden sinking feeling. We were heading in the direction of the police station and the jail. Uh-oh . . .

But before I could dwell on this, Claudia managed to sidle over to me when Mary was studying a garden and whisper, "Don't worry—my lips are sealed!"

At a little after nine we headed back to the boat. Thank heavens it was a cool evening. Sailboats, especially wide, shallow-hulled ones like catboats, can get terribly hot. So hot they don't cool off until the next morning. But I put the galley exhaust fan on and we opened the forehatch, putting a screen in its place, and soon the interior was cool enough to lie down and rest. You could not stand upright in it, though—it's the price you pay for having a little boat that you can beach or haul almost anywhere.

I lay on the cockpit cushions while Mary and Claudia talked below after making coffee. I was looking up at the darkening sky, watching the gulls glide overhead, mewing softly. I didn't need coffee—I was too wired.

When it got good and dark, about ten-thirty, I told the women I was taking a stroll, to check things out. I walked up the dock and over to Water Street, turned left, and walked until I was opposite Munder's Boatyard, where the *Esmeralda* was hauled out. There was no missing that enormous high bow sticking up over the workshops and warehouses. She may have been a small coastal freighter, but in this harbor she was the QE II. I had taken the binoculars, and scanned the place quickly enough so I wouldn't stand out. Munder's was surrounded by the ever-present high cyclone fence topped with razor wire and looked completely deserted. I looked for evidence of a watchdog and could see none. Big halogen lights lit the place up, casting an unnatural orange-yellow glow everywhere—I sensed that this and the fence were the main defenses against theft or vandalism. But, as Claudia had told us, there wasn't really anything to take off this hauled-up cargo vessel. Unless you were into stealing heavy-duty electric winches, or unless you've always craved a 2,200-pound Danforth anchor for the front yard of your beach cottage, you were mostly shit out of luck. With the aft superstructure locked, there just wasn't anything to take.

But how about alarms on the doorways I was going to explore? Uh-oh—hadn't thought about it. But it was too late to change plans now.

I returned to the boat and found Mary there alone.

"Claudia was restless and thought she'd take a stroll around," said Mary. "She said she'll be back in a few minutes."

Thinking nothing about this, I again reclined on the cushions, hoping to catch a catnap before becoming a cat burglar. But the more I thought about Claudia Ramos strolling around downtown Fairhaven with the crew of the *Esmeralda* everywhere around this little town, my apprehension grew. Some of them might recognize her, and tell Smitty. Or Smitty himself, who was no doubt within a seven-iron shot of where I was lying, might recognize her. Then what?

Then an even more sinister thought emerged: what if Claudia was, as Joe believed from the start, a spy for Larry Kelly's gang? And her stroll was the opportunity to fill them in on the operation I was about to pull?

This thought did me no good at all, and I was more wired than ever.

She returned at eleven-thirty, all charm and smiles. Was this really her, or the front she was wearing? She curled up on the seat cushion and looked at the water, showing a lot of tan leg and thigh.

There was no doubt about it: Claudia Kelly/Ramos was delectable. She smelled wonderful close up and had a great voice. She was smart and sassy. She was also mysterious and probably dangerous. And she was definitely this: someone I should *not* allow myself to get close to.

Naturally, I was tremendously attracted to her.

Why does that always happen, anyway?

The three of us sat and sipped coffee until midnight. I only had half a cup. Then we decided to try and sleep. The women went below and stretched out on the two bow bunks while I returned to the cockpit and watched the stars and clouds.

At two forty-five I stuck my head inside the companionway hatch. I heard light snoring.

"Charlie?"

"Yeah. I'm going now. If I'm not back by four, you take the cell phone and call Joe's pager number. You know he's never far from it. Have him raise hell down here."

"Kiss me before you go."

I crept down the companionway and leaned over to kiss her full lips. She looked a bit paler in the moonlight—

"Over here, dummy. That's Claudia!"

"Oh . . . Sorry . . ."

"I'm going to kick your ass when this whole thing is over."

I had my dark clothes on, and only wished the dinghy were blue instead of white. Anything white stands out on still water at night like a searchlight.

I cast off and began working the two miniature oars, heading for Munder's Boatyard two docks down.

27

I WAS THERE IN UNDER TEN MINUTES, AND IT WOULD HAVE been sooner if I hadn't been making every effort at silence. Peering at the brightly lit yard, I had two options with the dinghy. One was to haul it up the ramp; the other was to creep in among the pier pilings on the side of the ramp and tie her up behind enough of them so it wouldn't be readily seen from the water. I opted for this. Before I left the small boat, I glassed the entire yard and the ship one more time. Nothing. No movement, and not a sound except for the buzzing of those damn spotlights. I don't know about most people, but, personally, when I'm sneaking around somewhere I shouldn't be, I like it dark.

Well, this was it. I left the bulky glasses on the thwart and placed one foot on the ramp, put my weight on it, then followed with the other foot. I was now technically—and illegally—in the yard. I walked around slowly, pretending to be an interested bystander, for about a minute. No sirens went off, no Rottweilers with studded collars and slavering jaws lunged at me. I carried only three things, besides the keys: my state shield in the pocket of my jeans, a powerful rechargeable flashlight in a belt holster, and my folding Spyderco "clip-it" knife alongside it on my canvas belt. What was there to be afraid of?

I was looking for a ladder, half expecting there wouldn't be one, but was pleasantly surprised to see a small version of a fire-escape-style zigzag metal stairway winding up alongside one of the enormous steel gantries that steadied the hull of the *Esmeralda.* This was perfect. I climbed up that ladder deliberately, as if I had important business there, like maybe a night watchman. Then I was at the top, looking down at the deck of the *Esmeralda.* Viewed from this angle she looked smaller because the deep hull was not visible. All I saw was the aft superstructure still looming above me: the lower deck, the upper deck above that, all with railings, then the bridge and pilothouse on top, just below the funnel. I could see closed doors with portholes on all the decks. The upper deck was smaller than the lower one and fully roofed over by the bridge. This was the location of the officers' cabins; that's where I was headed. Above these decks were the bridge and pilothouse, with the radio shack directly aft. There wasn't much to explore here, about as much as a small bungalow.

The main deck of the ship stretched forward below me for over a hundred feet. There were three hatchways, all with the hatch covers removed. The ship appeared empty. The single derrick, positioned in about the middle of the deck between the first and second hatchways, was tall but immobilized; its booms were fastened down.

Now, I've been on enough of these midnight expeditions—usually with Laitis Roantis, who's a pro—to look for an alternate escape route if things get dicey. I saw that the opposite side of the giant gantry on which I was standing had an identical ladder. That was good. But that was *all.* In other words, if I got cornered on this vessel, either by the law or by some bad guys, and they were on both of the stairways, the only place for me to go would be the hold or the engine room, or try to hide in one of the cabins. That was it, besides the ultimate option of jumping from the stern into the shallow water of the harbor four stories below.

Hell with it; I climbed over the topsides and hit the deck with quiet feet, then made my way aft. The going was a bit too easy: the ship was canted up in the ways—going aft was going downhill. I climbed the small stairway that led to the poop deck, where the superstructure was. Then I ascended the ladderway to the lower deck. This big deck, according to Claudia, held the crew's bunks, the galley, the mess, and a small machine shop. I went to the first doorway and tried the big brass key. No go. But I didn't expect it to work. I walked all around this deck, which was partially covered by the deck above, trying the big brass key and inspecting the portholes. Everything was fastened up tight; every single porthole was closed and fastened. Walking around it was awkward, though, because of the cant of the ship. Reminded me of walking up the leaning tower of Pisa.

Next was the upper deck. I went up another ladderway, and did a full circuit of the deck, from the railings forward of the captain's cabin to the afterdeck. I was not in much danger of being seen from either the shore or the harbor now, since this deck was covered with a steel roof. If I stayed close to the bulk-heads, away from the railings, it would be difficult to spot me. With a pounding heart I tried the key on one of the after cabins. It went in and I turned it, hearing the lock mechanism work. I turned it back and forth several times. There was no doubt: the key fit, and worked.

But the doorway did not open because a new lock, standard pin-tumbler type, had been installed in the doorframe above the original one. Well, I had what I had come for: proof that the key Chris Ramos left us went to this ship.

That meant that Smitty and his crew had somehow doctored the paperwork on the vessel, or simply bought forged documents to show that he was the skipper-owner. But we could now prove him wrong. This ship was Claudia's.

But suddenly another thought entered my head: Chris hadn't told Claudia about the keys or their hiding place. He had told me. And Tony DeSilva. This, at least, according to DeSilva. But Joe had said priests can lie.

Hmmmmm . . .

Was it possible? Was it at all possible, given what Brady had told me in his office, that Chris Ramos's bequeathing of the keys to me on his deathbed meant that *I* was the owner of this ship? Once again I recalled the garbled message of the dying man:

Listen, Doc . . . anything you can find is yours . . .

Hmmmmm . . .

In the dark, underneath the eerie orange glow of the lamps, I smelled the ocean, felt the sea breeze on my cheek. If I let my imagination go ever so slightly, the reddish glow of the halogen lights became a tropical sunset. I stared off over to New Bedford, saw the twinkling lights . . . felt the breeze again, and smelled the water . . .

. . . before long I was conscious of a drumbeat . . . a steady thumping bass—an invitation to the dance . . . Peering over the side from the railing—my railing on my ship—I could once again see the old stone quay below. The samba beat oozed out from the cafe that reeked of cheroots, sweat, and cheap rum. I glanced beside the old doorway and there she was again, the girl in the Gypsy blouse and cotton skirt slit up the side. I realized now it was definitely Claudia. She didn't mind that I was now the skipper of her father's tramp steamer, although she missed me dearly on the long voyages. We were living in Montevideo now, in a hillside villa clogged with children and servants. I waved to her. She threw me a kiss and cocked her hand on her hip provocatively. . . .

Thump!

The dream vanished. What was that? A noise from some-where on the ship. Or was it in the boatyard? Or even out on the street behind me? I walked slowly around the deck on the star-board side, keeping close to the bulkheads, and looked toward the bow. The deck and hatches and derrick booms stretched out before me, silent. I waited for over a minute before moving again. Whatever the noise was, I did not hear it again. In all probability it was a car tire thumping over a pothole on the street. I returned to the task at hand and this time I decided to try for the big money: the captain's cabin itself. I advanced to the starboard doorway, inserted the key, and turned the lock.

Then I noticed that this door had no new lock affixed in the frame. With a trembling hand, I grabbed the brass knob, turned it, and pulled. The captain's door opened.

I pulled the flashlight from my holster and shined it around. I saw a wood-paneled interior, and enough light coming through the eight fastened portholes to douse the flashlight. I crept inside and looked around. A large bed to my left, along the aft wall. A microphone on the forward side, no doubt to communicate with the bridge, engine room, etc. A table in the center of the wide room, with four chairs. Perfect for a card game or quiet dinner. A smallish door that led to a private bathroom. Bookshelves that held books and personal articles. Posters of famous soccer players and reggae singers. This was Smitty's room all right. More navigational equipment. Not much else I could see in the semidarkness. I smelled incense and the faint reek of marijuana. I opened a locker and shined the light inside, seeing a row of gaudy flowered shirts. I was not about to search the place.

Then I noticed a third doorway in the center of the aft wall. I approached this and saw it was bolted shut—but from the captain's side. I turned the bolt locks and opened the door. I was looking down a small narrow hallway. Directly ahead of me, straight aft, was the door I had tried earlier. So the mates came into their cabins through this hallway, which they entered from the aft door. There were doorways in the corridor. I passed a toilet and a shower stall, then came up to two doors opposite each other. These I assumed were to the mates' cabins. I tried the door on the port side, and it opened. This was a much smaller version of the captain's cabin, without the wood paneling or the table. Just a bunk and a desk, some shelves and clothing lockers. I left it, shut the door behind me, and was about to enter the starboard cabin when I became conscious of a distant ringing sound coming from the other side of the door.

What was this, some kind of alarm system? The ringing sound was extremely high pitched. I tilted my head up, toward where the radio shack should be. Perhaps it was some kind of communications equipment.

But the sound wasn't coming from above; it seemed to issue from the room I was standing in front of. If that were the case, then perhaps opening the door would set off the alarm.

I remained there in the dark corridor, bracing myself against the slope of the floor, for several minutes before I opened the door a crack. The ringing was intense now, so loud and high it hurt my ears. I shined the light around the interior of the room before going inside. Rough cotton clothing hung on the walls. Two Panama hats. A native drum from Africa or the islands stood two feet tall in one corner. Then the beam of the flashlight swept by a big galvanized iron tub. I focused on that tub, convinced the ringing was coming directly from it. I advanced into the room and stood over the tub. A screen was placed on its top, with a conch shell on the screen.

I reached down, picked up the conch shell. I would have put it to my ear to hear the ocean, but the other noise was too damn loud. With the light in one hand, I reached down again, shaking now, and picked up the screen.

And there they were, hundreds and hundreds of them.

Frogs. As small as half my little finger. Hopping about like mad crickets, making their awful song.

And red.

As bright shiny red as hot chile peppers.

28

WELL, THAT WAS IT: THE FINAL PART OF THE MESSAGE CHRIS left me before he died. No, wait. Not the final part. There was one element still missing. One part of the grisly puzzle we still had not run up against: the headhunters. Personally, I wasn't even that keen on the frogs. I could skip the headhunters altogether, thank you.

I continued to shine the light on the frogs, though—they fascinated me. There was some brownish water in the bottom of the tub, and some sticks propped up on the sides so that the little critters could climb up out of the water and jump around. The light seemed to excite them. I knelt down next to the tub and looked closely at them. They looked exactly the way frogs are supposed to look: tympanic membrane, bulbous eyes, long, folded legs, and the curious, active throat that pulsed underneath, and swelled up when they made their cries. I realized that the steady ringing sound was actually the combined small noises of maybe two or three hundred tiny frogs. The eyes were different than the frogs I had seen before, however. They were jet black. And, of course, their red skin. It was surrealistic. Also, I noticed a yellowish, oily sweat that seemed to bead up on their bodies.

Four or five of them jumped out of the open tub and hopped along the varnished wood. I grabbed one and flung it back inside the tub as fast as I could. I felt no bite or sting whatsoever. Then the animals couldn't be that dangerous—or else why would Smitty keep them on board, in just a galvanized tub? I looked at my hand. It was fine. So then I grabbed the rest of them, but by the time I got them, some more had gotten out. Hell with it. I stood up, rubbed my hand dry on my pants, replaced the screen and the conch shell, and made my way out the door.

I was out on the afterdeck when I began to feel a tingling sensation on my hand. It was not unpleasant, but was growing in intensity. I decided to return to the bathroom in the corridor and wash my hands. After this, the tingling abated somewhat, but was still present. It would be best to go out the way I had come in; that way no doors would be left unlocked. So I went back through Smitty's cabin, locking the aft door behind me, and then exited through the starboard doorway again. When I was back out on deck, I shut the door and locked it again with the big brass key.

As I did so, I heard a noise.

I froze, trying my damnedest to locate its source. It wasn't a thump—more like a scrape. Perhaps a scuffing of a foot. Was it related to the noise I'd heard earlier? I crept forward to the end of the bulkhead and looked ahead at the empty main deck of the *Esmeralda*. Nothing down there that I could see. I looked to my left, toward the port side. The upper deck I was standing on was vacant. I put the flashlight back in its holster and drew the Spyderco knife from my pocket. It only had a three-and-a-half-inch blade, but its serrated edge could cut through cable. I eased along the forward side of the upper deck now, my feet making no noise on the steel decking. At the bulkhead's edge, I dropped to my knees and peeked around the corner, my head only two feet from the deck, the way Roantis had taught me. Nobody there.

Perhaps the noise had been a bird or some nocturnal animal. I stood upright and walked to the port ladderway, which descended from a rectangular hole in the deck to the lower deck below. A ladderway is a combination ladder and stairs, a very steep set of stairs with railings on each side. The steps are like those on a stepladder—steep enough that many people are afraid to go down a ladderway facing forward. I wasn't; I wanted to see exactly where I was headed. I went down the ladderway fairly quickly, knowing that only one more was between me and the huge main deck, and safety.

But as soon as I reached the bottom step, a shadow came up on my left and hit me on the side of the head.

I went down on one knee. My head hurt terribly and it was all I could do not to fall over. The shadow approached again. I saw dark blue jeans and black gym shoes moving closer. Where had I seen those gym shoes recently? On the feet of Missaels Smits, that's where. I managed to look up, but it was a white face that stared back. A middle-aged man with a thick face, pale complexion. He looked rough—maybe another prizefighter. I ducked my head again, pretending to be dizzier than I was. Then, with all the strength I had left, I lunged up at him, swinging my right arm in a wide sweep with the knife in my fist. I heard a ripping sound, and hoped I had connected with more than his clothing.

But apparently not. Next thing I knew, he had chopped me on the side of the neck. As I went down, I saw the silvery flash of the Spyderco disappear over the side as he kicked it away under the railing. I heard it clatter on the deck below us. Then he grabbed me from behind, twisting my arm up in a hammerlock, and pushed me along toward the next ladderway.

"C'mon, goombah. We got an appointment."

"If it's with Smitty, you can let me go; I'll walk by myself."

"Hell no. It ain't with that niggah. You got the wrong side of the fence, wiseguy."

"I'm on the side of the law; you should know that," I said between gasps. "I've got a badge I can show you."

"Don't want no badge. He just told me bring in the doctor. And get the friggin' keys—"

He patted me down fast and had the ring of keys jerked out of my pocket before I knew what was happening. But he kept his hold on me, and kept pushing me toward the stairwell. It looked like he wasn't going to kill me on the spot.

"Where . . . are we going?" I asked in a faint voice. I was feeling stronger as each second passed. But I remembered Roantis's lesson: pretend you've barely got enough strength to move. Then, when he least expects it, throw yourself on the enemy with everything you've got. I didn't think I could do that—but I still faked it. If nothing else, Mr. X would use up his strength half carrying me.

"Who are we going to see anyway? And why?"

"We're gonna go see the big boss. So you can help him get what he wants."

"The big boss, is he the guy with the whisper voice?"

"The whisper voice. That's a good one. He'll be tickled you called it that. Oh, tickled *pink*."

We were almost to the ladderway that would take us down to the main deck. But as we approached it, I could see we would pass by an open porthole. This was curious; they were all shut when I came aboard.

"Why . . . why does . . . he want to see me?"

"He'll tell yah."

I sagged lower. The man gave me a shot to the kidney with his fist. He was a pro at pain, that was for sure. I slumped down again, and he yanked me up, now almost dragging me along.

Then he let go of me, and I fell to the deck.

"Shit!" he yelled, loud enough for anybody on Water Street to hear. He slapped his neck hard, and swore again. I rolled over and was getting to my knees when he snagged me again. "Fuckin' bug stung me . . . Now stay in line—or I'll use the sap on yah. . . ."

We half slid down the ladderway, with him holding me tight and leaning way back. I could hear his breathing get more labored with each step. Finally we were down. He paused to catch his breath, then led me over to the gantry stairway. Our descent of this was a nightmare, with him panting and coughing, and threatening to kill me if I tried anything. By the time we were halfway down, I had grown to fear him much less for reasons I was not sure of. Perhaps I realized he was, while strong and tough, pitifully out of shape. He knew the moves and punches, but I ran thirty miles a week.

I resolved to wait until we were down on the ramp, then make my move. I didn't think he had a gun. Just his fists and feet, and the sap he'd tagged me with. I thought maybe I could sucker punch him and run like hell.

But run where? I couldn't get the dinghy under way fast

enough. And the fence was still twelve feet high and topped with razor wire. Maybe just lead him on a run around the yard until he dropped from exhaustion . . .

Then I remembered my caveat to Mary and Claudia, and I felt optimistic. I had given them an hour to wait for me. I was sure most of that hour had already elapsed. Time was on my side.

When we got to the bottom of the zigzag metal stairs, Mr. X could scarcely stand. Something was wrong with him. I suspected he could be in the first stages of a heart attack.

"Sit . . . sit down!" he rasped, pointing at the huge rough planks of the ramp. I did as he told me. He collapsed near me, smacking the leather sap against his palm. I saw he was dressed in a dark blue sailor's jersey with a navy blue watch cap pulled down over his head. The dark blue jersey had a wide rip in it. He was thick-bodied and strong. But suddenly he didn't look so hot.

"Feel . . . tired . . . don't . . . try any-ting . . ."

"Where are you taking me? Is it far?"

He shook his head. "Nah. Just ovah the big bridge."

"Which bridge? To New Bedford?"

"N-nah. The othah way . . ." He tried to motion with his arm, but it fell limp on the wood.

"The Cape?"

He nodded. He was still trying to slap the blackjack against his palm, but he was missing half the time. His eyes had a dazed and distant look. I got to my feet.

"Siddown . . ." he mumbled, trying to focus his eyes.

"Don't worry. I'm just going to stretch. What's your name?"

"Hmmmm?" His head was weaving now, his mouth wet. His legs were twitching slightly. He looked like a floored fighter on the canvas.

"Your name. What's your name?"

"S-S-Sid."

"Goodnight, Sid," I said, and spun half around, landing a kick on the side of his jaw. He crumpled, and did not move at all save for the twitching of his feet and hands. I took the sap and went through his pockets. Nothing but the keys he had taken from me. I took them back. He had a sleeve knife taped to his forearm, hidden by his dark jersey—a Gerber Mark II fighting knife. I left it there.

Then I took off for the dinghy, leaving him lying there on the ramp, right in the bright light of Munder's Boatyard.

I got in and began to cast off. But just then I heard a low rumble from the front of the boatyard. I stood up in the tiny, rocking boat so that I could see far in that direction. I recognized the sound: a motorcycle starting up. Then I saw it, with its black-clad rider, cruise around the end of the boatyard and disappear behind a warehouse. Then the sound again, much fainter, as he sped away.

WHEN I RETURNED TO THE *ELLA HATTON* AFTER MY MIDNIGHT skulk, I told the women of my adventures, and my narrow escape from the clutches of another of Larry Kelly's resident bad boys. I told them about the red frogs, too, and held out my hand so they could shine the flashlight on it. It had turned black and blue, and was aching now. But I felt fine. In fact, I felt great.

I thought the whole thing was bully.

They thought I was an idiot.

So what's new?

I fished some tonic and ice from the cold locker and constructed three very stout gin and tonics. We sat whispering in the cockpit, sipping our drinks, until the eastern sky began to gray and the gulls came to life. Then we collapsed back into our bunks. I had rigged the gizmo tarp the previous evening, that square canvas awning that fastens over the boom and comes down to within a foot of the deck on each side of the cockpit. It makes a wonderful canopy to sleep under. The women retired to the bunks below while I stretched out under the tarp and crashed.

But I awoke much sooner than expected; there was a commotion on the docks. I heard voices, full of sound and fury, not too far away. Also, flashing blue strobe lights from police cars were invading my sanctuary under the awning. I looked out to see them flashing off the buildings of the Fairhaven waterfront. Then I looked at my watch. Seven twenty-five. I assumed the workmen at the yards worked from seven until three or four. Ergo, they had discovered something when they showed up. And it looked like it happened at Munder's Boatyard.

Uh-oh . . .

"Charlie? What's going on, anyway?"

Mary was standing in the companionway in her nightshirt, scratching the side of her hip with one hand and running the fingers of the other through her long dark hair. Claudia, still blessed with youth, slept on.

"I dunno. But it seems to be coming from Munder's."

"Ohhhhh shit . . ."

"A coincidence, surely," I said, trying to appear calm. But already I was weighing the two choices that were presenting themselves. Either make sail and head for the canal ASAP, or go ashore and see what the commotion was all about. It did not take me long to realize that only a coward would run.

"I say we get the hell out of here pronto," Mary hissed. "Let's not even wake Claudia—just start the engine and we'll motor on out."

"An excellent decision," I said, fitting the engine key into the little slot under the helm.

But I knew it was no good. I was so deep into this thing now that Joe and Company would come looking for me even if nobody else did. I squared my shoulders and put on clean shorts and a knit pullover, some faded canvas Top Siders, and placed the state badge in my pocket. I was so tired I was almost reeling, but go I must.

"I'll be back as soon as I can. But I've got a hunch it will take longer than expected."

As soon as I approached Munder's, with a bunch of uniformed cops standing around the high fence, I knew my hunch was correct. I was willing to bet serious money that my assailant, Sid, had been discovered dead by the riggers returning to the *Esmeralda*. I flashed my badge and got through the gate.

"Oh no! Not you again!" came a voice. I turned and recognized the face of a young cop who'd been on the scene at Rivet Street. I forgot his name, but gave him the thumbs up and walked on toward the group of intense law enforcement and EMS people hovering over a too familiar part of the big haul-out ramp. I fought my way close enough to look down, and there he was, in the same exact position I'd left him in.

Did my kick kill him? I thought not. I wasn't skilled enough to deliver a kick that precise or powerful. Also, the man was hurting, and hurting bad, before I even made my move. I glanced down at my hand again in the full daylight. It looked as if three NFL linemen had stomped on it wearing hobnailed boots. The entire back of it from midfingers to wrist was now almost black. But the pain was diminishing, and my fingers were still mobile. I felt the worst was over. Still, I knew I'd better get it looked at.

And considering all this, it didn't take a genius to surmise that if I had been stuck through the skin in the back of the neck by a pellet or dart carrying this poison and it went through my bloodstream, I would be in the same condition as poor Sid.

Telling people I was a doctor, I showed my badge again and convinced those around me that I should touch the victim. I moved his head sideways and peered at the back of his neck. Sure enough, the red mark was there, and the tiny puncture mark in its center.

"Somebody please get hold of Joe Brindelli of the state police and ask him to meet Doc here as soon as possible. If I'm not here, I'll be on my boat. Okay?"

On my way back to the boat, I realized I had seen this man's face earlier. Then I remembered when it was: in the parking lot of the Concord Professional Building. The guy named Sid had asked me to help him with his car. But that made sense when I thought about it more. If the Big Boss, the Man Who Whispered, wanted to bring me in, he'd get someone who'd seen me up close before.

I slept a bit before Joe showed up. Then we walked back over to Munder's and I walked him through my midnight escapade, step by step, and showed him where Sid had ambushed me at the base of the ladderway. Then I went back to the *Hatton* and crashed again. *Hard.*

"Guess what, kiddies? We're going for a sail." It was a grim Joe Brindelli who gave these orders. A man whose patience had been tried beyond the breaking point. "Now. Just the four of us. I want to be close to all of you and far away from anyone who might overhear. This small boat is perfect. Doc, Mary, get ready and let's take off."

"I hope you don't need me," said Claudia cheerfully. "There are things I have to do that—"

"I want to talk to you *especially*," he growled, pointing his finger right at her chest. "And in my capacity as a detective."

Well, that shut her up. Soon we were outside the breakwater, the great groundswells of the North Atlantic making the small hull lift and fall, lift and fall. Mary was anxious, alternately looking at my discolored hand and watching Claudia with cat eyes. Did she want to see this younger rival brought low? As for Claudia, she kept peering toward the horizon with longing on her face. I was fairly neutral. I knew Joe was on my side, even though I knew a lecture was forthcoming, but above all I dreaded that the episode of my unfortunate incarceration—and Claudia's rescuing me—would surface. We had what seemed to be a fifteen-knot breeze, so I headed the *Hatton* downwind and let the mainsheet out. The boom swung out perpendicular to the hull and the sail filled. I nodded to Mary, and she cranked up the centerboard. Now the catboat would really fly. And fly she did—jumping the swells and barely skimming the surface of the brine, hissing like a banshee as she bounced over the waves.

"Okay, we've got several serious problems here," said Joe, opening a Heineken and lighting a cigarette almost at the same time. When it came to personal pleasures, this big man had the speed of a featherweight. "One, is *this*." He drew a sealed plastic bag from his coat pocket. Inside was a silver knife with a three-and-a-half-inch serrated blade. My Spyderco folder. It was open inside the bag, just as the lab team had found it. My knees began to tremble slightly.

"Look familiar, anyone?" he asked with the face and manner of a game-show host. I could almost hear the exaggerated tick-tocking and the insipid theme music as we thought up our answers.

"Let's begin with you, Mary. Ever see this before?"

"It's Charlie's." She turned to me. "Jesus, you didn't stab him, did you?"

"No. He did not. But almost. The victim, now ID'd as Sidney Foster, had a large rip in his clothing. The fibers of his jersey match those on this knife." He paused to let the words sink in. "In addition, notice the sides of the body of this knife. Pure, flat stainless steel. Perfect for fingerprints."

I was trying to watch the sails and the weather and the waves, etc. But now I looked at the women. They were looking at me as members of a jury might. I shuddered.

Joe withdrew the knife from the bag.

"Fortunately, I wiped this down with my handkerchief shortly after I found it."

He folded the blade in and toyed with the knife in his big hands, tossing it this way and that. Then we all heard him say, "Oops!" As the knife went over the side.

"Joey!"

"How careless of me."

We watched it flash and wink and then it was gone. My spirits soared.

"Okay. Problem two: the dead Mr. Foster. Career criminal. Associated in the past with Gary Walsh. Another former pugilist, but way out of shape. Doc showed me the frogs aboard the boat. From the looks of his hand, I'd have to agree the little critters are poisonous. Deadly poisonous. Karl Pirsch at the state lab has contacted animal poison experts. His initial findings are that the frogs are called simply dart-poison frogs, from Central America and the Amazon Basin."

"That place!" said Mary. "There's that place again!"

"They're bad news," continued Joe. "The worst of these fellows is bright yellow. Aptly named *Phyllobates terribilis*, its poison is so strong it's doubtful Doc would be alive now, just from touching them. Next in line are the red ones. I don't have much doubt that when the right people check for the venom in the tissues of Jacob Breitz and Sid Foster, they'll find it in abundance."

"So then Charlie's in the clear," said Mary. "I don't see what's to worry about then, except for finding Smitty's girlfriend."

"We're working on that night and day," said her brother. "But I don't expect a good outcome. Smitty's now got his own problems, too. The frogs aboard his hijacked ship constitute a lethal weapon. Even if he wasn't here when Breitz got it, the state won't have much trouble linking him with the killing in some way. But that's not what I want to discuss now."

"What is it, then?" Mary asked.

"I want to discuss Claudia's role in this business."

I glanced over at her. She looked at Joe steadily with a firm set to her jaw. Her eyes showed absolutely no fear. Claudia was her father's daughter, all right. All spunk and guts.

"Now, Claudia, I know Doc thinks highly of you, and appreciates the gift of the diamonds you gave him last month. But I must say certain things have been bothering me lately. Things that have no logical explanation except that somebody's not operating on the up-and-up. And, frankly, I think that person could be you."

"Can you be more specific, *Detective* Brindelli?"

"Yes, I can. The first incident was Doc's mugging in his office parking lot. It was more than coincidence that he would be mugged just after you gave him those precious stones."

She half rose off the cushions, leaning toward him, her eyes boring into his.

"Listen, Brindelli, you better have some hard proof before you go accusing me of stealing my father's own gift back. You obviously didn't know Daddy and what a fine man he was underneath. He wanted to pay Doc back for getting him off that hellhole they call Deer Island. And he obviously wasn't petty enough to make vague accusations."

Bravo Claudia, I thought. I looked in Mary's direction and saw she was impressed as well. Joe remained passive. But I knew what he was doing. He was a pro at his job, and I had seen this routine before. He would get a suspect and grill him unmercifully, and watch the reaction in the suspect's face. Generally, he told me, hostility and vehement denial is an indication the suspect is falsely accused. But, of course, the suspect could be an artful deceiver. So we had the same old question regarding Claudia: was she a good guy or a bad guy?

"The next thing that happened is Doc's getting arrested in your warehouse," Joe said, pointing his finger in the direction of Fairhaven, just beyond the breakwater. "It was as if he were being followed. And then you show up at the perfect time and help him out."

His words caused me to freeze up. I couldn't believe what I was hearing. Joe was revealing the jail/bail incident. And then Mary would find out about—about—

"Ready about!" I shouted. "Hard a-lee!"

I put the tiller down and the boat swung hard to windward; the boom came flopping all over the place and we had to duck. And since we had been running before the wind, the centerboard had been drawn up. When the gusts caught us as Mary took hold of the mainsheet, the boat wallowed and heeled over dangerously. We recovered—I had Joe drop the centerboard cable immediately—but it gave Joe a chance to remember what we had agreed upon.

"I did not press charges against Doc for breaking into my warehouse," Claudia said in a cool voice. "I even gave him back the keys he dropped there." She turned and looked me in the eye, steady as the horizon itself. "So what else is bothering you about me?"

"It's this: you told Doc you found out he'd been arrested because you talked to Tony DeSilva. You claimed that you two are old friends and you call him often. Yet Tony talked with Doc later and said he never talked with you; he was at some church function in Brockton. Well?"

Claudia never missed a beat.

"I never told you that I talked to Tony. I called the parish house and some kid answered. He was the one who told me the cops had Doc. So I hurried on down there."

"The cops had Charlie?" said Mary. "Hey, I never heard about this part! Okay, Claudia, what exactly did you do to help Charlie out?"

"That's not important right now, Mary—" Joe began.

"Oh, it's not, eh?"

Well, there it was. The cat was coming out of the bag, as always. Suddenly the boat seemed awfully small for the four of us. I was considering grabbing the nearest life vest and jumping overboard.

One of Winslow Homer's most popular oils is called *Breezing Up*. It depicts an old salt at the helm of a catboat with three or four youngsters with him. The boat is scudding along in a fresh breeze. Perhaps Homer painted it during the happy summer he resided on Gloucester's Ten Pound Island—right in the middle of the harbor. Anyway, our party aboard the *Hatton* resembled the Homer painting in that there were four of us aboard a catboat, scudding along. But here the resemblance definitely faded. While the party in the painting were having the time of their lives, our dismal group was in the process of accusation, insinuation, and slander. Not good.

"Okay, one more point, and then I'll finish," said Joe. "I know I've opened some wounds here, but it must be done to get at the truth. The final event that seems a bit too coincidental to be genuine, Claudia, is the fact that when Doc boarded the freighter in the wee morning hours last night—when everyone should be off the vessel or at least asleep—who should surprise him but Sid Foster, the same guy who set up the mugging in the parking lot. Now, c'mon. Don't you think that's just too convenient? Remember, there were only two people who knew the plans: you and Mary. Well?"

"What are you saying?" asked Claudia.

"I'm saying that Doc—who's not the best at snooping

around, granted—is either being dogged by people who are watching him twenty-four hours a day, *or . . .*"

Here he paused, ostensibly to light a ciggie—but I knew better. I knew the pause was for dramatic effect. Joe would make a great courtroom prosecutor.

"Or—we have a spy somewhere. A spy for the other side, which appears to be the Larry Kelly side. And he raised you, Claudia. So if for no other reason than that, you're a contender."

Claudia folded her arms across her chest, then looked out at the ocean. "I could not stand Larry Kelly. Neither could my mother, God rest her soul, which is why she died early. No matter what any of you may think at this point, I have nothing to do with the remnants of his gang. Nothing."

"Okay, then. That leaves the only other person I can think of who is passing information."

"Who the hell could that be?" demanded Mary.

"Antero DeSilva."

Silence here. A lot of it. Then a chorus of derision directed at Joe. None of us could believe a man of the cloth would do such things.

"I know it's hard for all of you to believe," he responded. "But not so difficult for me. I know the priesthood from the inside out. Believe me, it's not the citadel of purity the public thinks it to be."

It was then that Mary grabbed me to break the tension.

"Hey, Charlie! We're almost back to the breakwater! What happened to our sail?"

"Personally, I'd just as soon be on the *Lusitania.* I've had enough of this pleasure cruise."

"Sorry," said Joe. "I guess I put a damper on things. But it had to be done; the more I can find out, the greater our chances, however slight, of recovering Celia Ibenez in one piece."

"How about the other reason?" Mary was scanning the shore-line now as we made ready to make the passage through the breakwater. "How about the treasure of Chris Ramos? Or has everybody written it off?"

"I pretty much have," said Claudia. "If it's not in the warehouse or aboard the ship in some hidden place, I don't see where it could be."

"Same here," I said.

Only one person had not answered.

"Joey?"

"Me? I personally think it's worth pursuing. Mainly because it breaks the tedium and heartbreak of everyday life."

"Whew!" I said. "We weren't expecting such a Sartrean response."

We returned to the marina, tied up the boat, unloaded our gear, and locked her up tight. We would leave the *Ella Hatton* in the Fairhaven marina for the time being. Mary was going to ride up to Boston with Joe to go shopping with Marty. But not before Joe dropped Claudia and me off in Sandwich where our cars were. I noticed Claudia was strangely silent. I guess I couldn't blame her after the grilling she had undergone. I told her to cheer up, that it was Joe's way of uncovering the facts.

"No, it's not that. I'm just thinking about what he said. About a spy. The more I think about it, the more I realize it must be true."

As we trudged up the pier, Mary drew me aside. "You're not planning on . . . hanging around with Claudia after Joey and I head up to Boston, are you?"

"Hell no! I'll just return to the cottage. I'm going fishing until I hear from the state cops if any charges will be filed against me."

"The thing is, Marty's been up in Boston alone all this time, and I still feel like I ditched her."

"Well, go on up, then. I'll take the car to Eastham and see you when you come back down. I bet Joe will be tied up full-time for a while though."

"Oh, my God!"

Everyone turned to see Claudia frozen on the pier, having dropped her duffel bag at her feet. She was staring wide-eyed straight in front of her. I followed her startled gaze but saw nothing.

"Claudia?" I approached her, grabbed her arm softly. "Claudia, you okay?"

She turned suddenly and stared at me. *"Kate!"*

"Eh?"

"Kate! Kate Winger. The woman I've been staying with in Cambridge, Doc! You know, the one the papers said I was having an affair with . . . Katherine Winger?"

"What about her? You're saying all that's untrue?"

"Of course it is! But what can you expect from the *Messenger-Express*, for God's sake. But that's not the point. The thing is this—and now I'm sure of it—"

"What then?"

"Doc, *she's the spy!*"

We were all around her now in a tight little group like a miniature football huddle. She sat down on the spot, right on her duffel bag, and proceeded to explain.

"I've been thinking about what you said out there, Joe. And it all made sense. Except I knew I wasn't the spy—and I couldn't believe Tony could possibly be. I mean, I've just known him too long. He's such a dear man. But you mentioned all those co-incidences that couldn't be coincidences, you know? And I knew you had a point. So I kept thinking, if there is a spy, who is it? Who do I tell everything to? The answer is Kate."

She turned to me. "Just before I went to meet you at your office, as I was changing my clothes and packing up the diamonds, Kate asked me where I was going. So I told her. No big deal, I thought then. Well, look what happened. Then, before I went on the boat with you and Mary, I told Kate about it, and our plans to board the ship in the night. And so on. She always knew everything."

"How long have you known her?" Joe asked.

"That's just it: not that long—maybe two months. See, when I decided to change my name and moved out of my old apartment, she offered to let me stay in her condo while I went looking around for one for myself."

"Where did you meet her?"

"At the Harborside Health Club. Thinking back on it, I realize now she kind of pushed the friendship. I didn't hear about her being a lesbian until later. And when I mentioned it, she didn't deny it. But she never bothered me about that. She was just real helpful. She said she wanted me to make this change in my life with as little trouble as possible."

"Ahhh . . ." Mary said. "And now we know why."

"Well, let's get moving," barked Joe, heading for his cruiser in double time. "This is the break we've been waiting for. We'll pick her up this afternoon when she returns from work. Claudia? Can you give us all the details about her schedule as we ride up there?"

So we drove up to Sandwich first, to get the other vehicles, all riding in Joe's cruiser. It wasn't more than a thirty-minute drive to pass over the Bourne Bridge and head up to Sandwich where we'd left our car and Claudia's Caddy.

As we said our good-byes I drew Joe aside and asked him what I could expect in the way of criminal charges from Sid Foster's death.

"Well, somebody's got to bring those charges up, first of all. Let's see how fast the lab can get back to us on the frog venom thing. As it now stands, I'm going to make the case that you are officially connected with the state bureau, and that you were investigating the possibility of a stolen vessel for that vessel's claimant, et cetera, et cetera. I doubt if Foster's higher-ups will surface over this. They didn't over Breitz's death. I'd say the party responsible is the one who was lurking behind that open porthole. Tell me, did you hear an air gun, or anything similar?"

"Nope. But I wasn't in a good position to listen. I wouldn't be surprised, though, if they used an air pistol—just like our friends a few years ago with the Moscow metal."

"Yeah, I agree. Well, hang in there and stay by the phone. But don't worry. I'll call tonight and tell you developments about Kate Winger."

"You taking Claudia with you?"

"If she's willing. She'll give us a better entrée."

So I watched Claudia's big boat follow Joe and Mary out of the lot, and I left in the other direction: for Eastham and the Breakers.

Later that evening, as the sun went down, I sat on the deck watching the gold and blue of the west, listening to the waves as the tide rolled in. After getting back that afternoon, I had run four miles up and down the beach, done some push-ups and sit-ups, taken two sauna baths with cold showers in between, gone up to the seafood market in Wellfleet and come back with fresh halibut, which I blackened on the grill and ate with French bread and fresh green beans with Parmesan cheese and sour cream on them. Then I sat thinking about the Ramos business. And thinking and thinking. I had the strange feeling that the solution was in my grasp, that I had an answer somewhere that was tucked away in my head but wouldn't surface. And as a man of fifty-plus, I also suspected that if I were half my age, I would have put the pieces together by now.

Oh, well . . .

The phone rang and I went into the kitchen to answer it, still looking at the sinking sun out the window. It was Joe.

"Doc, we went to wait for Kate Winger to show up at her Memorial Drive condo after work. Claudia let us in and kept us company. We waited until past seven-thirty but she didn't show."

"You think she's caught on that we're getting wise?"

"Possibly. Claudia says she's never home late from work. I guess we'll try waiting again tomorrow, and keep an eye out. Meantime, Smitty got another phone message at the Seamen's Bethel. The voice—the same guy who can't talk—told him that tomorrow night they would call and tell him where to drive to get Celia back."

"Is that promising?"

"I guess it's better than nothing. But the thing is, we traced the call . . . to Lowell."

"*Lowell?* You kidding? That's entirely the wrong direction."

"We think so, too. Don't you get it?"

I thought for a few seconds, then admitted it was lost on me.

"Well, remember what happened at Flynn's? We traced the call to there and thought we'd outfoxed them. So we set up an ambush there . . ."

"Yeah, and walked into an ambush ourselves."

"Right. Point being: these guys know how to use the phone to set us up. Here, they definitely assume the call will be traced.

What we figure is, they're operating around here, just like Smitty says. They drove up to Lowell to make the call, thinking that we'd be drawn up there."

"In short, you think the call is a ruse."

"Definitely. So we're staying put down here, and alerting the locals up in Lowell to be on the lookout just in case."

"Anything you want me to do?"

"Yeah. It's the main reason for my call. Leave the cottage, Doc. Leave it now. Don't wait."

"What? Why the hell should I—"

"Just do it. Whether Kate's the spy or not, these guys seem to know everything almost before it happens. They probably know about your summer residence, and you're as high on their list as Smitty himself. Get out and get out fast. Go to a convenient motel, but not by a direct route. Make sure you're not being followed. After you check in, call me here at home."

"You're not kidding, are you?"

"Hell, no. And we've gone to the mattresses here, too. The gals ain't going out unescorted, and all the doors are locked up tight. This bunch is nothing to fuck around with. Your Beretta is here. Do you have any firepower down there?"

"Yep. Shotgun and a 380."

"Take 'em both with you. Keep the scattergun loaded in the car with you, not in the trunk. Carry the 380 on your person. You can do it, you know. You've got a permit to carry and a state badge. Take no chances. *Arrivederla.*"

I went back out onto the deck. The sky now looked all wrong. In the space of about three minutes, it had grown cold and threatening. I scanned the beach and the grassy sand dunes all around the place. Vacant. At least I thought they were. I went back inside, locking the door behind me, and gathered up enough stuff for a three-day stay. On my way out I had a duffel slung over one shoulder and binoculars over the other. The Remington 20-gauge pump was in my left hand. Stainless barrel, synthetic stock—it was waterproof. I had two boxes of shells: number four pellets and number one buckshot. The pump shotgun had an extended magazine that would hold eight rounds. I fed them in, alternating fours and ones. The Taurus 380 auto had two magazines, each holding thirteen rounds. It was riding on my right hip, the spare magazine in my pants pocket. I locked the front door behind me and went to the car.

"Well, this is it, Hotshot," I murmured to myself. "You've been scratching around the surface of this rough stuff, but now it's really here."

I zoomed out of the drive and headed to Chatham. There I drove around town for a few blocks, then doubled back to Route 6. Couldn't see anybody behind me—at first, that is— but after a few miles, I noticed a motorcycle that seemed to be staying with me, three or four cars behind. I exited at Falmouth, drove into town, and did the same routine of cruising around. Then I went back onto Route 6. This time, I saw no motorcycle. But then again, it was dark out by now.

Confident I was alone, I headed for the Bourne Bridge. I remembered some motels right near the canal. At the rotary I doubled back and took the first exit. There it was, a Best Western motel with a bar called the Canal Club Lounge attached to it. I pulled into the lot and checked into a deluxe suite on the canal side, overlooking the water and the huge steel bridge that spanned it. I paid in cash for two nights and gave a false name, just in case interested parties came looking for me.

I went into my rooms, then out onto the stone terrace. The bridge was all lit up with lights placed along the steel beams, like a fallen Christmas tree. It sure was big.

After all, Sid had told me the "Big Boss" was just over the big bridge. Well, I was looking at the biggest bridge around.

I went into the bar and ordered a gin and tonic, called Joe on the pay phone and reported in, and spoke to Mary briefly, telling her I was all right and I would stay put until ordered otherwise.

Then I took a deep breath, praying I was doing the right thing, and called Claudia's number in Cambridge.

30

"But I don't want breakfast, Doc. I wanted dinner. I wanted dinner last night with you."

"How's that?"

"Dammit, I wish you'd invited me out here last night instead of this morning. When you called, I just . . . got so excited . . ."

Claudia Ramos sat in the booth across from me in the motel restaurant. From the booth we could look out the window at the canal and the Bourne Bridge. And the parking lot. I was looking at an all-black motorcycle that had not been there when we sat down. How and when it had arrived, I had not the faintest idea. It had appeared like magic. Like an apparition.

I had ordered her breakfast, but she wasn't eating it. She played with her cold juice glass, running her pretty fingers up and down it, and looking at her plate of French toast. Then she looked up at me, her dark eyes going right through me. God, she was gorgeous.

"Well?"

"Well what?" she said. Pout.

"Aren't you going to eat anything? We might have a big day ahead of us."

She stared blankly at the tablecloth, then put her cool hand on my forearm, rubbing it ever so gently. "We could have had a great night behind us, too. I just can't help thinking about that."

Then she looked up at me again. I almost wilted, but I fought it.

The look said: *There's still time, dummy. We could get out of this booth, walk right back to your suite, get naked and jump in the Jacuzzi and . . . just see what happens.*

"Claudia, as gorgeous and desirable as you are, it would not

235

have been a good night. I would be clumsy and disappointing to you. I would feel terrified and guilty every second. I would regret it later, resent you for it—and Mary would find out."

She slumped down and sighed, drumming her long fingernails on the white tablecloth and looking out at the canal. The superstructure and funnel of a large cargo ship was sliding past. We couldn't see the hull because of the bluff.

"Doc?"

"What?"

"Do you feel any attraction for me?"

"Oh, shut up. You know I do."

"Don't you see my disappointment? Last night at nine you call me, saying you're at a motel and you want me to drive down."

"But I meant tomorrow. That is, today. Not then."

"I know—but I wanted so much to come down anyway. I could have been ready in a wink."

"Joe and Mary know where I'm staying."

"So. I would have chanced it."

"Fine for you to say; you've got nothing to lose. By the way, Joe knows you spent the night at the cottage last week."

"Really? He didn't act like he knew."

"I didn't tell him about your midnight visit."

"What would happen if Mary found out?"

"She would kill me. Then divorce me."

"But you didn't do anything . . . except feel my bare buns."

She flashed me a warm smile.

I glanced away, then picked up my coffee cup only to see my hand tremble in front of my face. I put it down.

"Doc? I don't want to take you away from her. I think Mary's great, and I know she loves you. I just want you for a while. A few stolen nights is all. Just for a fling . . . No risk involved."

I looked down at my finished plate. "Nope. Can't be done."

"Why not? You said you liked me."

"Because nothing is free. There would be a price to pay that's too high."

"How do you know?"

"Because I've got twenty-plus years on you, for one thing.

Tell me, do most people your age feel the way you do? Just good times for the short haul?"

"I think so," she said vaguely, as if in a dream, her gaze wandering. "I mean, the short haul may be all we have. We've got to live life while we can."

"That's true, but you might be trading the long term for the short haul."

She threw her folded napkin on the table, as if signaling an end to the discussion, and said, "So why did I come down here, then?"

"I want to learn a little more about this friend of your dad's who lived along the canal bank many years ago."

"Ivan? I only met him twice, I think. I was real little, so the memory is faint. And this was just his summer place. I think he lived in Jamaica Plain, or Dorchester, Mattapan . . . somewhere like that. He was in politics in one of those towns. A selectman or something. Actually, I think Dad said he was more powerful than people thought. Worked his way up through the rank and file until he was sort of a big shot behind the scenes . . . Know what I'm saying?"

"Oh, certainly. Massachusetts politics never changes."

"Right. And maybe Ivan was even—you know—connected."

"Oh, really? Hmmmm, that's interesting. Did he use this position of power to give your dad any breaks? Any contracts?"

Claudia shrugged. "Wouldn't surprise me. But, like I said, he used to sit on his porch and smoke cigars—or was it those strong Turkish cigarettes?—and watch the canal. Dad would call him from Southie when one of the tugs pulled out, and Ivan would watch for it—see if it was on time. Stuff like that. If the boat didn't show, or was real late, he would call the office and let Dad know."

"But you said Southie."

"Right. That's where the office was."

"Who are we talking about here? Chris or Larry Kelly?"

"Larry. My dad."

"You told me Chris was your dad."

"Yeah, my real dad. In both senses, too. But Chris is Daddy. Larry Kelly I call Dad."

"So this Ivan guy was friends with Larry, not Chris."

"Oh, yeah, right. As a matter of fact, Doc, Ivan hated Chris.
They never got along."

These words kept echoing in my head as I stared out at the
big bridge. With increasing swiftness, the pieces of the puzzle
floated into place.

"He hated Chris? Nobody I ever heard of hated Chris Ramos.
Why did he hate him?"

She shrugged. "I think I might have heard it was over a
woman. But hey, that was so long ago, Doc, I really—"

"Did he hate Chris enough to help frame him? To send him to
prison for much longer than he deserved? To use his political influence to get him sent to Deer Island?"

She gripped the edge of the table and stared at me.

"Claudia, I think I'm finally piecing together what happened
about twenty years ago. Okay: In the mid-seventies, somewhere in there, the scrap metal business goes downhill. Both
Larry and Chris are hurting. SEAMATT's in trouble. Larry begins to smuggle drugs to get the needed extra cash to stay afloat.
Chris follows his lead, but reluctantly. Chris's charisma and
charm, which helped him found the company and win so many
friends, are his undoing, because he seduces your mom, and
maybe has a fling as you call it—see about flings, Claudia?—
has a fling with some woman who this Ivan is in love with. So
there you have it; from that point on, the die is cast. Larry, who's
been buddies with this political honcho, Ivan, tells him about
his suspicions. Ivan says, Funny thing, I think the same thing
happened to me. . . . Bingo, they turn on Chris, arrange for him
to be caught with a lot of contraband, and be convicted and sentenced. You follow so far?"

"Yes . . . Oh God, yes . . . You're right, Doc. Go on."

"Well, Chris is sent off to prison. Rumor has it that he has a
fortune stashed away somewhere. Fine, this gives Larry and
Ivan plenty of time to find it. But search as they might, they
have no luck. Yet they're convinced Chris has it safe somewhere. But he won't tell them. Maybe they try to make a deal:
tell Chris if he spills about the loot, they'll try to get him out
early, something like that. But Chris Ramos, the tough Portuguese

who worked his way up from scratch, isn't about to cave in. So what happens next? Larry and Ivan, knowing he'll get out within six or seven years, put on more pressure. Somehow, using Ivan's political muscle—and maybe a promise of a cut of the loot to helpful parties—they get Chris transferred over to the infamous Deer Island, hell on earth, and wait for him to cave."

She buried her face in her hands. I saw her shoulders shaking as she sobbed. Then I looked around the restaurant and realized some of the patrons were staring at us. I quickly signed the check and put down my room number, then took her by the arm and we walked out to the parking lot. She held on to me for a few minutes until she pulled herself together.

We walked out across the grass and to the edge of the bluff and sat down where we could look down at the canal. Finally she wiped her eyes.

"Go on, Doc. Finish it. I know it's true now. Every bit of it. I've been trying to make sense of it all for the past fifteen years. It's never made sense—until now."

"There's not much more, kid, You know the rest as well as I. You remember that hijacking of the prison van in ninety-two? Well, Chris claimed it was engineered by people who wanted to kidnap him so they could force him to lead them to the treasure. At the time, of course, everybody, including me, thought he was nuts. Then Larry Kelly died. That changed the picture a bit. Maybe it gave Chris the courage and hope to hold on longer, even inside Deer Island. I don't know much about Ivan, but you said he got sick."

She nodded. "He got TB and moved away. I think to Florida to get the sun."

Right then another bell went off in my head. I remembered Smitty's remark about Jake Breitz's boss. But he couldn't remember the last name. So I asked her if she could.

"Ipassis. Ivan Ipassis."

"That's it! That's the name Smitty couldn't remember. Smitty claims he moved to Florida, too."

"Yep," she murmured, looking down at the water. She had grim determination in her dark eyes. I knew she had Chris's guts and courage in her. "And until now I was sure he'd died. You think he's still alive?"

"Before he died, Sid Foster told me his boss lived 'right over the big bridge.' What bigger bridge is there but this one anywhere around here?"

Claudia sat up straight now, still wiping her eyes. "Then what made him come up here again?"

"He heard about Chris's death. But back to the story for a bit. Here's your father, in a hellhole. Some people who know him start making inquiries and writing letters on his behalf. They're pretty sure he's been unfairly treated. Maybe by some unseen power who held a grudge. One of those is me. Another is Tony DeSilva. When Chris knows he's dying, he calls both of us to his bedside—"

"And Smitty too, you said."

"Yep, and Smitty, too. It wouldn't take long at all, if Ivan were still alive, for the local news to get to him down in Florida via one of the surviving members of the smuggling ring Larry started and Ivan assisted in."

"How are you sure he was part of the smuggling?"

"C'mon, do you really think all Ivan did was watch this canal for Larry to make sure his boats were running on schedule?"

"Well . . ."

"As soon as you said that, I thought it was a little strange. No: Ivan was eyes and ears for the ring—and he had the political clout to ensure that Kelly would get off lightly if he got caught—"

"And Chris would get clobbered if *he* got caught—"

"Exactly. So, Chris is dead. Larry's dead. Ivan Ipassis figures he's the one left to get the loot, wherever the hell it's hidden. Somehow he hears about Ramos's last-minute deathbed visitors. So he returns here and begins to get the old gang together . . ."

"And meanwhile, Smitty, Daddy's old-time smuggling partner, comes back too."

"Sure he does; he's one of the deathbed visitors."

"But he . . . Daddy never told me . . ."

"No, and for good reason. You know how many people have been killed so far? Know how they died?"

She nodded slowly, tears again filling up her pretty eyes.

"Now, let me ask you one more question, Claudia. What did Ivan Ipassis's voice sound like?"

She shrugged. "Kind of gruff. He smoked all the time. Those Turkish cigarettes—he was from Turkey, or Syria or Greece or somewhere like that—and his voice was raw."

"Raw, yes, but not heavily damaged? Like his vocal cords were gone? Like he was always whispering?"

She slowly shook her head. "No. Not that bad."

"Well, shit, then. Maybe he's not the one after all. Maybe it's somebody else, and Ipassis did die. Did he cough a lot?"

"Yes. And the tuberculosis—"

Silence then.

"The tuberculosis what?"

She slowly stood up, turned, and looked at me.

"Doc. It all fits now."

"What?"

"I remember Dad telling me. He said, 'Honey, Ivan's got TB, but it's not the usual kind.' "

"Really?"

"Uh-huh. He said, 'He's been diagnosed with tuberculosis of *the throat*.' "

31

"CAN YOU USE A GUN?" I ASKED HER.

"A little. I took a pistol course a few years ago up in New Hampshire, at a camp."

"How about a shotgun?"

"Uh-huh. We did some clay pigeon shooting there too."

"What kind of camp was this?"

"Sort of like Outward Bound, but it was designed especially for people who want to be prepared to defend themselves."

"Well, good for you. That's a better answer than taking our guns away from us. Follow me."

We went to the car, and I opened the back door, lifted up a beach towel, and showed her the shotgun on the backseat.

"It's loaded, with a round in the chamber. Those are high brass rounds in there with a lot of punch. Know what I mean?"

"You mean it'll kick when I fire it."

"Right. Throw it to your shoulder and flick off this safety button, here. You know how to work a pump gun?"

She nodded. I put the towel back and she got in. From under the seat I extracted the little 380 and stuck it in my belt holster.

"Do you have any idea where Ivan's cottage is?"

"Both times I met him was at the cottage. I know it's real close by. Do you really think he still owns it?"

"It's all we've got. He may have sold it. But if he didn't, he could have put the deed in another name if he was still connected, as you say. Let's try to find it first, then hang out in the bushes and watch to see who comes and goes. Okay?"

"Fine with me. Let's try this road by the motel first. I know it's one of the nearby ones."

We got in my car and started off. I cruised around the parking lot and stopped, rolled down my window, and studied the asphalt.

"What's going on?" she asked.

"Remember that black motorcycle that was here? So black you couldn't even see a brand name on it?"

"No."

"Never mind."

We drove down the road the motel was on, past a sporting goods store and a small grocery, then wound down toward the water. Soon we were passing small cabins and trailers set on blocks. Claudia grew agitated, swinging her head this way and that, sinking down low in the seat to scan up the hillsides. We finally stopped at a gravel parking area not far from the water's edge. She got out to look up the canal.

"Let's try the next road over."

So we backtracked and took the next one. As we passed a row of fuel tanks on a rack, she got excited.

"This is it! I remember those tanks. Only they were painted red then, not silver. Keep going . . . There, now bear left."

We entered a wooded area so dense the trees hung over the road and we drove through a narrow tunnel of trees. I looked at her face; it had an expression of intense anticipation. We wound down again on the curving road and were now going parallel to the water.

"There!" she yelled, and pointed up to her left past me, almost sticking me in the eye with her fingernail.

"Shhhh! Okay, hush now. And don't point or stare. We're just going to drive by, okay? Get a good look. A real good look and remember what you see."

It was a white ranch-style house with two cars in the drive. White planks or siding, a small front stoop with an aluminum awning and wrought-iron railings, a picture window with the curtains closed, and a carport on the far side. As we went past, I noticed the top of the carport was a terrace with aluminum beach chairs on it. The terrace was empty.

"Doc, there's Katherine's car!"

She was on my side of the car, leaning over me, pointing. I pushed her back to her side and told her to sit down. We passed by and kept going. We drove on for almost a quarter of a mile, then turned around. There were very few houses, and they were widely scattered.

"You sure it was Kate's car?"

"Positive. White Nissan Altima."

"There are tons of those around."

"Not with a Radcliffe sticker and a pink triangle on the back bumper."

"So your hunch was right."

"What do we do now? Call your brother-in-law?"

"Uh-huh. But not just yet. I want to get around behind the

house and watch it for a while. See who comes and goes. Then maybe we can figure out what's going on and who's inside."

We drove on past again, and it proved to be a mistake. Claudia, in the passenger seat, leaned her head fully out the window as we went past, scanning the place. Just then, I saw a woman on the terrace turn and look, then snap her head around fast and hurry through the screen door into the house.

"Uh-oh, she saw me!"

"Did she recognize you?"

"I think so."

"I think not; you have your sunglasses on."

"Doc, I think she knows we're here."

I kept driving, and we wound our way back up the bluff.

"Hey, Doc: there's a motorcycle behind us."

I looked in the mirror and saw the bike. Where the hell had it come from so fast?

"He's following us," I said. "I'm going to pull off on a side road and let him by."

I did this, and the black bike swept on by, but the rider looked back at us. He was also dressed in black, with a black full-face helmet on.

"You ever see him before?" I asked.

"Not that I remember."

"Well, I have. Listen: if Kate recognized you, we could be running out of time."

"What should we do now?"

"Go back to the house and watch it."

"Shouldn't you call Joe?"

"If we get time. But if the whistle's been blown, they may take Celia into a car and go somewhere else. Then we'll be back to first base."

"How can we follow them if we're on foot?"

"We won't follow them; we'll intercept them."

I swung the car around fast and went back down the hill.

"You're going past the house *again*?"

"Nope. I'm looking for a road just above the house, or someplace to hide the car and sneak up on foot."

I took a gravel road to the left that I judged would take us at least partway into the woods above Ivan's cottage. We drove in as far as we could and stopped where the road branched into two driveways. I pulled in between two small trees so as not to block anybody, then got out. We walked fast up both driveways to see if we could get to a phone, but both cottages were vacant and locked.

"Take the shotgun. Remember, it's loaded."

She got it from the backseat; we shut and locked the car, and walked into the woods, hunched over low and dodging branches.

"Can you recognize the place from the rear?" I asked her.

"As well as you can, I guess."

Within ten minutes we had worked our way low enough down the hill so we could see occasional shingled roofs below us. I didn't know if the vast space between the houses was to our advantage or not. After another hundred yards we saw the distinct terrace affixed to the green-shingled roof below us. We half slid down the slope until we were within sixty yards or so of the house. I glassed the place. Kate's Nissan was still in the drive; its back end was visible just past the terrace, which was now empty again.

We kept sliding downhill until I could see a big window through the trees. The kitchen light was on, and I could see the white refrigerator against a pine-paneled wall. Soon an old white-haired man with stooped posture shambled past the window. I could see a thin cigar dangling from the corner of his mouth. Ivan Ipassis. The Man Who Whispered. The man who sent Christos Ramos to Deer Island . . .

I handed the glasses to Claudia. "Recognize him?"

"That's him all right. The slimy son of a bitch!"

Next I tried the window at the other end. Usually the bedrooms are on the opposite side from the kitchen. But the blinds were drawn; I had no idea who was in there. Back to the kitchen. A woman with light brown hair came in carrying a tray with a glass and dishes on it. It was Kate Winger; I recognized her from the funeral. This was promising; she had taken food to someone in the bedroom. I was almost positive that person was Celia Ibenez. I handed the glasses to Claudia again.

"That's her, Doc. Jesus, how did she get mixed up in all this?"

"She was in it before she met you, Claudia. That's *why* she met you."

"What happens now?"

"What happens now is this: you take the keys and sneak back to the car. Drive to the nearest phone and call nine-one-one. Say you've got information on a kidnap victim and want to speak with anyone from the state Bureau of Public Safety. Got it?"

"Yep. State Bureau of Public Safety."

"And listen: make sure they understand this is an emergency. Life and death. Otherwise they'll give you the run-around. Now off you go."

She took the keys and scooted, leaving the shotgun on the leaves and dirt next to me. I continued to glass the house. If they came out alone, fine. But if they had Celia with them, I was going to charge down there and hold them with the shotgun until help came.

Then I heard a sliding noise behind me. Before I could turn my head to look, a huge weight fell on top of me. My face was shoved hard into the leaves and dirt. I couldn't breathe. Then I felt a sting on the back of my neck; a tremendous hot jolt shot through me, and I couldn't move.

I opened my eyes and saw the leaves and dirt. I knew something had gone terribly wrong—but, thank God, Claudia had gone for help. If I could just stall them until the police got here . . .

"Stand up."

I tried, but couldn't. Whoever was standing over me kicked me until the effects of the stun gun wore off. A very strong and big arm grabbed me around the waist and yanked me upright. A big paw patted me down and found the small automatic. Took it.

"Turn around."

I did, and was looking into a familiar face. The last time I had seen it was in the back room at Flynn's waterfront tavern in Southie. The man with this face had been beating the shit out of my brother-in-law. Gary Walsh stood there, tucking my auto-

matic into his pants pocket. Then he picked up the Remington
and pointed it at my chest.

He was scary enough. But the person I saw with him scared
me even more.

It was poor Claudia, a big bruise on her pretty face. Hands
fastened behind her back. Gag around her mouth. And tears in
her eyes. This meant we were both done for. I knew what she
would have said to me if she could talk. She would have said,
"I'm sorry."

32

WALSH WALKED BEHIND US WITH THE SCATTERGUN AS WE
went down the hill toward the house. I tried to piece together
what had happened in the last ten minutes. It was clear now that
Walsh was the motorcyclist. He'd been following me from our
cottage in Eastham all the way to the motel. He'd heard about
the cottage from Kate Winger, who was told everything by
Claudia and then passed it on to Ipassis.

In short, they'd been expecting us. And now I was certain
that Kate's appearance on the terrace had been deliberate—bait
to lure us into this trap. I thought of the dead people in the house
on Rivet Street and my knees went all shaky. I felt sorry especially for Claudia, young, smart, rich, and beautiful, who was
not going to live a full life.

And then I thought about Mary and the kids—and how goddamn stupid I was not to call Joe first.

We were three feet from the back door. I saw the old man
come toward it. I swear he was smiling.

And then I heard a noise. It was a slap. Gary Walsh slapping

Claudia around. I turned and faced them, and was surprised at what I saw.

Walsh was hunched over holding his neck; his huge hand was wrapped around it, his ugly mouth opened in a painful grimace. Straightening up, he flung his hand from his neck, wiped the wound with his other sleeve, and resumed standing, holding the shotgun level at his hip.

We went inside when the old man opened the door. I smelled his horrific breath, and heard him speak in that almost silent gasp: "Ah! Dr. Adams. Finally you come!"

It wasn't until Walsh came in and staggered toward the kitchen counter, unsure of his legs for a half second, that I had any hope.

"Is Celia Ibenez here?" I asked, trying with all my might to sound confident. "You should know that the police have ID'd you and are on their way now."

"She's not here. You are here, with my good friend Claudia. Dear, how are you?"

Ipassis went past me to Claudia, a big smile on his face as false as a government promise. When he got within range, she tried to kick him; it was all she could do. Then Ipassis showed his true colors, getting behind her and shoving her roughly against the refrigerator. I was watching Walsh out of the corner of my eye. He was standing straight up now, holding the shotgun level. But his eyes had a funny look. And just then I saw something else, just outside my field of vision: a long black shape disappearing behind the open back door.

Then Kate Winger came into the kitchen, looking at Claudia with no emotion whatsoever.

"Take her in back," rasped Ipassis. "Put her in the other bedroom. We'll leave in a few minutes."

We heard a soft thump behind us and turned to see Walsh now sitting on the floor, breathing heavily.

"What's the matter with you?" demanded Winger.

"I'm tired."

"Well, get up!" she barked, and started walking toward the hallway door, pushing Claudia in front of her.

Then another sound came from behind me, a pneumatic hiss,

and I saw the back of Winger's blouse punch in like a collapsing tent.

"Shit! Oh shit!" she screamed, and turned and came my way, thinking I had done it. She tried to hit me—I guess she assumed I was tied like Claudia. But I wasn't. My arms were free; I hit her hard just beneath the sternum and she bent way over, unable to straighten up or get a breath.

"Shoot him!" whispered Ipassis, but Gary wasn't listening; he was staring at the floor, inches away, with a confused look on his putty boxer's face, the shotgun lying across his lap. I sprang over and grabbed it.

Just as I did this, a black figure leapt into the room, helmet and all. He had a commando knife in his brown hand, a double-edged dagger. He held his other hand up to me in some sort of greeting, then plunged into the hallway, headed for the back bedroom.

Ipassis now stood in the middle of the kitchen, rage in his tiny gray eyes. Claudia came back into the kitchen; the cyclist had cut her bonds. She took the shotgun from me.

"Go follow him, Doc—he may need help with Celia—"

I went down the hallway and met the mystery man, who was holding Celia Ibenez gently, walking her up the hallway. They had to step over Kate Winger's writhing form before coming into the kitchen. Claudia had Ipassis against the far counter, holding the scattergun directly in the center of his chest.

"You sent Chris to Deer Island, didn't you?" she said through her teeth. The old man tried his fake smile again. No go. He tried to talk nice to her, like he'd missed her all these years. No go.

"Just say you're sorry," she demanded, her whole body shaking with rage. I was getting a bad feeling then.

"Claudia, don't do anything rash . . ." I managed to say.

Just before the gun went off.

An explosion that shook the room. Even Gary Walsh opened his confused eyes for a second. Before closing them again. Forever.

Ipassis was thrown back over the counter momentarily, then oozed back down, leaving a wet red trail on the white cabinets as wide as his body used to be. He half sat on the floor for a second, then swayed over and collapsed in a heap, piles of bloody sponges and shattered bones where his chest and neck had been.

I looked around. The motorcyclist was standing behind me, a pistol in his hand now. I realized it was an air pistol. And I knew exactly what was in there, too. Kate Winger was on her back, fighting for air. Celia Ibenez had collapsed on the floor, sobbing, no doubt from exhaustion, horror, and final relief. I went over to Walsh and retrieved my 380 and the spare magazine. Not much fight in him now, I thought. Behind me I heard Claudia murmuring something to the guy in black leather. When I turned around, she had her hand outstretched to me. In it were my car keys. I took them, and she came even closer.

"I'm trusting you to keep Celia safe until the police come," she said. "I need to get out of here." She flicked her head in the direction of the cyclist. "I'm going with him."

I found myself saying, "Good luck," before I knew it.

The two walked to the back door, but then she came running back.

"One more thing, Doc."

She put her arms around me and gave me the biggest kiss of all. Then she was crying.

"Oh God . . . I wish you were going with me. . . . I'll never forget you . . ."

Then they were gone. I heard the cycle rev up, then zoom away up the hill.

My first duty was to Celia. I led her gently into the living room and sat with her on the sofa until she calmed down somewhat. I knew I had to make the call; I just wasn't in a big rush. I did want Claudia to have enough time to make it back to the parking lot, jump in that new blue Caddy, and get a good start.

33

ALL I CAN SAY IS, IT'S A GOOD THING CELIA IBENEZ WAS THERE to vouch for me. Otherwise they would have found me there with my shotgun and three dead bodies. They grilled us for hours, but our story held because it was the truth.

No, I didn't know who the motorcyclist was. Never saw him before, never saw his face clearly. Yes, he was black—probably one of the Cape Verdeans whom Chris Ramos had helped out years ago. No, I had no idea where Claudia Ramos went. Probably far away, since she pulled the trigger. But it was not premeditated murder—it was clearly a crime of passion.

Joe and his buddies on the state force were no less than ecstatic the way it all turned out. They had Celia back in one piece—something they clearly had not expected. Most important of all, Gary Walsh was dead. Tommy Mahoney, the young officer gunned down in the alley behind Flynn's, was avenged.

Some other interesting things came to light as well. It turned out that Ipassis had been presumed dead, and had been living under an assumed name on Amelia Island, Florida, right near Jacksonville, for the past nine years. The police, FBI, and DEA uncovered all sorts of bad stuff he'd been into. His death was thought to cripple the organization badly. Good news. Another thing, he had a niece who was involved: Kate Winger.

They found Claudia's Cadillac at Logan Airport the afternoon after the showdown at the Ipassis cottage. Where she flew away to was anybody's guess. My choice was Portugal.

Smitty was reunited with Celia and her lovely little daughter. He continued to lay claim to the *Esmeralda*, and even had the documentation to prove it. But as Claudia had told me, the papers were probably forged—you can still buy anything you need along that line in Panama. He and his crew spent most of their time aboard that ship, refitting her for more trading voyages to the Caribbean and back, and maybe points further south.

As for the rest of us, we were all well and glad this business was behind us. But all we had to show for it was the ring of keys.

Which is why Joe called me up the next Saturday afternoon and asked me to take him back to Chris's warehouse down on the waterfront in Fairhaven.

So there we stood in the semidarkness, right in front of that row of new metal gym lockers.

"You're out of your mind," I told him. "That beating you got from the late Gary Walsh has rattled your gray matter."

"Perhaps. But I bet the gin has done worse damage over the years."

"You know? You may have a point. Are we here legally?"

"Yes. I've done all the necessary paperwork. And you know what? Your friend Brady Coyne—"

"—*former* friend—"

"—former friend Brady Coyne was correct about the deathbed gift. And with Claudia gone, who's the only remaining heir and contestant . . . You just might own this place."

"Yeah, and the freighter, if I can ever prove it."

"You ask me, don't go after the freighter. You don't want that frog juice under your skin."

"Whew! No kidding."

He held up the key ring, jingling it ever so slightly.

"Now, listen, we know the Schlage key works, right?"

I nodded.

"And we know the brass admiralty key fits the *Esmeralda*'s officers' deck. Correct?"

I nodded again.

"Finally, we know that these two little lever keys fit those two lockers, and they also work."

"Right. So?"

"So. Why? Why the hell would Chris Ramos, as clever as he was, leave these two little keys on the ring that he so carefully hid behind the Station of the Cross in his beloved church?"

"I have no idea."

"Neither do I. But I know it was deliberate. Now, Jeremiah Chubb invented the lever lock two hundred years ago. To this day, it's still almost impossible to pick. That's because the entire cylinder rotates with the key. That's why safe deposit box keys are still of this type. The cheap-looking, flat keys."

"Good, you figure it out. We've already looked inside all the lockers. I'd like to go to lunch."

He felt around the innards of lockers 106 and 107 again. Suddenly I heard a clank. Joe shouted, "Aha!"

I went over and looked inside. He was holding the edge of the shelf inside locker 106.

"Watch."

He moved the hanger bar underneath the shelf a half inch or so to the left, then raised the edge of the shelf upward. It went up about five inches, making a clank as it hit the top.

"So? The shelf's loose," I said.

"Nope. Not loose. Look: if I don't move this bar over, it stays put. Just where you'd want it to put your shaving kit and car keys, right? But when I slide the bar over . . . See? It goes up. And notice, too, it's not hinged from the back panel of the locker. See the angle when I raise it? It's connected to something else behind the locker. Look: see those two metal slats that run through the locker wall? Hah! They're connected to . . . something . . ."

"Hey, that reminds me—" I said, walking back to the first locker and opening it. Not there. I kept opening the lockers and looking until I drew the curiously shaped piece of one-by-two board out of locker 104. Joe took one look at it and went apeshit.

"Yes! This has to be it! Doc, we're on the verge! We're on the verge of the greatest treasure since the *Whydah*!"

"*Shhhhh!* Not so loud, guy. We'll have the whole waterfront crowd down here in a minute!"

"Follow me, sport."

I followed him back to locker 106. He jerked the rod over, lifted the shelf up, and inserted the stick, notch end down on the bar. Its blunt end rested underneath the raised-up metal shelf, keeping it raised. It was a good start, and I had to agree that it seemed that the wooden stick was fashioned exactly for that purpose.

Thing was, after another forty minutes of probing, tugging, pushing, tapping, and scratching our heads, we were no closer to finding the stash than ever. The shelf raised up when the bar was moved, and stayed in the raised position when the wooden stick was inserted under it. Big deal.

In the dim light I looked over at Joe, who was sweating with heat and frustration. I suggested we go take a lunch break.

We went back to that sub shop in South New Bedford—the one with Portuguese written all over the front. We ordered two large linguiça subs with lettuce, hot peppers, tomatoes, and their special sauce. These were giant subs: over a foot long and five inches wide. Weighed as much as an engine block.

We spent almost an hour in that cozy little store, attacking the subs—the hot linguiça sausage was delicious—and chugging two huge cups of Coke and ice. Went through six napkins apiece.

When we were almost finished—in more ways than one, judging by the way my stomach felt—Joe suddenly slammed his big palm down on the Formica. I turned to see everybody in the store—maybe fifteen people—staring at us. He leaned over close and whispered: "I got it. The shelf isn't the opening mechanism."

"It isn't?"

"Nope. It's the bolt release."

"Bolt release?"

"Yep. Listen, remember what I been telling you about locks of any kind: it's the bolt that opens the door, not the key. The key merely allows the bolt to move. Got it?"

"Got it."

"So, the clanking sound when the shelf is lifted? I thought at first it was the bolt itself. That's why I busted my ass for almost an hour trying to find any panel that opened. No luck, and now I know why. We've only solved half the puzzle. Now we must find the bolt. Find the bolt and how to slide it. See?"

I nodded, and waddled out of the place behind Joe, burping all the way.

Back in the warehouse again. I told Joe I really hoped nobody saw us come in again through the back way. He shook his head, telling me we had no worries—we had legal clearance.

"Now, if my reasoning is correct, the bolt should be behind the lockers, running horizontally."

"There's a fire extinguisher on the wall around the corner."

He turned and scowled at me.

"So? You smell smoke? There a fire in here or something? Are you listening to what I—"

"Just thought I'd mention it. I showed you the trapdoor when we first arrived; you saw how well Chris could conceal things."

He advanced to me slowly—menacingly, it seemed.

"So what about this fire extinguisher? Why should I care?"

"When I tried to pull it off the wall, it wouldn't budge. I didn't pay it any mind at the time, but think about it. Aren't fire extinguishers supposed to be easy to grab?"

"Excellent, Doc. Excellent. Lead the way, please . . ."

We walked around the corner to the big brass can on the wall. Joe pulled at it. No motion whatsoever. He took out his pocket flashlight and had a look.

"No wonder. Look: it's been wired to the wall bracket. Now why is that, do you suppose?"

"Maybe it's how the bolt is withdrawn."

Joe went around and grabbed the extinguisher, then pulled back in a quick jerk, using all his 230 pounds. No motion.

But we both heard a muted *thunk* deep inside the wall behind the lockers.

We stood there in the dark, staring at each other. He then shined his light at the wall bracket that held the extinguisher. There were big hex-head bolts holding it to the plaster wall.

"I don't see how we can get this thing to move without removing those bolts, Doc. Shit, I wish we had a socket wrench set with us."

"Give me one of your cards."

He did, and I swept it between the wooden bracket plate and the wall. The card passed right underneath the bolt heads. Same on the other side.

"Well I'll be damned—they're fake!"

"Listen: I'll go raise the shelf and put the stick in place, then you pull on this, okay?"

He nodded. When everything was in place, I told him to pull. Pull he did, and the extinguisher and bracket came right off the wall, sliding in front of three massive steel rods that were perfectly machined. It stopped eight inches out, and we went back to the lockers.

We fooled with locker 106 for a long time until Joe said: "Then why did he include the other key, eh? Are we bozos or what?"

After only a few minutes shining the light around inside locker 107, we saw a small metal shim extending from beneath the shelf. It was scarcely noticeable. But when Joe slid it sideways an inch, we heard a click.

Then we pushed on the back wall of the locker.

It swung open.

There was space behind it, all dark.

We shined the light in. A brick wall two feet away.

And a ladder affixed to the wall.

With steps going down.

34

"WELLWELLWELLWELLWELL," WHISPERED JOE. NO DOUBT Howard Carter said the same thing back in 1923 when he peeled back that fake wall in a minor tomb at Luxor and found King Tut's treasure trove.

I tried to say something too, but I was breathing too hard. I was breathing hard to keep my heart from coming out of my mouth and dancing around on my shoulders.

"Is this the greatest hiding place ever, or what?" Joe said.

"Yep. And I can't wait to follow you down there, buddy."

In a few seconds, after my comment sunk in, he turned with the flashlight and faced me.

"Excuse me? *You* follow *me*? *Au contraire,* my good man. It is you who are elected to go first."

"Now, why is that? You found the thing. You're the cop. You wanted to come back down here, not me."

"Okay. Then does that mean the treasure's mine?"

"No, it does not. After all, I have the keys. And Chris's blessing."

"Then perhaps we better get a few things straight right now, pal. Like how we're going to split this up. Eh?"

I thought for a second and informed him that he was certainly entitled to thirty percent.

"Thirty percent! You cheap bastard you!"

"Hey . . . Keep it up and I'll drop it to twenty—"

He stood up straight then, deliberately towering over me.

"All right Doc, if that's the way you wanna handle this—"

"Gentlemen . . . Gentlemen . . . please, no hostility!"

The deep basso voice was no illusion; Joe and I turned into the darkness of the warehouse.

"Who's there?" demanded Joe, moving his hand down to the bottom of his pantleg.

"Uh! Uh! Please, Lieutenant, don't grab for the backup gun. I would not like to be forced to shoot you—especially with *this* weapon. Hah hah hah . . ."

"Smitty!"

"Ahhh, the very same, sah. At your service."

We heard the soft scuff of feet approaching us. Many of them, it seemed to me. Soon a tall thin silhouette began to appear and grow closer.

"What the hell are you doing here?" said Joe in his official voice.

"Ahah . . . ahah . . . Well, sah, I think you and Doc can guess, eh? Hah hah hah . . ."

A light came on and played over both of us. A small, quick man came forward out of the darkness and in a twinkling had jerked Joe's Smith Bodyguard Airweight out of his ankle holster and patted him down, taking his pager off his belt. Then he patted me down, finding nothing.

"I think I can resolve your dispute for you," continued Smitty in his singsong voice. "I believe I will send one of *my* men down first. How's that? Hah hah hah . . ."

A second backup man sprang forward and went inside the locker. He was tall, not as tall as Smitty, but lithe and muscular. By the way he walked, I could have sworn he was the motorcycle man. We saw faint light swerving around inside the locker, growing fainter and fainter.

"What's it like down there, Lewis?" asked Smitty, still holding his flashlight on us.

"Very small, sah." His voice echoed eerily from within the deep stone vault. "Small and damp and cold, sah . . ."

"See anything we might like?"

"No, sah. Just old plastic buckets, sah . . ."

"Bring one up if you please, Lewis." Smitty then walked over to me. "Lewis is a very brave man, Doc. You owe your life to him."

So he *was* the mystery cyclist.

"You owe your life to Lewis *twice over*, sah."

Much clattering and banging in the locker now, and Lewis reappeared toting a tall white plastic bucket. The kind with a tight-fitting lid, used to hold joint compound or other building materials. He set it on the floor under the flashlight's beam.

Smitty bent low and pried off the plastic cover.

If you ever saw the 1951 version of *King Solomon's Mines*, starring Stewart Granger and Deborah Kerr, you know what we were looking at. Heaps and heaps of stones. Some multicolored, mostly red, green, and white-gray. Rubies, emeralds, sapphires, and diamonds. Uncut, raw stones. Some of them huge.

"And you say there are more down there, Lewis?" chuckled Smitty. "Whoooooeeee! Hah hah hah hah . . ."

"Just one more, sah."

"Well, let's get it, and get out of here. Gentlemen, it would be safest for me to transport the two of you down below and lock you inside the treasure hole—"

A deep chill went through me. I cannot stand close confines. Now this was ending like the movie did: with the adventurers being trapped in the cave by a deliberate avalanche—doomed to suffocate slowly in total darkness and silence.

I was just leaning my body forward, ready to begin a sweeping upward kick at Smitty's balls, when he added, "But it would be terribly uncivilized. And you two have been my friends throughout. You especially, Dr. Adams."

He reached into the bucket and grabbed a big handful of stones, then handed them to me.

"Put them in your pocket please, sah. Then I must ask you to place your hands behind your back. I regret this, but it must be done to ensure we escape safely."

"You're not going by ship," I said. "You'll never make it."

"Ahhhhh. Right you are, sah! The ship is Claudia's, anyway. I leave it for her. Ready?"

I put my hands behind me and felt the steel cuffs go on. They were doing the same to Joe, who obviously wasn't pleased.

"How the hell did you know we were here?" he demanded.

"We've kept all places under our watchful gaze, Lieutenant.

Even your fancy apartment. It is true I'm not leaving you with the bulk of the treasure, gentlemen, but after seeing your dwellings, I am convinced you are not in sore need of this find."

"And you are, I suppose?" said Joe with cynicism in his voice.

"Ahhhh, more than you might think, sah. And many I know are dearly in need of it. Yes. We saw you enter these premises—which we searched earlier, to no avail—early this morning. I sent Lewis in behind you—he's as quiet as a cat, you see—and he overheard your every word. When you decided to go to lunch, it gave the rest of us the perfect opportunity to enter, lie here, and wait. Again, we thank you for your genius, gentlemen."

Lewis struggled up the ladder and out of the locker with the remaining bucket.

"Give each of these gentlemen a long drink of water," commanded Smitty. Canteens were held up to our mouths and we drank our fill. Then we were recuffed together around one of the warehouse pillars, and gags were fastened in our mouths.

"I regret you have a long wait in store. But be assured that this evening a call will be made to the police here in Fairhaven, and you shall be found and released. Once again, gentlemen, my sincere thanks—and thank you so much for your efforts on behalf of the colored community here. Cheerio!"

And with that, he and his entourage were gone, leaving Joe and me to sit there in the dark until help came.

35

JOE WAS NURSING HIS PREPRANDIAL G&T ON THE DECK OF THE Breakers, watching the tide roll in and the sun go down. It was two weeks after the episode in the warehouse. We were all enjoying a summer weekend at the Cape. We had a special guest for dinner, too: Tony DeSilva.

"I sure was pissed off at the time," Joe said to Marty, "but for some reason, I'm not anymore."

"Maybe that's because you realize what he said was true, Joe. We really didn't need that loot . . . and a lot of other people did."

"Yeah, but do you really think, hon, that Smitty gave some of it away?"

"Well, he did to *me*," I said, checking the heat from the grill. We were going to have marinated halibut steaks for the main course. "Mary tells me that our handful will bring us over fifty grand."

"Really? Well, where's my cut?"

I went over and sat next to my brother-in-law. Put my hand on his shoulder. "Do you remember what happened just before we were going to go down that ladder?"

"Yeah. We got into a fight about splitting the take."

"See? There's a moral here somewhere. No wonder those pirates of old killed their companions and put them in the hole when they buried their treasure. Money corrupts. It ruins friendships. It's a good thing Missaels Haagmann Smits made off with it, you ask me."

"I didn't ask you that. I asked you, what's my take? What's Marty's and my take?"

"Oh, Joe—don't!" said Marty.

"Your take," said Mary, entering stage left from the kitchen door, "is to go with Charlie and me on our next vacation. That's what we've set this stash aside for."

"Really? Where to?"

"That's what we can take the next several months to decide. Together."

Then Tony DeSilva came forward, reaching into his shirt pocket. He was wearing a loud Hawaiian shirt with big flowers on it. No black frock with a turned-around collar at the Breakers. No, sir.

"May I show you all something?" he asked.

We looked as he unfolded a piece of paper. A long piece of

paper. A long piece of paper with a specially marked ink pattern all over it. We perked up. Then I saw the words "Grand Cayman Bank, Ltd." and I really perked up.

The check was a cashier's check for two hundred thousand dollars. It was payable to the parish of Saint Bernard's, Fairhaven, Massachusetts.

"May I read the note that accompanied it?" asked the padre. We gave him permission.

Dear Tony,

Here's a little something from Smitty and me. I hope you have the authority to use these funds as you see fit. We both hope it will be to continue and improve the halfway house you started. Give our love to Doc, Joe, Mary, and Marty. We really hope we can see them again sometime.

Affectionately,
Claudia.

"*Claudia?*" Mary was sitting bolt upright in her chair. "She was in on it?"

"Doesn't surprise me," I said. "I don't think she was from the start. But I think as things got scary, she might have teamed up with Smitty a bit. I know we'd both have been killed if Lewis hadn't been there at Ipassis's cottage with his air pistol."

"Uh-huh," added Joe. "And the time before that on board the ship when he zapped old Sid from the open porthole."

There was a silence then. Just the wind and the waves and the gulls. The soft hiss and crump of the incoming tide. I heard words in my head . . .

"*Oh, God . . . I wish you were going with me. . . . I'll never forget you . . .*"

I sighed. Was it regret? No. Was it missed adventure and excitement? Definitely. But I'd had enough of that. God bless her, I thought, and keep her safe and happy.

I fished for something in my canvas shorts. Drawing out a small cardboard cube, I tossed it to Mary nonchalantly.

She grabbed it, studied it. Her eyes grew wide when she read the logo of Concord Jewelers on its top. She opened the box, and we all huddled over her. Oooohs and ahhhhs all around. It was impressive all right. The one stone of the three Claudia had given me that remained safe in Toby Gustafson's vault.

"Thanks, sweetie! I love you," purred Mary.

I sat her on my lap and kissed her a good one.

"I love you, too."

"Boyer is up there with the best."
—*The Boston Globe*

If you enjoyed

THE MAN WHO WHISPERED,

don't miss the first episode

in the Doc Adams series:

BILLINGSGATE SHOAL

by

RICK BOYER

BILLINGSGATE SHOAL

by

RICK BOYER

*Winner of the Edgar Award for
Best Mystery Novel of the Year*

First, a fishing trawler runs aground on the Massachusetts shore. Then a young scuba diver sent to investigate the wreck is found dead in the water.

Doc Adams, a friend of the dead diver, sets out through the stormy seas and blood-flecked sands of Cape Cod to plumb a murder he should have prevented. There he uncovers a hidden treasure in illegal arms and is nearly killed in the process.

Published by Ivy Books.
Available at your local bookstore.

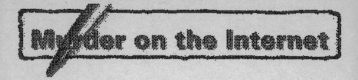